IDENTITY

NORA ROBERTS

IDENTITY

PIATKUS

PIATKUS

First published in the United States in 2023 by St Martin's Press
First published in Great Britain in 2023 by Piatkus

1 3 5 7 9 10 8 6 4 2

Copyright © Nora Roberts 2023

The moral right of the author has been asserted.

A CIP catalogue record for this book
is available from the British Library.

ISBN: 978-0-34943-396-7 (hardback)
ISBN: 978-0-34943-397-4 (trade paperback)

Printed and bound in Great Britain by
Clays Ltd, Elcograf S.p.A.

Papers used by Piatkus are from well-managed forests
and other responsible sources.

MIX
Paper from
responsible sources
FSC® C104740

Piatkus
An imprint of
Little, Brown Book Group
Carmelite House
50 Victoria Embankment
London EC4Y 0DZ

An Hachette UK Company
www.hachette.co.uk

www.littlebrown.co.uk

To family
The one you're born with
and the one you make

PART I

Plans

It's a bad plan that can't be changed.
—Publilius Syrus

To be happy at home is the ultimate result of all ambition.
—Samuel Johnson

Chapter One

Her dreams and goals were simple and few. As a former army brat, Morgan Albright spent her childhood moving across countries and continents. Her roots, directed by her father's work, grew short and shallow to allow for quick transplanting. From base to base, from house to house, state to state, country to country for her first fourteen years, before her parents divorced.

She'd never had a choice.

For the three years following the divorce, her mother had pulled her from place to place. A small town here, a big city there, looking for . . . Morgan had never been sure.

At seventeen, closing in on eighteen, she'd dug those roots up herself to plant at college. And there she'd explored those goals and dreams and choices.

She studied hard, focused in on a double major. Business and hospitality—choices that led directly to her dream.

Planting herself. Her own home, her own business.

Her own.

She studied maps, neighborhoods, climate, while narrowing her choices on just where to plant those roots once she'd earned those degrees. She wanted a neighborhood, maybe old and established, close to shops, restaurants, bars—people.

And one day she'd not only own her own home, but her own bar.

Simple goals.

With those degrees hot in her hand, she settled on a neighborhood outside of Baltimore, Maryland. Old houses with yards, and, as yet to be gentrified, so affordable.

She'd worked her way through college, waiting tables, then tending bar when she'd hit twenty-one. And she'd saved.

Her father—the Colonel—didn't make her graduation. And though she'd graduated with honors, he sent no acknowledgment of her accomplishments.

It hadn't surprised her, as she knew she'd simply ceased to exist for him even before his signature on the divorce papers dried.

Her mother and her maternal grandparents attended. She hadn't known it would be the last time she'd see her grandfather. A robust seventy, an active man, a healthy man, he died the winter after her graduation. He'd slipped off a ladder. One slip. Here, then gone.

Even in her grief, it was a lesson Morgan took to heart.

He left her twenty thousand dollars and memories, as precious, of hiking the Green Mountains of Vermont on summer visits.

With the money, Morgan moved out of her tiny apartment and into a small house. Her house. One that needed work, but had a yard—that needed work.

The three small bedrooms, two tiny baths meant she could take in a housemate to offset the mortgage, help pay for that work.

And she worked two jobs. She tended bar five or six nights a week at a neighborhood bar, a happy place called the Next Round. Considering homeownership, she took a second job as office manager at a family-owned construction firm.

She met her housemate at the local garden center as she puzzled over foundation plants. Nina Ramos worked in the greenhouses and knew her stuff. Handy with a yard that needed help, Nina turned puzzlement into joy, and, in that first blooming spring in a house of her own, Nina moved in.

They enjoyed each other's company, and knew when to give the other quiet and space.

At twenty-five, Morgan had achieved her first dream, and by her calculations would reach goal number two before her thirtieth birthday.

Her one splurge sat in her narrow driveway. The Prius would take her a few years to pay off, but it would get her to work and back dependably and economically.

In good weather, she rode her bike to her day job, but when she needed a car, she had one. Nina called the car Morgan's subgoal.

The little house on Newberry Street boasted a pretty yard, fresh white paint, and a new front door she'd painted a soft, happy blue.

Her boss at Greenwald's Builders helped her refinish the old hardwood floors, sold her paint at cost, and guided her along the path of repairs and maintenance.

She'd planted those roots, and felt herself blooming.

It made her smile to see daffodils playing their bright trumpets along her newly paved walkway. Late March brought changeable weather, but all those lovely signs of spring. She and Nina had planted a dogwood in the front yard the previous fall, and she could see the buds wanted to burst.

Soon, she thought as she walked her bike to its rack and locked it.

A good neighborhood, but she didn't see the point in tempting anyone.

She unlocked the door, and, since Nina's not-very-dependable car sat at the curb, called out.

"It's me, running late." She crossed the living room and, as always, thought about how much more open it would be when she took out the wall that blocked off the kitchen.

She had the money for that project earmarked, so maybe in the fall. Maybe before Christmas. Maybe.

"I'm not running late," Nina called back. "And I've got a date!"

Nina always had a date. But then again, Morgan thought, she was gorgeous and vivacious and only worked one job.

She paused at the open bedroom door.

Several outfits—obviously rejects—littered the bed while Nina modeled another in front of a full-length mirror. Her raven-black hair spilled down the back of a red dress that hugged every curve on her tiny body. Dark eyes sparkled as they met Morgan's in the glass.

"What do you think?"

"I often think I hate you. Okay, where are you going and who are you going with?"

"Sam's taking me to Fresco's for dinner."

"Fancy! Yeah, the red's a killer."

Which she envied a little. The only genuine disappointment between the housemates came from the fact that with Morgan's long, coltish frame and Nina's petite, curvy one, they couldn't trade clothes.

"Go for it. Isn't this nearly three solid weeks of dates exclusively with the hunkified Sam?"

"Almost four." Nina did a twirl. "So . . ."

"I'll be very quiet when I get home."

"I really like him, Morgan."

"So do I."

"No, I mean *really*."

"Oh." Angling her head, Morgan studied her friend. "I already know he's in serious like and more when it comes to you. It's all over him. If you're heading there, I'm giving you the full friend approval."

After flipping that gorgeous hair, Nina let out one of her dreamy sighs. "Pretty sure I'm already headed there."

"Full approval. I've got to change for work."

"From work for work. I've got to put all this away and clean up this room. I don't want Sam to think I'm a slob."

"You're not a slob." Chaotic, Morgan thought, but Nina kept her chaos contained to her own space.

Unlike Nina's cheerful chaos, lavender walls, a vanity top littered with makeup, hair products, and God knew, Morgan's space was just contained.

She used the third bedroom—closet-size—as an office, so this was sanctuary. Quiet blue walls, some art she'd bought from street artists in Baltimore, the white duvet and pillows, a small but cozy reading chair.

She took off office manager—gray pants, white shirt, navy blue blazer—put on bartender—black pants, black shirt. In the bathroom, she opened the drawer where she kept her makeup organized for easy choices. And changed day to night.

The short, angled cut of her blond hair worked fine for both jobs, but the bartender went for more drama on the eyes, deeper on the lips.

With years of practice, she finished the transition inside twenty minutes.

Since she wouldn't be eating fancy at Fresco's, she dashed to the kitchen, grabbed a yogurt out of the fridge. She ate standing up, imagining the wall gone, new cabinet doors and hardware, some open shelves, some—

"*Amiga mia*, you need to eat food."

"Yogurt's food."

Nina, now in a robe, put her hands on her hips. "Something that requires a knife and fork, and chewing. You've got that long, slim build naturally—bitch—but if you don't eat, it'll turn to skinny and gaunt. Seriously, one of us has to learn to cook." She shot up a coral-tipped finger, then pointed it at Morgan. "I nominate you."

"Yeah, I'll take that up in my spare time. Besides, you're the one with a mother who cooks like a goddess."

"You'll come with me for Sunday dinner. Don't say you've got work—your spreadsheets, or whatever. You know Mama and Papa love you. And my brother, Rick, will be there."

With the yogurt in one, the spoon in the other, Morgan waved her hands as if erasing a board. "I am not dating your brother, no matter how cute he is. That way lies madness. I'm not losing you as a roommate because your brother and I date, have sex, break up."

Nina held up a gold hoop at one ear, a dangle of three circles at the other. "Which?"

Morgan pointed at the dangles. "Fancier."

"Good. And maybe you'll date Rick, have sex, and fall in love."

"I don't have time. Give me two years, maybe three, then I'll have time."

"I like schedules, too, but not for love. Now you've distracted me. You have to eat."

"I'll get something at the bar."

"Dinner Sunday," Nina insisted when Morgan tossed the container, rinsed the spoon. "I'm telling Mama you're coming, and once I tell Mama, it's done."

"I'd love to go, honestly. Let me get through this week. We've been so damn busy at Greenwald's. Spring makes everybody think of remodeling or painting or building decks."

She grabbed her purse and kept going. "Have a great time tonight."

"You can take that to the bank. I'm calling Mama before I get my gorgeous on."

"Your gorgeous is never off."

Morgan jogged to the car. Pleased she'd already made up a little time, she drove the five-point-four miles to the town center.

The shops along what the locals called Market Mile (actually one-point-six) would close within the hour. But the restaurants and cafés would keep Market Street lit and busy well into the night.

Most of the buildings—rosy or white-painted brick—kept the retail to street level and held apartments above. The Next Round was no exception and tended to rent to patrons or employees who had no issue living above a bar.

She swung off Market, circled around the back of the bar to the parking lot. With her car secured, she crunched across the gravel to the back kitchen door and stepped into the heat and noise.

The Round ran to burgers, steamers, nachos with sides of fries, onion rings, fried pickles, and three varieties of wings.

When she opened her own tavern, she intended to spread out to a few more, hopefully surprising, choices of bar food.

And she should probably learn how to cook first, because you never knew when you'd have to pitch in.

"Hey, Frankie," she called out to the woman working the grill as she put her jacket on a peg. "How's it going?"

"Good enough." With her poof of ink-black hair tucked under a white cap, Frankie flipped three fat burgers. "Roddy and his brothers are grabbing some dinner before their dart tournament. Be glad you weren't on for happy hour. We were slammed."

"I like slammed."

She exchanged greetings with the two line chefs, the teenage dishwasher, and the waitress who swung in to pick up an order of loaded nachos.

Though she had ten minutes before her shift, she walked through the door and into the bar.

A different kind of noise, she thought. Not the sizzle of meat on a grill, the whack of knives, the clatter of dishes. Here voices filled the big room with its long black bar, its tables and booths. Music pumped from the juke, but not loud enough to overwhelm conversation.

She saw Roddy and his brothers—regulars—at their usual booth near the dartboard, drinking beer and chowing down on bar nuts. Coors for Roddy and his brother Mike, she thought, and Heineken for brother Ted. If their father joined them, he'd order a beer—on tap—and a bump.

She took the pass-through behind the bar where the bartenders worked.

She'd relieve Wayne, currently adding a slice of lime to a bottle of Corona.

"Got a little bit of a lull," he told her, and gave her his full-wattage smile. "Guy at the end of the bar's running a tab. He's on his second vodka tonic, so keep an eye."

He served the Corona to another stool sitter, exchanged a few words before he slipped back to Morgan.

"Waiting for his date—Match.com—first time. She's late, he's nervous."

Cute, Morgan decided, on the nerdy side. She'd put down money he had a full gaming system in his living room.

"Got it."

"I'm gonna clock out then. Have a good one."

As always, she checked her supplies—the ice, the limes and lemons, the olives, the cherries. She filled a couple of orders for tables, and was about to work her way down to Corona when she spotted a woman of about thirty step in, look anxiously around before she approached the guy at the bar.

"Dave? I'm Tandy. I'm so sorry I'm a little late."

He brightened right up. "Oh, don't worry about it. It's nice to meet you. Do you want to get a table?"

"This is fine. Is this fine?" She slid onto the stool beside him.

Morgan shifted down the bar as they smiled at each other with expressions of anxiety and hope.

"Hi. What can I get you tonight?"

"Oh. Um. Could I get a glass of Chardonnay?"

"You sure can. I love your earrings."

"Oh." Tandy put one hand up to her left ear. "Thanks."

"They're really pretty," Dave added. "You look great."

"Thanks. So do you." She laughed as Morgan poured the wine. "You really just don't know, do you? I was so nervous, I walked around the block. That's why I'm a little late."

"I was so nervous I got here twenty minutes early."

Ice broken, Morgan thought as she served the wine.

And this, she admitted, was one of the reasons she loved working in a bar. You never knew what might start, might finish, might bloom or break in a friendly neighborhood bar.

By the time Roddy and his brothers plowed through their burgers, the place started filling up. The Match.com couple decided to get a table after all, and a platter of nachos.

Morgan made a mental bet on a second date there.

Vodka Tonic cashed out, left a miserly tip.

Darts thwacked against the board to cheers and catcalls of onlookers.

A man in his early thirties came in. He made her think of an incognito movie star with his dark blond hair, chiseled features, gym-fit body in jeans, boots, and a pale blue sweater—looked like cashmere. He slid onto a stool.

She stepped down to him. "Welcome to the Next Round. What's your pleasure?"

"I've got a lot of them." He grinned at her—easy, charming. "But we'll start with a beer. Any local beer on tap?"

"Of course." Though they had lists printed in holders on the bar, she reeled them off.

"Maybe you can pick one for me."

"What're you looking for?"

"Another loaded question."

She shot him a smile. Looking for some conversation, she judged, along with the drink. And that was fine.

"In a beer."

"Smooth, but not bland. Rich, but not overpowering. Toward the dark side."

"Let's try this." She got a tasting glass, pulled a tap.

As he sampled it, he watched her over the rim. "That'll do. Good choice."

"That's my job."

Before he could speak again, one of the waitresses came up. "Girl table over there's stuck in the nineties. Four Cosmos, Morgan."

She carried the tray of empties into the kitchen while Morgan got to work.

"You know what you're doing," the new guy commented as she mixed the drinks.

"I'd better. Are you in town on business?"

"Don't I look like I belong?"

Close enough, she thought. His clothes said upscale, but not in-your-face. "Haven't seen you in here before."

A cheer erupted across the room.

"Dart tourney," she said.

"So I see. Serious?"

"Oh, in its way. Can I get you anything else? Would you like to see a menu?"

"Is the food any good?"

"It is." She pulled out a menu, laid it beside him. "Have a look, take your time."

With the Cosmos ready, she moved down the bar. Took orders, filled orders, chatting with regulars as she did. She worked her way back.

"I'll try a Market Street Burger, unless you tell me I'm making a mistake."

"It's a classic for a reason. If you like a kick, a little heat, go with the spicy fries."

He lifted his hands. "You've never steered me wrong."

She laughed, plugged his order in the machine.

Roddy, all six-four and two hundred fifty pounds, walked over to the bar. "Another round, sweets. How's it going?" he said idly to Handsome Guy while Morgan filled the order.

"Cold beer, beautiful bartender, live sports. It's a good deal."

"Yeah, it is. I took the lead in the semis. Give me some luck for the finals, Morgan."

She leaned over, touched her lips to his. "Go get 'em."

"Damn right." He took the beers and walked off.

"Boyfriend?"

She looked over at her customer. "Oh, no. Roddy and his brothers— the dart players—are regulars. I actually work with his girlfriend at my other job."

"Two jobs? Ambitious. What's the other?"

"Office manager for a construction company. What do you do?"

"I'd like to say as I please, because at least I try. I'm in IT. I'm in the area for a couple of months doing some consulting."

"Where are you from?"

"I travel a lot. San Francisco originally, but I'm based in New York now, or for the most part. Is this hometown for you?"

"It is now."

Another waitress came up, rattled off another order.

"Army brat," she said as she filled it.

"Then you know the traveling life."

"I do. And I'm happy to have left that behind."

When his order came out, he gave the plate a long look. "You don't skimp on portions here."

"We don't. Would you like a table?"

He sent her that charming smile. "I like the view right here. I'm Luke," he added. "Luke Hudson."

"Morgan. Nice to meet you."

He ate, ordered a second beer, stayed through the tournament.

He asked questions but didn't seem intrusive. Bar conversation, in Morgan's mind. She asked her own.

He was staying at a local hotel. His company would rent a house for him, but he liked hotels, and enjoyed getting into the local flavor wherever he traveled.

He asked where her father had been stationed, which places she'd lived she liked best. Easy breezy while she mixed drinks, mopped the bar, chattered with other customers.

"I should get going," he said. "I didn't intend to stay so long, but it looks like I've found my local watering hole."

"It's a good one."

"I'll see you again." When he rose, he surprised her by offering a hand to shake. And held hers while he smiled into her eyes. "It's really been great spending time with you, Morgan."

"It's been nice talking to you."

"We'll do it again."

He paid in cash, leaving a very generous tip.

A couple nights later, Luke wandered in later in her shift. It was trivia night at the Round, and the noise level boomed as various tables and groups shouted out answers.

"Pick another local draft," he told Morgan. "Something . . . adventurous." He glanced behind him at the game players. "No darts tonight?"

"Trivia night. It's a free-for-all, so shout out whenever you want."

"What's the prize?"

"Satisfaction." She offered him a tasting glass.

"Interesting and adventurous," he decided. "Got some dark cherries going. Let's go for it."

As she pulled the tap, she smiled over. "Anything to go with it?"

"Just the beer for now. Had a long day."

"Life in the tech world?"

"Like the beer, it's interesting and adventurous. How are things in your world?"

"Busy, but I like busy."

She filled orders, working her way up and down the bar, but with trivia in full swing, she had a lull.

"What do you do when you're not busy?" Luke asked her.

"I'll let you know if I ever get there."

"Gotta take some downtime. Mind, body, spirit, and all that. Paint me a day off."

"Paint's accurate. My house needs more of that, but it's not quite ready. And with spring coming on, we'll work on planting."

"We?"

"My housemate."

"So he's handy?"

"She, and she's terrific when it comes to curb appeal, planting. She works for a garden center. Inside, Nina's not so much, but I'm not bad."

"Construction company job." He pointed at her. "Handy."

"It helps."

"A lot of maintenance when you're a homeowner. I guess that's why I've never gone there. I'm not handy. And there's the job." He pointed at her again. "Army brat, so you wanted to plant roots."

"Exactly right."

She mixed a whiskey sour, pulled two beers before he caught her attention again.

"What made you pick this area—if you don't mind me asking."

"It had what I wanted. Four seasons, close enough to the city without being in it, not a small town, not a big one. Right in the middle."

She set out a fresh bowl of pretzels for him.

"It's a nice area, prime for some of the upgrading you seem to be doing with your place. That's why I'm here. Homeowners and businesses looking to bump up their tech, a couple of developments where people want to option smart homes. Old houses, new buyers looking to flip or just refresh."

He shrugged. "What I do is part of the infrastructure. Everyone has home offices now, and I can set them up. You must have one."

"I do. It's not especially smart, but it works."

Trivia ended with cheers and boos, and a run on drinks and snacks. As she worked, she noted he chatted up another stool sitter. Baseball. He appeared to know enough to keep that conversation lively.

"Ready for another?"

"Yeah, thanks. How about you, Larry? On me."

"Don't mind if I do. How's Nina's car running?"

"Barely."

Larry shook his head, rubbed at his short beard. "She's gotta bring it in."

"I'll tell her. Larry's the best mechanic from here to Baltimore," she told Luke. "He's kept Nina's car running well beyond its expiration date."

"I do what I can. You still liking that Prius?"

"It's perfect."

She set their drinks in front of them, filled another round for a table of six. Larry's conversation turned to cars and engines, and Luke appeared to know enough again to hold up his end.

"Gotta get on." Larry pushed to his feet. "The wife'll be home or getting there. It's her book club night, which is a front for drinking wine and gabbing. Nice talking with you, Luke. Thanks for the drink."

"Anytime."

"Another round?" Morgan asked him.

"Two's the limit. I should get on, I've got my own busy day tomorrow." He paid his tab, tipped more than well. "I'd say don't work too hard, but pretty sure you will. Nice seeing you again."

"Good luck in tech world."

He sent her a grin and strolled out.

He showed up again on a packed Friday night. She worked with the part-time weekend bartender to handle the crowd. Luke leaned on her end of the bar, as butts filled every stool.

"Surprise me. It's been a damn good week."

"Congratulations. Weekend off?"

"Ah, some paperwork and planning tomorrow, but yeah. Any suggestions on how I should spend the rest of it?"

"You could drive into Baltimore. Inner Harbor, aquarium, and it's opening day for the O's at Camden Yards."

"Want to keep me company, show me around?"

She couldn't say the offer came out of the blue. She knew when a man was interested. She played it light—part of the job.

"Can't do it. Homeowner's stuff on Saturday, and I'll be right here Saturday night. Sunday's already booked. But I appreciate the offer."

He sampled the beer she offered. "I'm getting an education on the local brews. It's nice, draw me one." He waited until she served him. "Look, if it's pushy or you're already involved, just say. No harm, no foul. But would you like to go out to dinner some night? A night when you're actually not working?

"No pressure," he added when she hesitated. "Just a meal and conversation. Do you like pizza?"

For whatever reason, the casual tone relaxed her. "I'm suspect of anyone who doesn't."

"The pizza at Luigi's is good."

"You hit the top of the line around here."

"So maybe pizza, some wine. I could just meet you there."

She hadn't had an actual date in . . . she didn't want to think about it. Why the hell not?

"I'm free Monday night."

"Seven o'clock at Luigi's?"

"Sure. Sounds good."

"Okay with you if we exchange phone numbers? I'm hoping you don't change your mind, but in case you do . . ."

She pulled her phone out of her pocket, took his so they could add their contacts.

"If you're planning on staying awhile and want a seat, the couple three and four stools down should be leaving after they finish their drinks and nachos."

"Thanks. I'll hover."

She shot him a smile, went back to work.

He grabbed a stool, had his two beers, and left just after midnight.

"Monday night," he said. "Enjoy the weekend."

"You, too."

"That is one fine specimen." Gracie the waitress looked after him. "And he's got his eyes on you, cutie."

"Maybe. He seems nice, steady—and he's only in the area for a few months."

"Strike while the iron's sizzling."

"Maybe," she said again.

Chapter Two

She spent her Saturday morning on the house. Laundry, cleaning, dreaming of opening walls, fresh paint, new counters. She did the weekly marketing, including Nina's list, left the receipt on the kitchen board for their monthly accounting.

When Nina got home from work that afternoon with a flat of pansies, bags of soil and peat, they hauled their pots out of storage. One day, Morgan thought, she wanted window boxes. But she also wanted new shutters, and a cute little front porch.

By her calculations, she could afford all that the following spring. And for now, pots of pansies filled the bill.

"Tell me more about this Luke."

With her hoodie zipped against the not-quite-April breeze, Morgan tamped down soil around happy-faced pansies.

"Not much to tell really. He's an IT guy, and must be good at it or his company wouldn't send him out for weeks and months at a time to take on a territory. Or whatever they'd call it. Plus, he dresses well. Not snotty well, just well."

"You said he was gorgeous."

"I did, because true. Good manners, friendly. Two-beer limit. It's a pizza date with a traveling man, Nina. We're not picking out china."

Nina pushed up her sun hat. "When was your last pizza date, or date of any kind?"

"Don't go there."

"You don't go there because you always smile and say no. Why did you say yes? Because gorgeous?"

Morgan shrugged, a little sheepishly. "It doesn't hurt. I can be shallow. But he's interesting, and he doesn't just talk. He listens. It's nice. I think he's nice."

"And temporary."

"Yes, and temporary, and that's a plus right now. It'll also be nice in say, five, six, maybe seven years to go for permanent."

Her eyes, bottle green like the Colonel's, went a little dreamy.

"Fall in love, take some time, think about starting a family. I've got to get me done first. God, these flowers are so sweet! How smart was I to get a gardener as a housemate?"

"The smartest. When my time comes—and Sam is definitely leading the pack—I want a big, crazy garden, so I have to have a big yard. Little house, no problem, but a big, giant yard."

She lay back on the cool grass. "Shade trees and ornamentals, paths meandering through cutting gardens and butterfly gardens. Crazy birdhouses and water features. I want the works."

Morgan stretched out beside her. "We should get a crazy birdhouse. I'm not sure what a cutting garden is, but now I want one."

"I can make that happen." She reached over, gave Morgan's hand a squeeze. "I do love it here. Not the big, giant yard of my dreams, but it's full of potential. Especially since you let me have my way."

"We play to our strengths."

"You should ask Gorgeous Guy over for dinner."

"We don't cook."

"We can put something together. I can ask Mama for something simple but impressive. She'll know. We'll clean this up, then go in and figure out what you'll wear on your date."

"It's just pizza, Nina."

"Today pizza, tomorrow who knows? We play to our strengths," Nina reminded her as she sat up. "Dating is my area. I think casually sexy for pizza date with Gorgeous Traveling Man."

"I may not have anything that hits that mark."

"Trust me, I can make that happen, too."

* * *

She'd wondered if Gorgeous Traveling Man would breeze into the Round on Saturday night—then asked herself what it meant about her that she was disappointed he didn't.

She told herself it was just as well, as they'd been slammed again. And she'd picked up a short afternoon shift when the Sunday bartender had an emergency appendectomy.

She'd gone straight from work to Nina's family dinner, enjoyed some amazing paella, a lot of laughs.

After work on Monday, she biked home. Since she'd spent part of her brief downtime over the weekend checking and rechecking her finances, projecting how much she could afford, she'd talked to her office-manager job boss about the costs of taking down the wall, redoing the kitchen—new appliances, new counters, new cabinets. The works.

With that number in mind she biked home, adjusting her plans to fit those finances. Paint the cabinets instead of replacing—for now, because she refused to give up the kitchen island of her dreams.

When she parked her bike, Nina came to the front door.

"You're cutting it close."

"I've got an hour and a half. Nearly."

"Get in here, *amiga mia*. We've got work to do. I'm doing your makeup."

"I know how to do my makeup."

"You know office-manager makeup, and just-flirty-enough-bartender makeup. But do you know sexy-casual-pizza-date makeup?"

"That's very specific, but probably."

"No probablys." Nina ticked a finger in the air. "My bathroom. I set it all up. I got a stool for you, since you're six inches taller than me."

"Six and a quarter inches."

"Rub it in, Legs."

Being Nina, she took nearly half the time Morgan had left to perfect her work.

"I think my face gained five pounds."

"Worth every ounce. Just look at that face. You've got those beautiful green eyes, but now they're amazing! I do good work."

She couldn't argue, not when her eyes looked huge and the green deeper, and her skin dewy and fresh despite (because of?) the endless layering and blending.

"The red gloss on the lips really works," Nina decided, studying the results of her labor. "The matte would've taken it over to sexy-sexy. This is good. You have perfect lips, just full enough, just wide enough. Go get dressed."

"What are you doing tonight?"

"Staying in." Nina followed her into the bedroom, just to be sure Morgan wore what she'd already chosen.

"Really?"

"Plenty of Mama's leftovers from last night. I'm taking a rest and beauty night. Bubble bath, hair mask, face mask. A *long* bubble bath with a glass of wine and candles. An evening of self-care. Then I want to hear all about your date."

"It's just pizza." And now all this prep made her nervous.

"You've got to start somewhere. God, you've got a great ass," she added as Morgan wiggled into snug jeans. "A yard of legs topped by a tiny little ass."

Morgan looked over her shoulder, shook that ass. "You hitting on me?"

"If Traveling Guy doesn't, something's wrong with him."

"I'm not looking for hits." Morgan slid into the bright blue sweater. "Maybe, depending, a subtle nudge could be acceptable."

Under Nina's watchful eye, she changed her earrings for some dangles, pulled on her best boots, then slipped on the stone-gray leather jacket, a Christmas gift from her mother.

"Do I pass?"

"Casual sexy personified." Nina took a small atomizer out of her pocket. "Walk through the spray," she ordered, and spritzed.

With an eye roll, Morgan walked through.

"Perfect. Now we're going to have a drink."

"I'm going to have a glass of wine with dinner."

"You're going to have a quarter of a glass now, just to smooth everything out. And if you go nuts and have two glasses with dinner, take your date on a walk around Market Street, down to the park and the pond and back. In fact, you need my blue floral scarf. It'll add just the right touch."

At seven on the dot, despite Nina insisting she shouldn't be right on time, she walked into Luigi's.

It hummed in the way she thought a good restaurant should, and smelled of sauce and spice and melted cheese.

It relieved her to see Luke already in a booth, and the smile he sent when he saw her didn't hurt her ego one bit.

He slid out of the booth as she approached, took her hand, kissed her cheek lightly. "You look amazing."

"Thanks. I hope you haven't been waiting long."

"Only just got here. Terrific jacket," he commented as he helped her take it off.

"A gift from my mother."

"She's got excellent taste. I ordered a bottle of red when I got here. I hope that's okay. We can change it if you want something else."

"Red's fine. How was your weekend?"

"Productive. I did take your advice, spent a little time at the Inner Harbor." He gave the waitress that smile when she brought the wine.

"Have you decided on what you'd like?"

"Maybe give us a few more minutes."

"No problem. Take your time."

Luke lifted his glass. "To a pleasant evening in good company. I really thought you might change your mind."

"And miss free pizza?"

He laughed. "What do you like on it?"

"Anything, everything, or nothing. Pizza is never wrong."

"You're talking my language. Now, how was your weekend?"

"Also productive. Nina and I planted some pansies. They make me smile every time I come home or leave the house."

"The housemate who works in a garden center."

"That's right."

"You're good friends."

"We are." The first real, permanent friend she'd made in her nomadic life. "It's great having someone who gets your rhythms. She's generally up and gone before I get up for work, and usually in bed by the time I get home from the Round."

"That probably helps. I mean you both have your own schedules, so it adds to having your own space."

"Yeah, so when we share that space, we enjoy each other. Is it odd not having a regular routine, neighbors, friends around?"

"Right now, this works for me." He sat back, a man comfortable with himself, confident in himself. And she found that very appealing.

"One day I imagine I'll want to stick, settle. But I get to see a lot of the country, meet a lot of interesting people." The quick, dazzling smile flashed. "Like you."

He had a good rhythm himself, she decided. Just flirty enough.

"You must like the work, and I have to think you're really good at it."

"I love the work. Creating systems that suit the clients. Fixing problems, making people's lives easier, expanding their horizons. Maybe you'll show me your house one day, and I could give you some ideas."

"Maybe."

He smiled again. "So, pizza."

She ended up drinking two glasses of wine, and enjoyed every minute. He told her stories, how he'd designed the smart tech for a ranch in Butte, Montana, and watched bison graze in the field.

And he listened to her plans for a new kitchen, even offered suggestions. Ones good enough to add to her list of hopes and dreams.

He suggested the walk.

The evening breeze kicked a bit, but felt good after the heat of the restaurant. And it had been so long since she'd taken a walk with someone, had someone hold her hand.

It was nearly ten, much later than she'd planned, when he walked her to her car.

"I'd like to see you again, like this. Not that I don't enjoy riding a stool at the bar while you're working. But I'd like to see you again. My schedule's flexible. I can work around yours."

Maybe Nina had crawled inside her head, but she found herself inviting him to dinner.

"Next Monday night at my place. It's the most open for me."

"You cook?"

"No. I'm going to have to add that to my list of things to learn, but no."

"Nina cooks."

"No, but her mother does, and she'll walk us through something if you're willing to risk it."

"Adventure's my game. Is seven good?"

"Sure. Seven's great."

"I'll be there. Got an address?"

She held out a hand for his phone, added it to his contacts. "I can give you directions."

"I'm good friends with Mr. Google. I'll still be dropping by the bar. I might even try my hand at darts."

"Roddy's a killer."

"I'll risk it."

He leaned in then, and she'd have called it a subtle nudge. Just the right amount of nudge the way his lips met hers. He didn't push, but made an impact. And the flutter she hadn't experienced in a long, long time added the perfect cap to the evening.

"Good night, Morgan."

"Good night. I had a really good time."

"Me, too. Drive safe."

She drove safe, though she floated a bit on the quiet rush of a good-night kiss.

And when she floated into the house, Nina, glowing from her self-care, cozy in her pj's, waited.

"Okay, I can take one look and know this was a major success in first dates. Tell! Did he hit on you?"

"The perfect amount. I really like him." With a happy sigh, she dropped into a chair. "He's just easy and fun to talk to. He's been so many places and tells a good story. He listens."

She lifted her shoulders, let them fall. "And when he kissed me good night, my stomach fluttered."

"What kind of kiss? Be descriptive."

"I'm going to say soft, and just a little dreamy. No push, no blast of heat. Just easy, and effective. I ended up asking him to dinner next Monday night."

"Whoa!" Jumping up, Nina did a quick dance. "Holy shit. He didn't drug you, did he? Or use some sort of mind trick?"

"He's a nice, great-looking, interesting man. That's it."

"More than enough. We'll have Mama help us cook something. Or do you want me to disappear Monday?"

"No." That came immediate and decisive. "Please, don't disappear. I wouldn't have invited him unless you'd be here."

"Should I ask Sam?"

"Yes, that evens it out or something. Nothing fancy, Nina. A nice, easy dinner. Let's stay casual."

"Casual sexy. We've got this, Morgan."

"If we don't, we'll get something delivered." She rose. "I have to get ready for bed. You should, too. You start at eight tomorrow."

"I'm going, I'm going, but I'm going to text Mama first so she can think about what we should make. I'm not going to tell you to have sweet dreams because that's a given. See you tomorrow. Oh, I can't wait to meet the guy Morgan Albright asked to dinner!"

Luke dropped into the bar Tuesday night. He slid right into conversation with her, and with some of the regulars. He honed his dart skills for a while—he wasn't bad. He had his two beers, some wings.

"Got yourself a boyfriend." Gracie wiggled her eyebrows.

"No. He's only in town for a couple months."

"Didn't say lifetime lover." As the lights blinked for last call, Gracie rolled her shoulders. "He sure is smooth. Me, I don't trust smooth. About fifteen years back I had an almost first husband. He was smooth. So smooth he slid right out of my bed into my cousin Bonnie's."

"Good thing he's not my almost first husband."

"So you can enjoy the smooth."

And why not, Morgan thought when he came in on trivia night.

The fact that he joined in earned him some points on her personal scorecard.

She had an interesting man obviously attracted to her and, given her schedule, not much one-on-one time. Which seemed okay with both of them.

It didn't mean she didn't look forward to Monday night with fear of actually cooking and anxiety, due to second-date syndrome.

She flexed some time, took off an hour early from her day job. Riding her bike home in air that had softened, really, finally softened into April gave her a lift.

In a matter of weeks spring would get serious and start popping out color. She saw some of the neighborhood's forsythia had already jumped in with their bright butter yellow, and the big willow on the corner of her block had its early green haze.

In her own yard, tulips bloomed lipstick red, and the azaleas that Nina had advised on their first garden center meeting had budded up and would pop their sweet pink in no time.

Maybe it was silly, but having them made her feel like part of the neighborhood.

She parked her bike, smiled at the pansies, and went inside where music pumped.

Obviously, Nina had beaten her home.

She tossed her keys in the bowl on the table by the door, hung up her jacket, tucked her purse inside the closet with it, then walked into the kitchen and chaos.

Nina had her hair back in a tail and wore an apron splattered with God knew. Nina's mama had given her an apron, and sent one home to Morgan.

Bottles, jars, shakers littered their stingy counter. From where Morgan stood, it looked like some of everything made up the splatters on Nina's new bib apron.

"I did it!" Nina's eyes stayed wide and a little bit wild. "I did the marinade for the chops. I did it, Morgan." She flung open the fridge. "See?"

Gingerly, Morgan leaned in, stared through the plastic wrap on the glass bowl—borrowed from Mama for this express purpose.

"I did it with these hands!"

"And it looks"—she leaned in closer, sniffed—"and smells just like it's supposed to. Do you need to sit down?"

"Maybe. You have to do the potatoes. Having men for dinner, meat and potatoes. And since April, asparagus. And we have to cook all of that, set the table and make it nice, and make ourselves look good.

"What were we thinking?"

"Too late for that now. The table's no problem, you've got that. But if you have trouble there, I can help. They're always showing table settings on HGTV. I can do those damn potatoes. If you can do the marinade, I can do the damn potatoes. Let me at 'em."

She donned an apron. By the time she'd scrubbed the potatoes, cut them into wedges as Nina's mother's recipe instructed—then fretted because the wedges weren't the same size, and what did that mean?—it pleased her to see her apron wasn't nearly as close to a Jackson Pollock painting as Nina's.

She followed Mama's instructions to the letter, and that wasn't a snap, as, rather than precise measurements, Mama had instructed her to: Use your eyes, use your nose.

So she started. Mixing spices together in a bowl, she sniffed, eyed. Then after tossing it all together, adding the oil, she spread the potatoes on a baking sheet and hoped for the best.

She left the table to Nina, where she shined, and dived into the kitchen cleanup, where she did.

Already exhausted, she changed out of her work clothes into cropped khakis and a bright pink T-shirt, and she wondered, sincerely, how people did this sort of thing every day.

And they still had the asparagus to deal with, the rolls to warm. She donned her apron again.

Nina, looking as fresh as a spring morning, met her in the hallway.

"So just olives, cheese, some raw veggies. We're good at that part. It's too bad the kitchen's so small, no real let's-all-hang-around space."

"Next spring," Morgan vowed. "It actually smells good in here, Nina. It smells like we knew what we were doing." In the kitchen, they stood hip-to-hip and stared into the oven. "It looks right, too. Are you sure it's only, like, ten minutes for the asparagus?"

"Mama knows," Nina said, voice solemn. "But we trim it before they get here, so that's now. Then, say about seven-fifteen or so, we really casually start the asparagus. Which five minutes do you want, sauté or steam?"

"God. God. Steam."

"That's the part I want. So." Nina held out a fist. "On three."

"Damn it." Morgan hissed when Nina's rock crushed her scissors.

By seven, they had the music down to a murmur, the oven on coast, the finger food arranged.

The knock came promptly.

"Aprons off!" Nina ordered.

They answered the door together, and found two men on their stoop.

"We pulled up at the same time." Adorable Sam in his horn-rims offered Nina a bouquet of pink tulips and Morgan a bottle of wine.

"I'll reverse that." Luke handed Morgan a clutch of purple hyacinths in a clear balloon vase. "Hi, Nina. I'm Luke." And offered her another bottle of wine.

And after all the work and worry, it was easy after all.

They crowded into the kitchen and the excuse for a dining alcove with glasses of wine. It seemed to her that Luke and Sam bonded quickly—the IT guy and the more-than-casual gamer had plenty to talk about.

Hoping their luck held, Morgan dropped butter into the skillet for the asparagus.

"Nothing like a home-cooked meal when you're on the road." Luke gave her a casual kiss on the cheek. "I really appreciate it."

"Let's hope it ends up being a home-cooked meal and not a cry for help."

He laughed. "It smells fantastic. Mind if I go wash up?"

"Sure. Hallway on the left of the living room, door on the right."

"Ten-minute countdown about to start," Nina announced, and Sam slid an arm around her.

"I can't believe you guys did all this. Worked all day, then made a meal like this."

"You haven't tasted it yet," Morgan reminded him.

"Worked all day," Sam repeated, and kissed the top of Nina's head. "And spent all this time making dinner."

Pleased, Nina lifted her face for a kiss.

"Okay, here goes." Morgan slid the asparagus into the melted butter, set five minutes on her phone. She stirred and shook it around, tried to use her eyes and nose with the salt, the pepper.

While she worked the skillet, Sam helped Nina take the chops and potatoes out of the oven, slide the rolls in to warm.

"Teamwork. That's my five. You're up, Nina."

They shifted positions, with Morgan arranging the chops on a platter—Mama's—and adding the fresh rosemary as garnish—as instructed.

"Sorry." Luke came back in. "I got a phone call, had to take it."

"No problem, we're coming down to the wire." Morgan looked over at him. "Everything okay?"

"Oh yeah, just a minor schedule change for tomorrow. Can I help here?"

"Why don't you top off the wine, in case we need it."

At the table, the cooking and serving done, Sam took the first bite. "Babe," he said to Nina, then smiled at Morgan. "Other babe."

Nina sampled a bite of chop. "Uh-oh. We're good at this, Morg. Now what?"

"Home-cooked meal on the road. Ladies?" Luke lifted his wineglass. "To the chefs."

"And to Mama. We did her proud, Morgan."

Despite the long day, Morgan enjoyed every minute. An actual dinner party, in her home—a first that didn't include takeout or delivery. Conversation, laughter, the occasional touch of Luke's hand on hers.

She found it sweet the men insisted on handling the cleanup, and relaxed into the lingering after, over coffee and—bakery bought— red velvet cake.

"I hate to break this up. Tonight's going to be a highlight of my trip. But the schedule change has me on-site at eight tomorrow."

"Where are you heading?" Sam asked him.

"They're taking me into Baltimore. House flipper bought a pair of row houses and wants to connect them into one, and wants it smart. It looks like I'll need to stay over a couple days. Maybe three."

He shrugged. "They squeezed it into my schedule the end of last week. A friend of one of the bosses."

"Eight a.m. in Baltimore. That's early to rise."

He nodded at Nina. "Yeah, it sure is, and a nice challenge. Converting a couple of old row houses into a smart urban mini-mansion— while maintaining the history of the place."

He glanced around. "I'd love to tackle this one for you. You've got good bones here, Morgan."

"I think so. When that wall comes down, maybe I'll add smart as well as space."

"When you do, you call me. I'll make sure I can work you in. That's a promise. Thanks, Nina, and thank your mother." He rose. "Everything was amazing. Really great meeting you, Sam. And I should be able to take a look at your system next week. There's always a way to add some bells to the whistles."

"That would be great."

Morgan walked him to the door.

"I'll stop into the bar when I get back. Couple of days. Okay if I text you now and again when I'm in my lonely Baltimore hotel room?"

"Sure."

"Can I take you out to dinner when I get back? Maybe a step up from pizza?"

"That sounds nice."

When he kissed her, just a little deeper than that first time, with his body pressed just a little closer, she thought it sounded very nice.

"Good luck in Baltimore."

"When you're good, you don't need luck, but I'll take it. Good night, and thanks, really thanks, for dinner."

She watched him walk to his car at the curb through an April evening that had started to mist with rain.

And when she shut the door, she thought maybe, in a strange sort of way, she did have a boyfriend. Temporarily.

Nina poked out. "I heard the door close, so . . . I really liked him!"

"Me, too." Sam poked out with her.

"So do I, so it's unanimous."

"You should invite him to dinner at Mama's next Sunday. She's your Maryland Mama, and she'd love it."

"Maybe. I'll think about it. I'm calling it a night. See you in the morning, Sam?"

"Survey says yes," Nina said, and made him grin.

She got ready for bed. Just as she slipped in, she got a text from Luke.

Wednesday, Thursday latest. I'll miss seeing you until then.

Even as she smiled, felt the warmth spread, she hesitated. Then shook her head and responded with the truth.

I'll miss you, too. G'night.

When she stretched out in bed, she was still smiling.

Chapter Three

Considering its age and lack of maintenance on the part of its owner, it was no surprise when Nina's car wouldn't start on Tuesday morning.

The obliging Sam drove her to work, the head-shaking Larry towed it into his shop.

She came home complaining about a scratchy throat and Larry's bad news on repairs.

"New battery a must, something about fan belts, and something-something *and* the transmission. Larry estimates five hundred." She flicked her hands in the air. "Poof, that's gone."

"Sorry. Really sorry." And because she was, Morgan added a hard hug. "You need some tea and honey. I'll fix it."

"Thanks." Eyes heavy, pretty skin pale, Nina plopped down. "I hate spring colds, and that's what this feels like's coming on. Between that and the five hundred, I feel crappy."

"How about some soup?" Morgan opened a cupboard, took out a can. "Chicken and stars. It ain't your mama's chicken soup, but."

"That'd be good. I think I'll take a hot shower, then snuggle into bed with chicken and stars, some toast and tea and stream a happy movie. Then sleep off this poopy day."

"You go get the shower and snuggle in. I'll make you poopy-day food and bring it in."

"Best landlord ever. I'd hug you again, *amiga mia*, but I don't want to give you whatever I might have coming on."

When Morgan carried the tray in, Nina was propped up in bed with her laptop and a box of tissues.

"Thanks. Big, giant thanks. I already feel better."

"Maybe you should take a sloth-in-bed day tomorrow." After she set the tray, Morgan laid a hand on Nina's forehead. "Doesn't feel like you have a fever."

"Just a stupid April cold, and we're really busy at work."

"You can take my car if you go in."

"I've got a ride in and back, but thanks. More big, giant thanks."

She lifted the tea, blew on it, sipped. "Oh, this is just the thing. I owe you."

"When that stomach bug hit me last fall, who took care of me?"

"I did, because girlfriends. I'll conk early, sleep this off."

"Text me if you need anything. I won't text you in case you're sleeping, but I'll look in, make sure you're conked when I get home."

"Got all I need, and I'm going to chug some NyQuil. That'll conk me for sure." She spooned up some soup. "It's not Mama's, but chicken and stars always work. Have a good one."

When she got home after her shift, she found Nina fast asleep. And when she woke to an empty house, assumed Nina had turned the corner.

Around midmorning, Luke sent a text that he'd likely be an extra day on-site in Baltimore. Morgan read it between generating an invoice for a finalized bathroom remodel and taking a phone call to set up an estimate on a deck addition.

She sat in her combination office/reception area with her view of the parking lot. She didn't mind the view; it provided a heads-up on who came and went.

A snake plant thrived in the corner—one placed, according to her information, by the big boss's wife some twenty years earlier. It now stood nearly six feet tall in a red pot she couldn't have gotten her arms around.

Bill Greenwald—second-generation boss—told her his mother

insisted it served as the business's good luck charm. As long as it thrived, so would the business.

Bill's wife, Ava, still donned a hard hat and tool belt to work with the crew. On-site, everyone knew Ava was the job boss and not to be messed with.

Bill's brother, Bob, a local lawyer, handled that end of things. Bill and Ava's two children, Jack and Ella, worked alongside their parents.

She often thought, when the day came to open her own place, she'd miss working for the Greenwalds, and their tight, squabbling family.

As she read the text, Bill walked through in his usual uniform of carpenter jeans, T-shirt with a flannel shirt open over it.

He had salt-and-pepper hair under a Greenwald's Builders cap, kind eyes behind square-framed metal glasses, and arms roped with muscles.

"I see that face. Got a message from your new fella?"

"He's new, but I wouldn't call him my fella."

He shot a finger at her. "When you know, you know. My dad hired Ava, and I worked with her for a month or more. Thought nothing more than she knew how to swing a hammer and takes no shit. Then one day, she lets out this laugh. You know that laugh."

Big and bawdy. "Yes, I do."

"The laugh sunk me. 'That's the one, Bill,' I told myself. 'No two ways. You might as well get used to it.' Twenty-seven years later come September, I'm pretty well used to it. So you'll know when you know.

"Anyways, I'm heading out to meet the inspector on the Moreni job. Gonna swing by the Langston demo after, see if I can hear that laugh. Things go as they go, I should be back by three. Or I'll let you know."

"I'll hold the fort."

"You always do."

And she liked it, Morgan thought as Bill left and she cleared up a little more work.

She filled her water bottle from the bubbler, then, sitting back at her desk, sent Luke a reply.

Hope that means it's going well. If you're back, and free on Sunday, would you like to join us for dinner at Nina's parents'?

It took a few minutes, but he responded.

Sounds great! It's going really well, and I'll be back.

Glad to hear it. Sunday dinner's on the early side. We usually go over about four, eat around five. Warning: Lots of people, lots of noise, lots of food.

I'm all in. Can I pick you up at four?

Sure.

Hope to see you Friday night, but absolutely on Sunday. Have to go.

He added a flower emoji.

When her smiley face emoji popped on his screen, he used his solenoid card to open the pathetic lock on her back door.

People, especially women, were so damn stupid.

He glanced around a house that rated dump on his scale. Still, the good bones, the location made it worthwhile.

In and out, he reminded himself, and moved straight to her home office. He'd uninstall the software he'd installed during his "bathroom break" the previous Monday night.

No bread crumbs left behind there.

Then he'd finish a very profitable few weeks in a matter of hours. Top it all off his way.

She'd see him before she expected to.

He imagined killing her in the parking lot of the bar, beside her car. But if she wasn't—as she usually was—the last one out, he'd be *in* the car, tucked in the back.

Then, surprise! And then the finale. Dump her body, drive the car to an associate in Baltimore. Make an exchange for the I'm-woke Prius, and be on his merry, merry way.

At least he hadn't had to fuck her first. Then again, he was a man who knew his marks, and had known straight off Morgan Albright wouldn't be an easy lay. Saved time, effort, and bullshit.

But boy, she'd been easy in every other way.

With hands covered in surgical gloves, he opened her laptop.

He booted it up, and honestly wondered why the woman didn't—or hadn't—spent any of her hard-earned money on newer equipment.

He'd already started the uninstall when he heard the pad of footsteps behind him.

He turned, innocent smile in place, as Nina—definitely not looking her best—stepped up to the doorway.

"Luke?" Voice hoarse, she coughed on the name. "What are you doing here?"

"Hey! I talked Morgan into letting me add some software to her laptop. I came in the back. Didn't want to wake you." No question she was sick, he decided, so time to improvise.

And put on his best sympathetic face.

"She said you weren't feeling well, probably sleeping. I'm sorry I woke you."

"Spring cold. Lousy. My boss sent me home, drove me home. I was just . . . How did Morgan know I was home sick? Did Angie call her?"

Too complicated, he decided. And she must've seen something in his eyes, because he saw something in hers. It said: Run.

Before she could, he grabbed the laptop, swung it hard. It cracked against the side of her head, and the other side of her head cracked against the doorframe.

She barely made a sound.

As she went down, he swung the laptop again—piece of shit anyway—and hit her again.

She'd fucked it up for him, and there'd be no capping it off his way with Morgan now.

So substitution.

"Wrong place," he said as he knelt down, dragged her onto her back so he could put his hands around her throat. "Wrong time for a sick day, bitch. Wrong girl, but you'll have to do."

It gave him a rush, always gave him a rush, to squeeze death out of life.

Though her eyes wheeled, her heels drummed, she never came fully around.

He left her and the broken laptop on the floor.

Adjusting, he hunted through the kitchen, found a trash bag. He loaded it with Nina's laptop, her phone, some jewelry he didn't judge as worth the pawning, found a hundred and fifty-eight dollars between her purse and her underwear drawer.

He went through Morgan's room. She actually owned a couple decent pieces of jewelry. Diamond studs—small, but good color and cut—a gold locket—looked old, probably a family piece. He tossed in some of the crap jewelry with it.

He thought waste not, want not as he loaded up.

Marks always squirreled some cash in the house. He found Morgan's—five twenties—rolled in a pair of athletic socks.

He grabbed her keys from the bowl by the front door, then went out the way he'd come in.

He used his elbow to break one of the panes of glass on the back door.

Daylight B and E gone bad, gone tragic—that's how it would look. Too bad, so sad.

He unlocked the car with the fob, tossed the goodie bag in the back.

He backed out of the drive and drove in the opposite direction of the city center. Humming along with Billie Eilish's cover of "Yesterday," he drove toward Baltimore.

A shower hit just as Morgan started to leave work. She checked the radar on her phone. A quick one, heading west.

She opted to wait it out and texted Nina to say so and ask if she wanted in on some Chinese takeout.

The lack of response made her frown.

"Lingering cold, maybe," she murmured as she watched the rain. "Post-work nap." She ordered some extra noodles and sweet and sour shrimp just in case.

Fifteen minutes later, she headed out in the damp air under sunny skies. She stopped for the takeout, secured it and her purse in the basket.

She expected a fairly quiet night at the Round, as Wednesday tended to be slower. They hadn't opened the outdoor seating area yet, but soon would.

When she got her place, she wanted a full patio area with a pergola, and she'd have heaters so customers could use it except in the coldest or rainiest of weather.

More seating, more sales, more profit.

When she didn't see her car in the driveway, her heart jumped. Then she realized Nina must have needed to go somewhere. Maybe more NyQuil.

Still, she always asked.

She went inside, nodded when she saw the empty key bowl. She hung up her jacket, stowed her purse, then detoured to Nina's room.

Definitely came home and went out again, she decided. The tissue box was back on the bed.

More tea and honey, she thought, and went to the kitchen to put the kettle on and stow the takeout.

She froze, simply froze when she saw the broken pane in the door, the shards of glass on the floor.

She backed up, breath already catching as she fumbled out the phone in her pocket. Her brain wouldn't function beyond nine-one-one.

"Nine-one-one. What's your emergency?"

"A break-in, a break-in. The kitchen door."

She looked toward the bedrooms, then toward her office.

And saw the hand, the forearm, the blood in the hallway.

"Oh God! Oh God. It's Nina!" She sprinted to the office, dropped to the floor. "Hurry, please hurry—229 Newberry Street. She's hurt. There's blood. She's not moving."

"Help's on the way. Can you give me your name?"

"Morgan. Nina's hurt, there's blood. I think—I think she's dead. No. No. No. What can I do? What should I do?"

"Morgan, is there an intruder in your house?"

"I don't know. I don't know. She's not breathing. I can't find a pulse. Help me."

"Help's coming. Can you hear the sirens? You should go outside now, Morgan, wait for the ambulance, the police."

"I'm not leaving her here. Should I do CPR? I—I took a class. She's cold. God, she's so cold. I should get a blanket."

"Nina's cold?"

"I'll get a blanket."

"Morgan, the ambulance is pulling up now. Do you hear the sirens? Go let them in, Morgan. Go open the door."

She veered off from her race to grab the throw off the sofa and yanked open the front door.

"Hurry, please. She's cold, and she's bleeding. She won't wake up."

She ran behind the EMTs, then stood with her hands crossed over her mouth.

One, a woman with dark red hair and soft blue eyes, looked at her. "Ma'am, how long has she been like this?"

"I don't know. I just got home. I was late, the rain, and the Chinese takeout, and I got home and saw the broken glass, and then Nina. Can you wake her up?"

"I'll call it," the other EMT murmured, and the female walked to Morgan.

"Let's sit down."

"Are you taking her to the hospital?" Something hard and heavy pressed on her chest. She couldn't get her breath. Something high and sharp rang in her ears. "She needs to go to the hospital."

"I'm sorry, very sorry, but there's nothing we can do. Your friend's dead."

"No. No."

"I'm sorry. You're in shock. Let's sit down."

"No. No," Morgan repeated, even as the EMT guided her toward the sofa. "I—I dropped the takeout. I dropped it on the floor."

"We'll worry about that later."

She eased Morgan onto the sofa, tucked the throw around her as she started to shake.

Then looked over as two uniformed officers came in the open door.

"DB down that hall with my partner. Nine-one-one caller's in shock. DB's cold, gone a couple hours at least. Can you tell me your name?"

"Morgan. Morgan Albright. She's Nina, Nina Ramos." Tears began to spill. "Please, can't you help her?"

"I'm going to get you some water. Sit right here and talk to this officer."

"Ms. Albright." The cop sat beside her. Morgan tried to focus on his face, but it blurred in and out.

"I'm Officer Randall. Can you tell me what happened?"

"I don't know. I don't know. It was raining. I didn't want to ride home in the rain, so I waited, and I wanted Chinese, so I got takeout. Nina didn't answer when I texted, but she has a cold, so maybe taking a nap, I thought. Maybe. And my car was gone, and hers is in the shop, so maybe she took it to get something. That's okay. She's knows it's okay."

"Your car? What kind of car?"

"Um. Thank you." Everything seemed distant now, far away. Like the wrong end of a telescope.

She took the water, used both trembling hands to lift it. "A Prius."

"What color, what year? Do you know the tag number?"

"It's blue. Dark blue. 2019. I—I can't remember the number. I can't think of it."

"That's all right. You came home and found Nina?"

"I came home, and I looked in her room. She'd come home from work because she had the box of tissues on the bed. She has a cold. And I was going to make her tea. I put the kettle on. I forgot I need to turn it off."

"I did," the EMT told her. "It's fine."

"I saw the broken glass. I saw it, and I got scared and I called nine-one-one. Then I saw her. I saw her arm, and the blood."

"Where were you before you came home?"

"At work. At Greenwald's Builders. It started to rain."

"Right about five o'clock. Didn't last long."

"No. I looked at the radar so I waited it out, and I called in the order for dinner."

"How'd you get home?"

"On my bike. I usually ride my bike to my day job if the weather's okay. And if Nina doesn't have a date and I have time, we usually have something to eat before I go back to work."

"At Greenwald's?"

"No, no. The Next Round."

"You're the bartender," Randall said. "I thought I recognized you from somewhere. I've been in a few times. Ms. Albright, is there someone we can call for you, somewhere you can stay tonight?"

"I live here."

"Maybe there's someplace else you can stay tonight?"

"I don't . . ." It hit her, hard, so hard, and everything came into vicious focus. "She's dead. Nina's dead. Somebody broke in and did that to her. We don't even have anything that's worth anything. We don't have anything."

"Why don't we look around just to see if you notice anything missing. How about in Nina's room?"

She got up, walked through the terrible clarity into Nina's room.

"I don't see her laptop. Her parents gave her a MacBook for Christmas. Not this one, the one before. It was pink. The cover. And her phone—iPhone. But it could be in her pocket."

She took a deep breath. "Someone's been in her dresser. She's messy, but she doesn't leave the drawers open like that."

"Can you look in without touching anything?"

"The boxes are on the floor. The clear organizers for her jewelry. She didn't have anything important, but she kept her jewelry in those boxes, and they're on the floor. She'd have had a little cash—I don't know how much—but a little in with her underwear. It couldn't have been more than a hundred dollars."

"Anything else?"

"I don't know."

"We'll look in your room."

She crossed the hall, took a long breath.

"I'm not messy. Somebody went through my things. I had, oh God, I had small diamond studs and an antique gold locket that was my great-grandmother's. Everything else was just costume. I had five twenties rolled in those socks on the floor."

She closed her eyes, felt herself want to sway. Stiffened against it.

"My laptop, back in my office. The room where—the other room. It was on the floor. It was on the floor and broken and there was blood. It didn't really register before. They hit her with it. It was broken and bloody on the floor. They hit her and they killed her. And I wasn't home to help her."

She swiped at tears that wouldn't stop falling. "The key fob wasn't in the bowl by the front door. They saw it, and just drove away in my car after they did this to her."

She drew another breath. "License number 5GFK82."

"That's very helpful."

"You have to find who did this. She'd have given them anything they wanted. They didn't have to do this. She works at Let It Bloom Garden Center. Somebody would have brought her home because her car's in the shop. So somebody knows when she got home. Her mama—"

That broke her, so she dropped down to the floor and let all the tears come.

They wanted to give her a mild sedative, but she wouldn't take it. Feeling was all she had, and she wouldn't let go of it. They urged her to stay somewhere else while they did whatever they had to do.

She wouldn't.

She sat outside, alone. Forced herself to call the bar, which set off more tears, and more offers to stay elsewhere.

Bill showed up—she supposed her night boss called her day boss. He said nothing, just sat beside her, put his arms around her.

"You're going to come home with me now," he said after she'd stopped the last bout of weeping.

"I can't. I can't. I feel like I'd never be able to come back if I left now. I feel like I couldn't ever live here if I left tonight. It's my home. I need my home."

"I'm going to fix that broken glass and put a dead bolt on the door. I'm not leaving until they say I can do that. And I'm going to have Ava bring over my car. You're going to borrow my car. I got the truck. I'm not leaving you here without a car. That's firm."

"Okay. Thank you. They have to find my car so they can find who did this. Then they have to go to prison forever."

"You bet your ass, sweetheart. Don't you come into work tomorrow. Don't you come in until you feel you can. You understand?"

"I want to—need to—go to Nina's family tomorrow. I don't want to intrude tonight. I just feel I shouldn't be there tonight. And Sam . . . The police said they'd talk to him, didn't want me to tell him yet. I'm not stupid, they want to make sure he wasn't here. He'd never have hurt her, but they need to talk to him. I need to talk to him tomorrow."

"If you need anything, there are plenty of people who'd jump to help. You matter around here, Morgan." He gave her a pat on the knee.

"I'm going to see about fixing that door."

When, long after midnight, she was finally alone—it seemed like days rather than hours—she looked at the card one of the cops had given her. For a crime scene cleanup.

The crime scene they said they'd cleared, like a table of dirty dishes.

The crime scene where Nina had died.

But she wouldn't call them. It was Nina, and she'd do it herself. The last thing she could really do for someone she'd loved like a sister.

So, late into the night in a house that echoed with silence, she got the bucket, the scrub brush.

They'd taken the laptop—evidence. They'd taken photos and videos and dusted for prints. The detectives had talked to her—questions, questions, over and over. But they'd left the blood behind on the floor, the doorjamb, the wall just inside her office.

It took a long time, longer because she'd gotten sick once, then broken down twice. But she managed. She'd do it all again in the strong daylight if she needed to.

She tossed the takeout, allowed herself a single glass of wine in hopes it would help her sleep.

And in the quiet, in the empty, she lay down in Nina's bed, hugged the pillow that smelled like Nina's shampoo.

Though she thought she'd emptied herself of tears, she wept again.

As dawn broke on another April morning, she finally drifted into the peace of sleep.

Chapter Four

Morgan tread water in a well of grief. She couldn't sink, couldn't allow herself to just go under. She had to talk to the police again. Answer questions, make formal statements. It kept the grief fresh and the water in the well deep.

Nina's family had become her family, and she couldn't help them if she sank. She sat with them, mourned with them, did her best to help with the funeral arrangements.

Both her bosses insisted she take a week off, and coworkers dropped off food. Casseroles, pasta dishes, ham, chicken.

She shared it with Sam. If he wasn't with Nina's family, he was with her.

He had his own well.

She sat with him while they both picked at the latest casserole.

"Still no word on your car?"

"No." Since he'd brought wine as his contribution to the meal neither of them much wanted, she sipped at her glass. "I guess it's gone. The cops don't say that right out, but what they do say makes it pretty clear. I filed the insurance claim today."

He gave her hand a sympathetic rub. "Nightmares?"

"Yeah, well."

"Me, too. Offer's still open for me to stay any night you want, or for you to bunk with me."

"I know."

"Or if you have a bad one, just call me."

Now she rubbed his hand. "Same goes. Bill's been great about lending me his car, but I need to start looking for one. Before I go back to work."

"If you want help with that, just ask."

"Thanks."

She didn't mention the insurance payoff would be a hell of a lot less than she'd paid for the car—already used and with significant mileage—minus her high deductible.

But that was a problem for another day.

"We finished packing up her room today. Nina's sister and mother and I."

He nodded, met her eyes. "I stopped to see her parents before I came over. The photos you helped them choose for the service are perfect."

"They don't blame me."

"Because you're not to blame."

"My head knows that. Or it's almost got that. But . . . I never, never imagined anyone breaking in here. Honestly, what did the son of a bitch get out of it? Even the car isn't worth that much. If I'd put in better locks, or invested in an alarm system."

"Stop." This time he took her hand, held it. "Stop that. She texted me her boss sent her home—so we could say what if her boss hadn't sent her home. We could say what if I'd come over to bring her some cold medicine, make her some soup or whatever. Plenty of what-ifs. But the fact is, nobody's to blame but the person who did this. Nobody."

Because she knew that, she nodded. And still.

"It was so hard to box up the last of her things, Sam, and take them out of her room. To go back in there alone, and there was nothing left of her there."

"She loved living here with you. I knew I was going to have a hell of a time talking her into moving in with me because she loved living here with you."

Tears rose into her throat, burned there. "You were going to ask her?"

"I was going to give it a little while longer." With a half smile, he tapped the side of his head. "Strategy. I know we'd only gotten serious for a few weeks, but I'd been serious about her a lot longer."

"She knew."

"Did she?"

And in his eyes she saw the sorrow, as immeasurable as her own.

"Oh yeah. You weren't a fling for her, Sam. It would've taken some convincing, some time, but she'd have said yes."

"How are we going to get over her, Morgan? What are we going to do without her?"

"I have no idea. I think about how we painted her bedroom before she moved in. I only had this place a few weeks before she did, so Nina was here right from the start, really. She had that lilac paint in her hair, on her face by the time we'd finished."

Morgan could see it, could see Nina, as clear as yesterday.

"And how she showed me how to plant flowers, and how she wouldn't take no, and dragged me to my first Ramos family dinner."

"Nothing like them."

"She wanted to set me up with her brother, Rick."

Sam swigged some beer. "Yeah, well. No."

That teased a half laugh out of her tight throat.

"I remember the night she brought you into the Round so I could size you up."

"We had tequila shots."

"You did. And oh God, the night we made dinner. When I came home from work, she was standing right over there. The kitchen looked like she'd set off a bomb. She was wild-eyed because she'd successfully made the marinade for the chops."

"It was a really good night."

"An excellent night."

He pushed more food around his plate. "You still haven't heard from Luke?"

"I think, like my car, that's gone. He never answered my text or call about Nina. Some people just don't handle, or don't want to handle emotional upheaval."

She shrugged. "It's good to know before things went anywhere."

"He seemed like a really solid guy."

"Transient—he was up front on that at the start. But solid in the moment." She shrugged again. "Gone now. It doesn't matter," she said, and meant it. "He doesn't matter."

Before Sam left he checked the locks on the back door, as he always did.

"I'll see you tomorrow. Or I can pick you up, take you if you want."

"I've got Bill's car."

"I've never been to a funeral Mass."

"Me neither." And even the idea had her stomach churning. "We'll stick together."

"Right." He hugged her, as he always did. "Lock the door behind me."

She knew he waited until he heard the locks click, just as she knew she'd obsessively check the back door locks again. Then the front door before she went to bed.

Alone, she walked into Nina's empty room, where the cheerful walls showed their deeper shades where pictures had hung.

Flower posters—always flowers for Nina. And the faded square where she'd had her corkboard to pin up drawings from young cousins, her nieces and nephews. She'd pinned up notes to herself, appointment cards.

Nothing left but those shapes to say Nina Ramos lived here.

She'd have to get another housemate. She couldn't really afford the mortgage and everything else without that income. But she didn't know how she could bear having someone else in this room.

She shut off the light, closed the door, and told herself she'd deal with it because she had to.

At ten the next morning, she sat with Sam in a pew behind the rows of Nina's family.

Her parents, grandparents, siblings, cousins, aunts, uncles, nieces, nephews, some who'd traveled in from out of state and as far away as Mexico.

Family, friends, coworkers, others she'd gone to school with, customers from the garden center, packed the church. One of her cousins sang, and beautifully.

Though her sister gave the core eulogy, others spoke. Since Nina's mother had asked Morgan to speak, she slid out of the pew, walked by the flower-draped casket, and talked of her friendship, talked of how Nina had helped her make her first home a home, taught her how to plant her first garden, had given her family when she'd been so far away from her own.

It was all like a dream, the ritual, the music, the flowers, the words— even her own words.

When it was done, she wondered why she felt no different than she had when it began. As she drove with the others to the cemetery, she thought that after the burial, after that ritual, those words, she'd feel some lessening of grief, some sense of closure—or the inching toward it.

But when again she sat beside Sam, this time gripping his hand as if she'd float away without that anchor, nothing changed. The priest said more words, and she sensed comfort in them even if she couldn't feel it.

She felt the cool April air on her face, saw the green of the grass, the grays and white of marble headstones. The flowers, so many flowers for Nina.

Somewhere—not far—a bird sang.

The sun dashed off the polished wood of the coffin. It illuminated the blanket of white roses over it.

She thought of Nina inside it, in the pale pink dress her mother had chosen. They'd had no viewing, but Mama wanted her to wear the pink dress, to have a white rosebud in her hair.

But she wasn't in there, Morgan realized. Nina wasn't inside the silk-lined box in her pink dress with a rose in her hair.

She'd gone to wherever those who leave us go. She'd gone before Morgan had come home to find her lying on the floor.

Already gone.

Graves and stones and words and music weren't for the dead, but the living they left behind.

Somehow, believing that, she allowed herself to sink, for a moment. For a moment, she pressed her face to Sam's shoulder, let the grief take her under.

When she could breathe again, feel that cool spring air again, she'd inched, just a little, toward closure.

She embraced the family, one by one. She gave and exchanged condolences through a headache that came on like a storm.

As she walked back to Bill's car, she thought, one more part. One more left in the ritual for the living. Back to the family home for food, for community.

It helped, more than she'd anticipated, that community. With the food, the drink, the tears, some laughter as people shared stories and memories.

Still, she slipped away after an hour as the headache raged and fatigue set in. She wanted nothing so much as to take off the black dress, one she knew she'd never wear again, then to lie down and sleep.

To be alone before she had to face what came after.

She'd have to face life again.

As she pulled into her driveway, two people got out of a car parked at the curb. She paused as they started up the walk in their black suits.

Not reporters, she thought. She'd learned to spot and avoid them over the last week.

More cops? she wondered. Insurance people?

Why now? What more did they want from her? What more could she say?

"Ms. Albright?" The male suit, graying hair, compact body, held up a badge. As did the woman, dark skin, hair in short, dark coils, deep brown eyes oddly cool.

"FBI Special Agents Morrison and Beck. Could we speak with you?"

As the headache pounded, pounded, Morgan stared at the identification. "FBI? I don't understand."

"We know you've had a difficult day, but if we could come in and explain."

"It's about Nina?"

"Yes, ma'am."

She felt that tiny inch toward closure slide away again.

"All right." She led the way. "I've talked to the police, and gave a statement. I honestly don't know anything else."

She unlocked the door, went inside.

"I can make coffee," she offered, only because she thought she should.

The woman—Beck—nodded slightly. "If it's not too much trouble."

"No, it's okay. Sit down. It'll only take a minute."

Instead of sitting in the living room, Morrison followed her, stood just inside the kitchen. "You have a nice house."

"Thank you." She saw his gaze shift to the back door as she started the coffee. "Bill, my boss, fixed the door. The police—the detectives that came after the other police that day, and the crime scene people—they said it was okay to fix the broken glass and put in the dead bolt."

"Of course."

"It just had the thumb lock before. He broke the glass, and just reached in and flipped it open."

"He?"

"He, she, they, I don't know."

"She was home unexpectedly from work?"

Again, she thought. She had to say it all again.

"They sent her home sick. She had a cold, and it got worse at work. The coworker who drove her home because her car was in the shop said they stopped so she could buy some DayQuil. She must've been in bed because the bottle was on the nightstand, and a box of tissues on the bed."

She kept her hands busy, got out mugs, creamer, sugar, spoons, a tray.

She'd say it all again, she thought, then they'd go away so she could sleep.

"The detectives said it looked like he went to my office, either to start there or to hide there if he heard her. The house should've been empty, but it wasn't. He was in there, and she walked in or started to, and he killed her.

"How many times do I have to say it?"

"Why don't I take that tray in for you?"

She let him because she wanted to sit down. She wanted to sit and get this all over with.

Beck picked it up as soon as they walked in.

"You kept your car fob in the house. In plain view?"

"Yes, Jesus." The reasonable part of her knew they did a job, but the rest of her just didn't care.

"I said all this, too. I kept it in that bowl by the door. Come in, put it in the bowl, always know where it is. He thought the house would be empty—that's what the detectives think."

Struggling, she pressed her fingers to her eyes.

Just get it over with.

"He broke in, killed Nina because she was here. He took her jewelry and mine—not worth much—I had a hundred in cash rolled in a sock, he got that and whatever cash she had in her drawer. It wouldn't have been much. He took her MacBook and her phone. No point in taking my laptop, since it broke when he broke her. It was five years old anyway, and not worth much. Then he took the fob out of the bowl and drove away in my car."

"I don't know anything else."

Beck opened a slim briefcase, took out a photo. "Do you recognize this man?"

His hair was longer and sort of carelessly, stylishly windblown, but otherwise . . .

The headache rolled nausea into her belly.

"Luke Hudson."

"How do you know him?"

"He came into the bar where I work nights, about three weeks ago. The Next Round. He came into the bar. I tend bar. He wanted a local draft, struck up a conversation. He said he was in the area for a few months. IT work, smart homes and offices."

Because her hands shook, she slid them under her thighs. "But that's not true, is it? Or you wouldn't be here. Did he do this? I don't understand how that could be. Did he do this?"

"Was he ever in here?" Morrison, ignoring the question, pushed on. "In your house?"

"Once. We had dinner. Me, Nina, him, and Sam—Nina was seeing Sam Nichols. We had them over for dinner the . . . the . . . the . . . "

She paused, pressed her lips together. "The Monday night before she died. My night off."

Beck wrote something in a notebook. Morgan began to rub her hands over arms that had chilled.

"I . . . He came into the bar a few times. Had local drafts, some food, conversation. He was friendly, but not pushy. He talked with some of the other customers. After he came in a few times, he asked me to dinner. Casual, pizza, and I decided why not? I met him at Luigi's and we had pizza and wine."

"Did you have a sexual relationship?"

She looked at Beck. "No. He came into the bar a handful of times. We had pizza one night, and Nina and I decided to have him and Sam to dinner—Monday's my night off. I said that already," she remembered. "I have Sunday and Monday nights off unless we're short-staffed at the bar."

"So he came to dinner," Morrison prompted.

"Yes." She tucked her hands under her thighs again. "We cooked— the first time either of us made a real dinner. And he had a change in his schedule, he said, and had to do a job in Baltimore, two or three days. He texted me a few times while he was gone."

"Did he leave the room where you were, the three of you were, at any point?"

"No, we . . ." She pulled her hands free, pressed her fingers to her eyes again. Now the headache lived there, too.

"Yes. Yes, he did. He asked if he could wash up. The half bath is down there." She gestured. "When he came back, he apologized for taking so long, said he got a call he had to take."

"How long was he gone?"

"I don't know. We were drinking wine, talking, and . . . Wait. Wait."

She shoved her hands through her hair. "Asparagus. I think . . . Yes, nearly ten minutes. Did he do this? Who is he? Why would he do this? For a MacBook and a used Prius? That's crazy."

"His name is Gavin Rozwell, and this is what he does. He's a psychopath, a con artist, a serial killer. And you, Ms. Albright, are his type."

"I'm his type? What type?"

"Slender blonde, single, between the ages of twenty-four and thirty. The androgynous name's a plus."

She heard the words as Beck spoke them, but they seemed to come out in some strange, foreign language. "What?"

"It makes it simple for him to steal your identity and become Morgan Albright. He would have selected you, researched you before he walked into that bar."

"Still crazy," she insisted. "Why would he want to steal my identity? I'm nobody. I don't have anything."

"You have this house," Morrison pointed out. "You had a car. You work two jobs, so you're bound to have a bank account."

"And first and foremost," Beck added, "he enjoys it. Do you have any credit cards?"

"I have one. I use it primarily for food and gas, pay it off monthly. It's good to build my credit rating."

"He's likely run that up, opened at least one more, and run that to its limit. Do you bank online?"

"Yes. My work schedule . . ."

"Have you checked your bank account in the last week?"

"No. Why would I? We just buried Nina. Today. We buried Nina today."

"Could you check it now?"

She nearly got up to go to her office and laptop before she remembered. And took out her phone.

What color she had left in her face leached away. "This can't be right. It can't be. It says I have less than two hundred dollars. I had over twelve thousand, just over. I've been saving for years. This is a mistake."

"It's cyber theft, Ms. Albright. I'm sorry," Morrison went on. "It's likely worse. You're a homeowner, and that's something he targets. It's very likely he used your identity and the information he got off your computer to take out equity loans, maybe a business loan. He'd have used lending companies rather than banks, agreed to a higher interest rate for the quick turnaround. The malware he likely installed on your computer in that ten minutes allowed him to channel access to your accounts."

"He's very skilled in this area," Beck continued. "It's probable he got into the house—he wouldn't have broken the window initially. He would have uninstalled the malware and walked out again. But Ms. Ramos was here, she saw him. He staged the break-in, took your valuables, the cash on hand to cover the rest."

"Ms. Albright." Morrison waited until her glazed eyes shifted to his face. "We've very sorry for what's happened to you. Very sorry for what happened to your friend. My partner and I have been after Rozwell for years. What happened here didn't immediately get our attention, as Ms. Ramos isn't his usual type, his target type. She was petite, dark hair, her name, no homeownership, and the clumsy burglary. Then an article came up in a search and mentioned you. Your house, your car."

"And you are his type," Beck continued. "When he was finished wiping you out financially, he would have killed you. He knows your schedule, your habits, had gained your trust. He'd have gotten you alone and done to you what he did to Ms. Ramos."

"But you're alive. You're the first one of his victims we've been able to speak with."

"I have to—" She shoved up, dashed to the half bath. When she was finished being sick, she splashed water on her face, scooped more out of the faucet to clear her mouth and throat.

In the mirror she saw a ghost of herself, sheet white, glassy eyes. Now that the sickness passed, all she had was numb.

She went back, lowered into the chair. "What am I supposed to do?"

"I know this is a shock," Morrison began. "I know this is a very, very difficult time. Can we call someone for you?"

"No. What am I supposed to do?"

"You're the first we've been able to interview," Beck repeated. "The only survivor we know of. We need you to tell us everything you can remember. What he did, what he said. You said he texted you, so we'd like to copy those. Regarding the identity theft, your situation? I'd advise you to hire a lawyer as soon as possible to try to deal with that."

"With what?" she demanded. "I'm broke. He came into the bar on a Tuesday night," she remembered, and told them everything she could think of.

It got worse, and kept getting worse.

Over the next six weeks, the full extent of the damage Gavin Rozwell wrought dropped hard. He'd managed to reroute her last mortgage payment, sucked up her last two direct deposit paychecks—one from each job. He'd run up her credit card to the tune of $8,321.85 as well as taking out two more major cards for a total there that hit over fifteen thousand.

He'd taken out a home equity loan on her house, in her name, using all her financial data. Her careful, hard-won home improvements had increased the value of her house since she'd purchased it, and her credit score was excellent. He'd taken out the maximum allowed, and had walked away with twenty-five thousand. And that in addition to a business start-up loan he'd wrangled, with her home as collateral, for another twenty-five thousand.

He shouldn't have been able to get two loans, two different lenders, but he'd done it—as she learned he'd done it before.

The insurance payment on her stolen car barely covered the amount she owed on it.

She had nothing left but debt, legal tangles, and grief.

Worse, somehow worse, he'd used the MacBook to wipe out Nina's meager savings in the hours between her death and when Morgan found her.

She had no pride left to swallow when she called her grandmother and asked for money to hire a lawyer.

Though both her employers offered her financial help, that she couldn't swallow.

And though it shamed her, she accepted the offer of Nina's car.

She had to work, and needed transportation to get there.

She planted no garden that summer.

On a Sunday morning in mid-July, she learned of yet another loan taken in her name when two men came to the house.

One look told her: bill collectors, so she turned off the lawn mower and waited.

"Looking for Morgan Albright."

"I'm Morgan Albright."

The two men exchanged a look. "Don't look like him."

"Because I'm not a him," she said wearily. "If this is about the equity loan, the business loan, the credit card charges, my lawyer's handling it."

"You're overdue, Morgan. Mr. Castle lent you the twenty in good faith. Full payment and interest due July first. Interest's doubling every day since the first."

"I don't know a Mr. Castle, and he didn't lend me anything. I'm dealing with identity theft, and can give you the contact for my lawyer and the FBI agents investigating."

"Mr. Castle's not interested in your problems, lady. Morgan Albright took the money, Morgan Albright pays."

"How about you give us ten percent, show of good faith," the second man suggested. "You don't want any trouble."

They might as well have asked her for the moon and a couple of planets.

"I have nothing but trouble! I don't have ten percent of anything because he took everything. You're looking for a man named Gavin Rozwell. He took this Mr. Castle's money."

She threw up her hands. "I work two jobs and I can barely cover the bills. I've got lawyer's fees piling up because he took out two other loans in my name, and it's a nightmare. For God's sake, he beat and strangled my friend. Go find him. Go find the son of a bitch because it doesn't look like the cops can."

"That's some story. It's going to buy you a week. Things won't be so polite when we come back."

She called the police, she called the special agents.

And the next morning she found the tires slashed on Nina's car.

Tears were finished. She might have trembled all the way to work, but tears were finished. She didn't tell Bill, or anyone but the police. Even the idea of talking about it exhausted her.

To help make the mortgage—nobody wanted to rent a murdered woman's room—she took extra shifts on Monday nights.

A gift from the boss, she knew, as she wasn't needed.

Rather than biking home, changing, maybe making a sandwich, she'd grabbed her bar clothes after she'd seen the tires. She changed in the bathroom at Greenwald's, did what she could with her makeup.

It would mean biking home after midnight, but she had reflectors and a headlight. It's fine, she told herself.

She served locals, mixed drinks for tourists.

A man sat on an empty stool. Stocky build, mid-fifties, ink-black hair worn with a hint of wave. He wore a baby-blue golf shirt—Lacoste—and summer-weight khakis.

"Nice evening," he said.

"It certainly is. What can I get you?"

"Bombay and tonic, twist of lime. Nice place," he added as he looked around. "Got a nice feel to it."

"We think so. First time in?"

"Yep. Just passing through. From the area, are you?"

"I am now." When she served his drink, he laid a piece of notepaper with a number on it. "That's what he owes me as of today." Then he held up a hand. "I didn't bring you any trouble. Came here to have a one-on-one, public place."

Her throat clicked as she tried, and failed, to swallow. "I don't have any money."

"I said this"—he tapped the paper—"is what *he* owes me. Not you. He screwed over both of us. My employees brought me your story. I get a lot of sad stories, lots of bullshit stories, but yours checked out."

He lifted his drink, watching her as he sipped. "Nice pour on the Bombay. So, I'm telling you, you won't have any trouble on my end." He put the paper back in his pocket. "It's not your debt to pay. Didn't seem right to add that to your list of troubles, so you can cross it off."

He drank some more. "He gave me a sad story. He's got a way with a story. No need to go into it. Pisses me off. Your name, your address, where you work. Both jobs. Anything about him you know I didn't read in the news reports and such?"

"I don't know. I didn't read any of it. I couldn't."

He just nodded. "I read about your friend, saw her picture. Beautiful girl. Only sick fuckers do that to beautiful girls."

He took out a money clip, peeled off two fifties.

"We're clear, you and me. My word on it, and my word's good. I'm sorry for your troubles."

"Mr. Castle." She nudged the bills toward him. "This is too much."

He shook his head. "I pay my debts," he said, and walked out.

When she stepped out of the house the next morning, Nina's car had four new tires.

Chapter Five

Summer rolled into autumn without any of Morgan's usual pleasure in the change of seasons.

Reality had to be faced.

Juggling, juggling, juggling, she'd tried to hold on. But the lawyer fees mounted to beyond what she'd asked her grandmother to lend her.

She couldn't bring herself to ask for more, not when she so clearly saw her life become an endless cycle of work, bills, debt, worry.

They wanted to come, her mother, her grandmother, but she couldn't face that either and put them off.

Even working nearly eighty hours a week, she fell behind. Nina's car—it would forever be Nina's car—needed more work, and though she knew Larry bottomed down his price for her, it cut into the budget.

Her washing machine decided to revolt and flood the day after she'd stolen enough from the budget to replace the balding tires on her bike.

Then her lights went off.

She'd paid the bill, but it seemed Gavin Rozwell had taken one more shot. Using her account number, he'd discontinued service. As she worked to straighten that out—with the power company rep insisting turning the power back on required a fee—she learned he'd canceled her homeowner's insurance and filed a huge fraudulent claim against her medical insurance.

It could all be fixed, the lawyer assured her. For more legal fees, more court costs, more money poured out in hopes of recouping it later.

By November she accepted she was in over her head, and she'd never come up for the third time.

With Sam, she visited Nina's grave with its pure white stone. The wind blew hard, scattered dead leaves, and overhead the sky held thick and gray with a rain that would come icy when it fell.

They hadn't brought flowers. They'd agreed Nina would hate for them to lay flowers that would wither and die in the cold.

"I know she's not here." Morgan tipped her head toward Sam's shoulder. "I still feel her in the house sometimes. It helps. Is that weird?"

"I don't think so." He slid an arm around her. "I go over for family dinner every few weeks because it helps. I haven't seen you there for a while."

"I barely have time to catch my next breath."

"I'm so sorry, Morgan. I keep hoping it'll level out for you."

"I'm putting the house up for sale."

"Oh, come on." Stepping back, he gripped her arms. "There has to be something."

"I can't hold on to it. If I pay the mortgage, I fall behind on something else. If I pay the something else, I miss the mortgage payment. I'm buried in legal fees, but the hits keep coming."

She breathed deep. "Can we walk? I feel like I'm dumping this on Nina, and that *is* weird, since I just said she's not here."

"We'll walk." He took her hand as they did. "There's got to be a way I can help. You have a lot of people who'd help, Morgan."

"I know that, but he didn't just ruin me, he's ruined this place for me. He sucked all the joy out, Sam. The house is a burden now, not my home, just another weight to try to lift every day. I don't know how long it would take me to get back on my feet, but I know it'll take years for me to get back to where I was."

"The son of a bitch. Why can't they find the son of a bitch?"

"I don't know. Way back, when he first started coming into the bar, Gracie—you know, head waitress at the Round—she said he was smooth. And she didn't trust smooth. God, she was right."

"What are you going to do?"

"Sell the house. The Realtor advised me to wait until March or April, and that it might take that long to sell anyway. But I've got to get started on that. I'll stick it out until it sells because I don't have a choice, but I have to get started."

She looked out at the headstones, the monuments, the flowers that would wither and die.

"Then I'm moving to Vermont."

"Ah hell, Morgan."

"I can't stay here, going backward. Moving into an apartment, knowing everything I had is gone. Seeing that every time I go to work, to the grocery store, put gas in Nina's car. I can't."

"I get it, Morgan. I do."

"I talked to my mother, my grandmother last night. They'll take me in. I guess they don't have a choice either."

"Maybe you could wait until after the first of the year on the house, give yourself a little more time."

"It's not home anymore," she said again. "And the jobs, they're just jobs now. Get up, go to work, turn around, go to work, go to bed, do it all again worried, all the time worried. I don't want to live like that."

"Take a break from all this. Come with me to family dinner."

"I can't, really. They'll push about Thanksgiving—they already are. And it's easier to make excuses over the phone. I can't pretend to be thankful this year. Don't tell them. Please don't."

She stopped, turned to take both his hands. "I'll tell them when the house sells."

"If that's what you want."

"It is. I've got to get back. I've got a long list of things the Realtor suggests I do before she shows it." Her eyes filled. "I have to paint over the lilac walls. Nina's bedroom."

"She wouldn't mind."

"No." Morgan looked back toward the white stone. "She'd understand."

Paint was cheap, and so was her labor. She painted the walls a neutral off-white she decided she personally hated. Taking her cues from HGTV, she went sell-this-house neutral everywhere.

She removed personal items, boxed up photographs, some sweet and silly knickknacks.

She cleaned every inch of what had been her home and now represented a fight she'd already lost.

The house sat on the market for six weeks without a single offer before the Realtor advised a slight price reduction.

Morgan agreed, and cleaned the house again for what the Realtor called a postholiday showing. By the middle of January, and a second slight price cut, she'd sold her living room furniture, which helped pay bills and allowed her one deep breath.

And she started researching bankruptcy.

An offer came in.

"It's twenty thousand below asking price, so they're lowballing you. I suggest we counter with—"

"Just take the offer." She sat at the table on a Sunday evening, knowing people had gone through the house yet again while she'd nursed coffee in a café. Gone through, judged, criticized, imagined what they'd change.

"Morgan, I know this hasn't been easy for you, but with settlement fees, that offer won't cover what you owe. Let me do what I do. Let me counter."

"All right." She stared into the bowl of canned soup she'd tried to eat. "But I'm giving you permission to take the offer if they balk at your counter. To take their counter to the counter if they make one. I need to move on."

"Understood. I'll get back to you."

"Thanks."

Pushing the soup aside, she pulled over the old laptop Sam had given her. *No arguments, Morgan,* she remembered him saying. *Just take the damn thing.*

She'd taken the damn thing and now did some calculations.

Belinda the Realtor had it right, of course. The offer on the table wouldn't cover her debt. But instead of owing about three hundred thousand, she'd owe roughly seven.

She could live with that. She was currently living with a lot worse.

Belinda called back. "The buyers are willing to split the difference. I'd like to counter."

"Take it, please. Just take it. It gets me out from under."

"I understand, but I hate for you to settle for less than it's worth."

"Belinda, a woman was murdered in this house. We both know that lowers the value to most buyers."

"You deserve better."

"I'll take what I can get. How soon can we settle?"

"Thirty days."

"Okay, I'll be ready. Thanks for this. I mean it."

She sat back, shut her eyes, and realized she felt nothing but relief.

Thirty days moved fast. She gave her bosses her notice, helped train her replacements. Since she'd have no need for them, she sold or gave away the rest of her furniture, the contents of her kitchen cabinets, even her cleaning supplies.

No matter how she'd braced for it, saying goodbye proved harder than she'd imagined.

On the morning of the settlement, when she locked the empty house for the last time, the relief she fought to cling to dropped into misery.

She'd cry later. She promised herself a champion-level crying jag, but later.

With the paperwork complete, the new owners beaming, she comforted herself that someone would love what could no longer be hers.

Maybe they'd take that wall down, and build a sweet little front porch.

She walked out of the settlement office with a check that totaled hardly more than two weeks' pay. Since it seemed best not to think about how thrilled she'd been when she'd walked out of that same office as a homeowner, she blocked it out.

She got into Nina's car with her suitcases already loaded, and drove north.

When she'd made her annual trek to Vermont for Christmas—except this past one, which she'd spent alone—she'd taken the train.

A happy little trip, she thought now, with her single suitcase, bag of gifts, and all that holiday cheer.

The drive from the outskirts of Baltimore to Westridge, Vermont, would take her a solid eight hours according to the GPS on her phone.

She hoped to make it without an overnight stop. And with bigger hope that Nina's car would make it.

She drove away from the first whispers of spring and into the firm grip of winter, with its shivering trees and a quick squall of sleet.

After skirting Philadelphia, then New York, she stopped to gas up, stretch her legs. In the parking lot she ate half the PB&J she'd packed and watched a couple walk a big, curly haired dog.

A dog had been in her long-range plans, she remembered, after she'd established her own business. Not a big dog, she thought, but not one of those pocket jobs either. A nice sensible-size dog who'd curl at her feet when she did paperwork and romp around the backyard—no digging in the garden. A sweet and quiet-natured dog she'd raise from a frisky puppy.

She saw her imaginary dog stretched out on her finished back deck to soak up the summer sun. Sitting patiently in her open, cheerful kitchen while she filled his food and water bowls. Greeting her with wagging tail when she came home from work.

She'd need a dog door, of course, leading out from the kitchen to the deck and yard. And . . .

She caught herself, closed her eyes.

"Stop. Just stop. That's done."

Appetite gone, she wrapped the second half of the sandwich and continued on her way.

She drove through Connecticut, into Massachusetts. Snow, white and thick, covered everything on either side of the highway, and the sky—gray as lead—surely held more. Wind streamed down from the rising hills, sent snow flying, drifting.

Traffic slowed to the point she felt herself drifting like the snow. So she pulled off again, walked in the frigid air. With light leaching out of the day, she nearly gave in.

A decent motel, a warm, quiet space, sleep.

She bought a large coffee instead and texted her mother she'd arrive in a few hours.

We'll be here. Got a big pot of beef stew waiting. Drive safe.

She added a heart emoji, and feeling obligated, Morgan answered with another.

Ignoring the signs of lodging, she crossed into Vermont and the Green Mountains.

There was beauty here—maybe frozen at this time, but beauty. She couldn't deny it, and had always enjoyed it on her holiday visits, her short childhood trips in summer.

Mountains and forests and valleys, snow drenched, made a winter painting, all Americana. She drove and wound through the dream of it, and felt something nearly release when the moon—just a slice of it—broke through the clouds to drop its blue light on the white.

She'd hiked the forest with her grandfather on rare and all-too-short summer visits. He knew every trail. It struck her that she missed him more here as she drove closer to where he'd lived his life than she did anywhere else.

He'd listened to her dreams.

To be fair, so had her grandmother and her mother. Though her mother had always seemed just a little distracted. But Pa had listened, as if nothing else existed in that moment but her words and wishes.

She thought of him now as she traveled through his world and remembered the little things he'd taught her.

How to hammer a nail without banging her thumb. How to use a compass. How to recognize a deer print, a bear's. How to fish, something she did not for pleasure but just to spend time with him.

He wouldn't be here this time, she realized, and that cold, hard fact ached in her heart.

She pushed on, veering west with the road out of the forest, through the towns, their outskirts, the villages and theirs.

And at last, at last, nearly ten hours after she'd begun, she came to the sturdy old Tudor riding its slope of snow with lights shining in the windows, smoke curling from its pair of chimneys.

After parking in front of the garage, heaving a sigh that she'd made it, she got out on her rubbery legs to drag her pair of suitcases out of the car.

The cold cut like knives sheathed in ice, and the moan of the wind crackled through the frozen trees.

But they'd blown the snow off the drive, away from the wide bricked path. At her limit, she bumped the suitcases up the pair of steps to the covered entryway and knocked.

The door opened quickly, told her they'd been waiting. In an instant it hit her, that study in shared DNA. So alike, the slim builds, the bold blue eyes, the beautiful forever bones of their faces.

An instant more enfolded her in female arms, the scent of women.

"Close out that cold, Audrey. Let me get a look at this girl."

Olivia Nash took Morgan's shoulders to hold her back and take a good study. "Worn to the nub, aren't you?"

"Long drive, Gram."

"Well, get that coat off. We'll get some stew in you. I'd say whiskey with it, but you never had a taste for it as I recall."

Her mother took her coat, scarf, hat, then stood holding them, taking her own good study. "How about some wine to go with that stew?"

"That'd be great." Though she didn't want either. She wanted bed and a dark room.

But she let herself be handled, taken from the foyer, past the living room with its roaring fire, then the study that had once been her grandfather's retreat, into what they'd remodeled into a great room with its cozy lounge, its dining area, its spacious kitchen that opened to the snowy yard and woods beyond.

All pin neat and, reflecting the two women who lived there, both practical and female.

"Sit right there at the counter," Olivia ordered. "Audrey, you get the wine, I'll get the stew."

They bustled, working in a way that told Morgan they knew how to work together, be together, live together.

Her grandmother had let her hair go gray as steel—like her spine—wore it short as a boy's. She didn't move, in Morgan's estimation, like a woman who had seventy in the rearview mirror.

From the pot on the shining stove top, she ladled twice as much stew as Morgan could have eaten on her best day.

Audrey put a glass of deep red wine on the counter, ran a hand over Morgan's hair. "We've got fresh sourdough bread, too. I baked it this morning."

"Baked it?"

"A friend gave me the starter last fall, so I needed to at least try. I like it, and I've gotten good at it. I think."

She cut a generous slice from a round on the cutting board.

She still wore her wheat-field-in-the-sun hair long, pulled back in a neat tail. Her hands—they'd always seemed so elegant, delicate to Morgan—nudged the butter crock over.

"Let me know what you think."

"Stick thin." Olivia set the bowl, a spoon, a cloth napkin in front of Morgan. "We'll fix that. We'll fix it," she said, and gave Morgan's hand a quick squeeze. "Let's all have some wine, Audrey."

"Oh yes, let's."

As her mother got more glasses—the Waterford, Morgan noted—she spooned up some stew. "It's wonderful." Then nibbled at the slice of bread. Surprised she could speak pure truth, she smiled. "It's all wonderful. Thanks for letting me come."

"I won't hear that." Olivia stabbed a finger in the air, picked up the wine with her other hand. "I'll hear none of that. You're my only grandchild. Your mother's only child. This is home. Whether you make another one down the road, this is always home. It's the three of us now."

She lifted her glass. "And here's to the three of us."

With a nod, Morgan lifted her own glass, sipped.

"You, ah, put glass fronts on some of the uppers. It looks nice."

"They light up, too." Walking over, Olivia flipped a switch that illuminated glassware, the good china. "Decided on it—when was that, Audrey?"

"Last spring, during our spring cleaning. I sent you pictures, didn't I, Morgan?"

"Yes, but seeing it . . . I'm sorry I didn't come for Christmas. I know you both wanted to come to me, but I . . ."

"Leave that for now." Olivia took one of the stools. "Leave all that for tonight. We'll talk about all of it, all you need to talk about, and I'll say again. We'll fix it. Tonight, let it be enough you're here."

Morgan nodded again, ate more stew. "How's the shop?"

"Oh, it bustles, doesn't it, Audrey?"

"Winter people." Audrey took her own stool. "They love coming into town and finding something local to take home. We're adding a wine-slash-coffee-slash-tea bar."

"Really?"

"She talked me into it. Nag, nag, nag." Olivia rolled her eyes at her daughter, then laughed. "I hate she's right about it when I dragged my feet. We should have it up and running next week."

"Fancy coffees and teas, hot chocolate this time of year. Iced coffees and teas, fresh lemonade, that sort of thing for the summer people. And wine all year round."

"Sounds great." Even if she couldn't imagine her mother thinking of it. "Where are you putting it?"

"That's the dragging of feet."

"She pushed until I gave in. We bought the dusty old fake antiques shop next door. Had to open up the damn wall between the buildings, fix the dusty old mess. She took advantage of my old age and weak mind."

"As if. We're putting in a few tables and booths, offering cookies, scones—simple things. People can shop, have coffee, or have coffee and shop. Or wine and shop more," Audrey said with a laugh.

"We opened the useless old fireplace in there, had it fixed up, put in an electric insert."

"That's—really smart."

"We went back and forth on it, didn't we, Mom? A real wood-burner would've had that genuine Vermont touch, but this is safer and cleaner."

They hadn't told her any of this, Morgan thought as she ate, as she listened to them talk about the details. Because they'd known she'd been mired in her own problems.

Eventually, she nudged the bowl away. "I can't eat any more. It's great. So's the bread, Mom. I'm seriously impressed. I just can't eat another bite. The drive wiped me out. If it's okay, I'd like to go up, settle in, and get some sleep."

"You don't have to ask for permission." Olivia rose. "Let's go get you settled."

They hauled the bags up to the bedroom she always used—two doors away from the master and across from her mother's.

But when she walked in, more changes.

No more old-timey rosebud wallpaper. Instead they'd painted the walls a quiet, soothing blue that held soft against the dark trim. The floors gleamed, as always, but now a blue-and-cream rug, a subtle floral pattern, graced them.

They'd changed out the bed to a queen-size with a brass head-and-footboard, covered with a white duvet, blue-and-white shams, and a throw folded at the bottom of variegated blues.

Instead of being on the walls, pink rosebuds stood in a vase on the dresser. A chair, with a little round table and reading lamp, nestled in the corner.

"It's just lovely."

"It gets better."

Olivia opened a door into an attached bath. A generous shower, a dark blue vanity with a white top veined with blue. Open shelves holding fluffy towels and the female touch of glass jars filled with bath salts, oils, cotton balls.

"It's so— You didn't have to do all this."

"Enough of that. Nash women—and you've got plenty of Nash in you," Olivia added, "do what they want to do. Maybe not at first or every time, but eventually and most times."

"We just took the room next door for the bath and closet. We still have plenty of bedrooms if we have a guest. It's nice we all have our own bathrooms."

"Easier to live together that way," Olivia finished. "Still got the full bath at the other end of the hall, and the powder room downstairs. This big old house needed some changes."

She narrowed her eyes at her daughter. "That doesn't mean we'll be tearing up the other baths anytime soon."

Audrey just smiled. "Eventually. Can we help you unpack, baby?"

"No, no, it's not that much."

"We'll let you get some rest." Olivia stepped forward, kissed her cheek. "There's bottled water in that cabinet under the shelves in the bathroom if you're thirsty. You know where we are if you need anything."

"I do. And you're going to have to accept me saying thank you. Thank you, both of you. This is really beautiful."

Audrey gathered her in, pressed cheek to cheek. "Good night, Morgan." They went out, closed the door.

Needing to get it done, she unpacked first without giving much thought to what should go where. Just get it all put away, out of sight, along with the suitcases.

Because it felt as if she'd worn her clothes for a year, she stripped down, pulled pajama pants and a shirt out of the dresser where she'd just put them.

She got in the shower, let the water rain down. Warm, so warm.

She had her crying jag while the steam rose and the water struck the tiles.

She'd lost, she'd failed. She had nothing left of her own.

She wept for Nina, her beautiful friend.

She wept for the home someone else now lived in. For the jobs she'd loved, the life she'd built, and the future she'd hoped for.

Emptied out, she turned off the taps, put on her pajamas.

As she'd been taught, she hung her towel to dry before going into her nighttime routine.

Then she sat on the side of the bed, listening to the wind, the settling of the house.

A house where she lived, had this lovely, lovely room, because of the generosity of two women who loved her.

"What now?" she wondered. "What do I do now? Where do I start?"

Tomorrow, she told herself as she climbed under the crisp sheets, the fluffy duvet. She'd figure it out tomorrow. Or the day after that.

Or, she thought, and turned off the light, shut her eyes.

And fell into sleep like a stone into a river.

Chapter Six

She woke disoriented, and for a moment thought she dreamed. The pretty room with all the soothing blues, the way the light slid through the windows, all seemed so strange and unfamiliar.

Then she remembered and had to fight the deep desire to just close her eyes, just escape into sleep again.

Not the way, she told herself. Hiding in sleep solved nothing. When she woke, Nina would still be dead, the life she'd built still in ruins.

She needed to move forward—somehow, somewhere. The only choice was to move forward. Move.

She got up, dressed. Out of ingrained habit she made the bed, fluffed the pillows before wandering downstairs.

Olivia sat at the kitchen island, wearing a black sweatshirt. Its white lettering said simply:

i dissent

She sipped from an oversize mug of coffee while she worked a crossword on her tablet.

Morgan pointed at the lettering. "To what?"

"Whatcha got? Let me fix you some coffee. We went for that fancy machine when we redid things around here."

"I can get it. I'm a bartender—was," Morgan corrected. "Coffee machines can't defeat me. I'm sorry I slept so late."

"After the drive you had, I expected you to sleep longer. How about some breakfast?"

"No, nothing now, thanks. Please don't fuss over me."

"Grandmothers are designed to fuss over their grandchildren. It makes us happy. Don't you want me to be happy?"

"Coffee machines don't defeat me," Morgan muttered as beans ground, as coffee streamed into the mug she'd set below, "but grandmothers do."

"Because we're so wise, and wisdom hones sneaky. And I see you still take some coffee in your cream and sugar."

"I thought you'd be in town, at the shop by now."

"Your mother's taking the morning shift. She only just left."

Sipping, nodding, Morgan leaned back against the counter. "Meaning you're taking shifts keeping an eye on me."

"Looks that way," Olivia said easily. "And I asked for this morning because I think it may be easier for you to tell your grandmother what's in your heart and mind right now than your mother. If I'm wrong—though when am I wrong?—I can switch with Audrey."

"What's in my heart and mind." Morgan closed her eyes. "I lost everything, most vitally my closest friend." She opened her eyes again. "Nina's mother told me you wrote her, so did Mom. It meant a lot to her."

"We only knew Nina through you, but that made her part of the family to us."

"After Nina . . . Well, I lost everything else. My savings—gone—my home—someone else's now. My car, and I know that's nothing really, but I loved that damn car. My plans, my goals, my pride, my sense of security and self. Poof." She flicked her fingers in the air. "A year ago, just one year ago, I had everything under control, everything lined up. Now? I've got nothing, literally nothing, and I'm living in my grandmother's house."

"All right." Olivia lifted her mug, sipped. "You're entitled to feel all of that. In fact, in your place, I'd have myself a first-class rage party."

Not pity party, Morgan noted. No self-pity for Olivia Nash. "I've had a few."

"Good, that's healthy. You deserve them. You're entitled to feel all that," Olivia repeated, "even when you're wrong."

"Where am I wrong?"

"You say you have nothing? You have Morgan Nash Albright, damn it, and don't ever forget it. And this is not your grandmother's house, this is the Kennedy-Nash family home. I'm giving your grandfather first billing on it.

"Now, you can take as much time as you need to wallow, to sleep late, to rage, to curse whichever deity works best for you. You were victimized, and for a strong, smart woman—and you're both—that's devastating as much as it's a pure pisser. When you're finished, you'll figure out what to do next."

"It *is* a pisser. It is a pure pisser. Why hasn't anyone said just that before now?"

"Because no one else is your gram. Haven't you said it yourself?"

"I felt guilty when I even thought it." But she didn't now, she realized, because Gram had said it first. "Everyone felt sorry for me, but—"

"Nobody got pissed for you—or showed it. Trust me, I'm plenty pissed for you. So's your mother, in her more delicate way. I'd like to kick that bastard's balls blue before I twist his dick off at the root."

With a shrug, Olivia drank more coffee. "But that's just not-so-delicate me."

"I can't say exactly why," Morgan said after a moment, "but that really helps."

"Good."

"I have to get a job."

"There's no 'have to' right now. Sit down, I'm making you an omelet."

"Gram—"

"Nobody turns down one of my omelets." Olivia rose. "Now sit. I'm going to ask you for a favor."

"What?"

"Take two weeks. Sleep, eat, read, watch movies, take walks, build a snowman, whatever." She got out eggs, cheese, fresh spinach. "The stress of this past year shows, baby of my baby. It shows."

Hard to argue that, Morgan thought as she sat. She saw it every time she looked in the mirror.

"You take some time. If you need something practical to do, fine. Come into the shop and we'll put you to work a few hours a week. Otherwise, it's time to catch up with yourself."

"I need to earn a living."

"You do, of course, and you will. Two weeks out of your life won't change that. And your mother and I want some time with you. I think—and again, when am I wrong?—you need time with us."

Morgan said nothing as Olivia whisked eggs in a bowl while a skillet heated on the stove.

"I feel like such a failure, Gram."

"You'll get over that, because you're not and never have been. You had your world fall away from under you. I know what that's like. I had mine fall away."

"When Pa died."

"Then, but we had a lifetime together, and all those memories. I can pick one out, like chocolates from a box, and every one has its own flavor. But a long time ago. I lost a child."

"What?" Morgan shot up straight. "When? I never heard—"

"Your mother was barely two, so she doesn't remember. I never talked to her about it until after Steve died."

"I'm so sorry."

"Steve and I built this house, this big, wonderful house, and planned to fill it with children. We wanted at least four, and when Audrey came along, we were so happy. Our beautiful girl, our first child. It was all so easy, really. And then, right on schedule, we had another coming."

She poured eggs in the skillet, added the cheese, the spinach. "I was eight months along. We were finishing the nursery, arguing over names, all the things you do. And something went wrong. Everything went wrong. I lost the baby and any chance to have another. A little boy. He never had a chance to take his first breath."

"Oh, Gram."

"With the grief—I know what Nina's mother feels because I felt it—but with the grief, I felt a failure. I lost my child and there would never be another."

She flipped the omelet with the panache of a French chef.

"We got through it, but it was hard. It was brutal. We had our beautiful daughter. Steve had his work. I started throwing pots." She laughed at that. "I was absolutely terrible at it, and never got better. I'm a businesswoman and no artist, but trying to be gave me a deep respect and admiration for artists, craftspeople. So it gave me a new direction."

"The lopsided green cup he kept pencils in on the desk in his study," Morgan remembered. "He told me once you made that in the long ago."

"It was supposed to be a vase." Olivia shook her head. "That man loved me. 'Sell the stuff, Livvy,' he said to me. 'You know what's good and you know how to sell. You just need a place to sell it.'"

"Crafty Arts was his idea?"

"Another chocolate from the box. So I gave up making bad pottery, and we started the shop, just a tiny place at first. But it grew, and so did Audrey. And I had a world again. A different one than I'd always planned, but a good world."

She set the plated omelet in front of Morgan. "You'll make new plans, build a new world. Now eat."

"Thanks. Thanks for telling me. Gram? Could I have that cup? The lopsided green cup? It'll remind me of him, and you, and finding new directions."

Olivia came around the island, pressed a kiss to Morgan's temple. Held on an extra minute.

"Of course you can. Now, you keep this in your busy mind. The man who did all this? He'll pay, one way or the other, whether or not you ever know about it, he'll pay. Karma's not just a bitch, she's a righteous bitch. And he won't break you, because you won't let him.

"Two weeks," she added.

"Two weeks," Morgan agreed. "I love you, Gram."

"Of course you do. I love you right back. Now eat."

So she ate, and she slept. She took walks and sat by the fire with a book. By the third day, she wondered how much longer she could keep it up without losing her mind.

Her grandmother might request two weeks, but Morgan's wiring demanded busy. On day three, with both Olivia and Audrey at work, she sat down at the secondhand laptop, opened the spreadsheet she'd created months before.

Reality hadn't changed since the last time she'd gone over it. Broke still equaled broke. But this time she worked on projections. No question she could live in the pretty blue room as long as she wanted or needed, rent free. But wiring also required she pull her weight.

She could take over some household tasks, but her ladies already had a weekly cleaning crew, and the trio of women who tended the rambling old Tudor had done so for a dozen years.

If she took over cleaning, she put people out of a job.

Unacceptable.

Laundry—the cleaning trio already dealt with most of that.

She could do the marketing—something—but she couldn't subject the ladies to her cooking unless she got a lot better at it.

Marketing, doing the dishes after meals? That should keep her busy for about three hours a week, which didn't begin to fill the hole.

She needed work. A job. Needed to earn an income.

To start on that? Drive into town, look around, visit the shop. And no, she wouldn't work there. It steered much too close to living rent free.

She put on makeup, and since she hadn't indulged in a professional cut and style in months, tried a few snips here and there.

She definitely wouldn't get a job at a salon, but it wasn't terrible.

She dressed in something other than sweats. Winter-weight leggings, boots, a red sweater over a thermal shirt. Before she could change her mind and just retreat to her room, again, she dragged on her coat, wool cap, scarf, and stepped out into the frigid, unrelenting grip of winter.

And prayed Nina's car started.

It coughed a little, wheezed a little more, but turned over.

In under ten minutes she broke through the snow-coated trees, crossed the narrow bridge over the frozen whip of river, and turned onto High Street.

Westridge ranked, she supposed, somewhere between big town and small city. Picturesque, certainly, especially in its winter coat. It drew tourists, she knew, in every season. Winter sports, summer sports, fall foliage, spring hikes. Hunting, fishing, birding.

The Resort at Westridge, with its classy cabins and classier hotel suites, drew the well-heeled into the area, offering all those activities along with exceptional food, an admirable wine cellar, two bars—a very casual lodge bar, and the more upscale glass-walled bar with a four-sided stone fireplace that catered to après ski, or après whatever the guests wished.

The town offered a banquet of restaurants, from diner style to five-star fancy, shops, boutiques, sporting goods, Vermont-flavored souvenirs, art galleries, and more.

Many of those nestled together on High Street, including her grandmother's Crafty Arts. Or, as the sign read now, Morgan noted, Crafty Arts and Wine Café.

Even this late in the winter season and before the spring thaw, it . . . well, it nearly bustled, she admitted. Since she really wasn't familiar with the geography, she had to hunt for parking. She remembered a small lot behind Crafty Arts but didn't know how to navigate around the hilly roads and busy intersections to find it.

Still, street parking—when she found it—offered her a chance to check out the main commercial areas and possible opportunities.

Restaurants, retail, cafés, a bakery, an upscale bar. She could wait tables if she had to, but the bar hit top of her list. On side streets, she spotted a gallery, low-rise apartments, more shops, a doctor's office, a wineshop—with a small wine bar. Next on her list.

On a less blustery day, she promised herself, she'd explore farther. But for now, she stopped in front of Crafty Arts and Wine Café.

Someone, she thought, had done a crafty and arty job on the display window. Tables and stands of varying heights held blown glass art arranged with wooden bowls, pottery. A soft gray throw draped over the back of a rocking chair.

Inside she found warmth, not just in the air, but the light, in the gleam of the wood floors. Paintings covered the walls. Old cabinets displayed handcrafted jewelry and small pieces of pottery, silverwork, copper. Another highlighted candles. Open shelves sparkled with blown glass.

A long antique bookcase transformed into the checkout counter where a woman chattered away with a customer while she wrapped up purchases. Behind her, a glorious stained glass peacock spread its tail.

The counterwoman glanced up, smiled. "Can I help you find anything?"

"Not yet, thanks. Just taking it in."

She wandered on. They'd done so much, she realized, since she'd last been in. Wood or ironwork tables held more pottery, lamps, cutting boards, platters.

She walked upstairs. If memory served, the second floor had once been used as storage and her grandmother's office. No more. Here she found textiles. Handcrafted scarves, gloves, hats, tablecloths, and runners.

Handmade soaps and lotions, more furniture, more art.

It occurred to her if she'd walked into this shop and still had disposable income, she'd never have walked out empty-handed.

When she walked down, she passed a couple heading up, and found the counter clerk just finishing up with another customer.

"Doing okay?"

"Yes. Sorry, I should've said, but you were busy. I'm Olivia's granddaughter."

"You're Morgan! Oh my goodness." Reaching out, she grabbed both of Morgan's hands. "I went to high school with your mother! It's so nice to meet you. I'm Sue Newton."

"It's nice to meet you, too."

"They're in the café—opening this Saturday. Some finishing touches going in. You go right on over. It's going to be great."

A sheet of plastic hung over the wide case opening. She pushed through into the light and bright. They'd hung plastic over the wide front window, something she found clever.

Keep people guessing until the big reveal.

She judged it would be big.

They'd carried the same wood flooring through for flow from space to space. The cream walls held more art—never miss a chance for a sale. They'd gone dark and moody on the millwork for contrast, and it worked.

The bar matched the millwork with a countertop of granite that married the cream with streaks of the dark. They'd scattered low tops, high tops, four tops, a few booths in deep blue leather.

And—not to miss a trick—had a small retail section of wine toppers, glasses, corkscrews, mugs, teacups, coffee and tea accessories.

They'd coffered the ceiling, adding the classy and the cozy.

Because she couldn't help herself, she walked behind the bar.

Shelves, a fridge, an ice maker, a wine cooler, a speed rack, a section for tools, another for bar mops. She pulled out a leather-bound menu and found her eyebrows rising up at the extent of the selection.

Before she could put it back and step out, her ladies came out from the back.

"It's going to work," Audrey was saying, then spotted Morgan. "What a surprise! What do you think?" She spread her arms.

"I think I'm stunned. It's amazing, everything. You changed the upstairs next door, and it's wonderful. And this? It's beautiful. Fancy but not fussy. Efficient but not staid."

"Still needs a few touches, but we'll be ready for Saturday." Olivia gestured. "Come look at the kitchen. We're offering baked goods, and that meant a damn commercial kitchen. But it'll be worth it."

She walked through the swinging door.

It shined, as the back of the house should. Stainless steel gleamed; steel shelves held cookware and tools. The big commercial hood over a six-burner stove top, the walk-in refrigerator said professional and impressive. Dishwasher, sink, mop sink, and the biggest, shiniest mixer she'd ever seen added more of the same.

"You've got it all. A really good use of the space."

"And it passed final inspection." Audrey swiped a hand over her forehead. Then bounced a little on her toes so her shiny tail of blond swung.

"We needed it compact because we needed room for . . ."

She opened a door.

"Holy crap!"

They'd created a wine cellar, filling three walls with racks, filling racks with bottles.

"You've got your whites," Audrey began, "domestic, French, Italian, and so on, then the reds, then rosés, then sparklings over here. The sommelier at the resort helped us."

"Because he's sweet on your mother."

"Mom."

"I speak truth."

The faint flush that rose into her mother's cheeks left Morgan stunned speechless.

"Maybe a little. Anyway, office and more storage upstairs. We're using the old office space above the shop for more stock."

"I saw. I went up. It's wonderful."

"It really is. We have a door—locked from the office side—so we can walk over and down if we need to. It's all so much, so I'm in a constant state of terror and excitement."

"I'm going to say, without bias or hesitation, it's brilliant."

"I'm so glad you're here." Audrey gave her a one-armed squeeze. "You can be part of it. You'll come on Saturday, won't you?"

"Absolutely. I'll help work the bar if you need it."

"Really?"

Audrey beamed; Olivia just smiled.

"Not for a job, for family. You've hired bartenders by now."

"We have two," Olivia told her. "We think one has managerial potential. But I know we'd welcome your opinion there. And it would take a lot off our minds if you'd more or less supervise on Saturday."

"Done. I'm going to start looking for work next week, but I'll pitch in here. If there's something I can do to help you get going, I'll do it."

"How about now, with those finishing touches?" Olivia gestured them out. "We need to dress the restroom."

"Unisex, ADA compliant," Audrey added.

"We need to choose the art. A table or console, something to go on it. We need to dress the tables in the café, and this and that."

"My schedule happens to be open at this time."

"Excellent. When we're done, I'm taking both my girls out to dinner."

She enjoyed it. For a few hours, she didn't think of what she'd lost and what she had to do next. She enjoyed spending time with both women, debating appropriate art and furnishings, placing them, changing them.

And maybe putting just a little bit of her own stamp on a family business with her idea of adding fairy lights around the big window for a little sparkle.

She enjoyed dinner out, which, instead of the fancy she'd assumed her grandmother would choose, turned out to be pizza and a carafe of red house wine.

By the time she went to bed, she felt she'd actually accomplished something. Maybe, hopefully, she'd pulled out of wallowing time.

For the next few days she split her time between polishing up her résumé and helping prep for the grand opening. She unpacked, washed, and stored the cups, saucers, creamers, and sugar bowls her grandmother had designed for a local potter to create.

White with a red clover—the Vermont state flower.

"They're perfect, Gram."

"They are."

"You need to price these for sale."

"I thought about it."

"I hope you do. I had this other thought."

"How much is it going to cost me?"

"I think it'll do the opposite, in the long run. It's a wine bar, yes, and you're tapping local vineyards for some of that. How about you tap local for your coffee beans, your tea? Then you can sell it—pretty tins of tea, classy bags of coffee. There are a couple of roasters local enough, and you could work with a tea farm. Vermont has a few."

"That's a thought." And eyes narrowed on it, Olivia considered. "That's a damn good thought."

"Crafty Arts is all about Vermont arts and crafts. It plays on that. I did a little research."

She reached in her bag, pulled out a folder.

"A little?"

"Well, once I got started. So it's something to think about, going down the road."

"And I will." Olivia put on the bold red cheaters hanging from the chain around her neck, skimmed the first pages in the file. "It's a good idea, Morgan. You've been an enormous help the last few days. Good brain, good eye, and a strong back. Much appreciated."

She lowered the file. "I can't talk you into managing the new space?"

"You don't need me, Gram. If you did, I'd at least get you started. But you and Mom? You've got this. I need to get my own."

"I expected that. So I'm going to tell you I heard Après—that's the main bar at the resort—is looking for a bartender/manager. Or will be next week. Their head bartender just gave his notice. His wife got a job offer in South Carolina, and they're relocating."

Olivia set the file down. "Because I love you, I sucked it up, and I spoke with Lydia."

"Lydia?"

"Lydia Jameson. She and I go back, farther than either of us care to remember, and her husband was good friends with your pa. She keeps her hand in—hell, both hands in. You can send in your résumé, and they'll take a look before they start the job-open process."

"At the resort. I've never been in Après, but I checked out their website, and it was on my list. Thank you." She pulled Olivia into a hug.

"It doesn't mean you've got the position."

"I know. That's up to me. But it's a chance, and a chance to do what I'm good at."

"You send your résumé to Lydia. I've got her email. Like I said, we go back. Write yourself a solid cover letter."

"I will. Thank you, Gram. I'll still pitch in here as much as I can, whether or not I get this job."

"We're counting on it."

That evening, she googled Lydia Jameson to get a sense, and saw why Lydia and Olivia went way back. Both born and raised in Vermont, both from New England stock. Educated, cultured women, rock-ribbed and steel-spined.

Businesswomen, both. Lydia's business dwarfed her grandmother's, but business was business.

She spent a solid hour drafting, revising, and refining a cover letter. Formal and respectful, she decided, with a personal touch in her thanks for the consideration.

After a deep breath, one hand on that lopsided green cup, she hit send.

A new chance. And she had others, she reminded herself. Maybe she hadn't landed where she'd expected, but she had opportunities here.

An opportunity to transplant those roots she wanted so much.

Restless, she went downstairs. Hair loose around her shoulders, Audrey stood in the kitchen pouring a glass of wine.

There came that light flush again.

"Caught me."

"How about I join you?"

"I'm so nervous. I thought a glass of wine might help me sleep. I can't believe we're opening the café tomorrow. It was an idea, then it was the planning, then the work and more planning. And now?"

She handed Morgan a second glass. "It's here, and I'm nothing but nerves. Your gram's up there sleeping like a baby. She has no nerves, I swear."

"Because she knows you've got a hit on your hands."

"You really think that?"

"No. I know that. Listen, retail, art—like the shop—that's not in my wheelhouse. But a wine bar is. I slipped into the wineshop a few blocks down, and its wine bar's lovely. Small, dark, and moody, well run, heavy wood, deep colors. Yours? Airy, arty, a different vibe. And the way you've opened it—or will tomorrow—to the very well-established shop? It's just damn smart. Like adding the coffee services, the tea options is smart. The baked on-site pastries and scones? It's all there, Mom."

"I keep telling myself that, but it sounds better when you say it."

She'd always considered her mother on the flighty side. A woman who couldn't settle down, couldn't make a decision and see it through. But she didn't see that now.

"I'm sorry I didn't keep in touch more, visit more."

"You had a life to build. And you did keep in touch. Sweetie, I have friends who only hear from their grown kids when they make the effort, only see them when they travel. You called every couple of weeks, you emailed, you visited every Christmas. Don't be sorry. I'm so proud of you."

"That makes one of us."

"You stop that. If I'd been in your place, I'd still be hiding under the covers. You're a doer, Morgan. You always have been."

"So were you," Morgan realized.

"Me?" Audrey laughed, sipped wine. "I was more of a going-alonger."

"I don't think—" She broke off as the phone in her pocket signaled. "That's my email tone. Who could that be? It's after eleven."

"Find out."

Morgan pulled out the phone, swiped, stared. "Oh God. I have an interview Sunday at eleven at Après."

"Oh! That's great! That's wonderful! Now we can both be nervous wrecks. Oh! Let's top off this wine, take it up, and pick out what you're going to wear. That's what I'm good at."

"I—sure. Yeah. I never expected to hear anything so fast."

"Lydia Jameson? In the race between the turtle and the hare, she's the hare. And she always wins. Let's play shop your closet."

Chapter Seven

Though she'd never attended an actual grand opening, Morgan rated the café's as pretty damn grand. Sharp at ten the doors opened, and sharp at ten, people streamed in. She helped serve the complimentary mimosas, coffee, tea, and scones offered for the first hour.

She met the mayor, a woman with a bubble of blond hair and a cackling laugh. The police chief, early thirties, handsome, lanky, killer blue eyes, wandered in—black coffee for him.

He also seemed to know everybody, which she counted as a plus in a police chief. When she noticed he left with a shopping bag, she figured he'd seen something he wanted or knew the value of supporting local businesses.

Maybe both, but it earned him another plus.

The new space rang with voices, approval, questions.

Her intention to pitch in for the first hour moved into three.

"You need to take a break," Olivia told her as Morgan bused another table.

"I'm good. I'm wired for busy, Gram, and feel more like myself than I have in way too long. See those women at the four top over there? Mimosas and scones? College dorm mates, ten years ago. They used to meet up for a week every summer. They all have families now, so they've taken it down to a long weekend this time of year. They're staying at the resort, came into town to shop—it's their last day."

"How do you know all that?"

"I'm a damn good bartender. People talk to me. They've had a great time, and consider finding this place a bonus. And as you can see from the Crafty Arts bags under the table, they'll be taking home plenty of memories. You should go say hello," Morgan added as she wiped down the table. "They'd love it."

"Then I will."

Eight hours after the doors opened, they closed. And the entire staff let out a cheer. Given the nod, Morgan popped a bottle of champagne and poured celebratory glasses all around.

Olivia ordered in pizza—who knew it was her grandmother's go-to?—adding much-appreciated fuel to the end of a successful day.

And at the end of that, when it was just the three of them, Olivia sat, put her feet up on a chair. "Not just resting my aching feet, but basking."

"We broke our single-day sales record in the shop, Mom."

Smug powered Olivia's smile. "So I'm told."

"And even with our opening-week specials, today's giveaways, the café pulled in a solid twenty percent more than we projected. Boom! Pow!" Audrey dropped into a seat, lifted her arms high, did enthusiastic jazz hands.

"You see here a woman who, as a child, couldn't keep a dollar in her pocket if I sewed it to the lining. Now she adds up profit and loss in her head."

"I was always good with numbers. Just not as much if there was a dollar sign involved."

She put her boots with their short, skinny heels up on another chair. And with a sigh, pulled out the silver dragonfly clip that had somehow, magically to Morgan's mind, kept all that hair scooped up and back all day.

"I'm basking, too." After scooping her hands through her hair, giving her head a toss, all that hair fell as if she'd just had it styled.

Magic, Morgan thought again.

"We didn't expect you to give us the whole day, Morgan. You were such an enormous help. And you're so unflappable. Every time I got, well, flapped, I'd look at you and see how you just breezed through it all."

"Do you want to know what I think?"

"Absolutely."

"I'm going to make us cappuccinos, and tell you."

She went behind the bar to the coffee station and began.

"It's just day one, and you won't pack them in like this routinely."

"Oh." Audrey's jazz hands dropped with flicks of her fingers. "Bubble burst!"

"But"—amused, Morgan glanced back at the table—"you have an unqualified hit on your hands. And here, as I see it, is why."

The machine hissed as it steamed milk.

"First, you have a lovely venue and you paid attention to the small details. It matters. You've put together a good staff. A couple of the new hires don't quite have their rhythm, but they're on the way. You, both of you, treat your employees with respect and, boy, does that matter."

She trayed the three coffees, added spoons and a sugar bowl, then carried the tray to the table.

"I don't know your business plan, and don't need to. But I do know you're serving an excellent product and doing it with class, casually, as the venue calls for. But."

"Uh-oh," Audrey muttered.

"You need one more hire. You're going to need—especially during high seasons—someone who can transition from business to business. Someone who can serve wine, make coffee, bus a table in a pinch, wait tables in that pinch, and handle retail in the shop. Someone knowledgeable or trained to be knowledgeable enough about the art, the crafts, and those who create them so they can answer questions. There were questions, and the staff—including this volunteer—had to refer the questions to you or one of the staff in the shop."

"You make a good point. Want the job?"

Morgan shook her head at her grandmother. "It's not what I'm best at. What you need is a coordinator, a kind of utility player. You've got time to find the right fit. And once you have that in place, you really need to do a photo book, with recipes from the café's kitchen and bar, with some of the arts and crafts included. Photos of wine, for instance, in glasses sold next door. The café's coffee cake displayed on one of your dishes, biscotti arranged on another, and like that. You have a local photographer do the pictures—that keeps it with your mission statement—and you sell it here, exclusively."

Olivia sat back. "Listen to you! I'm cursed with clever progeny."

"You started it," Audrey reminded her. "A photo book, like a coffee-table book. I can see it! You know who'd be great for the photos?"

"Tory Phelps," they said together.

"Hive mind." Olivia held up a hand. "The new hire first. Morgan's right there. The days of either of us working eight to ten hours a day, seven days a week, are done, Audrey."

"Agreed. But I can feel Tory out, just see how much she thinks she'd charge for something like this. That way we'd know if it's even feasible. She's good," she told Morgan. "We carry some of her work in the shop, had a showing for her last year. She teaches photography at the community college."

"Your mother does love a new project."

"She does." Morgan looked around the café. "This one turned out really well."

"Can't argue with truth." Olivia gave her daughter's hand a pat. "Now, let's get our tired butts home. This one has a job interview tomorrow and needs a good night's sleep."

She didn't get one, not when her mind refused to turn off.

What if she didn't get the job? She could look elsewhere, of course she could. But . . .

Should she tell her ladies she'd take that coordinator's job? She could handle it. She could learn about the arts, the crafts, the artisans and artists and craftspeople. She already knew how to manage staff, how to manage a business.

Maybe it was time to put away her goals and dreams and accept what stood in front of her.

But she wasn't ready to, not ready to just bury everything she'd worked toward.

Still, if she worked five years, lived here and worked and saved, she might be able to really start again.

Maybe.

She fell asleep on the maybe, then woke early to lie in bed and go over it all again.

When she went down for coffee, her mother sat at the counter with her laptop. She'd braided her sun-kissed hair back this morning and wore a candy-pink robe.

"Good morning. I'm researching how to produce coffee-table books. It's a lot!"

"I guess it is."

"It's such a good idea. Now it's in here." Audrey tapped her temple. "I can't let it go. I want to get as much calculated and organized before I hit your gram with it. That way works best with her."

Morgan started to reach for a mug and saw the Crafty Arts box beside the coffee machine, and the card with her name on it.

"What's this?"

"Just a little something from Gram and me, for good luck today. If you hate them . . . pretend you don't. I put it there since I wasn't sure if you'd be up and around before we left for work."

Prepared to lie if necessary, Morgan opened the box. The diamond etching on the silver, cuff-style earrings made them sparkle.

She didn't have to pretend.

"They're beautiful."

"We thought they'd go well with what you picked out to wear today."

"I think you picked that out."

"Well, I helped. But the outfit was in your closet, after all. Do you really like them?"

"I love them." She put them on to prove it. "How do they look?"

"Like you. Smart, just a little sleek, and very well-crafted. How about some breakfast?"

"Can't." Morgan pressed a hand to her belly. "I'm nervous."

"Of course you are. Who wouldn't be? But all you have to do is be Morgan. The resort will be lucky to have you, and I'm saying that as a business manager—something I never thought I'd be in my life. I watched you yesterday, baby, and you know just what you're doing."

"I used to think so. And I'm not going into this with a negative attitude. I need a boost, I can't pretend I don't. I need someone who isn't my mother or grandmother to tell me I'm good enough."

"That bastard did a number on you."

Morgan's eyebrows lifted. "Listen to the mouth on my mother."

"Oh, I've always had that. You just didn't hear it. Maybe that was a mistake, me always putting on the everything's-fine face for you. But I can't go back and change that now. You go in there today, and you be Morgan. If they don't give you that boost, they're idiots."

Audrey closed her laptop, rose. "I've got to get dressed. We'll probably be gone before you have to leave." Eyes on her daughter's, she lifted a hand to Morgan's cheek. "Will you let us know how the interview goes? Text, even drop by the shop?"

"I will. Thanks for the earrings. I can feel the luck pumping off them."

She put on the mother-approved outfit. The sage-green shirt, the slim black pants, the tall black boots. Added the butter-soft leather blazer. And had to admit, as usual when it came to fashion, Audrey hit the mark.

She looked professional, confident, and like herself.

Now, she just had to remember to act that way.

Downstairs, she gave herself a pep talk while she donned her outdoor gear.

You know what you're doing.

Your résumé's solid.

You may decide you don't want the job—but you'll take it because you need it.

Hissing against the cold blast, she walked to Nina's car. Let out a relieved breath when it started. And knowing the heater wouldn't do a damn thing until she got out again, shivered her way into town.

A quick glance showed her a couple coming out of the café entrance. Both held shopping bags. Boded well for day two, she thought, and drove through town and out again.

She turned left, bumped over a bridge where the water below shivered its way over rocks the way she shivered at the wheel.

Another turn with snow-drenched woods on either side. She tested the heater as she climbed a hill, and when it coughed out cool rather than cold air, decided to take it.

She spotted the first cabins tucked in those snowy woods and admitted she'd never understand the appeal of a winter vacation that involved winter.

A tropical beach, now, a sun-washed Italian villa, those made absolute sense. But a cabin in the Vermont woods, paying to freeze on a ski lift or skate on a frozen lake?

Forget it.

"And you can just keep those opinions to yourself if you hope to bag this job."

She followed the signs to the hotel, winding her way.

It stood, white against the white, dignified rather than glamorous, rising four stories with its straight, sturdy lines.

The first story jutted out on either side, which she already knew from poring over their website.

Inside she'd find shops, two restaurants, two bars and lounges, an indoor pool and fitness center, a small spa, meeting rooms, a ballroom for weddings and events, and fifty-two guest rooms, including a dozen suites.

Behind it, the mountains rose up, and the ski slopes streaked down. She decided on the spot she'd have to be dragged up there at gunpoint, and even then, a bullet might be the better choice.

She turned into the parking lot, noted that even on this edge of seasons she had to hunt for a space. They offered valet, but she considered that for guests, so hiked what seemed like a football field from Nina's car to the front entrance—a wide, stone, heated portico.

Inside, more white in the sparkling spread of marble floors, a four-sided roaring fire where people in cushy chairs or sofas enjoyed a late-morning coffee. A round table simply smothered in a gorgeous flower arrangement that smelled of spring.

Breathing in, breathing out, she crossed the lobby, walked through a wide archway and into Après.

She'd studied the website; she knew what to expect. But all she could think when she stepped in was: Oh God, oh God, I want this job.

A glass wall opened the bar to the world outside. The mountains, the slopes, a slice of the lake, the woods and trails, what she supposed would be gardens around a generous patio outside when winter loosened its grip.

Tables gleamed, dark wood, again dignified, and each held a small glass-domed tea light and a bud vase. The chairs and booths invited lingering on the soft, stone-gray leather.

The bar spread along the side wall, giving those behind the stick a full view of the room. Dark wood like the tables, it looked antique with its deep carving, its four-columned backbar with mirrored arches.

She instantly coveted it for her own.

The coffee maker—copper and elaborate—stood on its own counter beside the backbar, with the cash-out in a discreet alcove on the other side; swinging doors would go to the back of the house behind it.

She made mental notes for her future—the decor, all class; the flow, excellent.

She really wanted to get behind that bar, check out the setup, check the taps—a half dozen of them on either side of the bar. She crossed to it—maybe just a quick peek—but a man came through the swinging doors carrying a tub.

Tall, on the gangly side, hair in short, neat twists. He wore a white shirt, black vest and pants. The brass tag on the vest read NICK.

"Good morning." He flashed a smile. "Après doesn't open until eleven-thirty, but they serve coffee, tea, hot chocolate in the lobby. I'd be happy to take an order for you."

"No, thanks. I'm here to meet Ms. Jameson. Nell Jameson. I'm a little early."

"Morgan Albright?" His smile widened as he set the tub on the bar, then walked over, hand extended. "Nick Tennant. I'm the day man. You're here for the manager's slot. Nice to meet you."

"You, too. Really nice bar."

"I'll say." His look read pride as he glanced around. "Of course, I'm biased. Worked here ten years—in Après. Four years more for the resort summer and holidays."

"Ten years."

"Yep." His deep-set brown eyes stayed on her face, assessing. "And I'll answer what you're too polite to ask. Didn't want it—the manager's slot. I like putting in my eight, going home for dinner. We just had a baby."

"Oh, congratulations. Let's see."

Grinning now, he pulled out his phone to display the screen saver, an infant with her father's soulful eyes and a curly cap of hair. The pink bow in it and frilly pink dress said girl.

"Looks like her daddy. What's her name?"

"Shila. Got her mama's mouth, but otherwise, that's me all over. You got kids?"

"No."

"Changes everything."

He gave the baby on his screen saver a last smile before he tucked his phone away.

"I thought about managing, taking the evening work that comes with it. Or the coming in when a problem hits. The scheduling, the paperwork. Bump up the paycheck, but . . . Nope, ten-thirty to six-thirty suits me. Come in at ten-thirty, check the stock, check the keg levels, make the garnishes. Hell, you know the drill."

"I do."

"Open her up, then man the stick, get her done, and clock out, so most nights home by quarter to seven to my girls. Best of both."

"It sounds like it."

"Have a seat at the bar. I'll draw you a soft drink."

"I'll take it. Could I . . . I'd really like a peek."

"Come on through." He led her around, got a glass.

Clean, shiny, organized, she noted—as it should be. Ice maker, speed rack, sink shining clean, cooler, shakers, corkscrews, knives, swizzle sticks, bar mops, cocktail napkins, all as pristine as the bottles and glassware on the backbar.

"Whatcha think?"

"I think the people who run and work in here know what they're doing."

He shot a finger at her, then put her drink on the bar. "I can text up to Nell's office, let them know you're here."

"That's okay. This gives me time to see the layout and gear up." She went around, took a stool. "I'm not used to sitting on this side."

"How long you been running the stick?"

"Nearly seven years. I started my last year in college, and knew that was where I belonged. I don't have to ask if you like working here. You don't strike me as someone who'd put in a decade—plus the four years of summers and holidays—if you didn't."

"It's a great place to work. I met my wife here. Corrine's in Reservations. Well, she's on maternity leave, but she wants to come back at least part-time when Shila's six months old. Made good friends here, get treated fair here. Hal? He's head butler on the Club Level? Twenty-seven years in. And that's not the record."

"It's not?"

"Mrs. Finski—and everybody, even the Jamesons, called her Mrs. Finski—thirty-six years when she retired, head of Housekeeping."

"That says staff loyalty."

"Earned it. The Jamesons are good people."

"Thanks, Nick."

Morgan's first thought was Nell Jameson—photo on the website—filled the air with energy.

She hit about five-four in her stylish boots, and presented a gym-fit figure in a knee-skimming dress of rusty red. She wore her beautifully highlighted brown hair back in a casual twist.

And though she took a damn good photo, Morgan concluded, she looked better in the flesh. Maybe it was that energy, or the depths of her soulful brown eyes.

She walked with utter confidence. "Nell Jameson."

"Morgan Albright."

They shook, and sized each other up.

"Am I late?"

"I was early." Be yourself, Morgan thought. "I wanted to get a feel for the bar before the interview."

"And what's your feel?"

"The actual bar?" Morgan ran a hand over the surface. "I want it for my own."

"Can't blame you. My grandfather had it shipped over from Dublin."

"I thought it was the real thing. The rest? It's wonderful. Classy, but comfortable with it. Organized, a good flow—things guests won't necessarily pinpoint, but they'll feel it. And the view, well, that's a gift."

"Thermal windows, tinted to cut glare. You can watch the slopes—do you ski?"

"Absolutely not."

"Okay then. Spring, summer, into the fall, there's a view of the ninth tee over toward the lake. Do you golf?"

"No. But I've sat in gardens, even planted some, and I assume the view of those when they're not buried in snow is pretty spectacular."

"They are. Well, we'll take a table and get started." Nell held up a finger. "Before the table, why don't we start with you showing me some practical application. How about you make me a Kir Royale?"

"I'd be happy to. I need to see your ID."

She heard Nick suck in a quick gasp, but kept her eyes on Nell.

"Are you serious?"

"I can't serve you otherwise."

"I'm twenty-seven."

"That's what they all say. Sorry. You could pass for twenty. Could be exceptional DNA and bone structure, but it's not worth the hit to this venue, or to me, to risk it."

"Is that your personal policy?"

"It is, and I hope it's your business's policy or I'm the wrong person for this position."

"I see." Nell set her briefcase on the bar, opened it. She took a slim leather case from one of the pockets, slid out her license.

Morgan studied it, smiled, said, "Thank you."

Her heart hammered as she walked around the bar. Then settled. She knew what she was doing here.

She filled a flute with ice and cold water, set it aside while she located a bottle of crème de cassis, a lemon, a paring knife.

"The website lists you as head of Hospitality."

"That's right."

Morgan took a bottle of champagne from the cooler. "So that's Après, the Lodge Bar, the restaurants, room service?"

"The juice bar in the fitness center, the snack bar attached to the lift, grocery runs for stocking the cabins per guest requests."

"A lot," Morgan said as she opened the bottle with an elegantly muffled pop.

"I have an excellent team."

"I've only met Nick, but if he's representative, you do."

She dumped the ice, eyeballed a tablespoon of the crème de cassis into the flute, tipped the glass to pour the champagne.

"Do you think it adds elements of comfort and challenge, working in a family business?"

"I do." Intrigued, Nell propped her chin on her fist. "Are you interviewing me?"

"Just making conversation." She used the knife, sliced the lemon, cut out the pulp and made a perfect spiral twist. Topped off the champagne, added the lemon twist, then set the flute on a cocktail napkin. "Enjoy."

Nell sipped, set the flute down. "Okay, that's perfect. I wasn't going to actually drink it, but I'm going to make an exception. Let's take that table."

When Nell walked to a booth by the windows, Nick gave Morgan a grin and a thumbs-up.

"I'm going to get this out of the way," Nell began when Morgan sat across from her. "I'm sorry about what happened to you, what happened to your friend. I'm very sorry."

"Thank you."

"Part two of getting out of the way. I was annoyed when my grandmother set up this interview. Stepping on my toes."

"Oh." Shit! "I can't blame you."

"Grandmothers." Now Nell shot out a megawatt smile. "Good thing I adore mine."

"I'm going to say the same for me and mine."

"All right, we'll close those doors for now." Once again, Nell opened her briefcase. This time she took out a portfolio, opened it. "Your résumé's impressive. But it doesn't list your managing the Next Round bar in Maryland."

"I tended bar there. I managed the offices for Greenwald's Builders."

"Your employer at the Next Round told me you often handled scheduling, inventory, ordering, even small repairs and maintenance."

"As needed."

"Two words to live by. He also told me that you were the second-best bartender he's had in the thirty-one years of owning the bar."

"Big Mac. Number one."

Nell smiled again. "Exactly. Big Mac beat you out because he could sing like an angel and intimidated any potential troublemaker just by his size. But you were more dependable and flexible—so it's a close call. He hoped to sell you the business when he retired."

"He—" That hit hard. "I didn't know that."

"Apparently, neither did he, until you relocated. Are you planning to stay in Westridge?"

It shook her, the idea she'd been just that close to having her own. She had to put it aside now, because that was gone. And this was the here and the now.

"I want roots. I've transplanted them here. I have nothing to go back to, and my family's here."

"You've lived a lot of places, being in a military family. Any favorites?"

"No. Not really. It's all temporary, and you know it going in."

"So don't get attached." Nell nodded, and though she had Morgan's résumé on the table, didn't look at it. "You worked in college, so you have experience waiting tables, serving the public in that way. Which should give you an understanding of what waitstaff handles. On the managerial side again, your boss at Greenwald's Builders sang your praises."

It amazed her they'd already checked her references, but she answered smoothly. "The Greenwalds were wonderful to work for."

"A family business."

"Yes, very much so."

"Your grandmother and mother run a family business."

"They do."

"I love Crafty Arts, by the way, and really need to get into town and check out the new café."

"It's terrific."

"But you don't want to work there?"

"A wine bar's lovely, but it's not a full bar. They could use me, but they don't need me."

"Do you find family businesses offer levels of comfort and challenge?"

For the first time, Morgan laughed. "Yes, I do."

Nell sat back, sipped her drink. "Why a bar?"

"I like people. People gather in a bar. When you're behind one, they look to you to serve them a drink. But you have to know how to gauge the mood. Happy, celebrational, looking to brush off a tough day, sad, pissed off, just looking for company. And that's what you serve up with the drink. I'm good at mixing drinks, and at gauging moods. I like bars. They're their own little universe."

"How so?"

"The world's revolving out there." She circled a finger in the air. "But in here, it's a respite. Your meeting tanked, you didn't get that raise? Respite. Your kid aced his spelling test, you got a promotion? A place to celebrate and share good news. A resort bar, more transitory clientele, but still some locals dropping in.

"Business meeting over there." She gestured to an empty table. "A couple of honeymooners mooning over each other there. Two couples, old friends, taking a mini-vacation together. A bridal party celebrating. I can see all of them from behind the bar—it's a smart layout—and still give my attention to the stool sitters."

"What do you expect from the waitstaff?"

"The same as I expect from myself. Serve, gauge moods, and play to them. Don't chatter unless they chatter first. You want tips? Smile, make eye contact, pay attention, and don't neglect one table for another. Friendly service still has to be efficient. Serve now, bitch later. If you need help, tell me. It's my job to step in. As needed."

"Okay. I've got about fifteen minutes. Let's talk terms, then I need to pass you to my assistant to show you around." She took another sip of her drink. "If we come to terms, you can start training next Monday. I'd want you to have a solid week with Don, our current manager, before you fly solo."

Morgan put her hands in her lap, folded them together, gripped them tight. "Just like that?"

This time Nell studied her drink before she sipped, before she met Morgan's eyes straight on. "I know how to gauge people, too."

Ninety minutes later, still dazed, Morgan walked into Crafty Arts. A half dozen customers browsed while Sue rang up a sale.

"Hey there, Morgan. Your mom and gram just went up to the office."

"Thanks."

She made her way up, found them both at the computer and her grandmother hovering over Audrey's shoulder.

"I think interest in, Mom, rather than experience in. We can train—Morgan!"

Audrey clasped her hands under her chin. "Were the earrings lucky?"

"As lucky as it gets. I'm hired."

"Of course." Olivia said it with a shrug, but her eyes shined as Audrey leaped up to grab Morgan and bounce. "The Jamesons aren't idiots."

"I start training tomorrow, and I'll work on a probationary basis for three months. After which? Automatic raise in salary. Jesus, they offered more than I was making at the Round, with benefits. And, and, oh God, I'll manage a team of twenty-three, including back of the house."

"We have to celebrate," Audrey declared. "We'll take you out to dinner."

Morgan followed impulse. "I'm going to make pork chops."

Audrey blinked. "You're going to cook?"

"It's Nina's mother's recipe. I made it once, I can do it again. I'm going to make pork chops and her spicy potatoes," she repeated, because it would close out an ugly memory. "And we'll use the good china and stemware. That's how I want to celebrate."

She drew back. "Thank you, Gram, for opening the door. Thank you both for the lucky earrings I may never take off. I'm going to the store, then making dinner."

She gave them both a squeeze.

"If it tastes horrible? Lie."

Chapter Eight

The depth of stupidity, laced with gullibility, in the human race never failed to amaze him.

And delight him.

After all, without those lovely weaknesses, how would he live his life in the style he deserved?

Gavin Rozwell had learned early on the female of the species offered almost endless opportunities to exploit and manipulate. The method, of course, depended on the mark. For some, it only required good looks.

He had those, and had been assured of it all his life.

Others? Add charm—and he could sprinkle it on, pile it on, shovel it out as the mark and situation called for.

He had that talent.

Then again, some liked the rough stuff and no problem. But he kept the rough on the easy side. Until the end.

There were those who fell for the lone wolf, the brooder, the poet, the laid back, or the tightly wound.

He had a million personas he could wear like a bespoke suit.

Sob stories provided openings for certain types. Try the recent widower, or the cuckolded husband.

The trick? Be who the target wanted you to be.

And he excelled at it.

Again, he'd learned from an early age, watching his own mother fall for line after line. She'd truly believed people held inside them a core of good—no matter how deeply buried.

Nobody, according to good old Mom, was purely bad, not through and through. And in her world evil hadn't existed.

God made the world, after all, and God was good.

She'd believed—no matter how often she'd been knocked flat—kindness triumphed.

His mother, the saint.

His mother, the idiot.

She'd considered him a gift—her handsome, clever little boy. Sure, his father had knocked her around on the rare occasions he'd paid any attention at all. Then came the excuses, from her—never him. *He had a hard day, he gets upset, I shouldn't have said anything.*

And when he'd dumped them, taking even the money she'd tucked away under her cheap, serviceable white bras and panties, she'd made excuses.

He loves us too much to stay.

So he—her gift—saw weakness, a woman's weakness, ripe for mining.

For her, he became the loving, devoted son while she worked menial jobs for assholes who barely paid her enough to make rent. A simple clutch of dandelions or a heart cut out of construction paper ensured she waited on him, hand and foot.

And either didn't notice, or never mentioned, the five or ten bucks he'd take out of the coffee can she kept tucked in the kitchen cabinet.

He did well in school. He had a good brain, comported himself with absolute politeness. And used the trust he'd carefully built to run short cons on students and teachers alike.

He had a knack for computers and, honing it, destroyed his eighth-grade history teacher's life.

Bastard gave him a B-minus!

The hacking proved remarkably simple once he got going. Loading up Mr. Stockman's home computer with child porn had presented a challenge he'd accepted.

Stockman lost his job, his wife, and his children and did six years in a federal pen.

There's your B-minus, asshole.

His speech as valedictorian at his high school graduation brought his mother—and others—to tears. He accepted a scholarship to Michigan State. Though he'd had several colleges to choose from, he'd claimed he needed to stay close to home, near his mother in Detroit, so he could drive back regularly to help her.

He did so, faithfully, waiting until the spring of his second semester to make her his first kill.

A shock! A tragedy! The senseless murder of a forty-one-year-old woman during a break-in of her rattrap of a rental house while her only son, her loving and devoted son, slept ninety miles away at college.

Her nineteen-year-old son, who'd broken to pieces at her funeral. And at nineteen, of age, clear of any risk of foster homes or legal guardians, he'd tasted freedom.

He cashed in her life insurance policy, one he'd convinced her to take out—only fifteen dollars a month for peace of mind—and Gavin Rozwell, a natural-born psychopath, hit the road.

He thrived.

For a while he just traveled, lived high. But the insurance money couldn't last forever.

He ran simple cons for a while, and that proved fun and profitable. Then he moved to identity theft, and that brought more profit and satisfaction.

But it lacked a genuine thrill. No big kick. No wild buzz.

So while he traveled, he planned, he plotted, and found his true calling.

He knew he killed his mother over and over with the termination of each mark. He'd aced his psyche courses, after all. But so what? He enjoyed it, each time, every time. Ending them, looking into their shocked eyes when he choked the life from them, brought back the moment of looking into his mother's.

Who said you can't go home again?

And it served as the culmination of the thrill, the pleasure of taking everything they valued first, just the way his father had taken everything his mother had valued.

Well, except for him, of course.

Now, on a lovely spring morning, going by Oliver Salk, he sat on the terrace of his hotel suite in Maui, taking in the air, the view while he sipped his second cup of coffee.

In the twelve years since he'd murdered his mother, he'd lived well, lived high. The quarter-million term policy had given him the means and the opportunity to pursue the lifestyle he'd been born for.

He lifted his cup, toasted. "Thanks, Mom."

He'd earned it, just as he'd earned every penny since, because it *was* work, and work that required time, skill, brains. The weeks, often months of research and planning took a toll. Then add in the expense of maintaining his looks while changing them just a bit along the way, the cost of acquiring new identities and the wardrobe to suit them.

Some of the marks expected sex, something he'd honestly never enjoyed. But he considered it the cost of doing business.

There'd been that one in Portland three—no, four years ago, he remembered. God, she'd been relentless sexually. Then again, he'd cleared nearly eight hundred thousand before he ended their relationship. And her.

He'd done very well for himself, enjoyed his life, his work, his travels. And his success rate had been perfect, because he'd earned perfect. He deserved perfect.

Until Morgan Albright.

The one that got away.

It grated still, and he could admit the miss had left him shaken. More than a little shaken. Enough to take a break, indulge in a long vacation.

The bitch would've talked to the cops, to those asshole feds, and maybe, just maybe, he'd let something slip with her he shouldn't have.

Not likely, but the nagging maybe pushed him to take a breather, to put a few thousand miles between them.

He could afford it, after all, some time in San Diego, then a couple of months in Malibu, before some island hopping in Hawaii.

Nothing better than a fine hotel on a beach, to his mind.

And as the saying went, all work and no play made Gavin a dull boy.

But even in fine hotels on fine beaches, he thought of her, and thought of her. He'd taken what was hers, but she'd lived. She'd broken his streak and that ate away at him.

He had to fix that, fix her, reclaim his luck. To add to it, he was bored. Work was play for him, and he missed it, and missing it, had gone into research mode.

He'd need to reclaim that luck, start a new streak before dealing with Morgan.

He had two likely candidates on the mainland, and he'd choose the lucky winner soon. But Morgan? She proved people were stupid, gullible, and always ripe for the picking.

She'd changed her passwords—as if that mattered—and had shut down her already sparce social media accounts over the last year.

But her mother had them all. She posted regularly for the family business in Vermont. Pretty photos, cheerful marketing, with a personal touch.

So he knew Morgan, flat broke, had moved to Vermont, back with Mommy and Grandma. And all those happy posts helped him keep an eye on her. He'd researched her family, the family home and business before he'd walked into that two-bit bar, so he knew the setup, the finances.

When he was ready, he'd use her mother's accounts to find a back door and hack right back into Morgan's.

When he was ready.

Maybe he'd been meant to miss her the first time around. The idea of "meant to" soothed him. She'd hurt him by living, he could hurt her so much more by letting her live awhile, then taking everything again.

A second shot required a change of tactics, a different method altogether. But with the potential of more, much more. More money, more pain, more pleasure for him.

What if, just what if, he killed all three?

Something to think about.

But first, he had to get back in the game. Time to choose that lucky winner, he decided, and started making a plan.

* * *

Morgan loved going back to work, the routine, the structure, the schedule. Putting on her uniform made her feel productive, capable. Meeting the staff meant she was, again, part of a team.

Training proved straightforward enough. Après was certainly a bigger and more upscale operation than any she'd worked in before, but she'd handle it.

Maybe her visit to the wine cellar left her a little breathless—those racks upon racks, and the vintages far beyond any she'd decanted in the past—but she'd handle that, too.

The menu from the back of the house ranked several classy steps above the Round, and guests received maple-roasted almonds and picholine olives with their drinks instead of pretzels and bar nuts, but that was all a matter of style.

She breezed through her training week, serving guests not unlike those she'd painted for Nell during her interview. Though she considered Nick the best of those who tended bar, she had no complaints.

As for the waitstaff, their training showed.

At the end of the week, she received a summons from Lydia Jameson.

She'd expected an elaborate office, something regal to suit the photo of the woman she'd studied and the biography she'd googled to go with it.

Instead she found a modest, workmanlike room, a serviceable desk with a chair as straight-backed as Lydia's spine.

She wore her dark honey hair in soft waves around a strong face of sharp points. Cheekbones, chin cut like diamonds. The decades of lines didn't detract from it but made her look wise. And formidable.

Her eyes were deep golden brown behind the lenses of black-framed glasses. Her poppy-red lips didn't smile as she studied Morgan.

"Have a seat." The voice matched the face—strong—as she gestured with a hand adorned with a wedding set with a blinding square-cut diamond solitaire. "And welcome to the Jameson family."

"Thank you. I'm very grateful to be a part of it."

"I see Olivia in you, and some of Audrey with it. I imagine you got the eyes from your father."

"The color, yes."

"I have a great deal of respect for Olivia, and in the last several years, for your mother. It's why you're here. Or I should say it's why you were given the opportunity to be here."

"I know that. I'm grateful for that."

"As you should be. I had Nell interview you, as I felt I should step back. I also have a great deal of respect for my granddaughter."

"As you should."

Lydia's eyebrows cocked up at that.

"Nell tells me, as did Don, you'll be an asset to the resort."

"I'm determined to be."

"Are you a determined individual, Ms. Albright?"

"Yes, ma'am, I am."

Lydia let that hang a moment while she continued to study Morgan in silence.

"It's difficult for a determined individual to start over, but without determination there's no chance of succeeding. Your previous employers also touted your loyalty. We prize loyalty here, and will give it in turn."

"I appreciate that, and I've already seen it. Nick Tennant, ten years; Opal Reece, twelve; Adam Fine, sixteen. And others with that much or more. People don't stay happily at a job if they're not treated well, if there's not respect and loyalty on both sides. I'm going to give you my best, Mrs. Jameson, and my best is solid."

"I'd expect nothing less from Olivia's granddaughter. Once again, welcome to the Jameson family." This time Lydia rose, held out a hand.

"Thank you."

As she walked to Après, Morgan let herself breathe again. She was pretty damn sure she'd passed the last test.

On her first official day as manager of Après, she wore her lucky earrings. And came in an hour before shift for a meeting with Nell and her mother—Drea Jameson, Events coordinator.

They met in Drea's office, a larger space than Lydia's that included a rosy-hued love seat and two floral-print chairs.

Morgan thought the feminine touches suited the woman, with her tumble of auburn waves, porcelain skin, and dreamy blue eyes.

She wore a plum-colored sheath with a waist-length jacket. Morgan imagined the slim-heeled gray pumps boosted the petite woman's height.

"I'm so sorry I haven't had a chance to come into Après and introduce myself."

"Two weddings, an anniversary party, a corporate banquet, and the Grototti family reunion over the last couple of weeks wouldn't leave you much time."

Drea smiled, and Morgan wondered if the fact her lip shade exactly matched the love seat was deliberate or a happy accident.

She voted deliberate.

"Nell said you pay attention."

"Events take tables in the bar."

"They do. So." She handed Morgan a folder. "Events scheduled for the next four weeks. Don liked both electronic and hard copies monthly. There will be changes. Additions, cancellations, and you'll see final numbers in red."

Morgan opened the folder, skimmed the printouts. "Busy. Busy's good. I'm fine with just e-copies for myself, but I'd like to post the printout in the back of the house—and I can generate that. Updating as needed."

She looked up. "Is it possible to have the events list four to six months out?"

"Of course. Don liked to keep things more compact."

"It would give me a bigger scope and more long-range planning for vacation time, requested shift changes, which events require bar setups and bartenders. And with those, full bar or wine, beer, soft drinks."

She turned to Nell. "I understand that falls under your supervision, but the private bars decrease the tables in Après, at least during the course of the event, but still require staff pulled from Après or the Lodge Bar."

"True enough." Nell cocked her head. "More?"

"Well, while corporate meetings are a relatively small part of the resort's business, attendees use the bar for networking, casual meetings, so six months out there would ensure I had enough stock on hand. We had to borrow a bottle of 1800 Silver tequila from the Lodge Bar last Friday night."

"Knox Seed and Soil," Nell said. "Friday night tequila shots. We should've been prepared."

"Don's head was out the door." Drea lifted her coffee cup. "And that's understandable. I can give you six months out on all booked events, with a two-month view, delivered to your resort inbox."

"That would be perfect, thanks."

Nell angled her head. "And still more?"

Après might not be *her* bar, but.

"Since I'm asking, I might as well try my luck with one more. I'd like to feature a seasonal specialty drink, like the spa does with scrubs and lotions for services. Apple's the state fruit, so we could try featuring a cider—hard and soft—cocktail for fall or winter, or maybe mulled for winter. A sparkling cider mix for spring, sangria for summer, that sort of thing. Or, if you approve, I could coordinate with the spa, play into whatever they're featuring."

"And if they're featuring lavender scrub?" Nell wondered. "That's coming up next week for the spring launch." Nell set down her empty cup. "Which I'm betting you already know."

As she did, Morgan was ready. "Lavender margarita, lavender gin fizz, lavender champagne cocktail. I'd need to know and order the simple syrup, and have the sprigs on hand for garnish. But there's a lot you can do with it for spring or summer drinks."

"I'd like a lavender margarita," Drea decided. "It sounds lovely. What do you think, Nell?"

"Resort-wide, or exclusive to Après?"

"That would be up to you."

"Yeah, it would. Let's try the spa coordination. Resort-wide if it takes. You can try it in Après next week."

"Great. I'll order what we need."

"I'll walk out with you." Nell rose.

"Welcome aboard, Morgan." Drea rose as well. "And tell your mother and grandmother I miss them in yoga class."

"Yoga class?"

"Studio Om, on South Alley off High Street. We try to make the nine o'clock class on Wednesday mornings, but with the new café project and my schedule, we've missed class for a month. More like six weeks, for me, I think. Tell them I'm determined to make it this week."

"I will."

"She meditates, too," Nell said when they walked through the outer office with its ringing phones and busy assistants. "Do you meditate?"

"Only when I'm unconscious."

With a laugh, Nell shook back her hair, left down to skim her shoulders today. A more casual look to go with the gray pants and navy sweater.

"Me, too. I don't know whether to be fascinated or baffled by the idea of a lavender margarita."

"Come in next week. I'll make you one."

"I just might." She pulled her buzzing phone from her pocket. "Well, no meditation or margaritas for me. Good luck tonight," she added, and fast-walked in the opposite direction.

"Busy's best," Morgan murmured.

She exchanged waves or nods with some of the staff she'd met as she walked toward the lobby, over the marble floors, and through the archway.

It was, she thought, starting to feel like she'd found her place.

The bar buzzed, as a bar should in her opinion, with people relaxing with a drink before dinner, or settling down for bar food. At a quick scan, she spotted a couple of corporate types, heads together, conversation intense. A trio of women laughing together over glasses of wine.

Then stopped short when she recognized the two men having a beer. More Jamesons, she realized. The patriarch, Michael "Mick" Jameson, the man who, along with his wife, Lydia Miles Jameson, had expanded what had been a handful of cabins and a twenty-room hotel to the Resort at Westridge.

He sat with Nell's brother Liam, the youngest sibling.

They made a picture, Morgan thought, the generations. The grandfather with his sleek pewter hair topping a craggy face, the younger with a careless mop of brown and a face smooth and unlined.

And yet you wouldn't mistake them for anything but family as they sat, first generation in a sweatshirt, younger in a hoodie, holding an animated conversation over their evening beer.

Business, pleasure, or both? she wondered as she made her way to the bar and behind it.

"You're early." Nick poured another round—Chardonnay, Zinfandel, and a Cab—she identified for the trio of women at table five. "Tabs running, all tables," he told Morgan.

"Two just sat down on the lobby side as I came in."

"Lacy's on it. She's in the back picking up a cheese plate for that side. Bosses at table eight."

"Saw that."

"Heady Toppers," he said, identifying the beer. "If they go for another round, add the cheese fries even if they don't order it. Mick loves the cheese fries."

"Got it. Go home. I'll log your tips."

"You're the boss now."

"Looks that way."

A man who looked like he'd just waked from a long nap slid onto a stool.

"Good evening. What can I get you?"

He gave her a dreamy smile. "I just had my first hot stone massage. You ever had one?"

"Not yet."

"Do yourself a favor. Only time I've been more relaxed is never. My wife's getting one, meeting me here. It's our first time coming here."

"And how are you enjoying it?"

"I'm thinking about moving in. My wife's going to want a glass of champagne. The good stuff. She doesn't know it yet, but she's gonna. Me, I'll try that local brew. Marie. That's my wife's name."

Morgan thought Marie was a lucky woman. And decided she'd been right when the lucky woman came in moments later.

Marie all but melted onto a stool. "God, Charlie. Where has that been all my life?"

She blinked when Morgan set a glass of champagne in front of her.

"Champagne?"

"You deserve it. Eighteen years," he told Morgan. "Three kids, and our first solo getaway in sixteen years."

"And now I feel like a princess. I know we're supposed to dress up and have a fancy dinner, but, Charlie, I'm a wet noodle."

"Right there with you. Is the food any good in here?" he asked Morgan.

"I can tell you it is. Why don't you take a booth by the window. I'll bring your drinks. Take a look at the menu, and if you decide to have dinner here, I'll cancel your reservation for you."

"That's so nice." Marie just sighed it out. "Everything and everybody's just so nice. I love this place. Charlie, we owe my sister a great big bouquet for telling us about it."

While Morgan took care of them, the Jamesons brought their empties to the bar and took stools.

"Another round. Heady Toppers."

Morgan put the empties into the sink. "Cheese fries with that?"

Mick broke into a grin, and for an instant looked as young as his grandson. "My reputation precedes me. How about it, Liam? Split some, and don't tell your grandmother."

"You're paying? It's in the vault."

She plugged the order in, began to draw the beer.

"I don't know what you said to the couple over there." Mick nodded in Charlie and Marie's direction. "But it made them happy. That's the goal here, make people happy."

"Hot stone massages had already done that job. They made me want one of my own." She served the beer, caught the signal Charlie sent her. "Excuse me a minute." As she walked over, she waved the server over with her.

When she came back, she got out a champagne bucket.

"The Glade's losing a reservation. Charlie and Marie are dining here: club sandwich for her, steak san for him—hold the onions because Charlie has plans." She wiggled her eyebrows as she filled the bucket with ice. "They're capping their first day of their first visit to the resort with a bottle of champagne. The good stuff."

"Champagne's on the house," Mick told her.

"Oh, that's—that's great."

"I'll just go say hello while you get a bottle chilled. Don't eat all the fries, Liam."

"That's all Mick," Liam said, shaking his head.

She cashed out the corporate types, made a couple of dry martinis, watched Charlie and Marie clink glasses.

"You've got an easy way with a hard job," Mick observed as he polished off his beer. "I appreciate what it takes to make a hard job look easy. Let's mosey, partner." He slapped Liam on the shoulder.

Mick slid three twenties onto the bar. "Keep it up."

"Thank you, Mr. Jameson."

"Mick. We're family here."

"You ski, Morgan?"

She shook her head at Liam.

"We're going to fix that."

"I don't think so."

"If it doesn't involve skis or hiking boots or zip lines, this one doesn't see the point."

Mick gave her a wink before they moseyed.

It surprised her to find both her ladies waiting when she got home.

"What are the two of you doing up? It's nearly two in the morning."

"First day as manager. We made a pot of tea with our new Vermont tea." Audrey poured a third cup. "Sit down, have some tea, and tell us how it went."

"I had to talk her out of coming into the bar, so be glad it's just tea in the middle of the night."

Morgan took the tea, then dropped down in a chair near the still-simmering fire. "It went great. I had the meeting with Ms. Jameson—Lydia Jameson—then met with Drea and Nell. Drea said to tell you she misses you at yoga and hopes to make it Wednesday."

"So do we. Did they like the idea about the specialty drinks, the seasonal ones?"

"I got the go-ahead to try it out. Then I met Mr. Jameson—Mick—and Liam in the bar. So that only leaves out the second generation—Rory Jameson—and the oldest of the siblings, third-generation Miles."

"The family's done a great deal for the area." Olivia sipped her tea. "We get a lot of business—and so does the rest of downtown Westridge—from people staying at the resort."

"They always have ideas to share. Like you." Audrey toasted with her teacup. "I definitely think the tea's going to be a hit."

"They certainly seem tight—a tight family. I really like working there. And since I am, and I'm drawing a paycheck—and damn good tips—I want to start paying rent."

"Absolutely not. I said no," Olivia continued as Morgan started to protest. "I will not take your money. Do I take yours, Audrey?"

"No."

"And there you have it. I'd have been alone in this house without Audrey, and I likely couldn't have kept it. Too much for a woman my age all alone, and too empty. Now I have you here as long as you want to stay. You'll make your own home again one day, but for now it's here. You want some other responsibilities, that's different. You can make dinner once a month on your day off."

"You want me to cook?"

"Your pork chop dinner was really good," Audrey reminded her. "We didn't have to lie. You can just stick with that or expand, whatever. Mom and I like to cook, but it'd be nice to have a meal we didn't cook ourselves or bring home."

"Preparing a meal teaches independence," Olivia added. "I'm always surprised you don't, since that's your middle name."

"My middle name's Nash."

"Exactly." And Olivia smiled with it. "And you can start saving up to buy a car, one that doesn't have your mother and me worried every time you drive off in it. We can be grateful to Nina's family and still know that's a breakdown waiting to happen. I can use peace of mind more than money."

"All right."

"We'll be gardening soon, and can use your help there."

"And, Jesus, child, stop snipping at your own hair." Olivia rolled her eyes. "Go to the salon. Styling right down from the shop does good work."

Morgan pushed a hand at her hair. "I thought I was doing okay with it."

"No." Audrey spoke definitely. "I know you've made a budget. That's her second middle name," she said to her mother. "Budget in hair. You meet the public every day now. You need to look your best."

"A facial wouldn't hurt."

Now Morgan slapped both hands on her face. "My face!"

"Is beautiful." Audrey smiled and soothed. "But you need some pampering. They do amazing facials at the resort, and you'd get an employee discount. You need to treat yourself. Now we should all treat ourselves to some beauty sleep."

"I've got the dishes. I can sleep till noon if I want." Wouldn't, Morgan thought, but could.

"Night then." Audrey wrapped her in a hug. "Congratulations on your first day as manager."

As Morgan dealt with the dishes, she considered that she'd always lived in a female household. Her father had so frequently been absent, then just gone. Then she'd lived with Nina.

But she'd never been outnumbered, two to one.

Chapter Nine

Friday night. The end of the workweek for many meant a busy night at Après. And that put Morgan right in her element. As she mixed, shook, stirred, tapped, she decided that despite the horrible last year, she'd rung the bell.

She'd needed a job because she needed to earn a living, and with the first swing, she'd landed one she enjoyed. And one that helped her find Morgan again.

The capable Morgan, the Morgan who made plans and worked toward them. The Morgan who had a knack for bringing a bright spot to a stranger's day.

Whatever Gavin Rozwell had stolen from her, she still had her skills, and after a bumpy road, she'd relocated her spine. She intended to make good use of both.

At the bar, she served Keith and Martin, a couple celebrating their fifth anniversary—dry vodka martinis, three olives—and listened to their weekend plans.

"He'll hit the gym." Keith, adorable in his navy blue glasses, rolled his eyes behind them. "And drag me along."

"Because I love you."

"Yeah, yeah."

"Then a swim." Martin took the first sip of his drink. "Whoa! Now *that's* what I call a martini. How about you come back to Burlington with us and make all our Friday night martinis? We'd treat you like a princess."

"Do I get a tiara?"

"Naturally."

"Sign me up."

She slid down the bar to fill a table order from one of the waitstaff.

And she knew Opal—twelve years in—had plenty of reservations about the new manager.

While Morgan filled the order, Opal—forty-three, sturdy build, brown hair in a no-nonsense bowl cut—rang up the check for a second table.

"When you're slow on the drinks, it cuts into our tips."

Morgan added an orange slice and cherry to a whiskey sour while she filled a pilsner from the tap.

"Are you getting complaints on the service?"

"Not yet."

Maintaining pleasant, she poured a glass of Merlot, completed a traditional sidecar. "Let me know when you do."

"Don worked faster." With that, Opal hustled off with her drinks.

Couldn't win them all over, at least not all at once, Morgan reminded herself. But if that kept up much longer, she'd try a one-on-one.

She filled another table order—no bitching about her speed on this one—served bar snacks and drinks to the stools. Flirted harmlessly with Keith and Martin because they liked it, before she cashed them out around midnight.

From the corner of her eye she saw a man slide onto a stool at the end of the bar. Looked like a solo, she thought as he scrolled on his phone, and she worked her way down to him.

"Good evening. What can I get for you?"

"Glass of Cab," he said without looking up.

She got a red wineglass. Loner, she decided. Conversation not required. Despite the flannel shirt and jeans, the mass of dense brown hair falling over the shirt's collar, something about him said "suit."

She set the wine in front of him. "If you'd like anything from the kitchen, they're closing in about ten minutes."

Head down, thumbs busily writing a text, he shook his head.

She left him alone with his wine and his phone.

Thirty minutes later, when tables started to thin out and nightcappers wandered in, he was still there, end of the bar, working on his phone, half the pour still in his glass.

Minutes before last call, a group of three men came in. Early forties, she judged, and they'd unquestionably enjoyed any number of drinks already.

Laughing uproariously, they plopped down at the bar. The one in the middle shot a finger at her. "You're new. I've been here three times before, and you were a man. Six months ago—was it six months?—six months ago, you were a man."

"You're half right. I'm new."

He gave her a thoroughly drunken smile. "You're a whole lot prettier now."

"Thank you. What can I get you?"

He leaned forward, grinned. "Guess."

"I guess if you're not staying at the resort, I'm getting you an Uber."

He blinked at her while he processed, then slapped the bar and laughed. "An Uber," he repeated while his companions joined the hilarity. "What's in an Uber?"

All smiles, she leaned forward to meet his glassy eyes. "You and your friends unless you're staying at the resort."

"We got us the presi-fucking-dential on the Club Level." Since he said it with pride rather than temper, pulled out his key card to wave around, she kept smiling.

"I hear it's fabulous. What are you celebrating?"

"My divorce. I'm a free man!" He tossed out his arms, clocked both of his friends, who found more hilarity. "How about you come on up and celebrate with me, cutie?"

"Oh, that's tempting, but how about I serve you your last drink of the night?"

"Aw. We're drinking boilermakers like men, in solidarity."

"You got it."

"She tried to emasculate me," he claimed, while Morgan began to mix the drinks.

"Since you're drinking boilermakers like men, she didn't succeed."

"Gave her twelve years." His companions patted his shoulder on either side, and dug into the almonds she set out.

"Here's to the next twelve." She set the boilermakers on the bar. "Drinks are on me."

"Aw. You know, cutie, if I'd been married to you, I'd still be married."

"That's the nicest thing anyone's said to me all night. Enjoy."

She handled the rest of the stragglers and nightcappers before moving down to the loner at the end of the bar.

"Last call. Would you like another Cab?"

"Ice water, still." Then he looked up. "You handled that well."

She went blank. His eyes were tiger eyes, tawny, focused, a little fierce. For an instant that's all she saw. Then the rest pushed through.

The sharply defined planes and angles, the take-a-punch line of the jaw. Add forty-five, fifty years, change the eyes to blue, he'd be his grandfather.

"Thank you, Mr. Jameson."

"Miles. That's how we run here."

He glanced down the bar at the trio while she got his ice water. "I let Security know. They'll make sure they get back upstairs safely."

"They're harmless. He's just sad."

"Is he?"

"Divorce, even when you want it, even when you need it, is bound to make you sad."

"He'll wake up with a banger of a hangover tomorrow and be sadder."

His phone signaled—the first notes of "Bad to the Bone."

"Hell." When he picked it up off the bar, she left him alone.

When the trio stumbled out of the bar, Miles got up, left a twenty behind, and followed them out.

She ended her first solo week with a slammed Saturday night—her idea of perfection. On Sunday—a day and night off—she watched her mother bake bread and her grandmother roast a chicken.

Her assignment? Scrub and quarter potatoes, peel carrots.

It felt homey, relaxing, and happy with her mother rhapsodizing about seeing crocuses blooming in the snow.

"It's going to go up to the fifties tomorrow and Tuesday."

"Snow showers on Wednesday."

Audrey sighed at her mother. "I know, but I'm telling you we're out of it. Snow *showers*. Spring in Vermont's only prettier because it takes so damn long to get here. You're going to do those lavender drinks this week, aren't you, Morgan?"

"I am, so let's stick with showers and focus on the crocus."

Out the window, the snow still blanketed, but she could see thinning patches, even some ground here and there. Shrubs and bushes shook off the white. Icicles dripped and sparkled.

She thought of the pansies she and Nina had planted just about a year ago. She'd buy some, plant some in memory, and to make her ladies smile.

She stepped back from the cutting board. "Did I do these right?"

"They'll do. Now you're going to toss them together in that bowl with olive oil."

"How much?"

"Use your eyes."

"God."

"After that, you're going to add a little honey, zest some lemon. Salt, pepper, oregano. You know how to mix a drink. Figure it out."

She figured it out—she hoped—then spread them on a baking sheet and stuck them in the oven.

"Mom measured when she made the bread dough."

"Baking's different."

Rather than argue, Morgan changed the subject.

"I forgot to tell you I met the last of the Jameson siblings. Miles?"

"Did you have a meeting?" Audrey asked.

"No, he came into the bar Friday night. Late. Nursed a glass of Cab for about an hour while he sent and answered texts on his phone."

"Workhorse," Olivia stated. "Always has been."

"Takes one to know one."

Olivia shrugged at her daughter, then chose a bottle of white from the wine cooler. "Show horses look pretty, workhorses get things done."

"He's not pretty like his siblings—too much rugged in the face for pretty. But he's a really good-looking workhorse." Morgan got out glasses. "They're all really good-looking."

"They are. My aunt—on the Nash side—married a Jameson cousin. I was flower girl. I guess I was six or so, and I remember how beautiful it all was," Olivia said.

"I didn't know that."

In her gray sweatshirt with its rainbow peace sign, Olivia looked back.

"Your great-great-aunt and uncle, they'd be. So you've got distant Jameson cousins scattered around. I wore a pink organdy dress and pink rosebuds in my hair." Olivia took the wine Morgan offered. "I remember that, too. And dancing with my father, then with my brother, Will."

William Nash, Morgan knew, who'd gone to Vietnam, and died there.

"Anyway, the families go back, and both had their share of show horses and workhorses."

Audrey took her bread out of the bottom oven, gave a little shoulder wiggle of satisfaction as she put it on the cooling rack. "Wasn't Miles engaged?"

"No. Came close, rumor has it, but didn't get that far. And Lydia's pretty closemouthed on personal family business, but I know she was glad it didn't."

"Drea never talked about her at yoga, now that I think about it. Who was she anyway? I can't remember. Not a local, though."

"Sugarhouse princess from down in Brattleboro." To rest her feet, Olivia slid onto a stool. "All show horse. Edgar Wineman's granddaughter. Society page darling. Do they still have society pages? I gave them up for *Rolling Stone* magazine way back in the day."

"Probably." Fascinated, Morgan sat beside her. "So what happened?"

"Couldn't say. But I suspect a grandchild of Lydia and Mick Jameson has more good sense than to tie himself up for long with a show horse who likes to flaunt and prance around instead of getting anything done."

"Okay. Give me an overview of the family, one by one. I've got Lydia Jameson, but the rest."

"All right then. Mick, smart, has vision, and isn't afraid to get his hands dirty. He'd spend all his time outdoors if he could—and he and Steve spent plenty of that time together. Born athlete. I had a terrible crush on him when I was about thirteen."

"Get out!"

"Lucky for you I got over it, or you wouldn't be here drinking that wine. Rory, firstborn, went into law. He handles the family's legal business. Got his own firm, and one of his sister's daughters works with him. His sister, Jacie—she's about your mom's age—studied architecture, and met her husband in college. They've got their own business in New York, but you'll see them at the resort a couple times a year. Second daughter there's in interior design and works with them."

"The families stick tight."

"So they do. You should have a sense of Drea from your meeting. She's a sharp one."

"And kind," Audrey added.

"She is, has Job's own patience, and I imagine needs it with handling the events. If you've got something sticky to handle, Drea's the one to ask for advice. Diplomats could take a lesson. Stir up those vegetables, Morgan."

She rose to obey. "And the third generation?"

"We'll start with the youngest. Liam's not just a pretty face, though, jumping Jesus, he's got one. Takes after his grandfather—athletic, outdoorsman, and they were smart enough to let him play to his strengths. More like his mother in that patience, I'd say. Cheerful sort of young man in my experiences with him."

"That's how he struck me," Morgan agreed as she sat again.

"Nell, a chip off her grandmother's steely back. Solid as a rock, suffers no fools. Doesn't flaunt, and makes sure she frequents the local businesses.

"Now, Miles." Olivia took a thoughtful sip of her wine. "Not as easy to figure, that Miles. He's got the family home now, all to himself. Lydia and Mick decided the place was too big for them—and it's big—and passed it to him. I'm thinking Rory and Drea are happy in their own, so they went down a generation. Where Liam has that cheerful nature and can—as I've seen it—talk to anyone about anything, his brother's more the quiet type. Polite, well-mannered, as I've noted, but keeps more to himself. Then again, with Mick and Lydia about half-retired, Rory with his law firm, he's running the ship, or will be."

"It's a layered and detailed ship."

Olivia nodded. "Lots of decks on it and a proud legacy to keep afloat. Are you happy there, Morgan?"

"I really am. It's not what I planned, but I feel like I've stuck the landing. It's a good place to work, and I can't ask for more than that."

"Of course you can." Olivia patted her hand before she rose to baste the chicken. "But it's a start."

Once a month—three o'clock sharp on Sunday—the Jamesons held a family meeting. Tradition decreed the meeting took place at the rambling Victorian where Miles's grandparents had lived more than a half century of their married lives.

Though the house had come to him, he still considered them the hosts and the head. As a child, he'd spent the meeting portion of that Sunday in the library with a book, or playing in the backyard, alternately torturing or ignoring his sister when Nell came along, lording over or joining forces with Liam when he arrived.

Good times.

At sixteen, he'd sat proud at his first meeting, and learned the responsibilities and challenges of running a family business that not only sustained family but brought revenue and employment and interest to the community.

Decades of family meetings meant they ran smooth, had structure, even as the dynamics of that family ran through them like a river.

He couldn't imagine it any other way.

He prepped for the meeting, reviewing spreadsheets, ledgers, reports, and projections in his office on the second floor of the east turret. It overlooked the front yard, the hills, and the little apple orchard where he'd once climbed branches and thought the long thoughts of child-hood.

The dog Miles never intended to have slept in front of the fireplace—one of the dozen the house boasted.

The dog Miles eventually called Howl, because he did, had laid claim to Miles and the house the winter before as a stray of question-able origin and quirky manners.

Review done, Miles took his laptop, his file of hard copies, and switched off the fireplace his grandparents had converted to gas along the way. Howl opened one eye, grumbled in his throat.

Ignoring him, Miles continued out, took the back stairs down to the kitchen.

The dog, as he always did, followed. He watched, a hulk of bushy gray fur with a sweeping tail and long, floppy ears, as Miles set his laptop and file on the dining room table, switched on the dining room lights, lit the fire.

Miles walked back into the kitchen, opened the French doors, said, "Out."

Howl plodded out onto the deck, down the steps, and into the yard, where he'd spend some time guarding the property from squir-rels, rolling in the patchy snow, and howling with the wind.

Through trial and error, fits and starts, Miles had trained him to come to the mudroom door when he wanted in. And Howl had trained him to keep a supply of old towels in the mudroom or deal with tracks of snow, mulch, mud, depending on the season.

Since his mother would bring a ham, he only had to provide the coffee, soft drinks for the meeting, the wine for the post-meeting meal. They rotated the food contribution, which required another spreadsheet and a calendar, but it worked.

He made the coffee, prizing what he prized most—the silence and solitude. He loved the house, for all its size and quirks. He loved the warren of rooms even while he appreciated his grandparents' decision to take down the wall between the kitchen and dining room to open the space. Just as he understood the practicality of converting all the fireplaces above the main level from wood-burning to gas.

Since he'd moved in, he'd changed little. Why change something when it suited you just fine? And change, he knew, rarely meant one thing. The dominoes kept tumbling.

Now he carried the coffee service, the cups into the dining room, set everything on the walnut sideboard. He poured himself a cup and stood at one of the windows watching the dog roll in a patch of snow as if it were a summer meadow.

But he also saw buds forming on the trees, swaths of green—anemic yet, but green—spreading on the ground. Before long, maintenance would switch from snow blowers and shovels to lawn tractors and fresh mulch.

Which the dog would roll in.

The trillium would burst color in the woods and along the hiking trails. The redbud would show its neon blooms before leaves unfurled back where, long before he was born, his father and grandfather had built a tree house.

Jamesons built to last, he thought, then heard the voices and footsteps of his parents—first arrivals—who'd come in while he'd been daydreaming.

"You can smell spring coming," his mother said as his father set the big platter on the kitchen island.

"I smell ham."

At home, his mother slid baking dishes into the ovens, set them on warm.

"It does smell good, but spring lasts longer."

"Where's that dog?" Rory held up a rawhide bone the size of a redwood.

"Outside, getting wet and dirty."

"As a dog should." Rory set down the bone before taking his wife's coat. He hung his and hers in the mudroom. "Want coffee, babe?"

"No, thanks. Hi, stranger." She gave Miles a hard hug. "I hardly saw you all week."

"Busy days."

"Don't I know it."

While Drea set up her laptop and files, Rory wandered to the door to look out. Tall, lean, he stood with his hands in his pockets. He wore a red corded shirt Miles assumed his mother had picked out, and jeans going white at the knees, his usual when lawyer garb wasn't required.

His hair had gone gray at the temples, and a few stray strands wandered through his thick brown hair.

"How long's that dog been out there?" he asked Miles.

"Oh, two or three days. I let him fend for himself."

Rory sent a look over his shoulder.

"Maybe ten minutes, and he likes it out there. Obviously."

"He likes it in here, too. I'm going to let him in. I'll wipe him down, Mr. Fussy."

"He misses Congo," Drea murmured when Rory went into the mudroom to call the dog.

"I know."

If he'd had the choice, Rory would've taken the old Boston terrier to court with him. As it was, he'd taken the beloved Congo into his office every day as his Silent Partner.

"I do, too. Seventeen years is a long time, and it's hard to say good-bye. I know we did the right thing, poor little guy was suffering. But until your dad's ready for another dog, he's going to lavish that love on yours."

He heard his father talking to the dog and the dog's howls of de-light.

"So I hear." And since he also heard his grandparents come in and knew their habits, he went to pour more coffee.

At three, the family sat around the dining room table, his mother with spring water, Liam with a Coke, and the rest with coffee.

They ran through reports, projections, closed old business, out-lined new. One of the new Liam presented was a ropes course.

"I did the cost analysis for the build, the insurance cost, and Dad's looked into the legal. Should be on your screens now."

"I know they're popular," Drea began, "but I honestly don't see why people want to climb around on ropes and swinging platforms."

"For the same reasons they want to go down hills on a pair of skis or snowboard. It's fun. And it would add to our warm weather Ad-venture revenue."

"Used to be hiking, canoeing, kayaking were enough for that." Peering through her reading glasses, Lydia studied the projections.

"Times change, darling of mine."

She glanced across the table at her husband. "Yes, they do."

"The climbing wall we put up five years ago worked. During the summer season, it's booked solid on weekends and between forty and seventy percent of running hours weekdays. The zip line kills it. We're going to incorporate them into an Adventure package this season. Add the climbing wall or zip line to your hiking or biking, kayaking. Complete three adventures, get fifteen percent off a purchase at Outfitters. We could add the ropes course this season if we build it in time. Or next."

Lydia tapped a finger on the table. "Miles, you haven't expressed an opinion one way or the other."

"Liam should make his own case, and I think he has. He nagged me until I took a trip to White River Resort to try theirs. It's challenging, but it's fun, and it works."

"White River is three times our size."

Liam grinned. "Small but mighty, Grand."

"Obviously, Liam votes for it." Mick spread his hands. "Miles, I'm assuming you do?"

"I do."

"Nell?"

"I'm an aye."

"My darling Drea?"

As she tossed back her hair, she sent her father-in-law a flirty smile. "I'll tell you, my darling Mick, I'll never understand why anyone would pay to hang on to a rope, but I'll vote yes."

"So does legal counsel," Rory added.

"And I'll add my aye. Want to make it unanimous, Lydia?"

"If you don't bend to changes, you break." She pointed at her husband. "Don't think for one minute you're climbing ropes, Irish."

"Spoilsport."

"Yeah! I'll get started on it with the designer and builder next week. Thanks. You never told me you went to White River."

Miles shrugged. "Last fall. I wouldn't have told you if I thought it sucked either. You made your case."

"Any more new business, Liam?"

"No, Pop. I'm going to take my victory and retire from the field."

"Drea?"

"Some seasonal changes in packages for Events. And Nell and I are working on the idea, for summer, of a midweek picnic. A set menu, every Wednesday evening, long tables by the lake, two bars, buffet-style food and carving stations, musical entertainment."

"Picnic by the Lake." Nell took up the theme. "I'm working with the Lodge chef on the menu—keep it simple, friendly—make sure there are kid-friendly options, vegetarian and vegan options. Basically what we do for Buffet Night in the Lodge on Sundays, but midweek and outdoors."

"I used to camp out near the lake when we were just the Lodge." Mick studied the cost projections, and his eyebrows shot up. "Price of these grills is a hell of a lot more than a cookstove or a skillet over a campfire."

"Times change," Lydia said, and he laughed.

"That's a touché. I gotta say, I like it. The long tables, people sitting together. Makes community."

"We'll have firm numbers before our next meeting."

"And the menu—which will be subject to change as needed," Drea added. "Hospitality is coordinating with the spa on a seasonal specialty drink, beginning with lavender-infused margaritas."

"What the hell kind of drink is that?" Mick demanded.

"The new Après manager's idea. I think it's a clever one. Nell's not completely sold, but I like it," Drea continued. "Especially since Morgan made me one."

"She didn't make me one."

Drea shrugged at her daughter. "You didn't say you wanted to try one. She also claims she can make a special drink with whatever scrub and lotion the spa highlights, and I believe her. In addition, I've shifted our policy in order to give her a list of events booked for six months."

"That I agree with. It keeps staffing more structured. She carded me during her interview. I still can't get over it."

"What do you mean 'carded you'?" Miles asked.

"I wanted to watch her make a drink, and she said she had to see my ID before she served me."

Rory let out a rolling laugh. "Baby love, take it as a compliment."

"What it was? Ballsy." Nell shrugged. "I have to agree with that, too. I hated losing Don, but I have to say she's better at managing staff. Opal complains she's slower mixing and pouring—"

"Opal complains water isn't wet enough when she's cranky."

"True," she said to Liam. "And the fact is, tips are up, and so—marginally, so far—is Après revenue."

"She's not slow," Miles commented.

Now Lydia angled her head. "Oh?"

"I was in there Friday night for a while. About midnight, I guess, and at that point she worked the bar solo. Good crowd in there, and the service was quick enough. I didn't see any bump in it even when she dealt with a guy over-celebrating his divorce and his two close-to-sloppy-drunk friends. All of them pretty well smashed by the time they sat at the bar."

Because he'd hit his limit, Miles switched from coffee to water. "She established they were guests of the resort before serving them, but in a way that didn't put their backs up. And when divorce guy hit on her, she deflected in a way that let him keep his pride."

"She's Olivia Nash's granddaughter, after all," Mick stated.

"You were at Après when you texted me?"

"You texted me first."

Nell opened her mouth, rethought. "Maybe."

"Both of you should be doing something besides work on Friday at midnight."

"They both texted me, and I was doing something besides work."

Nell turned to her younger brother. "What's her name?"

He just grinned.

"And with that, this meeting is adjourned." Mick winked at his grandson. "Let's eat."

Chapter Ten

On her day off, Morgan bowed to pressure and sat in a chair at Styling salon.

The stylist, Renee, wore her pink-tipped golden-brown hair in a gorgeous fishtail braid. She took one look at Morgan's hair and sighed.

"Woman, what have you been doing?"

"I just . . ." In defense, Morgan pushed a hand through her hair. "Snipped a little."

"We're going to make a deal."

"We are?"

"If you like what I do, you never snip again." Now she combed her fingers through Morgan's hair. "Nice and healthy. Natural blonde, too, like your mom. You're a lucky one. What are you looking for?"

"Simple, easy to deal with. I used to wear it a little shorter, more angled. But I was afraid to snip that much."

"Praise Jesus." Renee narrowed her eyes, studying Morgan in the mirror. "You've got a good face, strong, pretty, diamond shaped. We're going bold and sassy."

"Oh, well—"

"Trust me. You're going to love it." After the shampoo, which felt wonderful, Morgan sat back in the chair. Sounds and scents bounced around the salon as Renee snipped.

She'd never spent much time in salons, just a quick cut every six weeks or so. In and out. Here people seemed to linger, holding conversations in the pedicure chairs or at the manicure tables, while more voices, the snap of scissors or buzz of razors carried around with voices from the chairs.

Like a bar, she realized, it was a kind of world with regulars, walk-ins, and those who served them.

"It's a good cut," Renee decided as she squirted something in her hands, rubbed them together. "And you got body, so you won't need a lot of product unless you want to fuss it up. You get some of what I'm using." She began combing her fingers through again. "Like this, before you blow-dry. Or you can use it between shampoos on dry hair."

"Okay."

Renee smiled as she began to wield the blow-dryer and a brush. "Watch what I'm doing here. It'll be easy to maintain. You're going to have the sassy, the layers, a touch of shaggy, right? And this long sweep of fringe from right to left. Got your bold. It's not going to look all done up, and it'll have nice movement."

Amazed, Morgan watched the transformation until she sat complete. Gone was the blunt, angled cut she'd worn before. Gone the admittedly inexpert attempts to trim.

Her hair looked fresh and fun, and no, not all done up, which she didn't have the time or skill to maintain.

What she had? Easy, casual, and—she supposed—bold and sassy.

She lifted her gaze to Renee's in the mirror. "I will never snip again."

"That's what I like to hear."

"Can I book an appointment for when you think I need it done again?"

"I like hearing that even more. We'll set you up."

She drove to the nursery a few miles outside of the town proper, bought pansies and pots and everything she needed to plant them.

When she heard her ladies come home, she poured wine.

"Morgan, the pansies! They're so sweet! Something smells so good. Did you cook? It's not your day to— Oh my God!" Her mother stopped dead. "Your hair. Your hair's adorable!"

"Is it?"

"Yes. Turn around, turn around. I love it. Mom, look at our girl!"

"I am. It suits you. Young, confident. What are you making here?"

"I found a recipe for leftover chicken, and it seemed easy. It always seems easier than it is, so I won't believe that again. But I think it's good. I tasted it, and I think it's good. Chicken chili."

"What a surprise. Three surprises at once. And all wonderful." Audrey took the wine. "What a busy day you've had."

"It felt good. It all felt good."

"Let's all sit down a minute." Olivia picked up her wine. "And feel good."

When Nell hustled into the bar just before noon, Morgan stood behind the bar handling the setup.

"First, great hair."

"Thanks. Can I get you something?"

"Not yet. Where's Nick?"

"In the dentist's chair getting a root canal."

"Ouch." Instinctively Nell sucked air between her teeth.

"Reminds me to get a local dentist."

"Are you working a double? Couldn't you get anyone to cover?"

"Charlene's kid's home sick. Rob has two classes today and finals coming up, so I didn't want to pull him in. I'd have tried Becs but she worked a double yesterday because Charlene has a sick kid. The Lodge has a private event so it didn't make sense to tap them when I could come in. It's fine. I've got it."

"How sick? Which kid? Jack or Lilah?"

"Jack, and his fever broke this morning. He's better." And it mattered, Morgan thought, that Nell had asked, and knew the names of Charlene's children.

"Okay then. My brothers are coming in. We're having a meeting, grabbing some food." She glanced at her watch. "I'm early. Miles will be on time. Liam will be late." Sliding onto a stool, she tapped the sign placed in front of sprigs of lavender in a bud vase. "So?"

"Moving nicely. Group of five—spa packages, annual repeaters—ordered two rounds. Want to try one?"

"Not yet. My mother said the one you had delivered to her was delicious. That was cagey of you, pinning her location, sending her one. I respect cagey."

"I'm glad she liked it."

"She did. Actually, I could use a latte."

"How about a lavender latte?"

The look that crossed Nell's face combined fascination with horror. "Are you joking?"

"I'm not. You game?"

"If I say no, I'm a weenie. And that's more cagey."

"You're no weenie." Morgan walked to the coffee machine. "If you don't like it, I'll make you a regular. I heard about the new summer event—the Picnic by the Lake."

"Really?" Shifting, Nell watched Morgan work. "Word travels."

"It does if you listen. It's a great idea. Yours?"

"Something my mother and I came up with brainstorming."

"Good brains. I'm going to have staff fighting duels to work it. And it's a way to keep things fresh and new. Like a lavender latte," she said as she set the oversize cup in front of Nell.

"We'll see about that. Have you heard about the ropes course?"

"No. I'm obviously not listening hard enough. You're adding a ropes course?"

"It's Liam's baby, and why we're meeting today, or mostly." She paused to take a cautious sip of coffee. Then another. "And okay, this is really good. Who the hell thinks of things like this?"

"I think it got its jump start in Asia."

"Wherever." She sipped again. "I'll have my assistant make up another sign. Which, from the smug look on your face, you hoped for."

"Is this my smug look?" Morgan patted her hands on her face. "I thought I put on my quietly satisfied look. Something like this wouldn't have gone over at the Next Round, but with your clientele, it'll work. Keep it priced for the season the same as a standard latte—the cost in additional ingredients and labor is minimal—and we'll move it."

"Done. Miles." Nell shifted again as her brother walked in. "Taste this."

He shook his head, looked at Morgan. "Black coffee. Did you shift to days?"

"Root canal," Nell began, "sick kid, finals. She's pulling a double. One taste."

"Jesus." He took a quick glug, then looked sincerely baffled. "Flowered coffee? Why?"

"Miles is a coffee purist. It's not coffee unless it's black."

"Then this should fill the bill."

"Right. Liam'll have a Coke when he gets here."

"Cheese fries with that?"

Miles held Morgan's gaze. No, not a pretty show horse, she thought again. But a really, seriously great-looking workhorse.

"Probably. We'll grab a booth in the back."

Still no suit, Morgan noted as they walked away. Black trousers, crisp blue shirt, good shoes—which he wore as easily as his blunt attitude.

She'd gauged Nell as a tough nut, but she'd made some cracks there. Miles struck her as tougher yet, but she'd find a way.

People began to wander in. With the private event at the Lodge, guests who wanted a casual meal would hit Après. Good, she decided as she filled the first drink orders. She'd keep busy.

When Liam rushed in—hiking boots, black sweater, jeans—Morgan gestured to the back booth.

"I'm a little late. They didn't order yet, did they?"

"No."

"Cool. Can I get a—"

She offered a tall glass of Coke with a lemon twist.

"Great, perfect. Read my mind."

He hustled back to the booth.

Not a tough nut, that one, Morgan thought. But kind of a sweetheart. Then she turned her attention to the two women, obviously sisters, potentially twins, who slid onto stools.

The one on the left frowned at the bar sign. "What's a lavender margarita?"

"Delicious," Morgan assured her.

She worked the double, and before five, placed the lavender latte sign on the bar. Nell was as good as her word.

At midnight, when she started to dream about a nice hot shower and a soft warm bed, she had six tables, five booths, and five of the eight bar stools occupied.

Miles came in, took a stool at the end of the bar, took out his phone.

The twins—thirty-eight, down from Middlebury for a three-day sister trip—came in for a post-fancy-dinner drink. Lavender margaritas. Once she'd served them, she moved down to Miles.

"Glass of Cab?" she asked.

He just nodded, so she poured the drink and left him to it.

Forty minutes later, she said good night to the twins, and wondered what her life would have been like if she'd had a twin sister. Or brother. Or any sibling at all.

When the boisterous table of six called it a night, the noise level dropped with their departure. That left her with two guys on stools with a couple of swallows of beer left in their glasses, a party of four polishing off a bottle of wine, a couple sipping their second martinis, and Miles.

"Last call, gentlemen. Would you like another round?"

They declined, cashed out. The party of four left minutes later.

"I'll cash out table three for you, Holly. You can call it a night."

"It was a night. I thought table three would be making the bedsprings sing an hour ago."

"Martinis as foreplay."

With a laugh, Holly went into the back for her coat, and Morgan poured two glasses of still water over ice. She set one in front of Miles.

"Thanks." He didn't look up. "You've hit last call, and Mr. and Mrs. Martini are still drinking so they missed the cutoff. You couldn't let Holly close the bar."

"The captain's the last to leave the ship. And Mr. Martini's married, but that's not his wife."

He looked up now, tiger eyes steady, curious. "How do you figure?"

"He's wearing a ring; she's not."

"Could be having it sized."

"Could. Not. She's twelve, maybe fifteen years younger."

"Nothing to that."

And seeing she'd gained his interest, thought she felt the first cracks in that tough nut.

"Not by itself, no." She glanced over at them as she sipped her water. "When they're not involved in the numerous PDAs they've indulged in, he expounds and she listens, wide-eyed, like he's the most fascinating man she's ever met, and when she went out to the ladies', he watched her ass. He didn't drool, but it was close."

"Maybe they're still very attracted to each other."

"He got a call when she was in the ladies', and I'm betting *that* was Mrs. Martini. It annoyed him. He was brief. You might say curt. Then he took a serious drink, scowled, and fiddled with his wedding ring. That's when he ordered the second round."

"Circumstantial evidence."

Morgan leaned on the bar. "Are you a wagering man, Miles?"

"Maybe."

"I'll bet you a crisp dollar bill I'm right."

"I might not have a crisp one on me."

"You can owe me. Anyway, he told his wife he had out-of-town business. She doesn't believe that, so she's called and texted several times. He's told his new to newish side piece he's in the middle of a difficult, protracted divorce. Maybe she believes that, maybe not, but either way, she's getting spa treatments and a classy hotel room and that platinum cuff she keeps playing with that came out of the resort's jewelry boutique. It was in the display window. It's gorgeous.

"Excuse me."

Mr. Martini signaled. Morgan put their bill in a folder.

Miles watched her deliver it, hold a quick conversation as he added a tip, signed the bill.

"Have a lovely night, Mr. and Ms. Cabot."

The woman giggled and snuggled up against Mr. Martini. "Oh, we're not married. Yet."

Morgan lifted the empties, wiped the table with the bar mop, and tucked it in her waistband.

"I owe you a dollar."

"Yes, you do. A crisp one." She loaded the martini glasses, the wineglass, the water glasses, the shakers, the garnish plates onto a tray, took them back into the kitchen.

When she came out, he was gone. With a shrug, she emptied the ice, wiped down the sink. She closed the register, locked the cash drawer, gave the bar and bottles a last thorough wipe down.

He came back, wearing a black coat and scarf.

"Sorry, sir, the bar's closed."

"I'll walk you out."

"Oh. Thanks, but you don't have—"

"I have to get my car anyway. Get your coat."

She got her coat, her knit cap, her scarf, her gloves.

He took one look at her bundled up. "Taking a side trip to the Arctic?"

"These cold Vermont nights don't translate into spring for me yet."

He turned off the lights, and she took one glance back—everything in order—before going through the arch with him.

They crossed the quiet lobby where the night man read a paperback at the desk.

"Good night, Walter."

"Night, Morgan. Good night, Miles. Drive safe."

They stepped out into the slap of cold. Not the blast it had been the month before, Morgan decided, but still a solid slap.

They turned left, down the wide walkway, away from the front gardens and guest parking to the staff lot. The owners had reserved parking with their names on the curb. His—a husky black SUV—sat alone, but he walked past it with her.

"I'm right over there. Thanks for the escort."

"Do you mean that?" He walked several steps closer to Nina's car. "You need more than a dollar if you're driving that."

Her hackles might have risen if it hadn't been pure truth. "I'm looking at cars." Soon, she thought.

"Look faster. I'll wait to make sure it starts."

"It'll start. Thanks again. Good night."

She crossed to it, got out of the cold air into the somehow colder air of the car. It grumbled, it coughed. She closed her eyes and prayed.

And when it turned over, she promised herself she'd look seriously for a car on her next day off.

But for now it only had to get her home. She glanced in the rear-view, saw Miles standing, hands in his coat pockets, watching her drive away.

And she thought, yes, she'd made that first narrow crack in the shell.

The week zipped by. She banked her pay, the bulk of her tips, then spent her Monday morning researching used cars online. She concluded she could afford a decent, dependable used car, but could better afford one if Nina's car lived one more month.

"One more month," she murmured.

Winter's back was broken, and if spring hadn't taken full advantage, if snow and cold continued to threaten, the worst still lay in retreat.

Another month meant a more substantial down payment, less to finance. And Nina's car only had to get her to work and back, run the occasional errand, get into town if she helped out at the café.

She put that aside, started to research easy recipes instead.

When that scared her off, she decided to take a walk.

Clear the head, she thought as she pulled on boots. Figure out what step to take next. She couldn't keep running in place indefinitely.

Yes, she had a job, she reminded herself as she stepped outside. A good job, one she liked a great deal. She had shelter, and she'd found living with her ladies an education.

She didn't miss her house. It hadn't been her home after Nina died. She missed Nina, and always would, and the friendship she'd had with Sam. Her coworkers and bosses who'd become her family when she'd rooted.

She paused, looked over the shockingly blue sky toward the mountains. She hadn't had this, she thought. Hadn't had this painting in her own backyard.

She'd have four seasons here, too. Couldn't she already see the first hints of spring? And yes, the change in the air, in the light.

The next step?

"The car, Morgan. You know it. Suck it up, and go find a car."

Because it wasn't just the money, it was letting go of that last piece of Nina, that last tie with the before.

She went back inside, dressed like a woman who knew her own mind. She got the paperwork—the title Nina's parents had signed over to her, her insurance papers, banking information, whatever she could think of.

With everything in a folder, she put on her lucky earrings. Negotiating a price and getting financing would take some luck.

She could expect the rockiest of rock bottom on a trade-in, but she'd make it work.

"Dealerships want to sell cars, don't they? They'd make it work, too."

She fussed with her hair—sassy and bold, she remembered. Then went downstairs, dragged on her coat.

When she opened the door to leave, Special Agents Morrison and Beck stood in the portico. Everything inside her froze.

"Ms. Albright. You're going out? We can come back."

She stared at Morrison. "I was just— No, it's not important. Come in." She stepped back like someone caught in a dream. "I'll take your coats."

When she had, she hung them, very precisely, in the hall closet. "I'll make coffee."

"Don't trouble," Beck told her. "Why don't we sit down?"

"Yes, of course. We'll sit down."

In the living room they each took a chair, so she sat on the couch. Gripped her hands together in her lap.

"He—he did it again, to someone else. You've come to tell me he's done it to someone else. Is she dead?"

"A woman in Tennessee, outside of Nashville. Single," Beck continued, "a slender blonde, age twenty-nine. She was found two days ago by her sister when the victim didn't answer calls or texts or report to work."

"Her bank accounts had been emptied. Multiple loans had been taken out in her name, using her house as equity. Her car was stolen.

The sister identified Gavin Rozwell as the man her sister had been seeing for a few weeks."

"I see." But she didn't. She just couldn't.

"He went by the name John Bower," Beck told her. "He claimed to be a freelance photographer working on a book. Her name was Robin Peters."

"I'm sorry. I'm sorry this happened to her. I'm sorry for her family. I don't understand why you've come all this way to tell me."

"Previously, he left nothing behind. If the victim wore jewelry, he took it, along with anything else of value. In this case, the victim was found wearing this."

Beck took out a photo, passed it to Morgan.

"That's—that's my locket. The locket my grandmother gave me. It was her mother's. There're pictures inside. My grandmother's parents inside. I don't understand. He gave this to her before he did this?"

Morrison waited until Morgan looked at him.

"We don't think so. The sister couldn't identify it. None of her coworkers had seen her wear it. Rather than the photos you listed in your statement at the time of the incident, this locket held these."

She took the next printout, and stared at the photo of her own face, and one of the man she'd known as Luke Hudson.

PART II

New Start

Tomorrow to fresh woods, and pastures new.
—JOHN MILTON

All beginnings are hard.
—GERMAN PROVERB

Chapter Eleven

Panic. It overwhelmed, rang in her ears, closed her throat.

"What is this? What does it mean? He can't possibly think of us as a couple. We never—it wasn't serious that way, not even when I thought he was . . ."

"Rozwell doesn't have relationships in the normal way, Morgan." Beck spoke carefully. "We believe you're the only woman he's targeted who survived, and as far as we know, this is the first time he's left a trophy he's taken from a target on a subsequent victim."

"Trophy," she repeated.

"Items he may keep," Morrison explained. "We know, as we've recovered some items, he tends to sell or pawn the more valuable, but there's no evidence leading us to believe he disposes of all. It's probable he keeps one or more objects from his victims."

"As trophies."

She'd heard of this, of course she had. She read books, she watched movies. But it brought fresh horror.

"Like—like a deer head on the wall. But he didn't keep my locket."

"He placed it on this victim, knowing we'd identify it as yours—even without the photos inside, we would have identified it as one of the items stolen on the day of Ms. Ramos's murder."

"Why would he do that?" But she knew. She already knew. "To scare me," she said before either agent could speak. "To let me know he hasn't forgotten about me. To—to allude we're connected. Why does he care?" she demanded. "He won. He killed Nina, he killed my closest friend. He took everything from me. I lost everything I'd worked for. I lost my home."

"You lived," Beck said simply.

"Nina didn't."

"He didn't want Nina. He killed her out of necessity, not desire. For the first time, he failed. He missed. You lived," Beck repeated. "And you're rebuilding your life."

Step-by-step, she thought. Brick by hard-won brick.

And now?

"You're saying—or he is—he's not finished with me. You're telling me he could try again. What am I supposed to do?" She pushed up, hugging herself as she paced. "Move again, go into hiding, change my name? And what good would any of that do? If he wants to find me, he'll find me."

"He wants you to be afraid," Morrison said. "He wants to live in your head. You live in his. And that burns, Morgan. It scrapes against his ego, and that burning, that scraping caused him to make a major mistake. We're forewarned, and so are you."

"What good does that do me?" She dropped into the chair again. "Now I live looking over my shoulder every day, waiting for him to come after me? What about my mother, my grandmother?"

"I'd advise you to install a security system."

"We have one," Morgan said wearily. "We never use it."

"Start," Morrison said flatly. "Morgan." He leaned forward. "I'm not going to say you have nothing to worry about, but you have advantages here."

"How about you name a few, because I'm not feeling it."

"You know what he looks like. He changes his appearance—hair color, facial hair, colored contacts, glasses—but you know him. He can't use his usual methods with you. He has to devise another way, and you can put up roadblocks there. Security system's number one."

"You work nights," Beck continued. "Buy a panic button, have your keys and the panic button in your hand when you leave work. Have Security or other coworkers walk you to your car. Check the tire pressure and gas gauge in your car before you drive anywhere. Never leave it unlocked, and check the back seat before you get in."

"We've already given local law enforcement Rozwell's photo. You should do the same for Security at your employment, and to the staff at your family's business. To hurt you, he has to get close to you. Make it hard for him to get close."

"He could just shoot me in the head from a distance."

"There's no satisfaction for him in that." Beck said it so easily, Morgan choked out a laugh.

"Oh, well then."

"For him, it has to be close. It has to be personal, because for him it is personal. It's possible he did this just to thumb his nose at us and frighten you. But I'd strongly advise you to take these precautions."

"Keep your phone charged and with you," Morrison added. "Get in touch with us, and the local police, if he makes any attempt to contact you. Contact us even if you just feel something's off. Taking a basic self-defense course wouldn't hurt. I'd give that same suggestion to anyone, frankly."

"Your best weapon against him is to live your life."

"With this criteria."

Beck's tone changed, softened just a little.

"Most of it's common sense. You're a sensible woman, Morgan. Stay sensible. I'm sorry we had to bring this to you. I'm sorry we haven't caught him. We believe he spent most of this past year in hiding because you spooked him. But he's come out now, and he's made some mistakes."

"The locket."

"And others."

Beck glanced at her partner, got a subtle go-ahead nod.

"Evidence indicates he kept this victim a prisoner in her own home for over twenty-four hours before he killed her. That's a risk he's never taken before. Her sister had a key, which he knew. She might have come in at any time. He spoke to one of the victim's neighbors during this period—deliberately went outside the house to start a conversation. In her statement, the witness described the conversation and his demeanor as odd, and she'd found it unusual for the victim not to come outside herself, as she was a keen gardener. She didn't report any of this, but she might have. He risked that, very possibly to stroke his own ego after his failure and time away from his work."

"And the woman is still dead."

"Yes. She didn't know him and didn't have the opportunity to take precautions against him. You do."

Beck put a manilla envelope on the table between them. "Inside are several photos of Rozwell, along with a description and list of his known habits and routines. My card and my partner's are also inside. We've spoken to the local police. Please give these to your employer, your family. If that's difficult or awkward for you, we'll do so."

"I'll do it."

"We're both available anytime, day or night." Morrison rose. "Take the precautions, Morgan."

She would, of course she would, she thought when she stood in the empty house. What choice did she have?

She'd start with the alarm system, something her grandmother had installed shortly after Pa died. And, Morgan knew, no one ever bothered to use.

She had to look up the instructions and the code in her grandmother's files, but she set it before she took the envelope and left the house.

She hated the way her heart hammered when she walked outside. And the trembling inside as she walked to the, yes, unlocked car, checked the back seat.

Three-quarters of a tank, so that was good, but she had no idea how to check tire pressure.

She'd learn.

Even on the short drive into Westridge, she found herself obsessively checking her rearview mirror, tensing up when a car approached on the other side of the road.

She locked the car in the lot behind Crafty Arts and walked into the warm welcome of the shop.

Sue and a customer laughed together like old friends. Maybe they were. Her mother stood at a display case while another customer tried on a pendant.

Audrey sent Morgan a smile as she spoke to the customer. "It looks wonderful on you, so good with your coloring. I like these earrings with it. They coordinate, but they're not matchy."

"You're the devil, Audrey." But the woman held one of the earrings up to her left ear.

"Try them on. You know you want to. See how they feel. What do you think, Morgan? Irene, this is my daughter, Morgan."

"So this is Morgan." Irene turned as she took off one of her own earrings, passed it to Audrey. "Your mom talks about you all the time. No wonder you said she was beautiful, Audrey. She looks just like you. And damn it, I love these earrings."

"They look wonderful on you," Morgan managed. "And the pendant's stunning."

"When you're right, you're right. Okay, Audrey, ring everything up. Then I'm getting out of here before my credit card bursts into flames."

"Is Gram around?" Morgan asked.

"She just went upstairs."

"Do you think you could come up when you're done? For a minute?"

"Sure."

She went through the café—three tables of tea drinkers—and managed to smile at the counter server before she went into the back and up the stairs.

Giving in, she sat on them a moment, between kitchen and offices, steadying herself. Get it done, she told herself, and rose.

She heard her grandmother's voice before she stepped into the office. Olivia sat behind the desk, studying her computer screen as she talked on the phone.

"If you can deliver next week, we'll take two of each for a total of six. Don't screw with me on the tonal quality, Al. The sound's as important as the craftmanship. I'm going to trust you. Tuesday works. We'll see you then. Bye."

She hung up the phone. "Wind chimes. Half a dozen. And we've got hummingbird feeders, garden stakes, birdhouses, and what-all coming in next week. That's a sure sign of spring."

She reached for her tea and took a good look at Morgan's face. "What's wrong? Something's wrong."

"I just—"

She broke off as Audrey rushed in. "What happened? What's wrong? I could see it in your eyes."

"Everybody sit down," Olivia ordered. "Take a breath, Morgan, then say it."

"He killed somebody else, a woman in Tennessee. Oh God. God. The FBI agents came to the house to tell me."

"Audrey, get your girl some water."

"I'm okay, I'm okay." After she reached for her mother's hand to stop her, Morgan continued. "My locket—your locket, Gram—he put it on her. He replaced the pictures inside with one of me and one of him. They said that was a mistake, but . . ."

She told them what they'd said about the murder, the sister, the neighbor.

"What twists someone into a monster?" Olivia murmured. "Are they born that way, or is it a choice? I suppose it can be either or both."

Rising, Audrey poured a glass of water from the bottle always on hand, gave it to Morgan. "Sip slow. You're not leaving, not moving somewhere else. I can see that thought in your head."

"If it's in there, it better get out. The Nash women are sticking together this time. And that's the end of that." With a slice of her hand, Olivia cut off the discussion.

"He killed Nina because she was there. What if—"

"What if, what if." Now Olivia threw up her hands. "What if he gets run over by a truck tomorrow? Listen to me. You're not leaving your mother and me to worry about you, leaving us in that house worrying if you're all right. We stick together, and that bastard's not going to split us up. Be done with that, Morgan.

"We start using that damned alarm system."

"I set it before I left. They said to do that, so I did. And I'm supposed to get a panic button. I want both of you to get one, too."

"Then we will." Audrey reached over to rub Morgan's arm. "We'll talk to the police chief. We'll talk to Jake."

"They already did. And they said you should have one of these pictures of him, and their cards."

After studying the photo Morgan gave her, Olivia nodded. "We'll post one of these right in the shop, and another in the café, where people can see his murdering face."

"Oh, Gram."

"We'll make copies, Audrey, and the other merchants, they'll post them. Let him show his face around Westridge. Let him try. Nobody fucks with my granddaughter."

"Mom!"

"I save that word for when it's most useful and appropriate. I expect they told you to give this to the resort."

"Yes."

"I don't know what else they told you, but so far, it sounds like sense. Here's what I'm telling you. You're going to turn in that rattle-trap you're driving and buy a new car. A new, safe, dependable car. I'm going to finance it."

"Gram."

"Don't interrupt your grandmother," Audrey told her.

"I'm going to charge you interest, and you'll make monthly payments to me just like you would a finance company. We'll do an amortization schedule. Your mother and I get peace of mind, and you keep your pride. Both matter."

"I've been looking at used cars—"

"New." Olivia sliced her hand again. "New, safe, dependable, and able to handle Vermont winters. I'm going to give you the name of the saleswoman I bought my last two cars from. We came to terms, and if she wants my future business, she'll do the same for you."

"Be smart, Morgan, and say thank you."

"I do thank Gram. I thank both of you." The gratitude burned in her throat, her heart, her belly. "But the fact is, I don't know if I'll have a job after I take this to the Jamesons."

"Don't buy trouble when everyone can get it for free," Olivia advised her. "Go do what you have to do. Then you go to the dealership. I've got her card."

She took out a business card folder, thick as a brick, flipped through. "Here it is. I'm going to call her, tell her what you're after, and what I expect."

Next she took out a checkbook. "Don't you come home without a decent vehicle." She made out a check to the dealership, dated, signed, left the amount blank. "We'll work out the payments when you get home."

"We'll be there when you get home." Taking Morgan's hand, Audrey brought it to her cheek.

"We'll be home, but we won't be able to get in the house without the damn code. What the hell is it?"

Surprised it was in there, Morgan choked out a laugh and told her.

Even though Nina's car wheezed on the drive to the resort, Morgan told herself not to think about cars yet. She could end up driving away from the resort unemployed, and if that happened a new car was pointless.

In the employee lot, she locked the car, headed down the walkway. Inside, the lobby boasted a fresh floral display, all spring, and she thought again how much she liked working here.

The people, the atmosphere, the energy, her responsibilities also appealed.

Now Gavin Rozwell could take it all away, take so much away again.

She might not work Mondays, but she had everyone's schedule in her head. Nell, direct supervisor, had a meeting finalizing the menu for an upcoming wedding.

Not only did interrupting that or waiting until it finished seem pointless, but she felt she should take this issue straight to the top.

And Lydia Jameson worked in her office on Mondays.

She made her way to the office area and found Lydia's door open, the woman behind the desk on her computer.

"Another double?"

"No, ma'am. If you have a minute?"

Lydia signaled a come-ahead. Morgan went inside, shut the door.

As she did, chief of police Jake Dooley sat in Miles's office. They'd been friends since middle school and he knew Miles as well as he knew himself, so Jake laid it all out, quick and clear.

As he listened, Miles studied the photo of Rozwell Jake gave him.

"Okay. Now give me your take. Not theirs, yours."

"He took stupid risks—talking to the neighbor, keeping her alive for a couple days when her sister had a key. The kind of risks everything in the file I've read says he's never taken."

Shifting, Jake leaned forward and tapped a finger toward the photo.

"He's not one of the types who wants to get caught, Miles. He enjoys what he does too much for that. He's not only a psychopath, a sadist, he's spoiled. He's greedy. And he's been, up until now, very careful.

"The locket?" Jake continued. "Not only leaving it on the victim, but replacing the pictures inside? Putting his own in there with Morgan's? That message is clear enough."

"Her statement is they weren't involved as a couple."

"Not a couple, no. But she's on his mind, she's connected. She's the reason his luck changed. And he wants her to know he's not done with her, to know and be afraid."

"If she's not, she's an idiot, and she doesn't strike me as an idiot. I'll talk to Security, to the family, to her."

"Good. When you talk to her, make sure she knows she can contact me, anytime. She has questions, I'll try to answer them. I know they've got a security system. If they're not using it, they're going to."

"Count on it."

"I'm going to hunt up Nell." Jake rose. "She's Morgan's direct supervisor, right? I want to lay this out for her."

"Fine. I'll let you know what Morgan has to say when I talk to her."

Alone, he spent another minute studying Rozwell's photo. Then he rose. He'd start with his grandmother, he decided, then work his way through the rest.

"You have trouble all over you," Lydia said to Morgan. "A problem in Après?"

"No, ma'am, it's personal."

"Sit down then. Let's hear it."

"You're aware of what happened when—before I—"

"Take your time," Lydia said when Morgan broke off. "This is to do with the man who killed your friend and stole your identity."

"Yes. The agents in charge of the investigation came to tell me he killed another woman a few days ago."

She said it all fast, got it out while her stomach churned.

"You've got his picture in that envelope?"

"Yes."

"Well, let's see it."

She fumbled, had to use both hands, but got one out, rose to hand it over the desk.

"Mrs. Jameson, I understand if you don't want to bring this trouble to the resort, to the staff, the guests, your family. I understand."

"Handsome. Slick-looking, though. Slick's never been my type." She set the photo down, folded her hands on it, then looked up at Morgan. "You've worked here about a month now."

"Yes, ma'am."

"I rated you as someone quick on the uptake—one of the reasons you got the job. Fast learner. But if you think the Jamesons are so weak-kneed and careless as to let you go over something like this, I was wrong about you."

It all just flooded through her, a tsunami of emotion, stress, relief. Bursting into tears, she dropped into the chair again, covered her face with her hands.

After one quick knock, Miles opened the door. "Grand, I—Well, hell."

"Give the girl a handkerchief."

"I don't have one."

"Come in here, close the door."

"Maybe I should just—"

"Now!" As she spoke, Lydia opened a drawer, took out a box of tissues. "Give her the tissues, get her some water. Don't be a jackass."

"I'm sorry. I just—"

"You cry it out. You're entitled. That murdering son of a bitch killed another woman in Tennessee."

Lydia gave him the details more coherently than Morgan had managed to give them to her. And though he already knew, Miles said nothing.

"She thought we'd fire her over it."

"Then she's stupid."

"She's not stupid, she's overwrought, as anybody with sense can see."

"I'm sorry." Struggling for composure, Morgan mopped at tears. "I'm sorry."

"What've you got to be sorry for?"

Morgan lifted her drenched eyes to Lydia. "I don't know. I just don't know. I wish I did." She pulled out more tissues. "God, I'm a mess. I can be sorry for that."

"Apology accepted. Miles."

"Sure. Jake—police chief," he added in case Morgan didn't know, "already spoke with me. We'll make copies of the photo, make sure Security has them. Reservations, check-in, restaurant and bar managers, and so on. Grand, we need to lend her one of the staff vehicles. You should see the pile of crap she's driving. A breakdown between here and the Nash place is inevitable."

"I'm going to get a new car. I'm going today. My grandmother wouldn't take no on it."

"Olivia Nash is a woman of sense. I expect the same from her granddaughter. You're also part of the Jameson family now, and we take care of our own. Understood?"

"Yes, ma'am. I'm very grateful."

"Continue to do good work, as you have been. That's thanks enough. Miles, walk Morgan to her car."

Morgan rose. "I'll do good work, and I'll still be grateful. Thank you."

"Let's go this way."

He led her to the left, past more offices, and paused at a restroom. "Go in and do something with your face."

"That bad?"

"Bad enough."

She went, saw he hadn't lied, and did the best she could.

"Better?" she asked when she came out.

"Close enough. Somebody from Security will walk you to your car after closing every night. Jake said you have an alarm system on the house. Use it. Don't buy another piece of crap. You need four-wheel or all-wheel drive."

Something about the blunt, no-bullshit-taken tone brought some strange sort of comfort. "I know."

"Have you ever bought a car before?"

"Yes. I had a nice Prius. He stole it."

"Don't pay sticker price because you're tired and have a headache."

Everything in her felt off and dull and stupid. "I am tired. I do have a headache."

"Don't pay sticker price or fall for all the add-ons." He waited while she unlocked the car.

She just nodded, got in the car.

He held the door open, looked down at her.

"Morgan, when something's your fault, you take responsibility for it or you're an asshole. When something's not your fault, you're stupid to take responsibility for it. None of this is on you. Go buy a car," he said, and shut the door.

Once again, he stood, hands in pockets, to watch her drive away. Then he went back inside to schedule an emergency family meeting.

It would take less time that way.

She bought a car. She didn't go into it or come out of it with the same pure joy she had before, but she bought a car. And she didn't pay sticker price. Still, Morgan credited that more to her grandmother's patronage of the dealer than her own negotiating skills.

Either way, she now owned a new compact SUV that would handle winter when it came around again. A hybrid that satisfied her economic and environmental values, and didn't wheeze, clunk, or cough.

She considered the fact that giving her anything but a pitying look as a trade-in on Nina's car was a bonus.

As promised, her ladies beat her home, and must have watched for her, as they both came out when she pulled into the drive.

"Oh, it's so cute!" Audrey clapped her hands together. "What a pretty blue."

"Looks sturdy." As she circled it, Olivia nodded approval. "And safe."

"Sturdy, safe, and cute. Good job, Morgan."

"It's a hybrid. I don't do a lot of driving, and they have a couple of charging stations at the resort, so it's practical."

"Hits all the notes then." Ready to soothe, Audrey put an arm around Morgan's waist. "You're worn out, baby. Let's go in, get some food in you. Gram made her smoked tomato soup. How about I make you a nice grilled cheese sandwich to go with it?"

"That sounds great, thanks." Inside, Audrey hung her coat before Morgan could. "They didn't fire me or ask me to resign."

"Of course they didn't. How about some tea? Why don't you put the kettle on, Mom?"

"A good stiff drink might put the color back in her face, but we'll stick with tea. Sit down, Morgan. You got through it, and getting through it's what counts."

She sat at the counter, pressed her fingers to her eyes. "I cried. God, I just lost it, right in Mrs. Jameson's office."

After turning the flame on under the kettle, Olivia turned back. "I doubt it's the first time Lydia's had tears in her office."

"Then Miles came in while I'm on my jag. He said I was stupid."

Busy slathering butter on slices of sourdough, Audrey paused, and her eyes fired. "For crying?"

"No, no, for thinking they were going to let me go. And I felt stupid, and relieved, and they were so kind. Matter-of-fact kind, so I felt even more stupid and relieved."

She dropped her hands. "He actually said they needed to lend me a car because I was driving a crap pile."

"Well, the crap pile part was true." Generously, Audrey layered sharp cheddar on bread. "No offense to Nina or her family."

"Nina knew it was a crap pile. I told them Gram decreed I get a new car, today, and Mrs. Jameson told Miles to walk me to my car, and he's telling me to fix my face because I look like hell. And I did, I really did after that crying spree. Then he's all 'Don't pay sticker price.'"

"There's a man for you." Olivia set the tea in front of Morgan. "Just assuming a woman doesn't have the brains to make a good deal."

"I more think it was because I looked like hell, and I've had this fog over my brain since I opened the door and found the FBI. Pretty sure it showed."

Tired, so tired, she knuckled her eyes. "I half expected him to tell me he'd go with me and make the deal so I didn't screw it up. Instead he said taking responsibility for something that's your fault means you're not an asshole, but taking it for something that's not makes you stupid. Or something like that."

"Did you screw it up?" Olivia asked while the sandwich sizzled in the skillet.

"I don't think so."

"Are you to blame for what this monster did?"

"No."

"Don't add the but. The answer's no."

Too tired to argue, Morgan nodded. "I have all the paperwork on the car, the total after the trade-in."

"We'll deal with all that tomorrow." Olivia ladled soup in a bowl while Audrey flipped the sandwich in the skillet. "We'll figure out the payment schedule, and you can make the first one on the fifteenth of May. Then the fifteenth of the month thereafter."

"Okay. It has a lot of safety features."

"And it's cute." Audrey set the sandwich, cut on the diagonal, by the bowl of soup, added a cloth napkin.

"It is cute. I know I'll love it when this fog lifts." She spooned up some soup, felt it slide, warm and soothing, through her battered system. "Oh, this is so good." Sighing out, she took a bite of grilled cheese. "It's so good."

When Audrey stroked her hair, Morgan turned her face into her mother's shoulder.

"It's all right, baby." She met her mother's eyes over her daughter's head. "It's going to be all right."

Chapter Twelve

The Jamesons gathered around a table in the small meeting room. Miles ordered sandwiches and side salads from room service, since scheduling conflicts meant they couldn't meet until nearly seven. In this case, since he'd taken the wheel, he sat at the head of the table.

"I can update the texts I sent out now that I've talked to the agents in charge. There's little to add to what we knew before we hired Morgan, and what she told Grand this afternoon. They have evidence holding Gavin Rozwell responsible for the murders of ten women, including the victim in Tennessee a few days ago."

"Ten," Mike murmured. "Good God."

"Over a period of thirteen years. Their profile tags him as a psychopath, a malignant narcissist, a sociopath incapable of feeling guilt or remorse. Jake adds sadistic and greedy to that, and he's not wrong."

"He ruins them financially." Nell studied the photo of Rozwell that Miles had passed out. "Then murders them. No, I'd say Jake's not wrong."

"The women he targets," Miles continued, "or has specifically targeted over the last four years—slender builds, blondes, single, androgenous first names, who own a home, a car or truck—represent his mother, according to their profile. His mother was the first of his ten victims."

"He killed his mom?" Caught between shock and disgust, Liam tossed his sandwich back on his plate. "Jesus."

"His father abused her, habitually, then took off—after taking out a loan on their home, clearing out the bank account, taking her car," Nell said. "Jake gave me some information. Basically, he's playing his father, using these women to punish his mother again and again."

"He's smart, and a very skilled hacker," Miles added. "Comes off charming, and takes on different looks and personas to appeal to the target of the moment. They believe he does extensive research on the women before he selects one, but generally only spends two to four weeks inserting himself into their lives before he assumes their identity to clean them out, and kills them."

"So ruining them financially isn't enough." Rory, still in a suit for a court case, considered the report. "He ruins them first, benefitting financially—that supports his lifestyle. He betrays their trust, and that isn't enough. He strangles them—very personal—using his hands."

"But he didn't get his hands on Morgan," Drea concluded.

"He killed her friend," Liam pointed out.

"But not Morgan, and she's the one he spent his time and effort on."

"Exactly." Miles nodded at his mother. "As far as the investigators know, she's the only one who survived."

"And a narcissist doesn't fail." Nell poked at her salad. "Can't admit failure, anyway. So the locket. Leaving that's toying with her, making sure she knows he intends to succeed. On his own schedule."

"The FBI agrees with you, and so does Jake. And I agree with them," Miles added, "on our part. Security has his photo and all salient information, as do all department managers. I've added guest services, doormen, valets, and the butler staff to that. One of the Security team will walk Morgan to her car after closing. She'll park in the guest lot, in front."

"Better," Mick agreed. "We have security lights in the staff lot, but the guest lot's in view of the front entrance."

"We'll put a single number, direct to Security, on her phone."

"She often closes Après alone," Nell considered. "I think she should have someone with her."

"Good point." Drea continued to make notes on her tablet. "This maniac is less likely to try to hurt her when someone's nearby. With everything else he is, he's also a coward."

"I could shift her to days. It's a waste of her skills, but we could move her."

"She'll balk." Miles shook his head at his sister. "I thought about it, but in addition to her pushing back here, people tend to be more careful at night. She isn't careless, so I don't see her taking risks."

"She's a sensible young woman." Lydia spoke for the first time. "We already have policies and protocol in place to ensure the safety of our guests and our staff. We add these layers to it for these circumstances. Are we all agreed on that?"

"Of course we are." Mick patted his wife's hand. "She's part of the resort family, and we look after family. I'm going to add I like her style behind the bar. Got a smooth way. I may not understand how anyone mixes lavender with tequila, but she's got a smooth way."

"The lavender margarita. I could use one right about now."

"How about I buy you a drink, babe, when the meeting adjourns?"

Drea smiled at her husband. "You've got a deal."

"That's all I have at the moment. I'm going to keep in contact with the agents in charge, with Jake, and we can adjust what we're doing, depending. Nell, will you text Morgan about her parking arrangements?"

"Can do. I'm going to ask her to come in thirty minutes early tomorrow so we can go over all of this. I'd also like to know why she went to Grand instead of me."

"She thought we'd let her go."

Liam goggled at his grandmother. "Get out. She ought to know better."

"Now she does," Miles said.

"Still. Anyway, I'll talk to the Adventure managers in the morning, cover that end. If we're done, I'm going to take off. I've got a date."

"Liam Jameson has a date." Now his sister feigned shock. "Alert the media!"

"You're just jealous."

"A little bit."

He poked her as he rose. "You'd have a date, too, if you weren't so picky."

"You'd have fewer dates if you were more selective."

"Maybe, but then I'd be heading to the movies alone. Night, all."

"Ah, to be twenty-five." Mick sighed.

"At twenty-five, you were engaged to me."

He grabbed Lydia's hand, kissed it. "Exactly. Why don't I buy *you* a drink, my own darling?"

"Why don't you?"

"Miles, Nell, want to join the previous generations in some libation?"

"I would, but I've got some work to catch up on." As he spoke, Miles gathered papers.

"I'll get in on it," Nell said. "Join you in a few minutes."

When they were alone, Miles looked at his sister. "What?"

"Do you think he'll come here?"

"I think it's a lot less likely he tries for her here than at her home, or on the road between there and here."

"That's what I think, and there's nothing we can do about that. Still, we take the precautions here." Nell rose, hooked the strap of her briefcase on her shoulder. "I like her."

"She's likable enough." He wrapped the sandwich he hadn't touched in a napkin.

"Bring that napkin back."

"Right. I'm going to finish up this work at home."

"I'll call room service, have them clear."

"Are you taking the other half of yours?"

"No, I'm going to hit Pop up for some bar food."

He grabbed another napkin, wrapped the second half of her sandwich. "I'll bring both back. Nell, walk out with the family when they leave, would you?"

"I'm not his type." She gave her own brown hair a tug.

"Just don't walk to your car alone. Indulge me."

"Consider yourself indulged."

Satisfied, he walked out with her, then peeled off to go home.

On her first drive to work in her new car, Morgan felt the first tiny sparks of joy. It ran so smooth, so quiet, it smelled so good. She loved the screen, and promised herself she'd program home and work and the shop into the GPS first chance.

For fun.

She didn't love the order to use guest parking, but she'd obey without argument. The Jamesons offered their full support, and they didn't have to. The least she could do was follow orders without complaint.

She caught the look in the doorman's eye as she waved on her way in. Word had spread. She wouldn't complain about that either, and she'd work on not feeling so odd and exposed.

More looks here and there as she made her way to the offices, and she told herself it was only natural. People were concerned or curious, or both.

Nell's door stood open. Inside she paced, energy vibrating, as she talked on a headset. She'd scooped her hair up today, and wore brown pants, a V-necked, sleeveless shirt. A cream-colored leather jacket hung over the back of her desk chair.

"Absolutely and completely ready with every detail in place. Yes, Hospitality will deliver everything requested to the bride's room at two, and make the delivery to the groom's room at two-thirty."

She shot Morgan a look, rolled her eyes, pointed to a chair. "I spoke with my mother just this morning. She has everything for the table settings. Yes, the favors, too. No need to confirm that with her. It's going to be a beautiful wedding, Mrs. Fisk. We have everything under control. Yes, we're looking forward to it, too. See you Saturday."

Nell disconnected, then dropped into a chair. "The mother of the bride."

"I had a feeling."

"I bet you a million dollars she calls either me or my mother back, or both of us, before the end of the business day."

"Even if I had a million dollars, I wouldn't take that bet. Or your job."

"Good, because I actually like my job. There may be something deeply wrong with me, but I like it. So, I wanted to tell you we have everything in place with security."

"I appreciate it, very much. I know it adds time and trouble."

"Very little of either. We have good security. Now we have aware-ness of a situation. I want to ask you, Morgan, why you didn't come to me with that situation. If you thought I'd be less sympathetic and supportive than my grandmother."

"No. Oh, God, no. You were in a meeting, the Saturday wedding."

"Oh Jesus, Mrs. Fisk again." She pushed a hand through her hair. "I didn't realize you'd come in during that time slot. Would you have come to me otherwise?"

"Yes."

The lack of hesitation had Nell nodding. "Okay then. I wanted to make sure you knew you could come to me. Because you can," she added. "Even if it's just to unload. I honestly don't know what I'd do in your place. I don't know how I'd handle it."

"You probably wouldn't break down in tears in front of your bosses."

"Plural?"

"Miles walked in right after the dam broke."

Nell's lips curved as she stretched out her legs. "I'm not smiling at you, but at his reaction, the one that just played in my head. It goes something like: 'Oh shit.'"

"Something like that. You could say I unloaded. I'm okay now."

"Are you?"

"What else am I going to do? I have to live, I have to work. We're using the alarm system at home. I'm supposed to check the gas gauge, the tire pressure before I drive anywhere. Lock the car, and still check the back seat. I ordered panic buttons, as advised. And I'm going to look into a self-defense course."

"On the last, look no further."

"What, you?"

"No, but . . . Don't I look like I can handle myself?" Nell curled up her right arm, flexed.

"I'd have said yes before. Now, I say: wow."

"Built by Jen. Personal trainer, and fitness center manager. Part of your benefits is use of the fitness center. You get personal training at a discount, and Jen teaches a self-defense course every quarter at Westridge High School gym. You just missed the spring class, but you should go see her at the fitness center."

Nell checked her watch. "You've still got nearly twenty-five minutes. Go see her now."

"Now?"

"Why wait? I'll text her, let her know you're coming."

Don't argue with the boss, Morgan reminded herself, and trotted her way down to the fitness center.

Inside fifteen minutes, she had her first session booked for the following day.

She had yoga pants. She didn't really do yoga, but she had the pants. She had a sports bra even though she didn't do sports. That seemed adequate, since she calculated she could fit a training session into her schedule once a week until she gained some skill with self-defense.

With the discount, the cost was doable even on her strict budget. Added to it, she learned that Jen—who looked terrifyingly fit—was Nick's sister. Morgan figured that gave them a bond that would translate into easy training.

As instructed, she arrived fifteen minutes early to warm up on her choice of treadmill, elliptical, or incline bike.

She liked to bike, but the incline looked weird, and the elliptical too complicated. Walking seemed the safest choice.

A few people scattered around using the scary-looking equipment, lifting weights, doing what looked like painful stretches on mats.

She stepped onto a treadmill, and after a brief study, programmed it for the allotted fifteen minutes at a moderate incline and speed. With the music from her phone singing through her earbuds, she felt righteous.

The rise and fall of the terrain outside the windows gave her a view of a few shrubs thinking about waking up for spring, and some brave daffodils and tulips in tight buds.

Pleasant, she decided. She could do this, even enjoy this. After all, now that she'd established a routine, she missed her weekday biking. Not the same, of course, as she just took this brisk kind of walk and stayed in one place. Maybe by summer, she'd hunt up a good second-hand bike, try out the hilly roads. She could even bike into town now and again.

She had more time now than she'd had before she'd moved. The idea she'd toyed with of getting a second part-time day job just didn't work. With that she couldn't cover any day shifts at Après if necessary, or help out at the café if her ladies needed her.

Still, even with the car payments, her budget worked and allowed her to start slowly building her savings again.

Six months, she decided. She'd take six months, then let herself start planning some long-term goals again.

It surprised her how quickly and easily the fifteen minutes passed. She gave herself a mental I-worked-out pat on the back and stepped off.

She spotted Jen, fit and fabulous in a red workout tank and tights with red and black swirls, which made Morgan immediately feel unfit and non-fabulous in her old black yoga pants.

She stood talking to a man in the weight section while he did curls. It took her a minute to work her way up long, strong legs in black gym shorts, a sleeveless gray shirt already showing a line of sweat, and the ripple of muscles to focus on his face.

Her initial wonder as to why sweat looked so damn sexy on some people turned to a jolt.

Who knew Miles was built like that?

And why, dear God, why did he have to sweat in the gym when she wore old yoga pants, a stretched-out sports bra, and an ancient T-shirt?

Obviously, she couldn't go over there, so she looked around for something to do that would look like she knew what to do.

She'd decided most of the machines looked like torture devices, when Jen hailed her.

"Morgan!" Jen lifted a hand, curled fingers in a come-ahead.

Oh well, Morgan thought as she started over. Miles shifted the weight to his other hand, kept curling.

"Sorry, I had a question for Miles."

"That's okay. No problem."

"You did your fifteen?"

"Yes."

"How far did you get?"

"Far? Oh, almost a mile, I guess."

"We'll bump that up next time. Let's get started. Thanks, Miles."

He said, "Uh-huh," and kept curling.

"I use this room for PT when the gym's crowded," she began. "Or for one-on-one yoga sessions."

Small, it had one wall of mirrors, shelves holding stability balls, medicine balls, bands, mats. A rack of free weights tucked into a corner.

"So, what do you do if you're attacked?"

"Punch him in the face?"

"Throat's better."

"Really?"

"But. Some hulking asshole comes after you, what's your real first instinct?"

Morgan hiked up her shoulders. "Scream and run."

"Exactly. If you can scream and run, you scream and run. If you can't, you hide. Either of those can come first, depending on the situation. If neither's an option, fight."

Morgan balled her fist. "Punch him in the throat."

Jen pivoted, grabbed Morgan from behind. "How? You don't have room to use your fist."

"Back to screaming?"

"Make all the noise you can, but defend yourself. We'll start with a basic: SING."

"I've heard of that."

"Solar plexus." Jen poked Morgan in hers. "Instep," she continued, demonstrating. "Nose. Gonads—or groin in polite company. Come up on me from behind, grab me, and watch it the mirror. I won't hurt you."

When Morgan wrapped her arms around Jen, Jen tipped her own weight forward. "You lean your weight forward to give yourself more room. Then?" She felt the light tap of Jen's elbow, solar plexus.

"The elbow's your strongest weapon. Stronger than your fist—use it and mean it. The idea is not only to hurt your attacker, but to loosen his grip so you have more room. His instep is a weak spot, hit it." Jen brought the heel of her foot down, gently, on Morgan's. "Most likely, his grip will loosen enough with those two blows for you to turn. This."

She held up her hand, heel out, tapped the heel with the other. "Strong, stiff, fast upward blow on the nose from the nostrils up, then recoil. Then knee, hard, sharp, straight into those gonads. These? Elbow, heel of the foot, heel of the hand, knee. They're strong and hard. They'll do damage."

"So I can run and scream."

"Damn right if it's an option. Let's just start with these four steps."

It felt good, almost like a dance. It felt like action.

"Good, that's the way. You don't have to think about it, you just SING. Next week I'll have a volunteer in here wearing a padded suit. You can really let it rip."

"I'd like that. Who knew I'd like the idea of hitting somebody?"

"But let's say he's got your back to the wall." After nudging Morgan to the wall, Jen pressed close. "And he's got his hands around your neck."

Jen lifted hers, then dropped them again, stepped back. "God, I'm sorry. I wasn't thinking."

"It's all right. I know you've been alerted. This is why I'm here. Show me."

"He's got you against the wall, you can't get your knee up or get an angle with your elbow. Most people's instinct is to claw at the hands cutting off their air. Don't bother. What's his weak spot in this situation? His eyes. Go for the eyes. Fingers are good, thumbs are best. Push your thumbs into his eyeballs like you're going to shove them right through the back of his head."

"Can I say ew?"

"After you're clear. Thumbs, and his grip's going to loosen because it's going to burn like the fire of a thousand suns. If you're upright like this, bust his balls, bring that knee up hard, elbow the gut. If you can get in a punch?"

She took Morgan's hand, balled it, brought it to her own throat. "Aim there, or here." Then shifted it to her nose. "Fist or heel of your hand, fast, recoil. Let's try that."

They practiced half a dozen times.

"Good, really good." Jen gave her a light, friendly punch in the shoulder. "You catch on fast."

"I still have to think about it and, well, I know you're not going to hurt me, so there's no panic."

"It'll get to be instinct, then instinct will cut through the panic. Trust me. I've been there."

"Oh, sorry."

"Maybe we'll exchange war stories someday over one of those lavender margaritas. But now, you've got twenty minutes left. We're going to shift focus. When I asked about your fitness regimen, you admitted you don't have one. You did use to bike in good weather about ten miles a day. That's why you've got strong legs."

"I sold it when I moved, but I'm thinking about getting one toward the summer."

"Good. You like biking so you'll do it. Meanwhile." Smiling, she gave Morgan's biceps a squeeze. "We're going to work on upper body strength and tone."

Defensively, Morgan crossed her arms as Jen walked to the freeweight rack. "Are we really?"

"Most men who attack women see the woman as weak, as a victim. We've gone over some of the actions and defenses you can take against an attacker, one who's likely stronger than you, bigger than you. That doesn't mean you can't get strong, and when you're strong, those actions and defenses are more effective."

When she carried over two weights, handed them to Morgan, Jen smiled again. "Let's get you strong."

For the next twenty minutes, she didn't just learn how to curl, extend, press, but how to breathe and stand—two things she'd assumed she knew how to do already—how to stretch the muscles she'd worked until they'd burned.

"Good, very good. You broke a sweat."

"I'll say."

"Same time next week. Meanwhile, I want you in three times a week to start."

Rubbing arms that made their objection known, Morgan fought not to just deflate. "In here?"

"Out there the other two days. Fifteen minutes cardio—and bump that up so you hit a mile or over. Fifteen upper body, fifteen lower, five—to start—on core, and a ten-minute stretch. If I'm not around to show you the lower body and core work, Ken or Addy will be."

"I don't always have an hour to—"

"Three hours a week—for now. Get motivated, make time. Rest days in between." She handed Morgan a bottle of water. "Hydrate. See you day after tomorrow."

"Thanks. Sort of."

Laughing, Jen went out.

After guzzling water, Morgan faced the mirror, flexed. Said, "Ow," and rubbed her biceps. "Three times a week? Three times a week so I'm not weak."

Okay, she thought, okay, she'd try it. For a month. Just one month.

She started out, then stopped, faced the mirror again.

"I can't wear this three times a week for a month. I'll look like an idiot."

Outfitters, she decided. With her discount, how much could it sting? It would sting, she thought, but walked out to where people lifted, sweated, ran—by choice.

One month, she promised herself, and she'd consider the gear she had to buy not to look like an idiot an investment in her own strength, fitness, and self-esteem.

It stung, even with the discount, more than she'd expected.

When she reported to work that evening, she reported with sore arms, a sore ass—damn squat lifts—and leg muscles that reminded her she hadn't fast-walked a mile in a very long time.

Nick beamed at her. "Jen said you did great."

"Your sister is a monster."

"Yeah, that's what they all say. Little sore?"

"What do you think?" After a quick scan of tables and booths, she breezed into the back of the house, did her check there.

"You'll get used to it," he said when she came back out.

"I don't think so."

"So . . . we had a crowd for happy hour. Our signatures are moving."

"Good to know. Catch that guy at the end of the bar, then you can clock out. I'll get this order."

"You got it. My mom's watching the baby, and we're going to the movies. I love that girl to pieces, but it'll sure be nice to go out with my sweetheart."

He drew a draft for the guest at the bar. Set a glass of white wine beside it. "Expecting his wife, running a tab, room 305. I'm out."

"Have a good time."

She poured and drew, mopped and served, and almost forgot about the nagging soreness.

Almost.

Near midnight, Miles took a stool.

She set a glass of Cab in front of him. "Not your usual night," she commented.

"I have a usual?"

"Friday night."

He shrugged. "I've got some work. Haven't seen you in the gym before," he said before she could move away and leave him to it.

"My first time. In that gym or any."

Amber eyes studied her face as if she were a puzzle to solve. "You've seriously never gone to the gym? Ever?"

"I had other priorities besides a gym membership."

"So you streamed workouts at home?"

"No." Why did that make her feel embarrassed? "Not everybody . . . some of us . . . I biked. I biked to my day job most days."

"Okay." But he picked up his wine instead of his phone. "And?"

"I biked," she repeated. "About ten miles round-trip. And things."

"What things?"

"Like . . . normal things."

A smile came into his eyes. She hadn't seen that happen before. Into irritation snuck a wish she could keep it there.

"Jen work you out?"

"It was supposed to be a self-defense class, and it started that way. Then it's 'Take these weights. Give me five more reps.'"

"Feeling it?"

"God, yes. Now she says I have to go into that torture chamber three times a week, and I'm afraid if I don't, she'll hunt me down and make me pay."

"You'll go in, but not for fear of Jen."

"Why else?"

"You're not a quitter."

Not sure what to make of that, she moved down the bar to fill a table order. When she glanced back, his thumbs were busy texting, so she left him alone.

At last call, she set a glass of still water on the bar. "Are you in here to keep an eye on me?"

"I had work, wanted a glass of Cab."

"Lou from Security came in at closing last night, hung around until I was finished. Is that what you're doing?"

"I'm about to finish this glass of wine and this work. But since I'm here, I'll walk you out to your car when you close."

"I'm wondering when your family may decide I'm more trouble than I'm worth."

Now he set his phone down. "First, that's not how we work. And if you think you're not worth some trouble, you should work on your self-esteem."

"I thought that's what I was doing today in the gym. It hurts a little."

"You'll get over it. Last table's leaving."

"Yes, I saw."

When he walked her out, he circled her car. "Big improvement."

"I know. I'm supposed to check the back seat before I get in, then check the gas gauge, the tire pressure. This car lets you know if your tires are low. I don't know how it knows, but it does."

"Good precautions."

"Do you take them?"

"No."

That made her sigh as she checked the back seat. "I'm going into that damn gym not because I'm afraid of Jen—though I'm a little afraid of her—and not because I'm not a quitter. I'm going because I won't be weak."

"That's basically the same thing."

"Maybe. Thanks." She pressed the fob to unlock the door. "Good night."

She checked the gauges before driving away. There he stood again, she thought, watching her go.

She was getting used to it.

Chapter Thirteen

Spring moved in. Flowers popped, leaves unfurled, and with gratitude, Morgan put away her winter gear.

While her grandmother wouldn't accept rent, Morgan knew she'd never refuse flowers. Her trip to the garden center flooded her with bittersweet memories of Nina. But having her friend's voice whispering in her ear as she wandered, as she chose plants brought comfort.

She spent a happy morning and afternoon selecting, buying, hauling, designing the arrangements in pots pulled out of the garden shed, placing colorful annuals in the beds with the sprouting perennials.

When her phone alarm signaled, she put her tools away, went in to clean up and change for work. A good, productive day, she thought. Not looking for something to do but *having* something to do.

Her day only got happier when she came down and heard excited voices.

"Oh, look at those colors! And how she's set those pots together that way, at different heights. Like a showpiece."

"I tell you what, Audrey, I meant to throw that old, rickety stand away. Look at it now."

"Spray paint and new screws," Morgan said as she stepped out onto the back patio. "You like it?"

"It's wonderful." Audrey leaned over to draw in the scent of heliotrope. "What a wonderful surprise to come home to. And the flowers you planted out front, all so pretty. You must've worked all day."

"It was fun. I didn't get to all of it." She gestured to the remaining flats. "But I thought you'd both like to have some fun, and some say in where."

"Did you buy the garden center out?" Olivia wondered.

"Not nearly. They're loaded. I didn't have a chance to get the patio furniture out and cleaned up, but I can do that tomorrow."

"I'd appreciate that, Morgan. I appreciate this."

Still glowing, Audrey looked around. "I had no idea you knew how to do all this."

"Nina taught me about plants. And when you're on a tight budget, things like wire brushes, sandpaper, and paint are best friends. Anyway, I've got to get to work. See you tomorrow."

"She looked so happy," Audrey murmured.

"She did. She's coming along. She's a girl who needs to do, and she's doing."

Audrey brushed her hand over the clouds of sweet alyssum spilling out of one of the pots. "I really didn't know she could do this, not like this."

"Now you do."

For a moment, Audrey took her mother's hand in a squeeze. "I guess there was a lot about me you didn't know."

"Daughters grow up and make their own. That's how it should be."

"I don't know where I'd be if I hadn't been able to come back and make my own here."

"You were, and you have."

"I know she may not stay, but . . . I hope the time we've got here, together, closes the distance. The distance is my fault."

"Stop it."

"It is," Audrey insisted. "I should've done better. I had choices, and she didn't. And I know she wouldn't have come back here, to me, not to me, if she'd had a choice."

"Like the lads from Liverpool said, all you need is love. Maybe I'd add comfortable shoes and an adult beverage after a long day, but love matters most. She loves you, Audrey."

"She does. I'm so lucky she does. Morgan and I, we became different people apart from each other. Now we've got this time to, well, grow together like the flowers she planted. I'm going to treasure every minute of that time."

"So will I. Why don't we take a look in the shed before dinner, see what else we meant to toss away that girl can play with, since it makes her happy?"

Instead of heading home when he left the resort, Miles detoured to Jake's. His friend lived on the edge of town in a compact two-story frame house with a small, covered front porch.

Miles had helped Jake build the deck off the back—and the pitched roof over it so Jake could grill year-round.

In Jake's world, if it wasn't takeout or delivery, it went on the grill.

When he pulled up, Miles noted the duo of hanging pots spilling something colorful above the porch rail. And that meant Jake's mother had stopped by at some point.

Jake would water them, out of duty to his mother—and a healthy fear of her wrath.

As much at home there as anywhere, Miles walked up to the front door, and in.

He could see straight back to the kitchen, where Jake stood at the counter, slapping ground beef into a hamburger patty.

"Hey. Want a beer?"

"Now that you mention it."

Miles opened the fridge, which held the beer, a quart of milk, Cokes, a jug of the mango juice Jake was inexplicably fond of, and a single lonely stick of butter.

"I just got in from breaking up a dispute over dog shit in Anne Vincent's newly tilled flower bed. You know her?"

"No."

"Avoid if possible. Convinced the shit had come out of her neighbor's Pomeranian—that's Gigi—Ms. Vincent scooped up the poop and proceeded to deposit it on her neighbor's front steps. As witnessed by said neighbor's eight-year-old son. That's Charlie Potter."

"Don't know him either."

"Charlie informed his mother—that would be Kate Potter."

Miles took a seat at the counter, sipped his beer. "Still don't know them."

"The ensuing altercation, which involved shouts, hard language, some shoves, alarmed young Charlie enough to have him call the police."

"That's where you came in."

"I was heading home. It's on the way." Since Miles was there, Jake started on a second patty. "Both women were—I'm going to reach back for the old-fashioned—het up. I can't say I feared for my life, but I did fear I'd have to haul a couple of women in."

"Not to mention the kid and the dog."

"Not to mention. The one's claiming Gigi doesn't leave the yard unleashed since the *one* time last fall the dog slipped through and dug in the neighbor's chrysanthemums. And the other's going off about barking and pooping when out comes Charlie, holding the suspect.

"Grab the buns and that bag of chips."

He gestured to the sliders and the deck before carrying the plate of patties outside to the already smoking grill.

"Now, while I do consider myself well versed in bullshit—you can't rise to chief of police otherwise—I don't claim to be an expert on dog shit. But it only takes one look at the size of that dog and the size of the shit to conclude Gigi's innocence."

The patties hit the grill and sizzled.

"Did you point this out?"

"I did, in more civilized and professional language. Further investigation—Charlie assists with some insight—reveals there are several larger dogs in the neighborhood, including, Charlie states, a big golden retriever named Stu just down the way who often escapes his yard and enjoys pooping elsewhere."

Jake flipped the burgers.

"In conclusion I tell Anne Vincent I'll remove the poop if she agrees to pay for the cost of having the evidence analyzed to identify the breed of the dog it came from. Which is, of course, bullshit. Otherwise, she'll remove it and clean the step, and Kate Potter will agree not to press charges. I advise her against taking similar action anytime in the future.

"She squawks—a lot—then says she's going to shoot the next dog that comes on her property."

"Jesus Christ."

"Yeah, avoid if possible. I tell her if she does that, she'll land in one of my cells in a half a quick minute. I put my hard-ass face on for that because I felt like one, and she backed right off."

He flipped the burgers back on the plate.

Since he knew his friend, Miles had already gotten the condiments and paper plates from the cabinet under the grill.

They sat at the table Jake had built in high school woodshop, doctored their burgers, opened the chips.

"So how was your day?"

"Not as gripping as yours."

"How's Morgan doing?"

"Handling it. The day you came in to tell me about Rozwell I walked into Grand's office, and she's in there. Crying."

"Well, it's a lot."

"It's a lot. Then I decide to go into the fitness center for a workout, and I see her on one of the treadmills. Strolling. What's the point of getting on one if you're going to stroll?"

He shrugged, ate.

"Then I find out she's working with Jen—self-defense, personal training."

"Jen the Destroyer?"

Miles grinned at that, shrugged again. "I stopped into the bar that night. She was feeling it. Anyway, she bought a decent car."

"Make, model, year, color? We want to keep an eye."

When Miles told him, Jake filed it away. Watching Miles, he crunched into a chip. "Sounds like you're keeping an eye."

"Security's on it," Miles began.

"No doubt there. I meant you. Personally."

"She works for us."

"So does a good portion of Westridge. I know when you're getting a thing."

"I'm not getting a thing. And she's got enough to deal with."

"Can't argue with the last part. Want another beer?"

"No, thanks. I brought home some work, and I've got to get there and feed the dog." But he sat another moment, nursing the rest of his beer. "Things are complicated."

"Tell me about it."

The gym didn't make Morgan happy, but she stuck with it. Maybe, she admitted as she ground her way through triceps kickbacks, because Jen intimidated her. And maybe, a little, because she felt a tiny bit stronger.

And a lot, she knew, because the three hours a week provided something to do, something active and productive.

Plus, sweaty.

Now, the self-defense portion did make her happy. It made her feel stronger and smarter and more self-aware. She had to admit she'd thoroughly enjoyed busting on Richie the bellman in the padded suit.

But she did *not* enjoy the lifting, the lunging, the mean machines, or any of the tortures Jen outlined for her. Still, knowing Jen's hawk gaze could zero in on her at any moment, Morgan squatted down into what her formidable instructor called the goddess position—screw that!—and began the biceps-burning series of curls.

"I've been texting you."

Morgan didn't quite defeat the snarl as she glanced up and saw Nell. Nell with her perfect sweep of glossy hair and makeup. Nell in her non-sweat-stained spring dress and pretty pink slingbacks.

"I'm working out. My hands are busy."

"So I see. Tracie said she saw you in here." As smoothly as a catcher behind the plate, Nell squatted down. "I need a favor."

"You need a favor?" Determined to see it through, Morgan shifted the weight to her other hand and began the second half. "If I say yes, will you do the core work I've got coming after this?"

"That wouldn't do you any good. I had Loren from the Lodge and Tricia from Après working the Janson wedding tonight."

"I know this. Can thighs split open?" Morgan panted out. "I think mine are going to split open. Why does Jen want to kill me?"

"Loren dislocated his finger."

"Working out?"

"Playing basketball. Right hand, ring finger. It's not broken, but it's in a splint, and will be for a while."

"I'm sorry. That had to hurt. Maybe as much as thighs splitting open. Maybe even more. Obviously, he can't tend bar at the Janson wedding tonight. You need another of my team?"

"I need you."

"I lost count, but I know that had to be fifteen." Morgan straightened slowly. "I finished the set. I finished, and I'm still alive. Everything burns, everything."

"It's supposed to. Listen—"

"Easy for you to say. You've got arms like Linda Hamilton in *Terminator Two*."

"Thanks. Morgan—"

"Yeah, yeah." She dropped down on a bench. "Even with the wedding—that's around two hundred—Friday's one of our busiest nights."

"It won't be as busy from seven to midnight, as the Janson wedding is fully thirty-five percent of our occupancy this weekend. Nick agreed to work a double. I couldn't reach you," Nell said when Morgan swiped at sweat and stared at her. "I asked if he'd cover if you took the event, and he agreed."

"He could work the event."

"He could, but. Tricia's on weekend days at Après because she's one of the best. Loren's the most experienced bartender in the Lodge. Nick's excellent, but I don't want him covering this after working a full shift, unless I have to.

"Ariel Jenson," she went on. "She's the bride. She's Mrs. Fisk—remember Mrs. Fisk? She's Mrs. Fisk on steroids. She puts the 'zilla' in 'bridezilla.' I need this perfect. My mother's also asking for this favor."

"You pay me. You could just tell me to do it."

"But that's not what we're doing. We're asking."

Morgan picked up the gym towel on her bench, mopped her face. "Do you know when I've sweat this much before?"

"No."

"Never. Wine and beer or full bar?"

"Full bar. Two full bars, one on the northeast corner of the ball-room, one on the southwest corner. She's got two signature cocktails. Her colors are lavender and peach, so an It's Peachy—a Bellini. And a Flying High, an Aviation, because it's lavender. I've got the recipe for the Aviation."

"I know how to make an Aviation."

"Really? I'd never even heard of it. Neither had Loren or Tricia—though they made them for the tasting and passed. This is why we need you. You already know."

"Fine. Sure. What—"

"Great. Many thanks. I'll text you everything, but you'll need to be here by six for the final briefing. Ceremony's at seven, plated dinner at seven-thirty, followed by dancing—live band—eight-thirty to midnight. If they go beyond midnight, it'll cost them, but Mom thinks they will. Plan on more like one."

"All right. You really won't do my core work?"

"I gave you a nice break. Plus, Jen says you're a machine."

Morgan nearly perked up. "Really?"

"A machine that needs a little more oiling here and there, but a machine." Reaching out, Nell pinched Morgan's biceps. "It's happening. I've got to run. I'll text you."

Morgan sat on the bench another moment, flexed, pinched. Maybe a little was happening.

Now she had to face the horror of crunches and bicycles and leg lifts before she checked to make sure Nick was set, then went home to shower and reschedule the rest of her day.

Though she'd worked weddings before, she'd never worked one so elaborate or formal—or so minutely regimented.

They'd transformed the ballroom into a spring garden and one that sparkled with crystals, shimmered with candles. Even her bar held a small arrangement of peach roses in a slim silver vase.

More arrangements, huge ones, flanked the raised platform where the band would perform. Currently a white curtain separated it from the rest of the ballroom.

The bride's demand.

Still more flowers flanked the ballroom doors where she would enter.

Tables, draped in lavender cloths with peach runners, held arrangements where the flowers sparkled with fairy lights. Chairs, also draped, had nosegays tucked into their back ties.

An arbor smothered in flowers stood at the end of a white runner. To its far left a string quartet would play before the ceremony, and would continue as the bride's attendants—eight of them, plus flower girl and ring bearer—made their procession.

They'd provide selected—by the bride—music for portions of the ceremony and throughout the dinner service.

Groomsmen would begin to escort guests to their assigned tables, staff would take their drink orders—limited before the ceremony to the champagne at the table, one of the signature cocktails, or nonalcoholic choice. Bartenders would fill the orders until seven—sharp— when the groom and his best man entered by the side ballroom doors.

Any guests arriving after the seven o'clock mark would wait outside the ballroom until the bride and her father reached the arbor.

No exceptions, by order of the bride.

"The ceremony runs fifteen minutes," Drea continued. "When the bride and groom are played out, guests are free to order drinks from the table, go to the bars while staff removes the arbor, the runner. The bulk of the photos are done, and the photographer and videographer will work the ceremony, but there will be another fifteen to thirty minutes of post-ceremony photos. The bride wants dinner service to begin at seven-thirty with the salad course. Then they'll announce the wedding party, the parents of the groom, of the bride, then the happy couple. Once they're seated, dinner service continues, and the bars are again open.

"At eight-thirty, the curtain comes down, and the band begins."

She ran through the rituals and their timing—first dance, mother-son, father-daughter, cake cutting, bouquet tossing.

At six-thirty, Morgan took her station and guests began to come in.

They suited the room in their black tie and sleek gowns. She thought the oohs and aahs as they took in the ballroom well deserved.

Then she got busy mixing peach and lavender drinks and pouring sparkling water.

She didn't know whether to credit the demanding bride or Drea, but it all ran smooth when at the dot of seven the music changed. The attendants, in their lavender gowns with crowns of peach rosebuds on their heads, proceeded down the runner.

The ring bearer and flower girl earned every smile—he in his tiny tux and lavender waistcoat, she in her frothy peach dress.

Then the dramatic pause before the bride, on the arm of her father, stepped into the doorway.

Morgan barely smothered an ooh of her own.

She wore a fairy princess gown, snow-white, miles of skirt, and a snug, strapless bodice that sparkled as it caught the light. Her hair, raven black, swept up and back with a few artistically, perfectly loosened strands to curl around her face.

She, too, wore a crown of flowers, more elaborate than her attendants' and with a veil trailing like a gossamer cloud down her back.

She may have been hell to work with, Morgan thought, but the way she looked at the man waiting under the arbor, the way he looked at her, said "love."

Drea slipped in, sidled over to Morgan. She said quietly, "Whew."

"It's stunning, everything is just stunning."

"That's what she wanted. And this?" She nodded toward where the bride and groom exchanged vows. "It's the first time I've seen her relaxed and happy in weeks."

She slipped out again.

Morgan watched the kiss, watched how the groom lifted his bride's hand to his lips when they turned to face their guests.

She wondered how it felt to look like a princess.

But more, she wondered how it felt to have someone look at you the way the groom looked at the bride. As if everything he'd ever wanted, ever would want, lived right there in her eyes.

Then they swept down the runner and out, and she got busy fast.

* * *

The band knocked it out. Playing to an audience of three generations, they wove in some old standards, pushed covers of current hits,
sprinkled in plenty of classic rock. The dance floor stayed packed,
clearing only for the rituals like the cutting of the massive four-tiered
wedding cake.

By midnight, Morgan estimated about half the guests had said
their goodbyes. But the other half kept right on partying.

It didn't surprise Morgan when she got word the father of the bride
agreed to an hour's extension.

She poured, stirred, shook, and enjoyed the music and the show.

It did surprise her when Miles walked in—and didn't look out of
place among the tuxes and gowns in his casual shirt and jeans.

She credited the invisible suit.

"I'm sorry, sir, this is a private event."

He glanced behind her at the few remaining bottles of champagne
on ice in silver tubs.

"How many of those did you go through?"

"Including the table bottles, you could round it up to a hundred.
The signature Bellini and straight champagne were popular. The Avia-
tions came in a distant third, by my estimates, behind the champagne
and beer."

"Sunglasses or pilots?"

"It's a drink, Miles."

On cue, the best man—sans jacket, tie, and waistcoat—came up
to the bar.

"How's it going, Morgan?"

"It's going great, Trevor. Another round for you and Darcie?"

"You got it. Best party ever. I'll be back for the drinks. Gotta dance!"

"You know that guy?" Miles asked.

"I do now. He and the groom—that's Hank, the one out there
with the crown of flowers on his head—have been friends since grade
school."

She dumped ice into a flute and a martini glass to chill them, then got out a shaker. "Trevor and Darcie have been an item for about ten months. It's serious," she said as she added ice to the shaker.

"An Aviation," she continued, "or, as one of the two signature cocktails, a Flying High. Gin, lemon juice, maraschino liqueur, and crème de violette."

As she shook the ingredients, she grabbed a bottle of champagne out of the ice tub. She lifted off the silver stopper, dumped the ice out of the flute.

As Miles watched, she managed to pour the champagne, strain the first drink into the martini glass. She added peach nectar to the champagne and had the drinks on cocktail napkins when Trevor danced back.

"All right!" He dug in his pocket, pulled out a money clip. "Only got twenties left."

"Don't worry about it," Morgan began.

"Nah, you're worth it." He stuffed a twenty in the tip jar. "Hey, this your girl?" he asked Miles.

"No."

"Making a mistake. Best bartender in the universe of bartenders. Plus, hot. Ah, don't tell Darcie I said that last bit."

"Lips are sealed," Morgan assured him. "Fly high, Trevor."

"Bet your ass!" He took a slug of the Aviation, then carried the drinks off to the dance floor.

"It's purple. Why is it purple?"

"Violet," Morgan corrected. "And because of the crème de violette."

"I get that part, but not why. They've got, what, about another fifteen?"

"About."

"I'll be back."

At quarter after one, only staff worked the ballroom while the band finished breaking down. She helped catering secure the alcohol, started to tie up her last bag of empties.

"Catering will haul that out to the bin," Miles told her, and glanced around. "You're clear."

"It's my first event at the resort, but I can say you guys know how to run one."

"We've got another one in here tomorrow, so we'll undress the tables and chairs, but leave some."

"With Loren out, do you need coverage?"

"No. Smaller, less elaborate, second-time-around event. You're clear," he said again, then took her arm. "I'll walk you out."

"Actually, I'm going to just swing by Après first."

"It's closed."

"I know that, and Nick's great. He's thorough and he's responsible, but he's also not used to closing, especially on a weekend night. Après is my responsibility, so I'm just going to check."

With a shrug, he led her through the hallways, around to the lobby, and the archway. When he flicked on the lights, she scanned the room.

Tables, booths, chairs looked clean. Housekeeping hit the floors every morning, the windows every week.

"Satisfied?"

Ignoring him, she walked in, circled the bar.

Clean, backbar tidy, tubs and trays clean and draining, sinks wiped down.

"Why don't you look tired?" he wondered as she did her check.

"I'm a creature of the night," she said absently.

"Owl or vampire?"

"Depends on the night, and despite the event, it looks like Après had a good night."

"I can see the stock."

He came around the bar himself, got a bottle of Cabernet off the rack. "I'm having a drink." He glanced at her while he drew the cork. "Are you having a drink? You're off duty."

"I . . . Sure." She set two red wineglasses on the bar, then fixed a wine keeper on the bottle after he'd poured.

"Booth." He gestured, walked over, and sat.

When she went over to join him, sat, she let out a sigh. "I do re-member how to sit. It's been awhile."

"You're entitled to breaks during an event."

"Yeah, Tricia and I worked them out." But it felt damn good to just sit. She sipped the wine, sighed again. "Do you do this a lot? Sit in an empty bar?"

"No. You?"

"Actually, yeah. Not drinking Cab, especially this label, but an empty bar has its own personality. This one's quiet comfort with a touch of subtle elegance. It's nice."

He shouldn't ask; he didn't like small talk. But he asked anyway because he wanted to know.

"Why bartending?"

"Well, I get to hang out in bars—and stay sober. I like bars. I like people. You have to when you're in hospitality."

"I'm in hospitality. I don't especially like people."

She studied him as she drank. Those eyes, she thought, sure knew how to focus in when he wanted to. "That's crazy. You have to work with people every day."

"Point made."

"Well, I like people. Working behind a bar's a busy place, but it's usually a cheerful one. People come in because they're ready to unwind or celebrate. You've got your lonelies who just want someone to talk to. That's what you're there for. Why do you come in on Friday nights, especially Friday nights when the bar's going to be crowded, if you don't like people?"

"Come into a crowded bar for a drink and it's not likely anyone's going to try to talk to you. I can get some work done, unwind, and have a glass of wine. Come in when it's not crowded? Somebody's going to try to start a conversation. 'Some weather we're having,' 'How about those Cubs,' something."

Aha, she thought. Now she got it.

"You use your phone as a force field."

He smiled a little. "I use it for work, and yeah, it doubles as a force field. What I wonder is how you got into tending bar, and, according to—was it Trevor?—have risen to the best bartender in the universe of bartenders."

"Trevor was flying high," she reminded him.

"I've seen you work, and I know why my mother and sister wanted you on that very demanding event tonight."

"I waited tables in college. Jesus, that's hard work."

Whether it was the empty bar, the Cab, or the company, she felt absolutely relaxed.

"It can be rewarding, but the fact is there are types—and a lot of them for various and situational reasons—who'll take out anything that doesn't work for them with the meal on the server. I decided I didn't want to waitress for a living or run a restaurant."

She settled back, sipped again. "Profit margins in restaurants are wafer thin. You make the money at the bar. For strictly cynical reasons, I took a bartending class and I liked it. I liked it a lot. So when I hit twenty-one, I quit waitressing and started bartending, and I liked it even more."

Feeling easy, she closed her eyes a moment. "The idea was to save up enough, get enough experience and save enough to open my own place. Nice little neighborhood bar. I had about three years to go, by my careful calculations. And then . . ."

She shrugged, sipped a little more.

"Yours is easy to figure," she continued. "Third-generation hotelier, oldest male sibling in gen three. Ever think about doing something else?"

"Sure."

"Like what?"

"Indiana Jones. My version of Indiana Jones, the lone adventurer/anthropologist."

"Every kid who's watched those movies wanted to be Indy."

"This was last year."

She laughed, shook her head. "You'd need the hat. Nobody could pull it off without the hat. But did you want this"—she gestured to encompass the resort—"and all the work that goes with it? Because your family puts in a lot of work."

"Nothing else I thought about wanting stuck. Yeah, I wanted this. We put in a lot of work because we all want this."

"It comes across. People who work here like the work and the conditions, so they're good at it. That comes down from the top. My day job before was a family business. Smaller scale, sure, but it comes to the same. And the bar where I worked last, good management. The one where I worked my last year of college, I can't say the same. But I learned, and that's what counts."

She set down her empty glass. "I'll pour you another if you want, but I have to get home."

"No, one does it."

She took the glasses into the kitchen. In the bar, she took a last look around before she shut off the lights.

"Nick's a serious asset."

"We know it."

"His sister's also a serious asset. She's the she-devil from hell, but an asset."

"They don't call her the Destroyer for nothing. No jacket?"

"I've got one in the car if I need it." She stepped outside into the cool and fragrant. "Don't need it. Speaking of assets, your grounds crew."

They crossed to the lot, circling the island where flowers bloomed in winding rivers of reds and whites and delicate pinks.

At the car, she checked the back seat before she unlocked it.

"Thanks for the drink and the escort."

"No problem."

She got in, checked the gauges. Of course he stood and watched her drive away.

And as she drove away she thought, in a weird way, they'd just had sort of a kind of date.

She didn't know what to think about that, and decided he probably didn't think of it that way at all. But if he did consider it a weird sort of date, she found she didn't mind.

Chapter Fourteen

She slept in on Saturday, and when she finally wandered down for coffee, she saw her grandmother sitting on the patio with a glass of iced tea.

Morgan grabbed a muffin—someone had made muffins—took it and her coffee out.

"Oh, feel that air! Perfect. Not hot, not cold." Loving it, Morgan sat, bit into the muffin. "Where's Mom?"

"She ran into the shop for a couple hours. One of our artists is bringing in a new jewelry line, and she wanted to get it priced and on display. I told her to go ahead, but I was going to sit out and enjoy the fruits of my granddaughter's labors."

"You and Mom put in some time. I love those wind chimes."

"How did it go last night?"

"I've never been to such a fancy wedding. We could use every flower we planted, and every perennial you planted before, double it, and still not have as many flowers as they had in that ballroom. Honestly, it was breathtaking. All of it. All those men in black tie, and the women in evening gowns. But the bride's dress—that was the showstopper."

"As it should be."

"She looked radiant, fairy princess radiant. And after driving Drea and Nell crazy for months, also looked happy and relaxed. God, it was so romantic. Flowers, music, candlelight. You have to give her credit for knowing exactly what she wanted, and the Jamesons for making sure she got it."

"And her father, I assume, for footing the bill."

"Had to be a whopper. I made over three thousand in tips."

"I'm sorry, what?"

With a laugh, Morgan lifted her arms to the sky. "Three thousand, two hundred and sixty-six dollars in personal tips. I've worked weddings before, and you can take home a nice chunk, but never anything like this."

"Maybe I went into the wrong business."

"It's almost like getting paid for going to a party. Not quite, because those people kept us busy. Worth it. Completely worth it."

"Obviously, you did an exceptional job."

"I like to think so. Open bars can go either way. Some people tend to tip generously because free drink, other people think free drink and don't bother to tip. In this case, generosity won the night."

She nibbled more muffin. "Toward the end, Miles came in. I guess he's my car walker on Friday nights." She shifted. "You've known him a long time. Have you ever noticed he doesn't really wear suits, but he does?"

"I don't follow."

"Well, like . . . Like Superman wears his suit under his clothes—which is ridiculous—but he wears his Superman suit under his civilian clothes so nobody sees it. With Miles, it's the opposite. It's like he wears this invisible business suit over his regular clothes. Like the power thing, Gram. Superman wears it under so you don't see. Miles wears it over, but it's invisible. It's still power."

"I can't say I've noticed."

"I can't quite figure him out."

And, she admitted, since he'd first sat at the end of the bar, she'd wanted to.

"I think I have the rest of them, but I can't quite figure him. Last night, after the event, I wanted to just check Après. Nick's not used to closing, and on a Friday night."

"My responsible girl."

"I am responsible. So we go in, and I'm doing my mental checklist. He gets a bottle of wine, asks if I want a drink. I think why not, so we sit down, have a glass of wine and an actual conversation. Then when

I'm driving home, I think it sort of—weirdly—felt like a kind of date. Do you think it was?"

"It's hard to say, since I wasn't there." Obviously intrigued, Olivia angled her chair a little closer. "Were there advances?"

"No. No. Nothing like that. It was just a drink and conversation. But, like I said, an actual conversation, which isn't his usual mode. Why bartending, and from me, did you ever want anything but the family business? You know, that exploratory sort of conversation you have on a first date."

"It's been a few decades since I had a first date, but I do remember."

"There was a vibe, even though it was just casual after-work conversation."

"He's a very attractive young man."

"Sure. They're all attractive."

"And are you attracted?"

"Physically? I'm a straight woman and he's gorgeous, so of course. He can be blunt and broody, and I normally wouldn't find that attractive, but it's offset by something, I guess, kind. He doesn't just walk me to my car—something he could pass off to someone else even when he's around. He waits until I've driven away. It's just an extra minute, but it's considerate."

"He'd have been raised to be a gentleman, to respect and value the people who work for him. He'd go out with Mick sometimes, hang with Steve in the shop."

Olivia looked toward the woodshop, tucked into the trees at the back of the property.

She'd given his clothes away, changed his office, but she'd never been able to clean out his woodshop.

"I didn't know that."

"Miles always struck me as an old soul. Something in the eyes."

"He's got great eyes."

"Mm-hmm. Would you be interested if he was?"

Morgan thought yes, then qualified. "Probably not smart to go there, is it? I do work for him. Not directly, but he's one of the big bosses. I guess it was just nice to sit down and have a drink with a good-looking, interesting man. It's been awhile. A really long while."

"You should get out, meet more people your age."

"Oh, Gram, I meet people all the time. Comes with the territory. I just haven't met anybody I want to sit down and have a drink with. Right now? I'm okay with that. I'm feeling like me again, even with everything that happened, even with checking the damn tire pressure every night, I'm feeling like me again."

Gavin Rozwell, now using the name Charles P. Brighton, strolled the French Quarter. He enjoyed the nightlife, the idiot tourists, the ridiculous drunks, and the ease of walking from the luxury of his hotel suite to shops, restaurants, music venues.

A man such as himself could blend so easily in the crowds.

He'd gone back to clean-shaven and had let his hair grow considerably. He'd dyed it a strong red as, in his experience, people would notice the mane of red hair and not much else.

If anyone were to ask, he'd come to New Orleans to research his novel, to allow himself to become absorbed in the culture, the ambiance of New Orleans.

Charles P. Brighton was a pompous ass, another character Rozwell enjoyed playing.

But despite his appreciation for the Vieux Carré, and the amusement of playing a pompous ass (with a tidy trust fund), he felt—as Charles would say—considerable ennui.

The last kill—RIP Robin—had left him oddly dissatisfied.

She'd been the perfect mark. Attractive, accommodating, trusting. With the loans he'd taken out on her house, accessing her bank account, what he'd netted on her spanking-new Hyundai, he'd cleared just over seventy thousand.

It had all been so easy.

Too easy, he thought now, strolling with his takeaway rum punch. No challenge whatsoever to play a woman so eager to start a relationship. And in Robin's case, she hadn't had close friends. The sister, yes, but they hadn't lived in each other's pockets.

She'd been prime for his skills, Robin had, and turned into a disappointment.

She'd nearly bored him brainless with her delight in his attention. While he'd been happy to kill her—at last—there'd been no crescendo, no rush.

It wasn't only about the money, after all. The money provided the lifestyle he wanted and deserved. But the kill? The kill brought him to the buzz, the bang. It offered the glory he could live on for weeks, even months after.

But not Robin.

And not with Morgan Albright's ridiculous roommate.

He needed that buzz, that bang, that fucking crescendo.

He deserved it.

Two women walked by him. Young, the one on the left a bit heavy in the ass for his taste. Tiny shorts, tiny crop tops—asking for it, no question. Add drunken laughter.

He could have killed them both, so easily really. Follow them into the next bar, strike up a conversation, pay for their drinks.

Entertaining the idea, he kept an eye on them. It wouldn't take much, he mused. Lure them up to his hotel suite. Women thought they had safety in numbers. Easy to roofie them both if he had to. Or just disable Fat Ass, then play with the brunette awhile.

Since it gave him a much-needed lift to imagine it, he tossed the rum punch and slipped into a hole-in-the-wall behind them.

A crowded hole-in-the-wall where the beer ran cold and the zydeco hot. People rubbed asses, women shook their tits on a dance floor the size of a silver dollar.

Since they stood two deep at the bar, he had time to study them.

Fat Ass had the better face, and blond hair if he ignored the solid inch of black roots. But the brunette had the longer, slimmer build he preferred.

Mash them together, he thought, noting the women ordered gin fizzes, and get one winner. And wouldn't housekeeping get a shock in the morning?

He started to step up behind them. Make that three! he'd say.

Boredom didn't excuse stupidity, he reminded himself. He could kill them—oh yes, he could see exactly how he'd do it—but then he'd have to pack, leave the hotel, leave New Orleans, and with only what these sluts had in their pockets.

Not how he played the game.

He wandered out, but since he couldn't get the idea out of his mind, stopped and bought a ball cap, a New Orleans Saints T-shirt, and a pair of goofy sunglasses.

Maybe mixing up the game would pull him out of his slump.

With his hair piled under the cap, the T-shirt layered over his own, and the sunglasses in place, he walked back into the hole-in-the-wall.

Fat Ass shook it on the dance floor. The brunette giggled with a couple of college-boy types at the bar.

He'd just order a beer, see if opportunity knocked.

Before he could, it knocked loud and clear when Fat Ass headed toward the back.

Maybe to pee, maybe to puke, but either way it looked like divide and conquer time to him.

He gave it a count of ten before he followed her back.

Plenty of people crowded on the dance floor, plenty of others massed at the bar or at the tables. The music pounded against the walls.

In his mind, he practiced the slurred *Oops, wrong door* if he found anyone else in the bathroom.

The music masked his entrance. No one stood at the single, wall-hung sink. Only one pair of feet showed under the stingy two stalls.

Opportunity knocked again, and louder.

He didn't see any point in ignoring it.

He locked the door behind him.

Risky, definitely risky, but he needed that buzz, that bang.

The instant he heard the slide of the stall lock, he moved.

Her eyes popped when he pushed in the door. Big, almost beautiful brown eyes that glazed over when he smashed his fist into her face.

She barely made a sound as she slid down, and he went down with her, closed his hands over her throat.

"Look at me, Fat Ass. I want to watch the lights go out."

Too drunk, too dazed from the blow to put up much of a fight, she just batted her hands at him, gurgled while a Cajun accordion went into a long, hot riff that pulsed against the bathroom walls.

He watched her die, waited for that buzz. And when he felt no more than a faint tingle of satisfaction, he punched her again.

"Bitch." He slammed her head against the side of the stall as he pulled off the small, cross-body bag she wore.

He tucked it into the back of his waistband and left her on the floor of the stall. When he went out again, the music still pumped, people continued to dance, and the brunette cackled at something the college-boy types said.

He wanted to kill her, too, just for being there, for having the right body but the wrong hair color.

After tossing the sunglasses, he walked another block, pulled off the cap, let it land on the sidewalk where he assumed someone would grab it up.

As he walked, he imagined the screams, the chaos when the next woman stepped into that hole-in-the-wall's bathroom. That, at least, gave him a little satisfaction. And wouldn't the brunette feel guilty? Flirting with drunks at the bar while her friend got herself murdered.

More satisfaction.

He decided the effort hadn't been wasted. Trying new things never hurt. He'd killed someone in a public place, so points for him.

Obviously, he needed to pick another target. He had other choices, and selecting Boring Robin from them just hadn't done the job.

Morgan would, no question of that.

But not yet, he thought as he walked back into his hotel.

Because when her turn came around again, he had to make it very, very special.

In the blooming time of May, Morgan's budget spreadsheet looked more promising. Maybe, she thought, life in general looked more promising. A good job with good tips provided her with more free time than she'd enjoyed in the previous decade.

She put it to good use.

When she heard her ladies talk about updating the powder room, she took a look at it herself. Some measurements, a trip to the hardware store, and a few hours' work would handle it.

She had nearly all the finishing touches in place when they got home.

"Morgan, we're home! What a day," Audrey continued. "A wine-with-dinner sort of day."

Morgan stepped back from straightening out the prints she'd hung and picked up the garden tub she'd used as a makeshift toolbox.

"Do you have time to eat before you—" As she passed by the open powder room door, Audrey stopped, stared, and actually let out a little squeal. "What— How did you— Oh my God, Mom, come see this."

"See what? I need to get these damn shoes off."

Then she, too, stopped at the doorway. After a long blink, she folded her arms. "Well, well," she said.

"Okay, I know you planned to call your handy guys, pick out a new sink, update the fixtures, paint, and so on, but it's a really small job, and the sink's great."

She ran a hand over the old-fashioned white porcelain.

"The chrome legs were dated, and the fixtures. I thought painting the legs matte black, getting the new faucet in the same finish showed it off. And with the walls this fresh blush color, it's like a little girly drama, especially with the bit of bling on the new light, and this old mirror I found in the attic. You've got a lot of great stuff up there."

"I bought that mirror before Audrey was born," Olivia murmured.

"And it's great, just needed some cleaning up. And painting the frame black ties it in. A couple of new guest towels on the black bar for fresh. I stole one of your African violets for the windowsill, picked up a new shade for the light. The fringe is like bling. I got the pretty soaps and the two prints from the shop. The little rug's from the flea market, but I thought the fact it's faded some added character."

Concerned she'd gone too far, Morgan shifted the garden tub. "Anyway, if it doesn't work for you, you can still call the handy guys."

"I love it. Mom, look how these sweet flower prints pick up the pink and black. It's all adorable. Classy, just a little girly, and adorable. Where did you learn to install faucets?"

"I learned a lot at my day job in Maryland."

"It was already in there." Arms still folded, Olivia studied the walls. "Got it from your grandfather. It's not what I imagined, and I thought that sink had seen its last days."

"It's a wonderful piece."

"It is now. It's not what I imagined. It's better. Now, I want to know what you spent on all this."

"I live here, too. I use this bathroom. And I enjoyed every minute of fixing it up."

"It's a gift, Mom." Audrey put a hand on her mother's shoulder. "Someone always told me to be gracious when offered a gift."

"Bit in the butt by my own words. Thank you, Morgan. Your grandfather's toolbox is up in the woodshop. You get that, and use it."

"I will."

"Next time we get ideas about buffing something up around here, we're coming to you first. Now we need to see about making some food. And I'm with you, Audrey, on the wine."

"I'll skip the wine, but I'll take the food. I'm starving. I just need to put the tools away and change for work."

After Morgan dashed away, Audrey took one more look. "Like the garden, I had no idea she could do something like this."

"But are you surprised?"

"No, I'm not. It made her so happy," she continued as they walked to the kitchen. "Not just our reactions, but figuring it out, doing it. She needs to pay you back, Mom. You need to let her."

"I know. It grates a bit, but I know. How about chicken and rice with a nice salad?"

"Sounds good." Audrey went to the pantry for the rice. "I don't know my daughter as well as I should."

"There was a time I didn't know mine as well as I should. We fixed it. You'll fix this."

"I hope I will. Right now it's enough she's here and happy. After yoga the other day? Drea thanked me for raising such a smart, capable daughter. All I could think was I had so little to do with it."

"You're wrong about that, Audrey, and when you fix it, you'll know that."

* * *

As May rolled into June, Morgan switched from lavender to apricot with apricot coladas and apricot tea—hot or cold. With her probationary period behind her, and Après open for outdoor seating, she dug in deeper.

After formulating her ideas, she went to Nell.

She found her supervisor leaving her office.

"I guess you don't have a minute."

"I have a few of them if you can walk and talk. I need to check on the setup for an event in the Presidential."

"Cocktail party for fifty. Loren's working the bar. Marisol and Kevin serving."

"You keep up. Wine, beer, soft drinks, hot and cold hors d'oeuvres, and a selection of mini desserts." After pressing the button for the elevator, Nell signaled for Morgan to come ahead, stepped in, tapped her card on the pad to access the Club Level. "What's on your mind?"

"The seasonal hires are working out well. Opal whipped the new waitstaff into shape fast."

"She would."

"Starting there, I'd like to recommend her for a bonus. She put a lot of time and effort into training the new hires, and it's paid off. I have a detailed report to send you."

"Do that." Nell stepped off, turned left.

"I love it up here. Rustic elegance. The high ceilings and beams, the warm colors, the use of American antiques and art. And the Lounge is really welcoming. The fireplace, the flowers, the sit-and-stay-awhile furnishings."

"We think so, too." At the end of the hall, she tapped her card on the pad on a set of double doors.

"Okay, wow. I've never been in here. Pretty presidential."

The generous foyer, papered in a dreamy blue, held a rustic bench. A hunt table displayed flowers, candles, with two high-backed chairs flanking it. She saw a bedroom on the right with a bed floating under a fluffy white duvet, and pillows massed against the headboard upholstered in dull, classy gold.

The foyer opened into a living area spacious enough for a pair of sofas and a long dining table draped in white and holding several warming stations. The portable bar already nestled into the corner.

But the star of the show shined in the wall of windows and doors that opened to a terrace and the stunning view beyond.

The lake, dotted with kayaks and canoes, shined blue against the green of rising hills, the rounded peaks of the mountains.

"I've seen the photos online, but you can't capture this."

"Two bedrooms, two and a half baths. What we think of as a butler's pantry we can stock with snacks and beverages at the guest's request. Or when booked for a party, like this, a place for the catering staff to stow dishes and trays and so on."

"It's beautiful, and still doesn't feel stiff and formal."

"We battled the interior designer to get our way. We won. What else can I do for you?"

"Sorry, distracted and dazzled. I'd like to train one of the new hires as a bartender. Bailey Myerson, she's a local, working her way through grad school. She's an excellent server, and she's expressed interest in learning. With the additional seasonal seating, we could use someone who's willing to shift where and when necessary."

"Did you ask Opal?"

"I wanted to run it by you first."

"And you have a detailed report already written."

"I do."

"Send it. Tell Opal I'd like her input as we're considering it."

"All right. Last, I'd like to promote Nick to assistant manager with the appropriate raise in salary. He deserves it, Nell. It wouldn't mean extra hours. He already stands in as assistant manager when I'm not there, and is ready, every shift change, to fill me in on any issues and ordering needs, and is always willing to pinch-hit when we need him."

"In his quarterly evaluations, Don indicated Nick had an excellent work ethic, was a team player, handled his job with skill, but lacked managerial skill and abilities."

"I disagree."

"So did I, which is why we offered Nick your position. What makes you think he'd take this one?"

"Because he's already doing everything I'd want in an assistant manager, and if at any point I needed more, he'd give it. What he's lacking is the title and the pay grade."

"It would be a salaried position rather than hourly."

"And he'd make more than he is now if compensated appropriately, which I believe you'd see to. He'd make what he deserves."

"Send me your report. Butler's pantry," Nell instructed as catering staff rolled in a table holding wine, and beer already on ice. "Ask him. Since we offered him your job, we'll certainly approve of this if he wants the position. Ask him, and if he does, tell him to contact me so we can discuss."

"Thanks. I've got about fifteen minutes before I'm on if you need any help with the setup."

"It's okay," Nell told her as another table holding glassware rolled in. "I've got it. Half behind the bar, half in the butler's pantry."

Satisfied, Morgan used her phone to send the reports as she headed down to Après.

Nick greeted her with his usual grin. "There she is! We're killing it with the patio seating. Who wouldn't want to sit outside on a day like this? And our apricot colada just hit number one on the cocktail list."

"Really?"

"You're going to need to order more puree."

He filled more orders when she stepped behind the bar, checked the night's schedule and inventory.

She waited for a lull. "The Jamesons are going to offer you the assistant manager position, with a salary commensurate to the job."

"What? Wait. They already have you."

"And they have you, and value you. You're already doing the job, Nick. It's time you're compensated for it. It won't add to your hours, but it will be salaried rather than hourly. I've recommended that salary, based on your experience, your skill, and what others in the position are offered."

When she named it, she left him long enough to serve the next two guests.

"Why would they give me that much more for doing what I'm already doing?"

"For the same reason you've worked here for years. Go home, think about it, talk it over with Corrine. If you want to pursue it, contact Nell and discuss terms and details."

"You went to Nell to say all this?"

"That's part of my job, like it'll be part of yours to tell me if I'm missing something."

He walked over, kissed her cheek. "Thanks. I mean it. Whatever we decide, I mean it."

He'd take it, she thought as he clocked out. She'd met his wife—and their adorable baby—and knew Corrine was a sensible woman.

She considered that duty checked off, then watched Opal on the floor. Hopefully she'd check off the next without too much resistance.

Chapter Fifteen

When she hit another lull—Morgan credited the party in the Presidential and the dinner hour—she called over one of the more experienced servers.

"I'm taking a break."

"You never take a break."

"I'm taking one. Cover the bar, watch your own section. Ten minutes. Things are slow right now."

She went out to the floor, tapped Opal's shoulder. "I need you for a few minutes."

"Do I look like I have a few minutes?"

"Yes. Suzanne, cover Opal's section. Ten minutes."

Though she followed Morgan out, she grumbled about it. "I need to keep an eye on the new hires. The patio's full."

"Yes, but the floor and the bar aren't." She went outside, kept going until they were out of eye- and earshot. "I want to talk to you about Bailey."

Opal went immediately on the defensive, hands on hips, eyes hot under bowl-cut bangs.

"She's doing fine. If you've got a problem—"

"She's doing more than fine. I want to train her on the bar."

"I barely got her trained the right way as a server. I can't spare her. You oughta know that if you know how to manage."

"I do know how to manage, and we can discuss your problems with me another time."

And since there were problems, Morgan thought, they needed to be dealt with.

"I can come in before shift any day you like and we'll sit down on that. Meanwhile, I can use another on-call bartender, and I see Bailey as someone with the ability and the energy to cover the bar and the tables, as needed. It would give her a small pay raise and another skill set. Nell wants your input."

The hands on Opal's hips balled into fists. "You went over my head?"

"No, I went to my direct supervisor to make this recommendation. That's my job. You head up the floor, so now our boss wants your input. Bailey wants to learn. I want to give her the opportunity. If you can't spare her and she's willing, I can train her on her days off. We'll coordinate the schedule."

"Could be the girl has a life."

"If it doesn't suit her, she can say no. Ask her yourself."

Now Opal folded her arms. "She says no, then you write in her eval how she's uncooperative and lacks ambition."

"Why the hell would I do that? Jesus Christ, Opal."

"Don't you swear at me."

Screw that, Morgan thought. Just screw that.

"Don't you accuse me of undermining one of the team. If she doesn't want the training, she says thanks but no thanks, and that's the end of it. It's her choice. Put up roadblocks if that's how you feel about it, but don't point fingers at me."

"Pick a day, half hour before shift. We need to have this out."

"I do my job."

"You do. If we can't resolve this, we'll both keep doing our jobs and rubbing each other the wrong way. I can live with that. Be sure to give Nell your input on Bailey."

Morgan walked back in, took over the bar, and tried not to steam.

In about ten minutes, Bailey came up to the bar.

"Opal said since we're slow right now you might have time to work with me."

"Sure." Satisfied Opal hadn't put up those roadblocks, Morgan gestured Bailey back. "Until you're needed back on the floor, you're going to backbar. Assist," Morgan explained. "Keep the ice well full, prep garnishes, replace bottles, clear and replace glassware. Right now, the stools are empty, so it's table service. It's well bartending, and for that you need good communication skills with the servers."

"I get that."

"Back here, it's clean, sanitary, organized, and calm—even when things get rushed and you fall behind, you need calm. If you stay organized, the calm won't be so hard to find. After you use a bottle, put it back where it goes. Every time, whether it's premium or on the speed rack."

She gestured under the bar. "Unless a customer calls the brand or label or specific mixer, these are your common go-tos. The two women just coming in? They're old friends taking a few days. They're going to take stools."

When they did, Morgan moved to greet them. "How were the massages?"

"Heavenly." The one on the left—about fifty, red-framed glasses, blond hair in a messy tail—sighed. "I'm surprised either of us can sit upright."

Her companion—dark mop of curly hair, sleepy brown eyes—laughed. "But we'll manage, because we're topping things off with those delicious apricot coladas."

"Got you covered. Charge to your room?"

"Please."

Morgan nodded approval when Bailey handed her a dish of bar snacks. "We use brandy snifters for these," she told Bailey as she added ice to the blender. "Build and blend. Apricot halves in heavy syrup. Pineapple juice concentrate, coconut milk, rum, and light crème de cacao."

"You didn't measure any of it."

"I did, but by eye and count." She hit the switch.

"Love that sound," the brunette said. "Pretty quiet in here tonight."

"Midweek quiet, and a private party on the Club Level."

"And they didn't invite us," the blonde said.

"Their loss, our gain."

Morgan poured the drinks into the snifters, garnished each with a slice of pineapple. "Enjoy."

Quick on the uptake, Bailey washed the blender. "I get the by eye, but not the by count when you're pouring."

"I use a four-count. With my pours, four seconds an ounce. You should take home one of the empties, and you can borrow a jigger. Use water. Measure it first, an ounce, ounce and a half, two ounces into a glass. Use another glass to practice your free pour. By eye and count."

"Like one-Mississippi, two-Mississippi."

"That's it. You've got people skills from serving. They're not much different behind the stick, but you need to study, get familiar with different types of alcohol, different kinds of drinks, and basic lingo."

"I know some of it just from serving."

"You'll pick up the rest. If you have a question, ask."

"I have one. How did you know they'd sit at the bar?"

"They were in last night and told me they liked to sit at the bar because you can meet interesting people."

They filled table orders, with Morgan talking Bailey through the process.

A quick study, Morgan thought again, and had to stop herself from her ingrained habit of backbarring as she went.

She caught a glimpse of Liam in the archway with a woman who had about a yard of red hair and what looked like barely a yard of black dress.

And heard Bailey's mumbled, "Shit."

She glanced over. "Problem?"

"No. I—I know her, the one coming in with Liam Jameson. We went to high school together."

"Let me guess. Mean girl."

"Oh God, so much mean in that girl. At least I know I won't be working her table."

"Calm," Morgan reminded her. "They'll come to the bar first, give me an order, then move to a table. That's Liam's way."

They did just that.

"Hey, Morgan, how's it going?"

"Moving right along. It'll probably start moving faster soon. The party upstairs should be breaking up. What can we get you?"

"What'll you have, Jessica?"

"A very dry martini, Hanger One and Carpano Bianco, three olives. I prefer picholine olives."

Automatically, Morgan chilled a martini glass.

"Sounds too sophisticated for me," Liam decided. "I'll stick with the usual."

"We'll have these sent to your table. Inside or out tonight?"

Before he could speak, Jessica let out a little laugh. "Bailey? Bailey Myerson? I almost didn't recognize you with what you've done to your hair. You're bartending now?"

"Hello, Jessica. It's been awhile."

"It really has. Bailey and I went to high school together." As she looked up at Liam, Jessica slid her arm through his. "So you moved back to Westridge?"

"For the summer."

"I'm just visiting for the week. I live in New York now. We really should catch up, shouldn't we, when you're not working. We should get that table, Liam, and let them get back to work."

"Sure. See you later."

"We're going to make her a perfect martini," Morgan began, "even though we don't like her."

While she had Bailey draw Liam's draft, she demonstrated.

"I'll take the drinks out." Bailey lifted the tray. "High school's over, and I'm a big girl now."

Within the hour, things started to pick up, as predicted. Opal sent word she needed Bailey back on the floor in fifteen.

"I learned so much already. Thanks, Morgan."

"Anytime. I mean it."

Liam slid, solo, onto a stool.

"Another round?"

"No, just a Coke. I'm heading home soon."

"And your date?"

"Not a date, just a drink. By the way, Bailey, I like your hair."

"Oh." Flustered, she brushed at it. "Thanks. I've got to get back to my station."

"Take your break first. You've still got ten coming."

"She's not working the bar?" Liam asked when Bailey hurried off.

"Training. Bailey's a summer hire, in grad school. You didn't go to high school with her?"

"We went to Lincoln—different districts. One of my friends dated Jessica back then for a while, so I knew her a little. We ran into each other in town earlier today." He lifted his Coke, rolled his eyes. "Some people just don't change. I like cats, but not the two-legged ones."

Now he winced. "That was probably really sexist."

"In this case, you get a pass. How'd she like her drink?"

"She said it was fine, the way you say 'fine' when you're tolerating something substandard. Before, when Bailey brought the drinks out, she needled her. You know?" With his thumb and forefinger together, he twisted them sharply. "And Bailey just smiled and said, like, it was so interesting to come home for the summer and run into someone from high school who hadn't changed a bit. All smiles, but it wasn't a compliment."

"Good for her. Awkward for you."

"Kind of fascinating really."

"I'd say you could chalk this up to a fortunate escape."

"You don't have to tell me twice."

She kept an easy conversation with him, and another with the group mid-bar, filled orders, watched the floor.

"You know," Liam said to her when she worked her way down to him again, "I did the backbar thing one school break."

"Did you?"

"Law of the Jameson Land. You put time in, in every capacity, so you know how everything runs. Or should. I'm pretty sure I sucked at it."

"I doubt that."

"I couldn't do what you do. I'm sitting here watching you do it, and can't figure out how you do it."

She leaned toward him. "I can't ski."

"I could fix that next season."

"You will never have the chance. Weird boots stuck to a couple of skinny boards, a hill of snow? Hard pass."

"Now you've made it a challenge." He stood, laid some cash on the bar. "I love a challenge. See you later."

"Have a good night."

Right before closing, Opal marched up to the bar. "Tomorrow, half hour before shift."

"All right. Let's meet in the wine cellar. It's private."

"Fine."

Really angry, Morgan noted. But at least—hopefully—she'd soon find out why.

She arranged her day to make the morning meeting with enough time to swing into Crafty Arts for an early look at the photos for a show her ladies had booked for the weekend. Before she left, she brought in the mail and sorted it into piles.

Though she assumed she'd find a solicitation from the one addressed to her from a credit card company, she opened it and prepared to toss it into the recycling bin.

Then stood, stared as her skin ran cold, then hot.

Three thousand, two-hundred eighty-six dollars and twenty-eight cents. On a card she didn't possess for purchases she hadn't made, in two stores in New Orleans, where she'd never been.

Everything inside her began to shake. Her throat slammed shut; her lungs shut down. For a terrible moment, her vision went gray. She didn't feel herself sliding, but ended up on the kitchen floor, clutching the bill, while her ears rang.

She clawed her way up, stumbled over to the sink, leaning over it until the nausea passed enough for her to splash cold water on her face.

Still trembling, she managed to get to a counter stool and sit. Then just lowered her head to the counter until she could breathe again, could think again.

Pulling out her phone, she scrolled through her contacts, called Special Agent Beck.

"He's—he's in New Orleans. Or he was."

"Morgan."

"I—he—got another credit card in my name. Morgan Nash Albright. He used my middle name with it this time. I got the bill in the mail. Over—over three thousand dollars."

"Morgan, I need you to stay calm."

"I can't."

"Stay calm. I want you to text me the bill. Take a photo with your phone and text it to me. We're going to send someone to pick up the hard copy from you, so don't destroy it. But text me a copy. Can you do that?"

"Yes."

"Are you taking the precautions we discussed?"

"Yes."

"Good. Morgan, I know this is upsetting."

"Upsetting." She had to press a hand to her mouth to muffle a quick, hysterical laugh.

"But I want you to hear me. This is another mistake. He's telegraphed where he is, or more likely was. He's given us a way to track him."

"Do you think he's coming here?"

"He knew you'd get this bill, and he'd know when you'd get it, within a day or two of when. It wouldn't make sense for him to come there now. He wants you to be afraid, upset, confused. He needs to believe he's in the front of your mind."

She closed her eyes. "The way I am in his. That's what you're not saying."

"If you are, it's causing him to make these mistakes, take these unnecessary risks. We can come to you if you need us to."

"No, no. Find *him*."

"We're working on it. I promise you. Send me the text."

"All right. I'll send it now. I—I have to go to work soon. If someone's coming to get this bill, they need to come to my work."

"We'll arrange that. If we have any new information, we'll be in touch. That's another promise."

She sent the text, then made herself walk to her grandmother's office for a manilla envelope. She sealed the bill inside, tucked it in her bag.

Instead of going into the shop, she drove aimlessly until she felt as calm as she could manage.

As a result, she was a few minutes late for her meeting with Opal.

"My time's as valuable as yours."

"I apologize." She offered no excuses as they stood facing each other in the cool air of the wine cellar.

Opal's eyes narrowed as she studied Morgan's face. "Are you sick or something?"

"I'm fine. You have specific complaints. This is the time to communicate them."

"Oh, I'll communicate them. If your grandmother and Lydia Jameson didn't go back, you wouldn't have this job."

"You're probably right."

"No probably about it. The Jamesons tend to promote from within, but not this time. You're not the only one on the resort who can mix drinks. And you're slow at it because you're so busy flirting with every man who walks in, coming on to them, especially the Jameson men. It's disgraceful, and it reflects on all of us."

"'Flirting'? 'Coming on to'? For fuck's sake."

"Don't you swear at me."

"Oh, fuck that, too. Report me. You're standing there calling me the next thing to a slut."

"If it fits. I saw you with Liam just last night, and you're sure doing whatever you can to snuggle up to Miles. Having him walk you out to your car after closing. It wouldn't surprise me if you'd try giving Nell a roll if you thought it would get you ahead."

Morgan let out a laugh at that, couldn't help it. "I'll have to tuck that one into my back pocket if I can't work out a three-way with Miles and Liam."

Hot color spread over Opal's face. "Shame on you."

"No, shame on you and the gutter your mind lives in. I engage with the guests—and the Jamesons—as I read them. Male or female. It's part of my job. I was not flirting with Liam last night. We were having a conversation, and one that mostly centered around Bailey."

"After you sent her out there to wait on that bitch."

"I did not send her out there. She wanted to go out there and she held her own. Just like she held her own at backbarring. Something Liam saw and appreciated, so if he didn't notice her skills before, he will now."

"Is he going to start walking you out after closing now? Maybe you figure to pit one brother against the other, playing defenseless woman. 'Oh, something bad happened to me, protect me.'"

Genuinely shocked, Morgan took a step back. "Yes, something bad happened to me. A lot worse happened to my closest friend. She'd dead. He beat her half to death, then strangled her. She was twenty-six years old."

A fresh flush worked up Opal's cheeks. "I'm sorry about what happened to her, but—"

"There's no but. There's no goddamn but. If she hadn't caught a spring cold and ruined his plans, I'd probably be dead. He wants me dead. He wants to kill me."

"So you say, and—"

"So I say. So the FBI agents say. So would the woman he killed a few weeks ago say if she could, since he left the locket—my grandmother's locket—he stole from me on her dead body."

It just erupted out of her now, everything locked inside erupted, hot as hellfire.

"You think this is a game to me? Some sort of game where I use it to get the Jamesons to, what, feel sorry for me? I'm going to warn you once, and only once, whatever problems you have with me, you leave this out of it. You leave this the hell alone."

"Everybody's got hardships. It doesn't mean you get hired out of the blue, get special treatment. And it doesn't give you the right to make time with another woman's husband."

"I haven't been making time with anyone. And if you're talking about your version of flirting with Miles or Liam, they're not married."

"Nick is."

"Oh, for— Even you have to know that's just ridiculous. And now I'll ask if you're questioning the Jamesons' judgment or their right to hire staff as they see fit?"

"No, but I've got a right to my opinion."

"Which you've given. As you hold such a low opinion of me, I'll again offer to switch you to days if you'd prefer."

"No."

"All right, then we'll just have to keep rubbing each other the wrong way."

She'd dealt with worse, Morgan thought. She *was* dealing with worse.

"I won't change who I am or how I work to suit your set of standards. As your manager, I'm sorry we can't resolve this in a more productive way, but as long as we both do our jobs well, we'll just deal. As a woman, I'm going to tell you to mind your own damn business.

"Now, is there anything else?"

"I've got nothing more to say."

"Okay then. Let's get to work."

She went up to a solid early evening crowd. Part of her relaxed in the familiar as she walked behind the bar. Before she took over from Nick, she drew a couple of drafts while he finished up.

"Talked to the boss last night. Came in, had a meet with Nell. Meet your new assistant manager."

"Yes!" She slapped high fives. "That's the good news I needed to-night. You need to go home and celebrate."

"I called my mom after I signed up. She cried a little. In a mom way."

"Aw."

"Then she said how I'd be manager inside six months."

"Hey!"

Laughing, he cleared a tab. "I said how could I give her more grandbabies if I worked all the time, and she changed that tune fast. Then said to thank you for pushing me a little bit."

"She's welcome. I'll see you tomorrow."

Then she stood at the bar, looked out at the floor, looked through the glass to the patio tables. She'd get through, she told herself.

She'd get through because she had to.

* * *

And she had to tell her ladies—no choice there either. When she came down in the morning, it gave her a lift to see the two of them, both dressed for work, sitting out on the patio, surrounded by flowers as they drank their coffee.

She'd put a damper on that morning ritual, but they'd get through that, too.

After making her version of morning coffee, she went out to join them.

"You're up early," her mother commented. "Gram and I were just luxuriating, since we don't have to go in until eleven. Maybe even stretch it to noon."

"And I'm thinking we bring home pizza. Should be early enough for you to grab a slice or two if you want."

"Who says no to pizza?"

Morgan sat and took a moment, just one more moment.

A hummingbird, bright as an emerald in the sun, gorged at the feeder while a downy woodpecker drilled madly at the suet. Flowers they'd planted in the spring bloomed, spiked, spread in cheerful abandon.

Here, in this one more moment, everything held good and sweet and lovely. Gavin Rozwell wanted to spoil that, to end that.

She simply couldn't let him.

"I spoke with the federal agents yesterday."

"What happened?" Quickly, Audrey straightened in her chair.

"I want you to know they're handling it, but I got a credit card bill in the mail. Not my card, not my charges."

"That creature," Olivia began, "because I won't call him a man, is relentlessly evil."

"No argument. But Agent Beck said he'd made another mistake with this. I believe her. He charged things in New Orleans, so they know he was there on those dates."

"He wants to scare you."

"And he did, Gram, but I'm okay now. Honestly, the confrontation I had—no, it was a fight, call it what it was. The fight I had with Opal Reece at Après was almost worse. And with this, the FBI's handling it, they'll deal with the credit card company, they'll track his movements in New Orleans. Maybe, with luck, figure out a way to find where he went after. It's too much to hope that he'd stay there, but they'll have a trail. I think."

"We should plan a little trip. A few days away. Go to the beach," Audrey continued. "Sit under umbrellas and drink mai tais."

"Mom." Morgan reached out to pat her mother's hand. "The answer isn't in beaches and mai tais. And it's way too soon for me to take time off. I'm being careful. Everyone's being careful, and it's a pain in the ass. What I want? I want to be able to sit out here just like this, looking at the garden, watching the birds, and knowing Gavin Rozwell is sitting in a cell looking through bars. The day I can do that is going to be a happy day."

"That's a day we'll drink mimosas instead of coffee," Olivia stated. "Meanwhile, what's this fight with Opal? She's the head waitress in Après, right? I don't really know her."

"I offered her an air-it-out meeting, and we had it yesterday. For my part, I wasn't in the best of moods with this credit card thing, but I didn't feel I could cancel it. Anyway, doesn't matter. She resents me. Resents that I got the manager slot through connections. She's not altogether wrong on that, but I'm also qualified, and I'm doing a damn good job."

"Of course you are."

"You'd have to say that, Mom, but I am. She bitches I'm too slow behind the stick, which is bullshit, plus the revenue's actually increased. Then she accuses me of flirting with men who come to the bar—especially the Jameson men."

"That's ridiculous!" Outrage shimmered in Audrey's voice. "And so what if you did? Flirting's not illegal in this country."

"If it were, a lot of bartenders would be doing time. It's not just about mixing drinks but making a connection. Making the customer feel special. Or being invisible if that's what they want. She's worked in Après long enough to know that."

"What are you going to do about her?" Olivia wondered.

"Absolutely nothing. She wants to work while seething over her manager, that's her problem. Plus, I *know* she expects me to write her up in her evaluation. I'm actually finishing those up today. Why would I do that? She's good at her job. More than good. She doesn't have to like me."

"Smart girl. In any case, she sounds like a very unpleasant woman."

"Only to me, apparently. From what I see, the waitstaff loves her, guests relate to her. Repeaters remember her, and the Jamesons value her." Morgan shrugged. "I can deal with it."

"Smart girl," Olivia repeated. "And a Nash-tough woman."

"Nash tough means tough. I'm actually going to go in and finish up those evaluations. I might as well get them to Nell a day early, since they're all but done."

"You could bring your laptop out here, enjoy the day while you're at it."

"Now that"—Morgan shot a finger at Audrey—"is a fine idea. I'll be right back."

Audrey watched her go inside, then looked over at her mother.

"She'll be fine, baby. We're right here."

"I know she will. Or I almost know she will. But."

"If worry's protection, she's wearing impervious armor."

"God, that's the truth. And at least we're not worrying from a distance."

"Not anymore."

Chapter Sixteen

Special Agents Beck and Morrison stood in the two-stall bathroom at a bar called Bourbon Beat. Two weeks before, Jennie Glade walked in, looking for her friend, and found Kayleen Dressler dead on the floor of the first stall.

The investigation remained open, and stalled with the conclusion of a random attack.

The victim, visiting her friend from Mobile, Alabama, knew no one else in the bar, or in the city.

"Local LEOs see it as a fatal mugging. No sexual assault," Morrison continued. "The assailant, likely male, followed her in, disabled her with a blow to the face, strangled her. Secondary blow, side of the head against the side of the stall, postmortem. She carried a small handbag, with ID, some cash—undetermined amount, but under two hundred—lipstick, a Visa card."

"It's Rozwell, Quentin."

"Not his standard method or victim."

"Neither was Nina Ramos. This one leans into that method. Strike, kill, strike after death. That's frustration, that battering after he kills them. He didn't get what he needed. Their fault."

Because he felt the same, Morrison nodded. "The victim was blond, and in the preferred age range. But this is new, Tee. Crowded bar, someone could have walked in. Or certainly seen him go in or come out, giving a description."

"He likely followed them. They hit several bars. He's restless, on the prowl, thinking about Morgan Albright. The victim hits the dance floor. He watches. She heads back to the john. Her friend's standing at the bar, talking to people, doesn't notice Kayleen go toward the back."

"People are drinking, dancing, looking to get laid," Morrison continued. "Nobody notices Rozwell follow her. Nobody notices for about fifteen more minutes that she doesn't come back—or notice Rozwell walk out, leave."

Beck walked to the door. "He gives her a minute, follows her. Steps in. If someone else is in here besides his target, game over. It's just oops, laugh, back off. But nobody was, so he's in. Locks the door behind him."

"He just has to wait until she opens the stall door," Morrison continues. "Blow to the face." He mimed a jab. "Knocks her back, down, dazes her. Music's playing, and it's loud."

"Even if she cried out, who'd hear? He's thinking about Morgan when he strangles Kayleen, Quentin, but it's not Morgan, and it doesn't give him that rush. So he slams her head against the stall wall, takes her bag, and leaves her. Back to his hotel, and he's gone that night, or the next day."

"Plays for me."

"Yeah, it plays. Good hotel, a suite with a view in a good hotel. In the Quarter."

"Yeah, yeah," Morrison agreed. "That's his style."

"Let's find it. When we do, when we're sure, I'll contact Morgan."

And the hits kept coming, Morgan thought as she set down her phone. She'd barely had thirty-six hours to adjust to the gut punch of the credit card bill, and now, another woman was dead.

By Rozwell's hands.

Some poor woman who'd done nothing more than go out for a fun, foolish night with a friend. He hadn't known her and, according to Beck, hadn't researched her. He'd just picked her out of a crowd.

They'd found his hotel. Though he'd either dyed his hair or worn a red wig, they'd located his hotel. He'd checked out the afternoon after the murder—after doing a little shopping on the fake card with her name on it—and had taken a cab to the airport.

But he hadn't gone inside, not according to the security feed.

Nothing she could do, Morgan reminded herself, but what she was doing. And that meant going to work.

A Friday night wedding rehearsal dinner meant an influx of wedding party post-dinner along with the weekend guests, the drinks-at-the-resort locals.

She had to thank the timing because it would keep her too busy to obsess.

She had Bailey working the backbar again, primarily, she felt certain, because Bailey had appealed to Opal. However it worked, Morgan put her to good use.

"You can fill this table order. A Shiraz, a Chardonnay, a house champagne, and a Pinot Grigio. Double order of cheese fries, four plates."

Trusting her, Morgan hit the blender for a trio of apricot coladas.

She worked on auto, filling orders, chatting, offering tasting glasses when a guest couldn't decide on a beer or wine or whiskey.

A guy rounding forty came up to the bar, crooked a finger at her.

"What can I do for you?"

"I'm playing stump the bartender with my table. I figure you're young, can't have been doing this for long, so my chances are good."

"What's the prize?"

"They pick up my greens fee tomorrow."

"Nice. What's the drink?"

Smiling, he ticktocked a finger in the air. "No fair googling."

She held up her hands.

"The Bone."

"I must be older than I look. Do you want Wild Turkey rye or bourbon?"

"Son of a—" Then he laughed. "Rye. Make it four."

"Four manly drinks. We'll bring them out to you. Sorry about the golf."

She chilled four glasses, got out two shakers so she could make two at once.

It boosted her mood, as did the couple who ordered a bottle of champagne to celebrate their engagement.

"God, this is fun!" Breathless, Bailey refilled the garnish tray. "I know it's super busy, but it's fun. Probably because it's all so new to me."

"It's not new to me, and it's still fun." Laughter burst from a back booth. "And not just for us."

The place filled up. Hikers, bikers, golfers, honeymooners, the wedding party, and more.

Around midnight, Miles came in, took his usual seat. And pulled out his phone.

She poured him a Cab.

"You're lucky to find a seat."

"Resort's at full capacity for the weekend. Sounds like half of them are in here."

"You should've heard it an hour ago. It's starting to quiet down."

She moved away to a couple polishing off a Merlot and a vodka tonic. "Another round?"

"Just in time. And we'll have some of those spicy fries with it."

"I'm so sorry. The kitchen closes at midnight."

"Oh, come on now." The man tapped a stiff finger on the face of his watch. "It's only five after. Maybe you should've gotten to us sooner."

"I'm sorry about the delay. Let me see what I can do."

Since she knew they'd already shut the fryer down in the back of the house, she ordered from room service.

"The fries will take a few minutes, so they're on me."

"That's more like it."

"Thanks for your patience." She moved steadily down the bar.

"Inside my head," Bailey murmured, "my eyes are rolling."

"As long as it doesn't show."

Face blank, Opal came up to the bar. "Two Bellinis, apricot colada, and a Corona."

"I've got the Corona and the empties. Thanks for letting me train tonight, Opal. I'm learning so much."

"I need you back in your section tomorrow."

"I'll be there."

With the blender whirling, Morgan got out the flutes, then handed Bailey the bottle of champagne. "You make them."

"Really? My first official cocktails."

With one eye on Bailey's pour, Morgan shut off the blender, finished the colada.

"Looks perfect to me. Good work." After setting the drinks on the tray, Morgan started to glance at Opal. A movement caught her eye.

She saw him, walking toward the glass doors to the patio. His head turned away, but she caught a glimpse of the profile. The gilded hair, the build, even the way he moved.

Everything in her went weak.

"Hey, Morgan, are you—"

Then everything went fierce.

She shot around the bar, caught him just before he reached the doors and grabbed his arm. "You son of—"

Startled, he turned, and she looked up at a stranger.

"I'm sorry. I'm very sorry. I thought you were . . ."

"Glad I'm not." He offered a puzzled smile. "Bad breakup?"

"I'm very sorry," she said again.

Turning, breath backing up in her lungs, gray closing in on the sides of her vision, she rushed out.

"Patio, table three." Opal pushed the tray at Bailey. "Serve it, cover the bar."

She darted out, ended up on Miles's heels. He came up short outside the women's room, just pointed.

Opal pushed in, found Morgan sitting on the floor, back against a wall, gasping for air.

"Slow it down." She crouched, put her hands on either side of Morgan's face. "Breathe slow now."

"Can't. Can't breathe."

"Yes, you can. Slow. Nice and slow."

"Hurts. Chest hurts."

"Sure it does. Push the air out, nice and slow. Pull it in again. It's a panic attack, so we're going to calm right down. That's it. In and out. My sister used to get these after some asshole jumped her in college. Keep it coming."

"I thought—I thought he was . . ."

"Yeah, I got that. You hold on."

Straightening, she went to the door, shoved it open. "She needs some water."

When she stepped back, Morgan had drawn up her legs, had her face pressed to them. "I'm okay. I'm all right. I'm so embarrassed."

"Don't be stupid." Opal walked over at the knock on the door. Took the glass. "Give us another minute," she told Miles.

"Drink it." She knelt in front of Morgan again. "Don't gulp it."

"Thank you. He just looked so much like him until I . . ."

"You're sure it wasn't?"

"Yes."

"Good thing you stopped then." As Morgan sipped water, Opal sat back on her heels. "You were winding up to punch him."

"Oh God." She lowered her head again. "That would've capped it."

"Shows you've got some grit. More than I figured. I figured you were stringing it all out, playing the victim. So I'm sorry about that."

"We'll call it a wash." Eyes closed, she leaned her head back a moment, then jolted. "Jesus, I left the bar. Bailey—"

"Can handle it for a few minutes. I've kept my eye on her. You're training her right. Of course, you've got prime material to work with."

"I do, but I have to get back."

"Well, your color's coming back, and you stopped shaking. Try standing up, and we'll see."

When she did, Opal nodded. "All right then."

She led the way out to where Miles paced in the hall off the lobby. "Over to you," Opal said, and went back toward the arch.

"Come on. I'll drive you home."

"No, God, no. I have to get back." Before he could order otherwise, and she saw that in his eyes, she held up a hand. "I need to. For myself, Miles, I need to. If I don't, he wins another round."

After a long look, he gestured to the archway.

"I'm sorry about—"

"Save it," he told her.

He went back to his stool; she went back behind the bar.

After grabbing a bar mop, she gave Bailey's arm a squeeze. "Sorry for running out on you."

"It's okay. You're okay?"

"Yeah, all good."

"The fries came in, and I filled a table order from the speed rack."

"Great. Can you do me a favor?"

"Of course."

"Find out what the guy I nearly accosted and his party are drinking. I want to send his table a round on me before last call."

"Sure."

Using the bar mop to keep herself steady, Morgan checked on the stools. The spicy fries couple didn't have much to say to each other, she noted. Alcohol and carbs couldn't always fix a bad mood.

The two women giggling together as they drank Chardonnay made her think of the dead woman and her friend in New Orleans, and her heart hurt.

At the end of the bar, Miles worked on his phone.

"Party of five," Bailey reported. "Two Heady Toppers, a mojito, margarita rocks, and a Merlot."

"Thanks. How about you handle the beer and wine?"

She took the drinks out herself, let the cooling night air wash over her as she crossed the patio.

"On me," she said as she served, "with a mortified apology."

"Well, thanks, but no big deal. Might've been if you'd landed that punch I think I saw coming."

"My right hook's devastating." Smiling, smiling, smiling, she flexed, and cleared a couple of empties while his companions laughed.

"I bet the ex is a handsome bastard."

"You've got him beat on the handsome part. Thanks for understanding. Enjoy."

Steadier, she walked back inside.

Spicy Fries finished up, and left a single dollar on the bar as tip. Giggling girls ordered another round at last call.

Morgan had Bailey serve them, then handed her the dollar.

"Keep this as a reminder. You can do everything right, and some people will still stiff you."

"What a jerk."

"Pretty sure his wife agrees. Regardless, if he comes in tomorrow, we still do everything right."

"Because we take pride in our work even when the guest's a stingy jerk."

"Even when. And because we represent the resort."

By one, a few guests lingered, inside and out, as staff cleared tables. Giggling girls called it a night, laughing their way out as not–Gavin Rozwell stopped by the bar.

"Thanks for the drink."

"You're more than welcome."

"If you ever want to talk bad breakups, over drinks on me." He put a business card on the bar, flashed a smile. "Glad you didn't land that punch."

"Me, too."

As he left, Bailey leaned over. "He was totally hitting on you."

"You'll have this." She stuck the card in her pocket. "Miles will want a glass of ice water, still, then you can clock out. You did really good tonight, Bailey."

"I can stay, help you close."

"You already have. You emptied the trash, replaced the liners, cleaned and locked the beer taps, cleared the ice bins. Cleaned and restocked glasses. I'm getting spoiled."

"Opal said I could have a couple hours Tuesday if Nick's willing. I work days on Tuesday."

"Good idea, and he will be. You'll see the different styles and rhythms."

With the last guests heading out, and the staff calling their good nights, Morgan continued the closing process, only pausing when Miles came behind the bar.

"Sit."

"I still have to—"

"I know how to close a bar. Sit."

"You don't necessarily know how I close a bar, plus it's my job."

Ignoring her, he began wiping down bottles. "I worked the

backbar for a couple months back when. Bailey's already got a lot of this done."

"She pays attention." And, Morgan thought, so do you.

They worked in silence. Once she'd restocked the beer and wine coolers, she started to lock them.

"Don't lock the wine cooler, and go sit. Is Cab your drink, or do you want something else?"

"I didn't say I wanted a drink."

"If you wanted one, what would it be?"

She'd never thought of herself as particularly stubborn, but even if she were, she didn't think she'd reach his level.

"Maybe something lighter. Pinot grigio."

He poured a glass of red, a glass of white, then locked the wine cooler.

"Let's take these outside. You may be tired," he continued, "but you're wound up with it. So wind down."

He took both glasses, waited for her to cross over and open the door.

When she'd closed it again, he took the closest table, sat.

"Did he really look that much like Rozwell?"

Shaking her head, she gave up and sat. "No. The build, the hair, and he was dressed in that I'm-casual-but-stylish way."

"Uh-huh. Did Jen teach you to chase down a murdering bastard and punch him in the face?"

"Of course not. I just . . . reacted."

"I was sitting right there. Security's a couple taps away on your phone."

"I couldn't think, sure as hell didn't think." She sampled the wine. Cool and light, like the air. "It's not an excuse, but I don't think I'd have reacted that way except he killed another woman."

"When?"

"I don't know exactly. A couple weeks ago. I just found out. He got another credit card in my name," she continued, and told him.

"They found his hotel. He either dyed his hair or wore a red wig. He checked out the day after he killed her and took a cab to the airport.

But he never went in the terminal. He stole a car from long-term park-ing. He had five days before the owner got back and reported it, so he could be anywhere."

"He wouldn't have gotten past Security and walked into Après."

"I didn't think about Security. I didn't think at all. I panicked."

"No." Miles kept his gaze locked with her. "You didn't panic until you realized you'd grabbed the wrong guy. Up until then, you looked ready to kick some ass. Are you prone to panic attacks?"

"Not before. Not ever. Since? I've had a few, I guess, but nothing like that."

"Mad's better, if you can hold on to it. Are you going to call him? The guy you mistook. He gave you his card," Miles added when she looked blank.

"Oh. No. Definitely no. First, it's bad policy whatever the circum-stances. Second? Circumstances. Add the last guy I dated—and only a couple times at that—turned out to be a serial killer. Sort of puts you off the process."

"You're feeling better."

She tipped her head back to look up at the stars. "I guess I am."

"Then there's the asshole with the fries."

"Oh yeah. He was a winner." She lifted her glass in toast. "The sort who knows leaving a single on the bar's more insulting than leaving nothing."

"What's his story?" Miles wondered. "You'd have one."

"He likes being an asshole. It makes him feel important, especially when it's to service people or underlings. He wore a Rolex, looked like the real deal, and his room number's one of the suites on the Club Level, so he can afford to be generous. He's just not made that way. He's a ter-rible boss, impatient, demanding, and rude because he can be."

Sipping his wine, Miles watched her. "What about his wife?"

"She didn't say a word, but she shot me one quick look. It said: *You think this is bad? You should see what I put up with.* I'd say she's about done putting up with."

She shrugged. "That's my take from behind the stick."

"It slides along with mine from the end of the bar. And yet, you like people."

"The guy I nearly hit was gracious about it. The two women at the bar—sharing a room not on the Club Level—left a twenty-five percent tip. Opal left her station—which she never does—to help me through that idiotic panic attack. And you're sitting here helping me shed a difficult night when you could be home in your boxers watching late-night ESPN. So yeah, I like people."

He studied his last sip of wine before drinking. "I mostly listen to ESPN rather than watch. And for all you know I wear briefs."

"No, absolutely a boxers guy. And that," she realized, "is absolutely inappropriate. I should clear and head home."

He rose when she did. "I'm driving you home."

"What? No. I'm fine."

"Better isn't fine. We'll take your car. One of the night men will follow in mine."

"I *am* fine."

He just held out his hand. "Keys. You know the drill."

"They're in my bag. This is stupid."

"Bad policy to call the COO stupid."

"I didn't say *you* were stupid," she muttered, snagged the glasses. "Although."

He closed and locked the door behind them, then waited while she dealt with the glasses, retrieved her purse.

"Listen, Miles—"

"Keys."

"Jesus." She yanked out the fob, dropped it into his hand. "I'm liking people less at the moment."

"Probably a step in the right direction." He shut off the lights.

Both cars waited at the entrance. Feeling ridiculous, she got in the passenger seat. Miles slid behind the wheel. "You've got long legs," he commented. "I barely have to adjust it."

She snapped on her seat belt. "When you leave the resort, you head into town, then—"

"I know how to get to your place."

"Oh."

"Grandparents," he said as he pulled away from the curb. "Yours, mine. Friendly. I tagged along with my grandfather sometimes."

Of course. Gram had told her that.

"Yours helped me build a birdhouse for a school project."

He glanced over. "I aced it."

"But you don't like people."

"I liked your grandfather."

"So did I." The stiffness in her shoulders melted away. "It was a highlight whenever I got to visit. It depended on where my father was stationed, but after the split, we usually had a week in the summer, maybe a few days at Christmas, depending on where we were."

"Lots of moves."

"Lots of moves," she agreed. "The army, and then after, my mother couldn't seem to settle. I never imagined she'd settle here. Or I would."

She shifted. And because she did feel better, because she wondered, she asked, "Have you ever thought of living somewhere else?"

"I like it here."

"If it wasn't for the family business and all of that."

"I'd still like it here."

She'd been right about that, Morgan thought. She liked being right about that. "It's the roots. They're deep. I always envied deep roots."

"You've got plenty of time to plant and grow them."

He drove smoothly along empty roads, then the quiet streets of Westridge.

Just because she'd lost time—and so much more—didn't mean she didn't have time. She'd planted herself here, she thought, by need rather than choice, at least to start. But she'd planted herself, and could feel those roots begin to take hold.

She liked the quiet streets as much as she enjoyed how they moved and thrived during the day. She enjoyed the solitude of a walk in the woods as much as a lively, crowded bar.

She didn't have a house she could transform into her home, but she had a home.

When he pulled into the drive, she didn't have to remind herself to be grateful for it.

He took her fob out of the tray. "Keys."

Reaching out, grateful for the hour he'd given her, she took his hand first, held it. "Thank you."

She lost a beat, just one quick beat, looking into his eyes. Then drew her hand and the keys away.

When they stood on opposite sides of the car, she hit the lock button. "Good night, Miles."

"Lock the door behind you."

He stood, of course, watching until she walked to the door, until she unlocked it. She glanced back once, felt a tug she didn't want to feel. Then stepped in, shut and locked the door behind her.

He'd been kind when she'd needed kindness more than she wanted to admit. Given the circumstances, she reminded herself as she walked upstairs, it wouldn't just be unwise but a huge mistake to let herself feel anything but gratitude.

An attractive man, she mused, and an interesting one. An appealing one, she admitted. So wasn't it natural she felt some attraction and interest and appeal? Absolutely, as long as she left it there. Right there.

She sat on the side of the bed, trying to ignore that flutter, that telltale flutter. And wished so much she had Nina to talk her through it.

Chapter Seventeen

He had Sunday off, and Miles intended to do little to nothing with it. No pressing work, no meetings—even family—no crises, small or large, on the horizon.

A handful of household chores, sure, but he could enjoy them when he didn't need to squeeze them in.

He did his version of sleeping in, so rolled out of bed before nine, let the dog out. Then, because he'd had the foresight to install a coffee station in his closet, he enjoyed his first Sunday morning cup on the bedroom terrace.

As usual Howl patrolled the perimeter of the backyard, defending against any possible invaders. Sometimes he wondered what went on in the dog's mind, and usually decided not a whole lot.

Trooping down to the basement and his home gym, he put in a solid hour, felt righteous.

He grabbed a shower, a long one. Sunday morning indulgence. After tossing a load of laundry in, he fed the dog, scrambled some eggs, toasted a bagel. With a second cup of coffee, he sat out on the back patio and read the paper on his tablet while enjoying breakfast in the summer sunshine.

And because of the sunshine, he hung the laundry out to dry.

He put fresh sheets on the bed, hung fresh towels in the bath, dealt with the dishes, and considered his indoor tasks complete.

Because the day called for it, he puttered around the gardens. They didn't require more than the puttering, as the grounds crew from the resort would tend to them if and when he didn't have time.

Still, he knew how to tend, as part of his training had been a summer working with the grounds crew.

Howl lay on the grass in the sun and watched.

He worked in the quiet because he prized the quiet when he could get it. Just the chirp of birds—which reminded him to fill the feeders—the occasional mutter from the dog, the hum of bees doing their work.

Deliberately, as he did every full Sunday off, he'd left his phone inside on the charger. If something vital cropped up, someone would come get him. Otherwise, he was, for one day, incommunicado.

As an experiment, he dug out a tennis ball, showed it to Howl. Then tossed it. And, as always, Howl sat, watched the ball fly, land, then looked at Miles as if to say: *What? Go get it yourself.*

"What kind of dog *are* you?"

Howl's grumbles and mutters equaled a canine shrug.

Miles got the ball himself, stuck it back in the garden shed.

By two, laundry dry, folded, put away, sun tea chilling, all chores stood complete. Now the day stretched ahead, tempted him to check his phone. He wouldn't, a matter of discipline, but it tempted him.

He could sit on the front porch and read a book. He could put on his boots and go for a hike. He'd have to take the dog because it seemed wrong not to.

A hike, then the book made sense, but if he reversed it, he could swing into town, pick up something for dinner, spare himself the cooking.

Whatever he did, it had to be outside, as he considered it a crime to waste a perfect summer Sunday afternoon lazing around indoors.

Besides, despite Morgan's ESPN comment, he didn't watch much TV, sports or otherwise.

Thinking of the offhand comment made him think of her, which he'd studiously avoided doing all morning.

He really had no business thinking of her, at least not beyond the bar manager. But he found her so damn interesting. No question she excelled at her work—and as Nell had concluded during the last family meeting, they were lucky to have someone who mixed creative and organized in equal parts.

He didn't like worrying about her but couldn't seem to stop. The way she'd gone from raging fury to helpless panic when she'd grabbed that guest stayed imprinted on his mind.

He'd admired the fury; sympathized with the panic.

She'd lost everything but had dug down deep to start again.

He admired that, too. And more, respected it.

She had dreams, goals, hopes, he thought as he picked up the book he'd barely started. How many of those had Rozwell taken?

Someone wanted to kill her, and wouldn't let her forget it. Yet she got up every day. She went to work, did her job, lived her life.

Or the one she'd started to make.

The combination of vulnerable and tough just fascinated him.

He could tell himself that fascination had nothing to do with her looks, but he didn't like to lie to himself. Those looks, he thought, the way she lit up when she laughed, the way she moved behind the bar— like it was a freaking dance floor. And those eyes, simmering green and somehow always alert.

And now, Jesus, he'd stop thinking about her. Metaphorically put her with his phone on the charger and go read his book.

When he started toward the front door, Howl howled. He could come out, of course, and Miles would leave the door open so he could come and go. But since he didn't carry the leash, the dog knew damn well he couldn't go beyond the front porch.

The road was a ways off, but still.

"Deal with it," Miles said, and opened the door.

And there she stood, like he'd conjured her up just by thinking about her for only a few minutes.

She wore a red T-shirt and faded denim shorts, and those long, long legs damn near killed him. In her hands she held some sort of container, and even with her sunglasses, he could see the awe in them as she looked up.

"You have turrets," she said, and the awe spread.

"The house does."

"Two turrets," she said again, then Howl walked onto the porch. "And a dog!"

Howl muttered, grumbled, let out a high trio of whines as he wagged from head to toe.

"Turrets and a talking dog!"

Miles felt the dog dancing in place beside him. He started to tell the dog to sit, then Howl broke a primary rule.

He raced off the porch and straight at Morgan.

Rather than alarm, she showed only delight, shifting the container under one arm so she could crouch down and greet him.

He licked, he rubbed, he rolled over on his back for a belly rub, making a constant series of happy noises.

Not even for his father, Miles thought, did the dog make such an ass of himself. But then, Morgan laughed, rubbed, cooed, nuzzled.

"Oh, what a good boy. What a very good boy! Aren't you hand-some? What's your name? What's his name?"

"Howl. He—"

To illustrate why, Howl howled and made Morgan laugh.

"He's not supposed to go off the porch without a leash."

"Oh, but— Oh, the road. Good policy. Come on, Howl, we don't want you to get in trouble. Sorry, my fault."

She straightened on those damn flamingo legs, and the dog pranced—he *never* pranced—beside her on the way to the porch.

"And sorry," she continued. "I got distracted, because turrets. I was just going to leave these on the porch, then text you. I didn't mean to interrupt your day off."

"Leave what?"

"I baked you cookies." She held the container out to him.

"You . . ." If he'd been thrown off before, now he was completely floored. "Baked me cookies."

"To thank you for Friday night. I'll admit it was my mother's idea, and they're good cookies mostly because she supervised every step. But the thank-you's sincere."

He took the container, opened it, then sampled a cookie while she turned the dog into a puddle by kissing his nose.

"They are good cookies." When Howl spared him a glance, Miles shook his head. "Not yours."

"No chocolate chips for you." Morgan stroked Howl's ears. "They're not good for you. What is he?"

"A dog."

"I meant what kind of dog."

"Nobody knows. Best guess is a sheepdog got busy with a beagle."

"Well, that's a combo. I'm trying to be sorry I ended up interrupting your day off, but otherwise I wouldn't have met Howl. And . . ."

Now she glanced up, and he already knew he'd have a harder time saying no to those eyes than Howl's.

"Do you have five minutes?"

"Probably."

"If I could just . . . could I see inside the one turret? Just a peek inside one of them."

"Probably," he repeated. "Why?"

"I've never been inside a turret. I have a thing for houses, and yours is a beautiful Victorian. The turrets just punch it up another level."

"Okay."

"Oh, thanks. Five minutes, I swear, then I'm out of your hair. And you have cookies."

He gestured her in.

"Oh, it really is beautiful. Just . . . You kept the interior walls curved at the base of the turret for the sitting room or reading room or morning room. Whatever-you-want-it-to-be room. The woodwork! You have ceiling medallions. Oh, the floors—are they original?"

"Yeah."

He thought she looked at the sitting room off the foyer as if he'd just opened Aladdin's cave for her.

"Gorgeous, they're just gorgeous. And the windows! And, sorry, I'm eating up my first minute. I love houses. Old houses especially. New construction's just so, well, new. You can really feel the history in here. I mean, look at the staircase!"

She walked over, the dog trailing her adoringly, to stroke the newel post.

"You get to use it if you want a look inside the rest of the turret."

"And I really do. It's so elegant, but not formal or fussy. Feels like a home," she said as she climbed the stairs with her fingers brushing the rail. "Which it is. It's yours."

"Now it is."

As he led the way along the second floor, he thought how completely odd it was, giving her a kind of house tour while he carried a container of homemade cookies.

She let out a sound sort of between a moan and a sigh when she stepped into his office. He ordered himself not to find that sound sexual.

He failed.

"Oh yes! It's perfect. It's just perfect. The curved walls, the view out the tall windows—all that wonderful natural light just pouring in. You have your desk facing the door because who could get any work done with that view?

"Curved shelves on curved walls, and the fireplace, the carving on the surround, the metalwork. It's absolutely magical. Then you have your high-tech computer on the handsome antique desk, chocolate-brown leather chairs. Respecting the history of the house while getting today's work done."

She gave him a friendly punch on the biceps. "Kudos. Major ones."

Then she bent to rub the delirious Howl again, and sent some gray fur floating into the air. "Do you curl up and sleep on a chair while Daddy works?"

"No to the chair, and a big no to Daddy. He's a dog. I'm not."

"Aw." But she smiled. "Thanks, big-time, for indulging me."

"You don't want to see the rest of it?"

"I'm dying to. I don't see how it can be more perfect than your office setup, but I'd really love to see."

She followed him out.

"It's a big house."

"I like space."

"Me, too. My house in Maryland was pretty small, but I was going to open it up some. Then, big plans, after I had my own super-successful bar, I'd add a second story. Bedroom level, and I'd have my office downstairs. Anyway . . ."

She trailed off when she stepped into the top story of the turret.

"And more perfect. It's like a hideaway. Somewhere to stretch out on that sofa, or sit by the fire in the winter, sip some whiskey, and think long, deep thoughts. Or just stand at the window and look out at . . . everything."

She sighed again, stroking the dog, who clung to her side. "Now I can cross standing in a turret off my list of things that must be done."

"You have a list?"

"I live by lists. Lists and spreadsheets. I didn't even know this one was on the list until I saw yours. Now it goes on and gets checked off in the same day. Pretty good deal for a couple batches of cookies."

She turned away from the window where the sunlight streamed over her.

He wondered how she could look as if she belonged there.

"And now, as promised, I'll get out of your way. Though it's going to be hard to say goodbye to my new best friend."

"You want him?"

"Stop that." She flicked a finger on his arm as she walked by. "I bet you have one of those enormous attics with exposed beams just full of treasures."

"You want to see that, too?"

"A promise is a promise, but I may find myself baking cookies again—which is harder than you'd think. My grandmother's house has one. I go on attic hunts on my day off sometimes."

"For what?"

"Treasures. You can get very creative living on a strict budget. I found this terrific old lamp up there a couple weeks ago. A new shade, some rewiring, and voilà."

He thought of those long, slender fingers. "You rewired a lamp."

"Google knows all, and for me, that was easier than the cookies. Added benefit, I'm now excused from making dinner on my days off—which had its hits and misses—and encouraged to rewire lamps or refinish an old table where I find them."

"We probably have old lamps up there."

"An attic staple. I really do appreciate it, Miles."

On the main floor, she turned to smile at him again.

"I got cookies out of it."

"Those are a thanks for knowing what I needed Friday night and making sure I got it even when I didn't want it. So . . ." She started to turn to the door, turned back again. "I want to ask you a question, and want to say either answer is absolutely okay."

"You want to see the basement?"

She laughed. "No—well, yes, but that's not today's question. I'd just like to take it completely out of the resort box, so just me is asking just you, if that's all right."

"How do I know if it's all right until you ask the question?"

"Right. It's a little awkward. The thing is, I'm pretty good at reading people. Well, with one major exception, but I'm pretty good at it. The new kid in school, in the neighborhood, on the playground learns to be. Or I did. So I'm asking if I'm just completely off on this, or if I'm reading there may be a thing, potentially a thing, here."

She gestured to him, to herself.

"Out of the resort box," she repeated quickly. "I know when someone higher up the chain's putting that kind of pressure on, those kinds of moves. I quit a job in college over that. That's not this, at all. And I don't mean to add pressure or moves from my side. I wonder if I'm reading it right from your end of things. If you're interested in me, outside the resort box."

"We're in the resort box, Morgan."

"Right. Yes. Okay then. So thanks for the turret tour and the dog fix. Enjoy the cookies."

He waited until she'd opened the door, told himself to wait until she was out of it. But he didn't.

"You're not reading it wrong."

She shut the door, leaned back against it. "Thank God. Okay, now it's a two-part question. Can we agree that if the potential thing becomes a thing, my job has nothing to do with it? I love my job, Miles, and—still reading—it's clear you love yours. This isn't about that, and I realize it's trickier for you, in your position, than it is for me, in mine."

"Maybe I'd get tired of you and fire you."

"First, Nell's my direct supervisor, and second, and more to the point, you wouldn't because you're not made that way. I could get pissed off, file a sexual harassment claim."

"First, I've got a killer lawyer—he's my father—and no one would believe you anyway. Second, and more to the point, you wouldn't because you're not made that way. I can read people, too."

"No, I wouldn't. We could spell it all out, put it in writing. How we entered into this thing due to mutual attraction and interest without pressure or coercion from either side. Your father could draw it up. Howl could witness it."

"It's good you added that so I know you're bullshitting. And the thing's called sex, Morgan. If we think we're going to have it, we should be able to say it."

"If the sex doesn't work out, I still promise not to quit, or hold it against you."

"I can promise not to fire you, or hold it against you. Even though if it doesn't work out, it'll be your fault. I'm good at it."

"Now you're bullshitting, but the sad fact is, I'm way out of practice—which accounts for a lot of the awkwardness of this conversation. You should initially grade on a curve."

He didn't know what to make of her, or this, but knew the moment mattered.

"Are you used to men grading you in bed?"

"The memory dims. It's been a few years."

"Did you say 'years'?"

Her shoulders hunched; her hands slid into the pockets of her tiny shorts. "Don't rub it in."

He held up a finger, then walked to a table to set down the container of cookies. "I'm going to prolong this ridiculous conversation, which I find strangely arousing, and ask why. I understand the last year, but you said 'a few.'"

"I was busy and focused on other things."

"I keep busy and focused, and still."

"I worked two jobs." When he said nothing, she sighed, shrugged. "All right, on top of that—and I know this is going to feed your ego— there wasn't anybody who flipped the switch so I wanted to make the time to be with them. Until now. It'll be fine if this turns out to be a one-off, or short-term, or—"

"I wish you'd shut up now."

"I'd be really happy to shut up now. I should go." She opened the door. Shut it again. Then moved straight to him, into him, fixed her mouth on his.

For someone who claimed to be out of practice, she had skills.

Dimly, he heard the dog's tail thumping on the floor as Morgan wrapped around him. He couldn't claim he found it easy, but he let her take the lead. This time.

Drawing him in, sparking fire in his blood. Then easing back again.

"I have something more to say."

"Do you always talk this much?" he wondered. "I think I'd've noticed."

"I think, in this case, we could dispense with the whole ritual of dating. Like drinks, dinner, movies, live theater, salsa dancing. Whatever's your usual pattern."

"I don't have a pattern."

"If you did, we could ditch it, and I could ditch mine—the whole taking-it-slow, give-it-a-few-weeks thing I've always run on—and jump straight to the sex."

His Sunday off shot like a bullet to the top of the best-of list.

"You're not going to buy me dinner first?"

"I'll owe you," she said, and took his mouth again.

He circled her out of the foyer, into the living room because, damn it, she'd lit this fire in him, and the bedroom was too far away.

As he circled, he tugged off her shirt, tossed it aside.

"Don't judge me on the underwear." Breathless, she dragged at his shirt. "I wasn't planning on sex when I put it on this morning."

"Let's just get it out of sight then." One-handed, he flipped open the back hook of her bra, made her tremble.

"You are good at this."

"Quiet." He tumbled her onto the sofa. "I like the quiet."

She couldn't quite manage silence, not with what he did to her body with his hands, his mouth. To be touched again, to feel a man's weight on top of her, to have his mouth just take hers over. She felt those shocks of pleasure in every cell of her body.

And the feel of him under her hands, warm flesh, hard muscle, rocked her already shuddering system. His mouth was everything she'd imagined when she'd let herself imagine. Hot and masterful. Her heart thudded under that mouth as it roamed and possessed.

With a bare brush of his fingers, he shot her to peak.

It ripped through her, tearing her breath, shattering her mind, electrifying her body. Giving her no time to recover, he drove her up again, smothered her cries with his mouth while her body arched under his.

Then he was inside her, deep, holding, holding until her hips began to pump, until the world went mad.

He watched her, those tiger eyes on hers, as she wrapped her legs around him, urged him to thrust, faster and deeper.

As he watched, he saw the pleasure on her face, the shock of it in her eyes. She had more, and it cost him to give more rather than take. But he gave, and gave, while her body rose and fell with him. He gave until she cried out again, until her hand reached back to grip the arm of the couch as if to keep herself from flying.

He gave until she went limp and lax and liquid under him. Then he took his fill.

She could have drifted on the echoes of pleasure for hours, maybe days. Weeks didn't seem out of the question. She let herself focus on the drift, and the pleasure, how it felt to have his heart racing against hers. She could add in satisfaction, as his body lay as lax and limp as hers now.

Out of practice, maybe, but she'd gotten the job done.

Since they were right there, she ran her hands over the muscles of his back.

"These don't really show under your invisible suit."

He didn't stir. "I have an invisible suit?"

"You wear it every day. Well, not right now, but otherwise."

"What does it look like?"

"Charcoal gray, single-breasted, in that fine Italian wool. Crisp white cotton shirt, steel-blue silk tie, single Windsor, black cap-toe oxfords. Italian, of course."

"That's very specific."

"If I had a million dollars, I'd bet you you've got something damn close to it in your closet. It looks good on you."

"Why is it invisible?"

"You don't need anybody to see it to know you're in charge. It just is. But now, we're naked, and it's really nice."

He levered up to study her. "Maybe sex dimmed your vision and I'm still wearing it."

She just smiled. "Nope. Naked. I got you naked. It was my idea, and I want full credit."

"It was more of a concept than an idea, and I got you naked first. But then, I didn't have a lot to deal with, since you were wearing those really tiny shorts."

"I was going to sand and paint this little bench after I dropped off the cookies, so . . . Oh shit! I have to text my ladies. I said I'd be right back."

"Your ladies."

"Mom and Gram. My phone's in the car. I really meant to just put the cookies on the porch. Then there was a turret and the dog and the sex. I need my phone."

"You're naked," he reminded her. "We're pretty private here, but you might not want to go out to your car naked."

"I'll get dressed first."

"Okay." He lowered his head, pressed his lips to the side of her neck. "You could do that."

"I will." She closed her eyes, went back to drifting. "In just a minute."

"Okay," he said again, moved to her jaw.

"No. Wait. Damn it. I don't want them to worry."

When he shifted, she wiggled out from under him and started to grab up her clothes. "Is it better if I make something up—not lie, that's not it. I can just say you gave me a tour of the house if that's better."

"Better for what?"

"If you don't want them—people—to know we had sex on your couch. It's fine if you don't."

"You think too much."

"I do." She pulled on her clothes while he watched. "I can't stop. I had to fake meditate when I went to yoga with my ladies. But I bet everybody else is faking, too."

"Way too much. Get your phone, tell your ladies you'll be awhile."

"I'll be awhile?"

"You owe me dinner. We'll figure that out after I get those tiny shorts off you again. As for the rest? Why the hell would I care if people know we're involved? And more immediate, when you do get back home, you're going to look like a woman who's had sex, and odds are your ladies will clue in."

He'd said "involved," she realized. Not sex on the couch, or not only.

"Stop thinking," he advised, and reached for his boxers. "Go get your phone. I vote we take this up to the bedroom."

"I'd like to see your bedroom."

"Great. We'll do that."

"I'll get my phone. I said boxers," she reminded him. "Howl's only pretending to be asleep," she added as she dashed for the door.

Miles glanced over to where the dog curled in front of the fireplace, one eye open.

"Mind your own business."

Chapter Eighteen

His bedroom lived up to the rest of the house she'd seen, or so she judged after she actually had the opportunity to really look at it.

And really looking at it from the middle of the glorious four-poster only added to it. An elegant marble fireplace, French doors leading out to a terrace, a cozy sitting area, local art displayed on walls of rich, deep blue set a tone of relaxed indulgence.

And lying under him, she felt both relaxed and indulgent.

She imagined the lovely cedar chest at the foot of the bed held blankets and throws, and the double mahogany six-panel doors opened to his closet.

She'd still bet that imaginary million he had a suit in there very close to her vision.

She'd gotten a glimpse through the open door to the en suite and its big freestanding claw-foot tub. But only a glimpse, as he'd been dragging her clothes off as he pulled her into the bedroom.

"You're thinking again."

"Not really thinking. More admiring. This is a beautiful room. If the third-floor turret room's a hideaway, this is a sanctuary. You don't work in here."

"Not if I can help it."

"It's a lot, what you do." Absently, she toyed with his hair. "It makes my job easier."

"How's that?"

"Most guests who come into Après are happy. They've had a spa treatment, or taken a hike, had an adventure or a good meal. They're just looking to continue the happy over a drink. The service shines, and that comes down from the top. The details shine, and ditto. It spreads out to the community when guests go into town, wander around the shops. Anytime I help out at Crafty Arts I see guests come in. And they rarely leave empty-handed.

"So it's a lot, what you do." Relaxed, so relaxed she realized if she closed her eyes she'd drop straight into sleep, she gave his back a last stroke. "I've been awhile. I should go."

"You owe me dinner. I took a couple of steaks out of the freezer when you were out on your phone. I'll grill them. You can handle the rest and we'll call it even."

"The rest? What's the rest?"

"It's steak on the grill, Morgan. You do something with potatoes."

He wanted her to stay for dinner, and that was wonderful. But. "I really only know how to do two somethings with potatoes that don't come frozen in a bag, and only one thing I've done more than once. And I usually have supervision."

"You'll wing it."

"I'll wing it."

Later, she got an up-close look at the bathroom and enjoyed a sexy, steamy interlude in the biggest shower she'd ever seen outside of HGTV.

She could regret she hadn't brought so much as a tube of lipstick, but he'd seen the rest of her naked anyway.

Then she got a look at the kitchen.

"Oh, this is so smart. Open this up, because this is how people live now, and still respect the origins. It's what Gram and my mother did with the Tudor. Do you cook a lot? Because this is a very scary stove."

"Not a lot, no. Enough to get by."

"My getting by used to be a salad, takeout, or order in."

"With frozen potatoes."

"My Tater Tots are excellent. I can make pork chops. It's my one thing. And Mexican potatoes—they're spicy."

"I like spicy."

She wandered to the glass doors. "Your back gardens are fabulous. And you have herbs, so I can use fresh. It's Nina's mother's recipe, but the problem is she—and everyone in my house—doesn't understand or believe in using precise measurements."

"You don't measure behind the bar," he pointed out.

"Don't attack me with logic when I'm obsessing over potatoes. Where are they?"

He pointed to a lower cabinet, where she found wire baskets and red potatoes.

"Do you have a scrubber thing?"

"Under the sink. How long do they take?"

"About an hour once I— Crap, I'm supposed to preheat the oven. See? Supervision. Jesus, there's a lot of knobs on this thing."

Because it amused him, he let her figure it out while he chose a bottle of wine. "I have white if you'd rather."

"No, the Cab's more than fine. There! Did it. I think. I'm already feeling the flop sweat."

While she scrubbed the potatoes, Howl sat beside her, head pressed to her leg. Miles went to the door, opened it. Said, "Out."

"He's not bothering me."

"He needs to patrol."

"He does?"

"It's his idea, not mine." After he closed the door, he turned to her. "Are you going to say this meal requires a salad or a green vegetable?"

"I'm absolutely not going to say that."

"I'm starting to think you may be, almost, the perfect woman."

He set a glass of wine on the counter beside her.

"I like salads and green vegetables fine, but I'm currently obsessing about potatoes. I don't have room for more than that. I need to use that cutting board and one of those knives you have on that magnetic strip like a restaurant kitchen."

"Go right ahead."

"Then I need the herbs and spices and olive oil and a baking sheet. And scissors or shears so I can cut some of the herbs out there. He actually looks like he's patrolling."

"Because he is." He set out a baking sheet, kitchen shears, and pointed to the olive oil dispenser, then to a cabinet. "Spices."

He watched her cut the potatoes into wedges. Amused all over again at the intensity of her focus, he leaned back on the counter, sipped his wine.

He enjoyed his Sunday solitude, he really enjoyed it. But he found it surprisingly pleasant to have her in his kitchen.

She muttered something about garlic, so he pointed again.

When she went out for the herbs, Howl interrupted his routine to race to her so they had another round of mutual admiration.

She came back in, chopped things up. Pulled more things out of the spice cupboard. Dumped things on the potatoes, used a wooden spoon to stir and coat. Grabbed the pepper mill, added that— obviously forgotten, as she stirred it all up again.

"Okay, I think I've got it. Anyway, here goes."

She put the baking sheet in the oven, set the timer.

"You said an hour. That's thirty minutes."

"Because that's when I'm supposed to stir it all up again. I don't know why, and don't care. It's just what I'm supposed to do."

She grabbed her wine, said, "Whew!" And drank.

"Did you have kitchen duty in your resort training?"

"Oh yeah."

"That's why yours is so organized. I skipped kitchen training. My mother cooked. When my father was deployed, we ordered in or went out about half the time. Otherwise, dinner at seven sharp, and there would be green veg."

"Strict."

"You bet. Looking back, I realize she'd get nervous when she started dinner. I'd set the table, but she'd check that. Everything lined up just so. Military precision. After the divorce, she kept that up awhile, then she'd toss something together or we'd order in."

She lifted a shoulder, sipped more wine. "Anyway, that might be where my kitchen phobia comes from. Now she and Gram cook together, talk, laugh. Mom bakes bread."

"From flour?"

"I know, right?" With a laugh, she tossed back her hair. "She says it relaxes her, and it really seems to. So far, I've managed to escape her attempts to teach me.

"What does Howl patrol against?"

"Uncertain. The occasional squirrel gets by him, but I've yet to see a bear or deer get through the perimeter. Let's sit outside."

He took the bottle.

Howl deserted his duties to prance to the patio table and lay his head on Morgan's lap.

"It's so quiet," she murmured. "You must love it."

"I do. See much of your father?"

"Hmm? Oh, no. None. I lack the desired chromosomes. For which I'm grateful," she added, "or I'd probably be saluting or being saluted right now."

"Plenty of women go into the military."

She rolled her eyes with another laugh. "The Colonel believes, firmly, women have their place. This is not in uniform unless assigned to office work or nursing."

"Strict," Miles said again.

"Oh hell, he's a down-to-the-marrow misogynist. I didn't know there was a name for it when I was a kid, but I knew what it was. Anyway, he married again right after the divorce, which made it pretty clear that was the reason he wanted out. I'd say we're all better off this way."

Maybe through her filter, Miles thought, but he couldn't see cutting a child out of his life that way.

"Does Howl patrol while you're at work?"

"What he does when I'm not here is his business."

"But when it rains? Then there's the winters."

"He's the one who decided to live here." Then he shrugged. "He's got a dog hut in the side yard."

As if he knew the discussion centered on him, Howl grumbled.

"Is that right? All those late nights, shivering in your hut."

"It's heated." He didn't like admitting it, but both the dog and the woman stared at him. "And the mudroom has a dog door."

"All right then. That's a good deal," she said to Howl. "You take care of your pet."

"He's not a pet. He's more of a tenant."

"A tenant." Her eyes laughed over the rim of her wineglass. Those eyes of sizzling green. "What's the rent?"

"He keeps bear out of the bird feeders and deer out of the gardens."

"Fair enough. I'm going to keep all that in mind if I ever get a dog. I wanted one when I got my own place, but it didn't seem right. Two jobs, hardly ever there. Right now, Gram's not ready, not when she lost Pa and their Lab within weeks of each other."

"Same with my father. Not ready, so he spoils this one every chance he gets."

"Who could help it? Look at that face." She crooned it while she took that furry face in her hands.

"Timer!"

She dashed to the kitchen.

"I can help it," he told Howl, then got up to turn on the grill.

When she announced she liked her steak medium rare, she edged closer yet to the perfect woman.

And the potatoes she'd obsessed over hit the right accompanying note. While they ate, Howl—fed and knowing the rules—settled down several feet away.

"So we're square," Miles announced as the sun began its western dip.

"If making half a meal qualifies, I'll take it. And I'm about to feed your ego again."

"I can make room."

"I'm so relaxed. I don't think I've been this relaxed in—probably never. Thanks."

"I'll say you're welcome, though it's been pretty obviously my pleasure."

"And all I had to do was bake cookies. I'll add to that by doing the dishes before I go. It's one of my top skills."

When they'd put the kitchen to rights, he gripped her hips, boosted her up.

"Let's finish where we started," he said, and took her back to the couch.

When they'd finished where they'd started, she got dressed again.

"Do I really look like I've spent the afternoon and most of the evening having sex?"

"Yes. I did my job."

She pushed a hand through her hair. "Then the reaction when I get home is on you. You be a good boy," she told Howl while she rubbed and stroked him into delirium.

"You've got tomorrow off."

"Monday's fun day."

"Not for me, but I should work it to get home by seven. Come back."

She looked up from the dog, met those fascinating eyes. "I could stop in town, pick up a pizza."

"That'll work. Get a large. Pepperoni, and anything but mushrooms."

"All right."

Back in his boxers, he walked her to the door. "See you tomorrow." Then he backed her against the door and kissed her until her bones melted and poured out of her body.

"Good night. 'Night, Howl."

He waited in the doorway while she got in her car, waited until she'd driven away before he closed the door.

When he did, the dog let out a mourning howl.

"You're a grown woman." Morgan lectured herself as she walked from her car to the front door. "A grown, single woman. You're allowed to have sex."

Besides, they couldn't ground her.

She went in, dealt with the alarm. And seriously considered the cowardly route of going straight up to her room. There, she could shut the door and do a crazed happy dance.

Because she hadn't just had sex. She'd had lots and lots of great sex and felt, simultaneously, as if she could sleep for the next three days and scale a mountain.

Cowardly and rude, she told herself, because she heard their voices from the kitchen. She strolled back, casually, she thought, to find them sitting at the counter over tea and cake.

Audrey smiled at her, blinked, then ratcheted up the smile.

"Just in time for some of Gram's famous pound cake. Did you have dinner?"

"Yes. Sorry I was gone so long."

"You should have fun on your day off. Sit, have some tea. We're thinking of adding the pound cake to the café menu. Have a slice and see what you think. We're toying with serving it with raspberries and cream."

Since they'd brewed a pot of tea, Morgan got out a cup.

"So, you and Miles went out to dinner?"

She felt her back itch as Olivia asked it.

"No, he grilled a couple of steaks. I made those potatoes I know how to make."

"Isn't that nice?"

The itch turned into a burn as she grabbed a dessert plate.

"And yes, we had sex. Lots of sex. And I'm going back for more tomorrow."

Silence rang for a beat, then a second while she lifted the dome off the cake plate.

"Well." Olivia sipped at her tea. "Those must've been some cookies."

At Audrey's burst of laughter, Morgan could only stare.

"Oh, sit down." Audrey patted a stool. "Gram and I remember what it was like. We're not going to pry. We really want to pry."

"It's killing me," Olivia admitted.

"But we won't. I'll say I missed your first time. I did miss your first time, didn't I?"

"Yes." Morgan got a fork, sat. "College. It wasn't wonderful."

"I missed yours," Olivia said to Audrey. "But I knew when you got home from spring break."

"That uniform. I was a goner."

"You're not talking about Dad? Dad was your first?"

"First and only."

"The only's your own fault. I bet that sommelier would put the look in your eye that Morgan's got in hers."

"Mom. Wasn't Pa your first?"

"Please." Snickering, Olivia ate a forkful of cake. "Remember the era. Free love, baby." She tossed up a peace sign. "No, he wasn't my first. But he was my best."

She looked over at Morgan. "I know Miles is a good man. A bit of a workaholic, but that would suit you, as you're the same. He wouldn't have pressured you into sex, and you don't wear the look of a woman who felt pressured. All that matters."

"I guess I sort of started it. He has turrets."

"Is that a sexual euphemism? Do I have to look it up in the Urban Dictionary?"

"No, Gram." Now Morgan laughed. "Literal turrets. On the house. He caught me goggling at them. And he has this adorable dog. I asked if I could see the inside of a turret, which is just wonderful. And one thing led to another."

"Do you love him? Is that prying?" Audrey wondered.

"I raised a very old-fashioned daughter. I'm still not sure how that happened. Audrey, they're young, healthy, single adults."

"I like him," Morgan qualified. "I'm attracted to him, obviously. He's so interesting, with all these layers. And yeah, I respect his work ethic and his dedication to the family business. We'll see where it all goes, but I'm absolutely fine with where it is.

"This cake is fantastic. I remember this cake now. And yeah, I can see the raspberries and cream. Pretty presentation, plus serious yum."

"You could take some for Miles when you go over tomorrow," Audrey suggested.

"That's okay—he has cookies. And I'm picking up a pizza on the way."

"Ah." Sitting back, Olivia sighed. "Pizza and sex—those were the days. It's hard not to envy youth. And now, since I'm old, I'm going up so I can fall asleep reading my book."

"You're not old, Gram." Morgan pushed off the stool to hug her. "You're timeless. I'll take care of the dishes."

"Timeless." Olivia gave her an extra squeeze. "Even if you weren't my only grandchild, you'd be my favorite just for that. Good night, ladies."

"She is timeless," Audrey agreed. "And I only hope I have her energy in another twenty-odd years."

Maybe it was the mood, or maybe it was the moment, but Morgan turned to her mother.

"I'm going to pry."

"I can't think of a thing I have that's worth prying into."

"Why no one since the divorce?"

"Oh, I don't know, Morgan." Audrey sighed a little, flushed a little. "I mean, at first I wasn't sure what to do or where to do it. You were still young enough to need me around, but I had to work. I wasn't good at anything."

"Why do you say that? That's just not true. You could pack up a house on a moment's notice, then unpack everything in a new place in no time. You ran the house, and when he wasn't around, you did everything. I barely had chores."

"I wanted you to make friends, have the kind of happy, easy childhood I'd had. Which was stupid because it wasn't at all the same for you, ever."

"It's not about me right now. I'm asking about you, and I realize I should have asked a long time ago. You weren't happy. You pretended to be, but you weren't. Why did you stay?"

"I loved him. Oh, I loved him so much right from the first minute, and it look me a long time to get over that."

Idly, she turned her teacup around and around in its saucer.

"Maybe that was the problem. I fell so hard, so deep, so fast. I only wanted to be a good wife, a good mother, and I didn't measure up on either."

"Stop that. I mean it."

"You never lacked for anything—other than a solid place, a solid group of friends—and those mattered so much to you. You hated moving, and I kept that right up after the divorce. I was so afraid of making a mistake, admitting I'd made one, that I kept making them.

"You made your own place, your own life, so—"

"Not about me," Morgan repeated. "Not now."

"All right." After letting out a long breath, Audrey nodded. "All right. I stayed because I loved him, and because I wanted you to have a father. I wanted—and it took a long time for me to understand it—but I wanted both of us to have what my parents had, what I had because of what they had together."

"They loved each other. They loved you."

"Always. Just always. I couldn't make that happen for me, for you, and it made me feel like a failure."

"He failed," Morgan corrected. "He failed us."

"Yes. Yes, he did. I've been careful what I've said about him because I kept hoping he'd soften toward you, reach out to his only child. But he hasn't, and he won't."

"He never loved me."

Audrey's eyes welled, but she shook her head, drank more tea.

"No, I'm so sorry. He never loved either of us. Or just stopped, I've never been sure. We weren't what he wanted, or felt entitled to, I guess. I'd get so nervous when he was about to come home."

"It showed."

"Parents can be so blind to what their kids know. I was afraid of him—not physically," she said quickly. "Not that. Never, ever that. But of disappointing him, which I constantly did. He didn't really want children, but if he had one, he wanted a son. Then I disappointed him by giving him a daughter. He wanted me to get my tubes tied after you were born. I was twenty-four—barely—and wanted more children. It probably stands as the only thing I absolutely refused him. So he got a vasectomy, and that was that."

"He's cruel in his way."

"No, no, not cruel, Morgan. Just always right in his mind, and rigid with it. I wanted a child, I had a child. As long as you were clean, well-fed, well-mannered, well-educated, he'd fulfilled his duty as he saw it. He didn't want me to work outside the home, so I didn't. You and the house, wherever it might be, they were my duties. My performance rating, on his scale, never reached above adequate.

"We weren't suited," she concluded. "I should've let go, taken you, come home. But that meant failure, so I didn't. Then he let go. He met someone he wanted, who suited him. So he told me he'd filed for a divorce, laid out the terms. I shouldn't have been shocked, but I was. Shouldn't have been brokenhearted, but I was."

"You cried at night for weeks after we left."

"What we think our children don't know," Audrey murmured. "Still, I didn't come home. Gram and Pa never liked him. They gave him respect as my husband, as your father, but there was never any genuine affection there on either side. So I didn't come home, because that meant I'd failed."

And that, Morgan realized, she understood perfectly. Hadn't she done the same thing after Rozwell?

"Instead, I dragged you from place to place, telling myself we'd find just the right one and settle. But I was running from that failure."

"You didn't fail."

"It felt like failure. He married again the day after the divorce finalized."

"I didn't know that. Not that fast."

"The very next day. God, that was a slap in the face. Replaced, just that easily, after all the years of trying to be what he wanted. So I kept running, then you went off to college, and I was lost."

"Mom."

"It came home to me that I'd needed you more than you'd needed me. You're so like Gram, baby. Strong, driven, independent, and Jesus, so clever. And somewhere in there, I realized I'd done a really good job raising you, and I'd done it on my own. After a while, I came home, and it wasn't like failure. It was coming home. And somewhere in there, I stopped loving him and saw things, saw him, more clearly. He failed, just as you said. He failed as a husband, and God knows he failed as a father. And we're still okay."

"We're more than okay. I never gave you enough credit for doing so much alone. I'm giving it to you now."

"It means a lot." She squeezed Morgan's hand. "I'm so proud of you. I can regret not coming home sooner, bringing you here, to your grandparents, giving you that solid foundation, but if I had, maybe we wouldn't be here right now, like this."

"I resented the moves."

"Oh, baby, I know you did."

"But they helped make me what I am. So no regrets. I thought you were weak, Mom, but what you were and are is incredibly strong. Nash women."

Audrey leaned over, hugged hard. "For purely selfish reasons, I'm really glad you had sex with Miles."

On a rolling laugh, Morgan leaned back. "Okay. Why?"

"Because, for whatever reason, it opened this door—one I kept closed too long, and just didn't know how to open again. Now we've walked through it together. And we're just fine."

"We're more than fine. I'm glad I came home. The reasons why are horrible, but I'm glad I came home. Did you keep his name because of me?"

"I . . . I didn't want you to have a different last name than your mom."

"You should let that go, too. Hell, so should I." The idea struck so right she wondered why she'd never thought of it before.

"You know, Mom, we both have the same middle name—Gram's name."

"Pa never minded she kept her name. 'Livvy Nash,' he'd say, 'come see this.'"

"I remember. We'd all have the same name if we both went with Nash. Legally. Nash women, Mom. It can't be that complicated."

"Is that what you want?"

"Same question to you."

"Nash women. Yes. Oh, I like that. I really like that."

"Let's do it."

"If you're sure, I can call Rory Jameson tomorrow, ask how we go about it."

"Yes. Let's be who we are, Mom. Audrey and Morgan Nash."

Later, in her room, she studied herself in the mirror. She couldn't say if she looked like a woman who'd had a lot of great sex, but she looked and felt like a woman who'd found a kind of contentment she hadn't expected.

Yes, the reasons for finding it began with horror, and she wouldn't thank Gavin Rozwell for it. She wouldn't thank the Colonel either, come to that.

But she lived in a household of strong women, had work she loved, and—at least for now—had a man she liked very much who liked her back.

"Morgan Nash," she murmured, and smiled to herself. "That's who I am, and nobody can take that away."

Chapter Nineteen

She had sex before pizza, which didn't surprise her in the least. And when they finally settled down to pizza and wine, and Howl to the rawhide bone the size of a Buick she'd bought before the pizza, she told him about the conversation with her ladies.

"So you were right about them knowing, and now I know my grandmother was at least a little bit of a free-love hippie before she married my grandfather."

"I already knew that."

"How?"

He lifted his glass. "I also have a grandmother. While she wasn't really a free-love hippie, she's expressed some admiration, and it strikes like maybe a little envy, for your grandmother's youthful lifestyle."

"Really? I think, given time and opportunity, I'm going to get Gram to reveal more about that youthful lifestyle. I also had a long, overdue talk with my mom about the Colonel. I was a kid, so pretty self-absorbed, and really didn't understand how hard he was on her. Or how hard the divorce was for her. She kept us jumping from place to place after, and I resented that. I wanted roots."

She glanced around at his yard, back at his house. "Like you have here. What I didn't understand is that she wasn't flighty or weak. She was coping. She loved him. It's hard for me to see why, but she loved him."

"Love's a strange and inexplicable thing."

"Apparently." She bit into another slice. "Ever been there?"

"No."

"Me neither. Attraction, serious like, but not that last tumble. He didn't feel it for us, and it felt good to really acknowledge that, between the two of us. My mother talked to your father today."

"Okay."

"About the legalities of dropping Albright and being—legally—the Nash women. My grandmother's name, both our middle names. Mom kept Albright because of me, I kept it because it was just always there. It doesn't have to be. The process isn't really complicated, but it's a lot of steps, starting with the county probate thing. Your dad's going to take care of it—lots of documents to change."

"Driver's license, social security, passport."

"Yeah, like that. We'll end up with spanking-new identification. It's not really new identities, though, just having a name that matches who we are. All three of us."

"Your mother's birth name would be Kennedy, right?"

"Yeah, but going with Nash all around feels right. It feels good, the whole thing. So another side benefit to us having all that sex."

"I'm planning on more, so we can see what else comes out of it."

She smiled at him over her wine. "So, can I ask how your workday went, or do you like leaving that back at the resort?"

"Work never stays just at the resort. That's running a family business."

"I get that, entirely. My ladies are always talking a new piece, a new idea. Just last night, when I got home, they were having pound cake because they'd decided to add it to the café menu. So, workday?"

"Monday morning meeting with department heads, a request from the head butler to update their kitchen and storage areas. Accounting reports, and I was spared from that for a too-brief period when Jake came by."

"Jake?"

"Jake Dooley."

"Chief Dooley?" Her throat wanted to close. "Is there—"

"No. We're friends, good friends. We went to middle and high school together. He's . . . Well, he's family."

"I met him at the café opening. I didn't realize you were friends."

"Not quite womb to tomb. More puberty and beyond. He wants to do a team-building deal with his force on the ropes course. He's working it out with Liam."

Just normal things, Morgan realized. How wonderful to talk of normal things.

"Have you tried it yet?"

"It's the Jameson way. You offer something to guests, you try it out. We excused my grandparents."

"How'd you do?"

"I did fine. Liam's like damn Spider-Man, but I did fine. You should try it."

"Maybe I will—in my next life. But I could probably do it. I'm getting beefed up."

"Uh-huh."

"I am! Comparatively."

"Wanna arm-wrestle?"

"No. But we can body-wrestle after pizza."

He took another slice. "Damn close to the perfect woman."

When she got home, slid into bed, she felt damn close to perfect.

In the middle of the workweek, he came into the bar one evening with his brother and sister. Another third-generation meeting, she decided when they grabbed a table in the back.

She filled their table order when their server came to the bar.

Three Après burgers, double order of cheese fries to share. Liam's favored draft, white wine for Nell, and the Cabernet for Miles. A bottle of still water for the table.

While she worked, she observed.

They talked. Some laughs, some headshaking or rolled eyes. Mild arguing—no, more debating, she decided. Pauses to speak to their server.

They stayed nearly ninety minutes, and stopped by the bar on the way out.

"Nice midweek crowd," Nell observed.

"We'd have more outside if we didn't have the summer shower."

"Speaking of outside, I need to talk to you—tomorrow's fine—about a last-minute booking for the patio. Surprise birthday party, twenty-six guests. They just decided they want to book the patio, next Thursday night, between seven and eleven."

"We'll make it work."

"We'll talk details tomorrow."

"I'll be here."

"Haven't seen you on the new ropes course," Liam commented.

"I'll get there in, oh, fifteen, twenty years."

"You've got to try it. I'll—ha!—show you the ropes. Have a good one."

"You, too."

When Miles walked out with them without comment, she simply raised her eyebrows and kept working.

He came back two minutes later.

"Another Cab?"

"No. I have the monthly family meeting on Sunday."

"Okay."

"So why don't you come home with me Friday night?"

She mopped the bar. "It happens my schedule's open."

"Good. I have something I have to handle now, so I'll see you then."

"Enjoy your evening," she said, very pleasant and professional.

And smiled to herself while she filled another order.

She helped with the yard work on Saturday—and proved she knew how to handle a garden. He liked the company more than he'd expected to.

When he had to go in to deal with some work-related calls and emails, she stayed outside with the dog.

He came out to find an old garden tub on the table holding flowers, and watched Morgan wing the tennis ball across the yard.

To his shock, Howl not only raced gleefully after it, but raced gleefully back to her with the ball clamped in his teeth.

"What the fuck!"

She spun around, the ball back in her hand. "Sorry. I saw the ball when I got the tub, and thought it was for Howl to chase."

"He ran after it."

"Well, yeah. He's a dog."

"He never does that. Give it."

She dropped the drool-laced ball in his hand. Miles tossed it; Howl sat and stared up at him.

"Oh," Morgan said, and the throat-clearing didn't disguise the laugh. "I see."

"Do you? Do you really?" On that, Miles walked across the yard, fetched the ball himself. He brought it back while she stood in her little black shorts and skinny white tank stroking Howl between the ears. He handed the ball to Morgan. "Throw it again."

When she threw it, Howl ran after it, tail wagging, eyes gleaming. He pranced back to drop it in her outstretched hand.

"What a good boy!"

"My ass. That's just insulting. Who feeds you?"

Howl leaned lovingly against Morgan's legs, and Miles knew he didn't imagine the smirk.

"Maybe he thinks your heart's not in it. Want to try again?"

"No."

She tossed the ball herself. "I thought since you have that family thing tomorrow, flowers would be nice. I can put them in a vase for you before I change for work."

"Sure, fine."

After praising Howl—and didn't the dog just lap that up—she put the ball back in the shed. As they went inside, Miles started to close the door on the dog, but Howl looked so, well, smitten with Morgan he didn't have the heart.

"Got a vase?" she asked while she washed her hands.

"Bottom of the dining room buffet. Take your pick. Want a beer?"

"No, thanks. Never got a real taste for them."

"Coke?"

"That'll work." She crouched down, opened one of the doors on the lower buffet. "Wow. Quite a collection."

"Grand took what she wanted when they moved. They're mostly her collection."

"This is beautiful." She held up a vase of smooth wood. "Is it from Crafty Arts?"

"Yeah. A guy I know makes them. He had a show there last fall."

"It's perfect." She brought it out, started on the flowers. "You must know a lot of people. The advantage of living in the same place, going to the same schools."

"Not everybody stays."

"No, of course not. But a lot do, don't they? Most of my staff grew up here, or have lived here for years. Not necessarily in Westridge, but the general area."

"Plenty of job opportunities." He handed her a glass. "Good schools, low crime, a solid arts community. It's scenic, offers an abundance of outdoor activities and interest, and it's close to the national forest."

"I don't suppose the chamber of commerce could do anything about the length of winter."

"You learn to embrace it." Because he liked watching her, he leaned back on the counter with his beer. "Skiing, snowshoeing, ice-skating on the lake, pickup hockey games, ice fishing."

"I don't get why anyone wants a fish enough to drill a hole in the ice and sit in a shanty."

"It's not for everybody."

She glanced over. "You?"

"Not in this lifetime. It's freaking cold." When she laughed, he shrugged. "But plenty go for it. It's not just the fish, it's the beer, the camaraderie. Liam likes it, but mostly he and our grandfather just like to sit there and hang out. Then he'll go around to the shanties, bullshit awhile, go back, and tell Pop the news."

"Liam's got the social skills of a cruise director. But then, he sort of is."

She stepped back, studied the results of her work, adjusted a couple of flowers.

"I could say the same about you."

"Me? Not really. His is natural, innate. I had to work at mine. You can't be shy waiting tables or tending bar—at least not if you want to pull tips. So that helped me push through."

"'Shy' isn't a word I'd use to describe you."

"Not now." She centered the vase on the island. "You didn't know me when. I didn't have a real date until college."

"Were all the teenage boys blind and deaf?"

That not only earned him a smile, but she stepped over, kissed him. "I was the skinny new girl who didn't have much to say for herself. The one who sat in class—fully prepared, because them's the rules—but prayed the teacher wouldn't call on her.

"Now, college, I knew I'd be there for four years, so I could reinvent myself a little. And I practiced."

"You practiced?"

"Sure. Today, I'm going to speak to three people, and I'm going to pay attention to what they say. Today, I'm going into that coffee shop, and I'm not going to sit alone hunched over the table, because I'm going to get a job. After a while I didn't have to think about it every time, or talk myself into it."

She patted his chest. "You've always been confident. Some of us pretend to be until we learn to be."

"Looks like you learned."

"I did." She walked back, adjusted one more flower in the vase. "I expect Liam was always surrounded by friends, or those who wished they were. Nell, popular girl, but not one of the mean clique. She had the looks, the style, the brains, and that sense of fair play. You? More the loner with a small, tight group of real friends. Like the police chief. None of you had to battle shyness because you always, always knew who you were. I had to figure out who I wanted to be, and, well, be."

"And did you?"

"I did." She leaned into him, comfortable, easy, with the flowers she'd arranged behind her. "He thought he stole that from me. Rozwell. That's his purpose, to take who you are, erase it. For a while I thought he'd succeeded. But he didn't. Whatever he took, I'm still me."

He stroked a hand down her back. "It seems to me that who you are isn't someone you had to figure out, just someone you had to dig out. She was always there."

"That's a nice way to think about it. And this." She lifted her face, kissed him again. "This has been really nice. Now I have to go up and get ready for work. I don't want to be late. The boss could fire me."

The dog followed her upstairs. Miles nearly did himself, before he told himself to stop being ridiculous. When she came back a half hour later, hair styled, makeup perfect, uniform crisp, he sat at the counter working.

"Have to go. Have a good meeting tomorrow. And you." She bent to the dog. "Be a good boy and play fetch with Miles."

"Miles will no longer participate in that activity."

"Hard-ass." But she kissed him yet again.

He walked her to the door battling the urge to ask her to come back, to just come back again after she'd closed. And told himself it was too much and too fast.

He watched her walk to her car with the dog whimpering beside him. Maybe he regretted not asking her, but they both needed their own space, their own time.

When he closed the door, he found himself annoyed by the silence, and annoyed he felt annoyed by it.

He liked the quiet.

He went back, grabbed what was left of his beer, his laptop, took them both outside. And went back to work.

The meal portion of the family meeting would consist of chops on the grill, basted in his grandfather's special sauce, his grandmother's potato salad, grilled vegetables, and his mother's strawberry shortcake.

But business came before food, and for this, they gathered around the dining room table with glasses of sun tea or lemonade.

Events—summer weddings, engagement parties, family reunions, a few new fall packages under consideration.

Nell discussed Nick's promotion, some changes to menus, and the success of—and the glitches in—Picnic by the Lake.

"The feedback from guests has been very positive," she continued. "Enough I'd like to continue into the fall, as weather permits. Vermont foliage is always a draw, especially if we add a campfire, offer guests the makings for s'mores. From the accounting, you can see what we lose at the restaurants and room service, we more than make up with the picnic bookings."

"Some lap robes, like we offer to patio guests," Mick suggested. "Late summer, early fall evenings can get chilly, especially on old bones."

"We'd need to order more. I think it's worth it."

He glanced at his wife, then at Miles. "Miles?"

"The feedback is positive, and so's the revenue. I'm good with it."

"Then it's over to you," Nell said to Liam.

He wound his way through his report. "And the Westridge police force's team building, Thursday. I'm going to work that myself, and get some shots for the website. I think we should try to market the same deal to the volunteer fire department, with the same discount."

"I like that." His mother sipped some sun tea. "With some marketing we might draw in other police and fire departments. But let's get the photographer, Liam. You're going to be busy with the group."

"The website needs updating. I've been working on it," Miles said. "We can add this in. I'll contact Tory." He made a note. "Make sure she has Thursday free to take the photos."

"Saves me. Your turn now anyway," Liam told him.

It took awhile, but he summed up the month's business, any staff changes, current and projected updates, offered a template of the progress of the website refresh, some new brochures.

"In addition, I had a thought that ties in, more or less, with the team building and that marketing. Ice fishing."

"Do we have to think about winter?" Nell let out a sigh. "I'm hardly used to wearing sandals again."

"It'll come whether we think about it or not. Ice fishing contest, three days running, cash prizes. For the most part," Miles continued, "this would involve locals. Some guests, sure, but I'd want it open to all comers. Keep the fee reasonable. We tag, say, a dozen fish. Dad, you could work out the legalities on it, but anyone who competed would need a license. Say, a hundred dollars for six of them. A thousand for the rest—except one. Ten thousand grand prize."

"That's a hell of a fish." Mick rubbed his hands together. "Let me at 'em."

"You already know we couldn't compete. Even with the entry fees, we could lose money, but it's good community relations, good marketing. If it works, we make it an annual event."

"I think it's a brilliant idea." Lydia tipped her head toward him. "You don't ice fish. Ever. What made you think of it?"

He shrugged. "Winters come, and they stick. We'd get a lot of free marketing out of it. Local TV crews, internet, word of mouth. We give it a blast on the website, on social media."

"I'm thinking two dozen fish—you figure that out, Rory," Mick told his son, "the ins and outs, the cash prizes, and how that works."

"Will do."

"Your hundred-dollar fish, your five-hundred, thousand, and the big kahuna."

"We could do prizes for the shanties—best decorated—wouldn't that make a picture?" Drea considered. "They wouldn't have to be cash. A free night or weekend, discount cards at the spa, the shops, the restaurants and bars. We set up to have hot chocolate, coffee, maybe some baked goods. Nell and I can work on that. Something like we do in January, Nell, for the ice sculpture event."

"We can rock this." Liam nodded as he made his own notes. "I should've thought of it myself."

"Take your ropes course victory," his mother advised.

"Oh, I do. Anything else? I'm starving."

"One more thing. It crosses resort business and personal."

"A family business." Drea lifted her hands. "So much does."

"It does," Miles agreed. "And in that vein, I'm letting you all know I'm seeing Morgan Albright."

He expected the pause, and maybe a moment of confusion. He got both.

"Ah, seeing Morgan," Drea said slowly, "as in dating?"

Nell gave Miles the sharp eye. "As in sleeping with, Mom. Damn it, Miles."

"Sorry. Did you want to sleep with her?"

"Aren't you just adorable? Are there not enough women in Vermont you can choose from without sleeping with someone who works at the resort, and in *my* department?"

"Apologies again. I've run through all the others. She was the only one left. Once I'm done with her, I'm hitting on New Hampshire."

"All right, kids." Their father held his hands up, palms out. "That's enough. First, this is Miles's personal life, and he's entitled to it just like the rest of us. Next. Everyone at this table, everyone who knows him would have no reason, whatsoever, to think he'd in any way coerce or pressure any woman, any employee into a sexual relationship."

"Morgan may not feel that way."

Liam let out an impatient hiss as he turned to his sister. "Come on, Nell, Morgan's worked for us long enough to give a solid impression. If she felt pressured, and I don't buy that, not with Miles, she'd come to you, or Grand, or Mom. Or, more likely, she'd tell Miles to back right off. I've seen her handle guests who come close to the line. So have you."

"I also know she's coming out of a trauma. Major trauma, and one that's not over."

"I'm aware." He spoke coolly—a clear warning signal. "And you're crossing the line if you think I'd take advantage of that."

"I don't. I'm saying she might. I need to talk with her. I do," she pressed before Miles could speak. "I'm her direct supervisor. I'm responsible."

"I have something to say."

When Lydia Jameson spoke, no one interrupted.

"Rory is right in that this is Miles's personal life, and his family needs to respect that. And his family should trust him, as he's never given any of us reason to do otherwise."

"Nell is right," she continued. "Though I have no doubt Miles is confident this relationship is on mutual and even ground, Nell, as Morgan's supervisor, should have an open and frank discussion with Morgan. She's Olivia Nash's granddaughter, and so I have no doubt Liam is also right. If she didn't want a relationship of this nature with Miles, she would make that clear.

"But," she continued after a pause, "we can't forget what she's been through, is still dealing with. Nell, I think we'd all appreciate it if you'd arrange to have a private conversation with Morgan tomorrow. I expect you'll have the answers and responses that allow all of us to let two unencumbered adults live their personal lives."

"I'll arrange it."

"That's settled then." Mick knocked a fist lightly on the table. "Miles will, no doubt, respect whatever Morgan has to say on the subject."

"Of course I will."

"She's a very appealing young woman." Mick smiled with it. "On several levels. And an asset to the resort. We look after our own. I'll add if Miles wasn't who Miles is, he wouldn't have brought this up at the meeting. And now, let's fire up the grill."

Outside, Nell made a point to draw Miles away. And watching them, Drea winced.

"Let them hash it out." Rory gave her shoulder a squeeze. "We didn't raise shrinking violets."

"That's my worry. I'd hate to see this end up in a fight."

"Wouldn't be the first time."

"Not even close. But you're right, let them hash it out. We can mop up the metaphorical blood later if necessary."

Nell drew Miles around to the side of the house. "Listen, I have to do this."

"So you've said, and so everyone agreed."

"It's not that I don't know you, don't trust you."

"It isn't?"

"No, and you damn well know it, so get off the high horse."

"I couldn't get in the saddle because you took up all the room."

She paced a few feet away, paced back again. "You're not going to piss me off."

"Wanna bet?"

"Miles!" She threw up her hands, then tapped her fists against her temples. "You can sympathize, you can be outraged about the idea of someone in power pressuring—in subtle or overt ways—a woman to have sex. But you can't know what it's like to be in that woman's position."

"And you do?"

"Yes, I do. I know what it's like to feel cornered by a guy who thinks I should be interested, or grateful, or compliant. And—"

"Hold the hell on." Taking her by the arms, he stared down at her. "Who? Who did that?"

She gave him a look, both affectionate and disdainful at once.

"Do you want me to start reeling off names since high school? I'm not going to do that. I handled it, and I'll keep handling. But I know what it's like, and you just can't. And yeah, Liam's right. I've seen her handle herself. But you're not a guest, not another member of the staff. You're the boss. So I'm going to talk to her and establish there's not any doubt or hesitation in her about having a sexual relationship with you.

"Is it just sexual?"

"Who's asking? The head of Hospitality or my sister?"

"I guess, in this case, it's your sister."

"Then I don't know yet."

She nodded. "That's fair. I never know either."

"My sister doesn't have sexual relationships. She's pure and untouched."

"That's right." Now she patted his cheek. "Just like our mother, who conceived and bore three children through a chaste miracle."

"That's my theory."

"I love you, Miles, and you didn't piss me off, so you lose the bet."

"Day's not over."

Nell went back and forth over where best to meet Morgan, and in the end texted a request to go to the Nash house on Monday at ten.

Somewhere, she thought, Morgan would feel comfortable, and after her family left for work so they'd have privacy.

When she arrived, Morgan answered the door quickly.

"Hi, thanks for seeing me. I'd forgotten what a lovely house this is. I don't get out this way often."

"Come on in. At first I was surprised you wanted to come by this morning, then I realized I shouldn't have been."

"Miles told you?"

"No, he hasn't said anything. But I know you had a family meeting yesterday, so I guess it came up that Miles and I are seeing each other."

"That's just the term he used. Isn't that interesting?"

"We'd better sit down. Why don't we go to the great room? I can make coffee."

"That'd be good. I have to say you can tell three women live here— and I mean that in the best possible way. It just looks feminine. Smells feminine. And oh, your yard! So pretty. I love the bird feeders."

"Me, too. Coffee, latte, cappuccino—your choice."

"I'd love a latte."

"We'll make that two. Have a seat."

"There's something so artistic and soothing about your backyard. I talked myself out of an apartment and bought a small house. Small enough, I told myself, so I could maintain it myself, with a yard small enough I could do the same.

"I failed."

"I'm going to say that's hard to believe."

"Something always got neglected or put off. I'll get to that tomorrow, or next week, and I know when you do that it's just going to pile up. So I told myself I'd be more efficient if I hired someone to maintain it."

"You're giving people jobs that way, and paychecks," Morgan pointed out.

"There's that. And still, your backyard is so much more appealing and creative than mine. Is that wind chime from Crafty Arts?"

"It is."

"I'm going to stop by there on my way to work and get one. Do you mind if we sit out on the patio?"

"One of my favorite spots."

Chapter Twenty

When they sat at the patio table, Nell looked around one more time.

"I'd want to live out here. Do you drink your coffee-flavored milk and sugar out here every morning?"

"Usually."

"Miles has a Zen place like this, and actually makes time to work in the garden every week unless he's really slammed. I guess you know."

"Yes, it's beautiful."

"Okay, well." Nell tucked her hair, loose today, behind her ear. "I don't want this to be awkward."

"Too late."

Nell made a small sound of agreement. "I guess there's no avoiding the awkward. I wanted to talk to you here, your turf, your home, and not my office, so you'd be as comfortable as possible."

"I appreciate that. I do. Can I cut to my personal end of the line and ask if you're firing me?"

"What? Jesus, no! No. Toss that out right now." As she spoke, Nell shot a hand in the air as if winging something away.

"Okay then." Morgan breathed out. "I'll throw out the worry and we can just stick with the awkward."

"I wish it wasn't awkward, because this is about your comfort, Morgan. I know Miles, obviously. I love Miles, but I stand—or sit right now—as your direct supervisor, and your support. I understand you and Miles now have a personal relationship, and I want you to tell me, to feel absolutely secure and safe in telling me, if you felt in any way pressured to enter that relationship. Even if Miles didn't—"

"You can stop there because that's a big, solid no. He didn't pressure me, I didn't feel pressured. He didn't make any moves. I did, and I thought that's why you might fire me."

"Oh. A minute?" She lifted her coffee, drank. "He didn't share that part, and of course he wouldn't. He's Miles. It would've been helpful. We'd still have had this conversation, but it would've been helpful."

"I can be helpful. He was more than kind to me after I had the incident Friday night—a week ago on Friday night. You'd know about that."

"Yes, and I'm sorry it happened."

"So am I. I also felt, even prior to that, he might be interested in me. He never said or did anything, but— Oh hell, Nell, you know, right? When a man's interested. You might misinterpret, but you get a sense."

"All right, yes."

"I wasn't going to act on the fact I was interested back because I love my job, and I need it, but I baked him cookies."

"Seriously?"

"My mother's idea."

"Oh, I get that, too." Now she laughed, shook her head, drank more coffee. "So you baked him cookies."

"With a lot of help, but yeah, then I was going to drop them off at his house, but I saw the turrets."

"It's a great house."

"It really is, and then Howl came running out, and I was so charmed, and Miles looked so baffled. I asked to see inside the turret. I still wasn't going to act on the attraction, I just really wanted to see. Then I was leaving, and . . ."

"Oh, don't stop now."

"And I just felt what I felt was mutual, so I asked if he was attracted or interested, and he was so careful I figured I'd misinterpreted. But then he said I hadn't, and we sort of talked through the situation and how to put that whole thing aside—mutually. Then I made my move, and one thing led to another."

Morgan shrugged. "Is that helpful enough?"

"He'd never have told me all that. I'm glad you did."

"If this is going to cause any problems . . . I don't know what to do. The job, living here with my ladies, now Miles? It all makes me feel more myself than I have in so long. I don't want to give any of it up."

"Why would you? You're an excellent manager, this is a lovely home that feels happy with it. And though as my brother, Miles can irritate the crap out of me, he's an interesting man, with a strong moral code. I needed to know where you stood and how you felt, and why. Now I do, and can say this now sits as your personal business."

"Good. Thanks. And whew. I know I'm probably not his usual type."

"I don't think he has one."

"Well, I mean like that woman he was seeing not that long ago."

"Carlie Wineman? Please." Nell rolled her eyes. "I know a ladder-climber when I see one, and okay, I didn't see it for a while. And I shouldn't say any of this, but the hell with it. I'm now Miles's sister, not head of Hospitality, and I'm going to say this. She's gorgeous and knows how to show off her looks. She knows art and wine, skis like a champ, speaks French like a native."

"None of this inspires self-confidence."

"I'm not done. After a while—it took awhile, because she could be very charming—I realized Miles was a step up for her. Socially, financially. And more, she just liked the way they looked as a couple. Everything about her is about as deep as a rain puddle, except her vanity."

"All right, maybe a dribble of self-confidence coming back."

"I like you. I like you for Miles. I don't know if this is just a sex thing, but—"

"I don't know either."

"Understandable. Once I got to know Carlie, I didn't like her. And I really didn't like her for Miles, and was thrilled when he broke things off. I do love my brother even when he pisses me off, which is with some regularity. I also piss him off with some regularity."

"Because you're so much alike."

Over the rim of her cup, Nell shot a long, cool look. "Now you'll piss me off."

"You have to know that. You're very self-aware. You came here because you wanted me to be comfortable and feel more in control. That's kind and respectful. Miles is kind and respectful, he's just more brusque about it. Liam's more freewheeling, but you all get the job done, and well. Part of that's work ethic, and part of it is a deep love for the family and the business it created."

"Maybe you should've gone into psychology."

"A good bartender is a psychologist who mixes drinks. Did you like that part of your training? Liam said you all trained in every area of the business."

"Did he? Well, he's right about that. I can't say I liked the work, but I found the training valuable. It made me understand it's a lot more than mixing those drinks.

"Now, though I'd like to just sit here for another hour in this spot—it reminds me what it is to relax—it's not my day off. I have to go buy a wind chime, then get to work and let you get back to your day off."

"I'm glad you came by."

"So am I." Nell rose. "I don't make real friends easily, but tend to keep the ones I make. And damn it, that's exactly like Miles. Anyway, we should have lunch sometime."

"Lunch?"

"Or drinks. And now it sounds like I'm asking you out. Maybe I am, in a way. A 'let's see if there's a possible friendship in here' sort of way."

"I don't make friends easily either. I'd like to try that kind of lunch or drinks."

"Great. I'll text you possible openings in my schedule, which is exactly why I don't make friends easily."

"I'm a big admirer of the schedule."

"That's a good launching point for possible friendship."

They parted on those amiable terms, then Morgan sat and let the relief wash over her. She wasn't going to be fired, she wouldn't have to choose between the man and the job when she wanted both.

And, over and above it all, Miles had told his family.

"Turning around," she said quietly. "It really feels like things are turning around."

Gavin Rozwell enjoyed the balmy ocean breezes and the golden sands of the South Carolina beach. The local seafood suited his palate. While the view from his front deck afforded views of sea and sand and sunrise, he had to admit he missed the terrace of his hotel.

But when a man booked a hotel for a couple of months, he earned notice and talk. A man who rented a beach house didn't. He'd have to make certain the reward was worth the sacrifice.

Here, he was Trevor Caine, a successful ghostwriter working on a project, and carving out time to—hopefully—finish his own too-long-neglected novel.

He'd gone for the casual scruffy look, as it seemed to reflect the beach setting and his current persona. He'd darkened his hair to a chestnut brown, added some sun-kissed highlights and a goatee. A spray tan completed the beachy look, along with a collection of shorts, T-shirts, distressed jeans.

He topped it off with a Mets fielder's cap he'd battered a bit so it looked well-worn, and a pair of Ray-Bans.

He decided he not only looked the part but looked damn good.

While he did, occasionally, stroll on the beach, he spent most of his time at his laptop. Instead of writing, he continued his research, refined the outline of his plan.

His target, Quinn Loper, had her own beach house—with some very nice equity therein—owned and operated a cleaning company that serviced the rentals, contracted through the booking agency.

She no longer did any of the dirty work, and for a sliding scale of fees, offered wipe downs, deep cleanings, window washing, and so on to other locals.

Quinn had an MBA and a solid business. She also had well-off paternal grandparents who'd relocated from New York to Myrtle Beach when they'd retired, for the weather and the golf.

Her mother had died in an accident when Quinn was six—so sad!

Boo-hoo!—and her widowed father moved her and her eight-year-old sister to South Carolina to be close to family.

Her father remarried seven years later and now lived in Atlanta. Her sister recently married another woman—he didn't get that, but live and let. They bought an old plantation-style house in Charleston, rehabbed it—and ran a B and B.

An enterprising family!

He considered Quinn a prime choice. She'd been on his list for a couple of years, and since Fat Ass in New Orleans—big disappointment!—he'd gone deeper into his research.

Single—and not gay like big sister—twenty-eight and athletic enough to run on the beach most mornings. She also had a membership to a local gym. She worked out of her home, saving the cost of office space, and ran a crew of sixteen, full- or part-time.

She supplied the equipment and supplies under the company name of Beachy Clean.

Too cutesy for his taste, but it worked. She had just over seventy-five thousand in equity built into her four-bedroom, two-and-a-half bath, two-level home—with front and back decks and a hot tub. She drove a Mercedes convertible and owned a Dodge pickup truck.

Her business account remained healthy, and her personal accounts—well, that MBA and those rich grandparents paid off handsomely.

He calculated he'd net between two hundred and two hundred fifty thousand before he killed her and drove off in the Mercedes.

The truck was loaded, newer, but the convertible was *sweet*.

With his research done and his cover firmly in place, he only had to engineer a meet-cute.

He headed to the beach just after sunrise. When she ran, that was her time. He ran two miles that day and the next without seeing her. He had to remind himself to be patient, remind himself he established a pattern for any other early risers who walked the beach or drank coffee on their oceanfront decks.

The guy in the Mets cap who jogs in the morning.

The third day she beat him there, so he fell into place behind her.

Long legs, tight body—the way he liked them. She had a long pony-tail through the back opening of her ball cap. Other than the length of the hair, she reminded him of Morgan.

Maybe she had more curves—but they reminded him of his mother, so it all worked.

Prime catch.

After a solid mile, she turned. He'd paced himself so they'd run toward each other just long enough. He flashed a smile, tapped his cap, tapped a finger in the air at hers.

"Go team!"

"Having a good year," she responded, only slightly breathless, and kept going.

"Hot bats." He ran on, then turned, paced her again, keeping about six feet between them.

When she slowed to a walk, he gave her a half wave as he ran by. She'd walk another quarter mile or thereabouts. He'd watched her routine through binoculars. She'd cool down with the walk, stretch a little, then walk up the path between the oceanfronts and back to her own house.

He stopped at that point, bent over to brace his hands on his knees, panted some until she walked closer.

With a half smile, he straightened. "It's a pretty run, but I'm not used to running on wet sand."

"You did fine."

"You did better. From New York?"

"Born there." Keeping a careful distance, she balanced on one leg for a quick quad stretch. "But I've lived here most of my life."

Which sounded clearly in her coastal Southern drawl.

"I inherited my love for the Mets from my grandfather. New York?" she asked in turn.

"I moved to Brooklyn right after college. Found my place and my ball team. Nice to meet a fellow Mets fan in South Carolina. They're playing the Mariners tonight. Bassitt against Castillo."

"I'm looking forward to it. So, you and your family on vacation?"

"No family, just me. Working vacation. Can't beat the view." He gestured back. "I'm two back from these big-ass oceanfronts. They call it Riding the Wave."

She'd check on him with that info, he thought. Just as he wanted her to.

"Ah, Trevor Caine." He offered a hand.

"Quinn Loper. Enjoy your stay."

"Oh, I am. Maybe I'll see you on the run tomorrow."

She shot a smile over her shoulder as she walked away. "Maybe."

He timed it well the next day, and she ran just behind him. He slowed just enough. "Hell of a game," he called out.

He hadn't watched it, but he'd gathered all the stats and highlights. "That double play in the bottom of the ninth? Sweet!"

They ran together for a stretch, tossing game tidbits back and forth. This time he slowed to a walk when she did.

"Taking a tip from you," he told her. "Walking it down. Too much sitting, I guess, and not enough time in the gym."

"Same for me if I fall off routine. What kind of work do you do?"

She already knew the basics of the identity he'd built, he could tell.

"I'm a writer, working on a novel. He's said for three years and counting." Sheepish smile for that one. "Ghostwriting pays the bills while I do."

"Ghostwriting? Like, you write a book and somebody else puts their name on it?"

"It's not as simple as that. It's more somebody needs something they've written fixed up, or has an idea, but it needs fleshing out."

"Books and baseball are my things."

And he knew that, hence the cap and the cover.

"Who have you written for?"

He gave her a smile and lifted shoulders. "The thing about ghosts is we're invisible. Can't say. It's a contractual deal. I decided to come down here, finish up a project for a client, and give my own some serious time."

He looked out over the water. "It's working. I think I can finish the contract book by the end of the week. Then, no excuses, it's my time, my story."

He looked back at her. Easy and casual, but let interest show through. "What do you like to read?"

"A good story. Thriller, mystery, romance, horror, fantasy. Just take me away for a while and we're good."

"That's the goal. What do you do when you're not reading or watching baseball?"

"I run a cleaning company. Beachy Clean takes care of your cottage."

"Seriously?" He tipped his cap back. "You clean my rental?"

"Not me personally. I run the operation that does."

Not own it, he noted. Being careful.

"I'm going to start picking up a lot more before the weekly cleaning so I don't get reported back to you as a slob."

Her smile came wide and bright.

"The crew's like ghostwriters. Very discreet. And I've got to get to it. Good luck with the writing."

"Thanks."

By day four he planned to run together, but she didn't show. He settled for day five. On day seven, she asked him out for a drink, beating his scheduled ask by two days.

He followed up with an invite to dinner—all casual, friendly, and a friendly good-night kiss before he deliberately missed a day.

"Pulled an all-nighter," he told her, and put on shining excitement. "It just started to roll, and I couldn't stop."

"Your book, right?"

"Yeah, all mine."

"What's it about?"

"Can't say—that's straight superstition. It's like if I talk about it, it'll stop rolling." He looked up as gulls winged and called overhead. "This was the right time, the right place. If I ever get it finished—and I will—and published—and I will—I'll send you a copy. I honestly think these morning runs with you got the engine going."

"That's great, Trevor."

"How about I take you to dinner—maybe tomorrow night—to celebrate?"

She smiled. "How about you do?"

It took nearly three weeks for the mating dance to end up at dinner at her place. It gave him an opportunity to study the layout and get a few minutes with the desktop in her office.

She wanted sex, and that was fine, not unexpected. He could handle it, could get hard imagining the kill.

Plus, she had a laptop in her bedroom, so he gained two points of access.

He met her grandparents, ate barbecued ribs on their deck. And since they just laid the opportunity out there, he took it, uploaded his program into the old man's office computer.

No reason not to add to his take with a chunk of their investment account.

He'd just add a couple of days onto his schedule.

It only took a month, and he'd given himself two. After securing the loans as Quinn Loper, banking the take, he drained her accounts, sweetened it with a hundred K from her grandfather.

He thought about killing the grandparents, but he couldn't find the thrill in it. Instead, he found the thrill imagining their shock, their tears after he'd killed their beloved granddaughter.

He slipped into their house while they slept—they left the windows open to hear the ocean.

Idiots.

He removed his program, slipped out again.

Quinn didn't leave the windows open, but her front door lock was a joke.

He moved through the darkened house, into the bedroom where she slept. He was tempted to wake her up first so she'd have more time to know what was happening, more time to feel it, fear it.

But she worked out, and he knew she'd put up a fight.

So he eased onto the bed, pinned her arms under his knees. Her eyes popped open when he closed his hands over her throat.

She couldn't make a sound, not more than a peep, but she bucked, tried to roll.

"You're just another whore." Tighter, tighter, cutting off the air, watching her eyes roll. "You think you're special, but you're not. I'm making you nothing."

Her mouth gaped open as she fought for air, beneath his hold on her arms, her fingers clawed at the sheets. Her heels drummed.

"I took everything I wanted, do you understand? Your house, your business. It's all mine now, and nothing you ever did will matter because now you're nothing."

She stopped struggling and convulsed. Even in the dim light, he saw the life drain out of her eyes.

And she was nothing; and he was a god.

Oh, the thrill. It coursed through him, hot, bright, strong.

But not, he realized, perfect.

She'd been good, much, much better than Fat Ass New Orleans, but not perfect.

Nothing would reach perfect again, until he finished Morgan.

Out of his pocket he took the bracelet he'd found in Morgan's drawer, and he slipped it on Quinn's wrist.

"Here, you can have this. I want to remind her I'm coming for her."

He took the keys to the Mercedes, drove it the short distance to his rental to load up the luggage he'd already packed. Just as he'd already shaved, as he'd already dyed his hair black and generated a new identity.

By the time anyone found her, he'd have traded the convertible to a contact he had in North Carolina, and with a new ride, head west for a while.

As he drove off into the night, he smiled to himself.

"And that's how it's done."

Morgan didn't want the summer to end. Every day, rain or shine, offered her another building block in her new life. A life, she'd discovered, she genuinely loved.

Nothing could change the tragedy that had set her on this new path, but she could, and would, not only walk it but appreciate the scenery on the way.

She could and would be grateful.

On a sunny Sunday, she intended to show some gratitude with a surprise.

"I really appreciate you helping out."

As they drove, Morgan reached up to stroke Howl, who pressed against her seat in Miles's burly SUV.

"I know you have a weekend routine."

"It's a routine, not a commandment carved in stone."

"Either way, I'll never move that concrete base alone, which is why it's been sitting in my grandfather's workshop for a dozen years. But the three of us can move it."

"Yeah, the dog'll be a lot of help."

"He's here for moral support, aren't you, Howl? And he gets an outing. It's like a little vacation."

"Every day's a vacation when you're a dog." He pulled into the drive at the Tudor.

"My ladies won't be back until after three, probably later. This is going to work."

"Every time you say that it comes out a little less confident."

"I just need to get started. I'm nervous, but that'll pass once I get started."

She led the way around the house, with Howl looking everywhere, sniffing everything on his doggie vacation.

"I set the solar panel for the pump out yesterday so it would charge, but everything else is in the workshop. There's a dolly, but I was afraid to try to move it by myself."

She grinned at Miles. "You're the muscle."

"Looks good back here," Miles observed.

"And when we finish this project, even better. It's the one thing that's missing. Or the one thing until I think of another thing."

The workshop, a faded cedar square with a bright blue door, stood at the back of the property, tucked among the trees and backed by a narrow stream.

"Just like I remember it. The dog your grandfather had when I was a kid liked to stretch out in the stream. Our grandfathers sometimes sat on a couple of old folding chairs, had a beer, bullshitting. He always had a cold Coke for me when I tagged along."

"He loved kids." She opened the shop door. "They wanted a big family, but Gram had complications."

"That's a shame. Jesus, it looks just like I remember in here. 'A place for everything, Miles,' he'd say. 'And everything in its place. Because when you need a tool, you don't want to waste time hunting for it.'"

Running her hand over a worktable, she glanced around at the power tools, the pegboard holding hand tools, the big red tool chest, the labeled mason jars holding screws, nails, washers.

"It still, somehow, smells like him. I think that's why Gram hasn't given away any of his tools, or sold them. It's been handy for me, with the little projects."

Miles walked over to a concrete pedestal, easily three feet high with a wide top.

"This thing?"

"That thing. I don't know why he had it—neither does Gram. I hope he approves of what I do with it. I've already drilled the holes in the frog."

Now he walked to the concrete frog on another worktable.

It sat cross-legged on a perch inside a wide copper bowl. Its hands lay cupped, palms up on its knees. It wore a beatific smile.

The holes in the cupped palms offered a clue.

"You're going to pump water out of his hands?"

"I knew what he should be as soon as I saw him. The submergible pump goes under his seat, and the wire for the panel goes down through the base—see the holes I put in? The sunshine runs it."

"Did your grandfather teach you how to work a drill that way?"

"Not really. I didn't spend that much time here—and that's a regret. But some basics—hammer, nail, measure twice, cut once. Then there's always a tutorial on YouTube. It's going to work."

While the dog explored the shop, Miles walked over to get the dolly. "Do you know where you want it?"

"The exact spot."

"Said every woman ever."

"That's very sexist. Possibly true, but very sexist."

He started to tip the base to slide the dolly under, stopped, and shot her a look. "Jesus, Morgan."

"I know, it's a ton, which may be why it's still in here. We'll get it."

Together, they maneuvered it onto the dolly. While Miles rolled it, she balanced it.

"If it goes," he warned her, "don't try to catch it. It goes, it goes."

"It's not going to."

It took some doing, a lot of muscle and sweat, but it turned out she did have an exact spot. In the full sun, beyond the shade of a weeping peach, and in front of a swath of thriving Nikko Blue hydrangeas.

"Okay, just hold it there!" She ran back for a slab of slate—hole drilled—then the pump and wire.

Once she had the pump set, they eased the base onto the slab of slate.

Miles gave it a push. "It'll take a tornado to knock this thing over."

"Exactly."

She ran back, Howl running with her, to get the frog and bowl.

"See, the pump fits into the seat, the seat in the copper bowl—that came from the shop, a local craftsman—and the frog on the seat, with the pipe going up, and into his butt. Could you get the hose?" She gestured. "It'll reach, I checked."

"I'm sure you did."

She didn't miss a trick, he thought, when he hiked over to turn on the hose, walked back with it.

"It's going to work," she muttered.

"Fill it up?"

"Please. I love how the sun plays off the copper. I thought about getting a regular birdbath bowl, but the copper just pops out. The frog's so cute. Totally Zen—which is what I call him. I think they'll love it. Okay, moment of truth."

She turned on the pump. Waited. Waited.

Water spurted out from the cupped hands in pretty fountains that spilled back into the copper bowl.

"It works!" She spun a circle, grabbed Miles, kissed him, spun another. "Oh, it's adorable, right? Adorable and quirky and unique."

"You're handy. You built a damn fountain."

"I learned to be handy, and it was more like putting pieces together. I love it. If they don't, they'll say they do, but I'll know. Let's sit on the patio, see how it looks from there. I'll get us a drink."

PART III

Roots

Beauty, strength, youth are flowers but fading seen;
Duty, faith, love, are roots, and ever green.
—George Peele

Love is strong as death;
jealousy is cruel as the grave.
—Song of Solomon 8:6

Chapter Twenty-one

As she filled two tall glasses with ice, Morgan did a little dance. Out the kitchen window, beyond the patio, the Zen frog tossed water into the air. Now she could imagine her ladies smiling at it while they enjoyed their morning coffee or evening wine. Through the rest of the summer and into the fall before the air blew too cold.

Picturing it perfectly, she opened the refrigerator for the pitcher of lemonade, then paused when the doorbell rang. A delivery, she supposed as she went to answer. Still, the rules of her life had become the habit of her life.

She checked out the front window first.

And all the simple pleasure of the day drained away.

She opened the door to the two federal agents.

"You'd have called if you'd caught him because you'd want me to know right away. That's not it."

"No, Morgan, I'm sorry. That's not it. Can we come in?" Beck asked her.

"Yes, of course." She closed the door behind them. "Who was she?"

"Let's sit down first."

"Sorry, yes. I . . ." She looked back toward the kitchen. "I'm not alone. I have my . . ."

What? She couldn't say "boyfriend"—he wasn't a boy. Partner, no, she didn't think of them as partners, not really. Lover was true, but not all.

"Out back. Miles—Miles Jameson. We're involved." That sounded reasonable and true. "He was helping me with a project. He knows about all of this."

"Yes, we've spoken with him." Morrison glanced back as she did. "Do you want to go out, include him in what we have to tell you?"

No, she thought. She wanted to sit in the sunshine with Miles and lemonade and watch the frog fountain.

But.

"He'll need to know anyway. I work at the resort. His family owns the resort. And, as I said, we're involved. I was just . . . getting lemonade. That sounds so normal." She laughed, shoved a hand at her hair. "So summer Sunday afternoon. I'll get two more glasses."

She walked them back to the kitchen. She could see Miles had already wound the hose back on its reel. Now he stood there with his hands in his pockets, studying the frog fountain.

"Can I help you with that?"

"No," she told Morrison. "I'll get a tray. You should go out. I need a minute. I just need a minute."

She worked on steadying herself as she got a tray. Now she saw Miles turn, saw his bemused, relaxed face tighten.

She filled two more glasses with ice, then carried everything outside.

They continued to stand, the three of them, while the sun struck light against the copper bowl, while the frog smiled his peaceful smile.

She couldn't say why it meant so much when Miles crossed to her, took the tray. He said, "Sit down."

Even though it sounded like an order, it steadied her a little more.

When she sat, he poured the lemonade into the glasses so the ice crackled. It sounded like machine-gun fire to her ear.

Howl laid his head on her knee.

"Who was she?" Morgan asked again.

Beck took the lead.

"Her name was Quinn Loper, age twenty-eight, single. She owned her own business in Myrtle Beach, South Carolina. She fits his profile, top to bottom, though she was substantially more financially well-off than most of his victims. And in this case, he was also able to access her grandparents' accounts. He didn't harm them physically but skimmed a hundred thousand. He could have taken a great deal more."

"He took their grandchild," Miles countered.

Beck nodded at him. "Yes, and maybe that was enough this time."

"He rented a beach house, a two-month rental, under the name Trevor Caine," Morrison continued. "While he may not use that identity again, you should keep it in your records. He posed as a writer."

They laid out the facts and evidence they'd gathered. Then Beck took over again.

"It's our conclusion he rented a house rather than booking a hotel because it's an area where beach rentals are common, and he'd attract less notice."

Beck leaned over, laid a hand over Morgan's. "Morgan, I know it might seem we've made no progress finding him, stopping him, but we were able to track him from New Orleans, and eventually, we found the agency where he rented the car he used to drive to South Carolina. He'd changed his appearance, but two of the staff there ID'd him, so we knew the name he used, the look he used. Using those, we tracked him to Myrtle Beach. We found the hotel where he'd stayed a couple of days."

Morgan said nothing, just nodded.

"We alerted local law enforcement. We'd begun canvassing the rental agencies when the alert on Quinn Loper came in. We missed him by hours."

"But she's dead anyway. I'm sorry, I understand how much time and work you're putting into this. But she's dead anyway."

"Yes, she is."

The regret came through, enough that Morgan wished she hadn't spoken the horrible truth.

"We weren't in time. But he made mistakes. He stole her car, a high-end Mercedes convertible. And he didn't disable the tracking system."

"I'm not sure what that means. I'm not in the high-end car club."

"It's an embedded system. It means they tracked him—tracked the car." Miles's eyes narrowed. "But you don't have him."

"No, but we have the individual who bought the car, and who's previously taken in trade or in sale other vehicles from Rozwell. We have this person in custody."

"He knows where Rozwell is?"

Morrison took over. "He claims no, and we believe him. He claims he thought Rozwell was a car thief, that he knew nothing about the murders. We tend to believe him on that, especially since facing potential charges of accessory after the fact, multiple counts of murder, he's cooperating."

"We know the vehicle he took in trade," Beck told them, "and the name he used for the registration. We have his description at that time, and which direction he took, when he took it. These are major mistakes, Morgan, a breakdown in his discipline. We have an APB out on the vehicle, on the name he's using."

"Is he coming here?"

"Our information is he brought up a map on his laptop while his new car was prepared for him. He mapped out a route west, likely as far as Kansas, so not here. Our conclusion is he's not ready for you yet."

Beck opened her briefcase, took out an evidence bag. "He put this on the victim."

"My bracelet." In the summer sunlight, her skin went cold. "The one he took when he killed Nina."

"He wants you to know he's thinking about you. To keep you on edge. But the fact is, Morgan, he's on edge. He wouldn't have made so many mistakes otherwise. He knows cars, he knows tech, but he forgot about the tracking system in the Mercedes."

"We can put you in a safe house," Morrison began.

"My mother and grandmother live here. What if he comes for me, and hurts them instead?"

The thought of it, the risk of it, turned the hard knot in her belly to ice.

"And how long do I stay shut away somewhere? A week, a month, a year? I can't live like that. No one can live like that. Miles—"

"No," he said. "You can't live like that. We're doing everything you advised us to do. If there's more, tell us and we'll do that. How many times is she supposed to let him take what she has, what she is? How many times does she have to start over?"

Saying nothing, Morgan watched him. His voice stayed absolutely calm, and turned cold enough to freeze the air.

The invisible suit, she thought. He put on the invisible suit. For me.

What he said, how he said it, meant, in that moment, everything.

"She shook his confidence, isn't that it?" Miles demanded. "You have profilers—isn't that the reason he's fucking up? She dented his shield, so she has to pay. But he has to make sure he dents hers, too. Shakes her confidence. Otherwise, he'd have gone after her right away. It's got to eat at him, but he's waited more than a year.

"She scares him. And he damn well should be scared of her."

"I don't disagree," Beck said. "But unless we stop him first, he will come sooner or later. Because yes, it eats at him. The three women he's killed since Morgan survived? They're substitutes, and a substitute never satisfies like the real thing."

"Then you'd better find him first."

Beck sat back, picked up her glass, set it down again. "If he'd waited one more day in South Carolina. We'd just walked into the agency he used for the rental. If we'd walked in a few hours earlier. But we didn't, and he didn't."

"It's hard for me." Morgan stroked Howl's head. "It's hard for both of you."

"It's the job," Beck began, then both her and Morrison's phones beeped. "Excuse me." She rose, stepped away.

"Is that your dog?" Morrison asked Morgan.

"No. He's Miles's dog."

"More or less," Miles muttered.

"It wouldn't hurt to get a dog. A dog's a good deterrent. You could—"

"We've got a break," Beck interrupted. "He checked into a hotel in Kansas City, Missouri. Local LEOs responding now. We've got to go. We'll be in touch."

Morgan stood to walk them out, but they were already rushing away. "Good luck," she called out. "Maybe this time," she said to Miles.

"Maybe. You're okay."

"You think?"

"No panic attack."

"There's that. I want to tell you, it meant a lot, what you said."

"I said a lot of things."

"That I'm not going to let him take my life away again, that he should be afraid of me. You stood up for me. It matters that I know I'll stand up for myself, that you believe I can and will, and you'd still stand up for me. It matters."

He said nothing for a moment, just watched her as she sat, the dog stretched out under her chair.

"Morrison had a good point. You should keep the dog with you. I don't know if he's much of a guard dog, but he'd make noise."

"And give up that fancy doghouse?"

"I'm pretty sure he'd sleep out in the rain if you'd give him a pat on the head."

Smiling, she gave Howl a rub with her foot. "You're his home, and his roots. I know what it's like to be uprooted, so no. But thanks. Those agents? This isn't just a job for them. They want to stop him, and it's not for a government paycheck."

She paused, drank some of her lemonade. "I think I did dent his shield, the way they said. If what happened to me, and what didn't, shakes him enough to help them find him, stop him . . . I'll be good with that. More than. And I hope he knows that despite everything he took from me, I have a good life here, with more than I knew I wanted. I hope that shakes him, too."

"I'm just going to get this over with."

He surprised her by reaching out to take her hand. He rarely made gestures of casual affection or intimacy.

"Am I going to like it?"

"That's not the point. I'm attracted to you. That's obvious or we wouldn't be here. I like being with you, and not just for the sex. For some strange reason I like the way you make a fountain out of a frog."

"You helped."

"I was just the muscle, and don't interrupt. I'd enjoy watching you work behind the stick even if it wasn't for us. It's like a freaking ballet. I like your body, and I appreciate it has a good brain to go along with it. But all that aside, as they're really just different aspects of attraction, I admire the hell out of you."

Her earlier surprise shot straight up to stunned. "Oh, well. Wow."

"Don't interrupt," he said again. "I don't know how I'd have handled what you've had to. If I'd lost what you lost, and the way you lost it. If I'd had to face losing someone close to me, family, the way you did. Because that's what Nina was to you. She was family. I sure as hell hope I never have to find out if I have that kind of courage."

"You can talk now."

"I'm pretty sure I'm speechless."

"That'd be a first."

Howl stirred, muttered, then pushed out from under the chair.

"I think your ladies are home."

Before he could draw his hand away, she tightened her grip, then reached out to take his other. "You've just turned a really hard knock around. I'll think of more to say later, but right now, you turned it around."

"Miles, how nice to see you!" Seriously pretty in pink, Audrey stepped out. "No, don't get up. Don't. Oh, and this is the sweet dog Morgan's told us about. Aren't you handsome?" Audrey all but purred it while she bent down to pet the wagging Howl. "And listen to you. I agree." She laughed as he talked. "It is a beautiful day. And a busy one," she added as she straightened. "We nearly . . . Oh, oh, *Morgan*! Where did you get that? It's wonderful. A birdbath, a fountain. A yoga frog! It's adorable. Mom! You have to come out here and see!"

Amused, charmed, Miles just sat and watched.

Morgan's mother, pretty as a cupcake in her pink sundress, bounced on her toes with her hands pressed together under her chin.

Morgan had that chin, he realized, and those long, narrow hands with long, slender fingers. Then Olivia Nash came out, teenager trim in white linen pants, a sleeveless lipstick-red shirt. And he saw Morgan there as well in that same chin, and the cheekbones.

"What in the world, Audrey. Hello, Miles, and hello, Howl. Don't you have the sweetest face?"

"Thanks," Miles said, and earned a laugh.

"Both of you."

"Mom, would you look?" To make sure of it, Audrey took her mother's arm with one hand, pointed with the other.

"Oh, for . . . Well."

"Morgan got us a yoga frog fountain."

"She built it," Miles corrected.

"I didn't build it. I just found the pieces for it and put them together."

"Morgan, that's the definition of 'build.'"

"It's that old concrete base your dad could never figure out what he wanted to do with, Audrey. And that's Doug Gund's copper bowl. I saw we'd sold it, but nobody mentioned we'd sold it to you, Morgan."

"I asked them not to. Is it okay there? Do you like it?"

Studying the fountain, Olivia patted a hand on Morgan's shoulder. "He would've gotten such a kick out of that." Then she bent down, kissed the top of Morgan's head. "He'd be so proud of you. I love it. I love it almost as much as I love that some of his cleverness rubbed off on you."

With a hand on Morgan's shoulder, her other holding Audrey's, Olivia turned to Miles. "I'm betting she drafted you into hauling that ton of concrete over there."

He just flexed his biceps.

"I hope you and Howl will stay for dinner. We picked up some nice tilapia on the way home, and I've a mind to blacken it. You like spicy, Miles?"

"What man would say no?"

"That's settled then. It looks like you've already had some company."

Morgan rose, picked up the agents' glasses. "Sit down, and I'll get some fresh glasses and tell you about it."

Audrey stopped her with a touch on the arm. "This is about him. About Gavin Rozwell."

"Yes, but it's not all bad. Let me get the glasses first."

Audrey watched her go. "I'm glad you were here, Miles. I'm glad she wasn't alone."

"So am I, but she's right. It's not all bad."

Olivia sat. "Whatever it is, we'll deal with it."

They listened, with the summer sun streaming, with the faintest breeze just whispering in the air. And he watched as Audrey took her daughter's hand, as Olivia never took her eyes off Morgan's face.

"He made her care about him," Audrey murmured. "He took all that time to gain her trust, and more, make her care about him."

"Because the cruelty is the point. He didn't kill her grandparents," Olivia continued, "because that's not what he does. But more? I think more, because he knew how much they'd suffer. The cruelty is the point. What a sick, twisted life he lives."

"It's time he lived it behind bars. It's way past time."

Morgan gave her mother's hand a squeeze. "That may be coming, Mom. He made that mistake, not disabling the tracking system, and they got all that information from his—I'm not sure what I'd call him—the car guy."

"He could switch cars again anytime," Olivia pointed out.

"He could, but they know where he is. I didn't get to the last thing. While they were here, they got an alert. He'd checked into a hotel in Kansas City. The local police were responding. They could have him already. It could be over."

He wanted to do some shopping, and walk around to stretch his legs and get a feel for the area surrounding his hotel. He always made a point of checking out the traffic patterns, the local hot spots. Plus, he'd grown tired of the beach look. His current identity called for a more arty wardrobe.

Italian sandals, a pair of animal-striped Vans, black jeans, some new shirts, and a straw boater.

He enjoyed himself enough to stop and take an outdoor table at a bistro, order a glass of Malbec and a French dip. With his shopping bags tucked under the table, he set up his laptop, checked out the news reports for Myrtle Beach.

There she was! A very nice photo, all smiles and beach-blond hair. The artist drawing of Trevor Caine—suspect—wasn't bad, he concluded. Then again, Trevor Caine was as dead as Quinn Loper.

He read the report while he ate, and found himself mildly disappointed they'd yet to connect him, the real him, to Caine or the murder.

They would. He counted on it. A man needed recognition for accomplishments, after all.

He wondered if those bumbling Special Agents Beck and Morrison were on the case yet. He hoped so. It gave him such satisfaction to frustrate them, time after time.

Had they told Morgan? Oh, he really hoped so. He made a mental toast as he imagined her shivering with fear in a dark room, door locked, while her mother and grandmother wept in concern.

His mother had spent plenty of time locked in dark rooms nursing black eyes, cracked ribs.

He congratulated himself on not disposing of the junk jewelry he'd taken from Morgan's drawer. Leaving those pieces on the women he'd finished? Inspired, if he said so himself.

And he did.

What would she think when she found out a corpse wore her cheap, tacky bracelet? He drew a picture in his mind of her curling into a ball, crying, hysterical, begging for someone to protect her.

He'd see that, he promised himself, in reality, in the fucking flesh. And that would balance the damn scales before he finished her.

He finished his wine, paid the check, and because his musings put him in a fine mood, added a generous tip.

Carter John Winslow III could afford generosity thanks to a hefty trust fund. It allowed him to pursue his art without worrying about a paycheck.

Not that he needed that background story at the moment. He wouldn't stay in Kansas City more than a couple of days. He planned to head south of the border, book a suite at a resort on the Pacific Coast. A nice R and R.

God knew he'd earned it.

If he hadn't taken that walk around, done some shopping, stopped for a bite to eat and a glass of wine, he wouldn't have seen the police cars and the black SUV pull up in front of his hotel.

He wouldn't have been half a block away when cops poured out and rushed into the hotel lobby.

He wouldn't have been able to keep walking, just keep walking with his heart pounding in his throat and sheer shock ringing in his ears.

How had they found him? *How?* He'd ditched the Caine ID before he killed the bitch. He hadn't left a trail.

He kept walking.

Somehow he had left a trail, and now his Winslow ID was useless. And his things—cash, other IDs, other electronics, clothes—they'd have those now.

The sweat that slicked his skin turned icy as he went into a drugstore. He needed hair dye, some haircutting tools, some basic supplies.

No Mexico now. No, he couldn't risk a border crossing now. North, he'd go north. Montana, maybe Wyoming, where cows outnumbered people and people minded their own fucking business.

He couldn't get to his car, so he'd have to steal one. Some old junker he could hot-wire. He had to find a place to deal with his hair. Cheap motel. He had cash on him, and ways to access his accounts.

A cheap motel, change his look, steal a car, get the hell out of goddamn Kansas City.

No, no, steal the car first and get out. Roadblocks, manhunt. His mind whirled with fear, with what-ifs.

He walked out without buying anything, and kept walking until he found a bus stop. He got on the first one to come by, kept his head down and turned. Buses had cameras like every other damn thing now.

He reminded himself he had the laptop, at least he had the laptop.

But his hands shook and more sweat pooled at the base of his spine.

It took him nearly an hour of walking, riding, walking until he found a likely car in the vast parking lot of a Walmart.

They hadn't bothered to lock it, and it stank of pork rinds and loaded diapers, but he thought the car seat in the back would provide some cover.

He got it fired up, wound his way until he hit Interstate 29, and headed north. He cursed when he had to stop for gas, but he needed it, needed to keep going until he got clear.

He paid at the pump with the Luke Hudson Visa card he'd kept to remind him of Morgan. A lesser risk, he thought, than going inside—camera—or using the Winslow card.

He'd get to somewhere in Nebraska, he decided, find that cheap motel. Deal with his hair. In the morning he could buy what he needed to generate a new identity.

As he drove, he beat a hand on the wheel. All of his things! All of them, gone.

He had to slow his breathing, concentrate on his driving. If he got stopped . . .

He wouldn't get stopped. Couldn't get stopped, so he wouldn't.

Get to Nebraska. He rocked back and forth to calm himself. Find some crap motel where they didn't look twice. He'd have to ditch the stolen car—airport, long-term parking—to buy some time. Some bumfuck airport in bumfuck Nebraska.

Or maybe a junkyard. They probably had plenty of those piled up in the goddamn cornfields.

Switch the plates, ditch the car. Maybe buy a new one for cash from some yahoo. Or rent one, wait and rent one once he had the new ID.

He couldn't decide. He couldn't *think*.

He had to find somewhere to hole up first, to hole up and figure out what he needed to do next.

Because for the first time in his life, Gavin Rozwell was on the run.

Chapter Twenty-two

Morgan sat in the quiet of the empty house. She still held her phone, and half expected to have to use it to call for help when the panic attack came.

But it didn't come, so she stood, stuck the phone back in her pocket.

She'd work, she thought. She'd take her mind off things with work. Summer would end, and with fall, new drink specials.

She could do some research, and maybe start fleshing out the vague plans she had for Après with Halloween.

She could sit outside and work, let Totally Zen keep her calm and level.

When the doorbell rang, she jumped, felt her chest constrict.

She pushed the air out, telling herself not to give in, and braced on the back of a chair, keeping that air going in and out until she could walk to the door.

Out the window she saw Miles and a man she didn't recognize.

She opened the door.

"Morgan, Clark Reacher. He's going to install your home security cameras."

"My what?"

"Miles laid out what you need, so you don't need the sales pitch." Reacher, a man of about forty with a pleasant face and a wiry build, smiled at her. "Best we've got."

"I'll explain it to her. Why don't you get started?"

"But—"

Miles just took Morgan's arm, steered her to the back of the house. "You'll have security cameras, front, back, and on the side door. Somebody tries to get in, you get an alert. With the doorbell package, you won't have to look out the window when somebody rings the bell. You just look on your phone, your tablet, whatever. Clark'll fix it up."

"I didn't order this. Did Gram arrange for this?"

"No, I did."

"But you just can't—"

"Let's go outside."

"Miles, you can't arrange for all this without talking it over."

"I did, so I can." He nudged her outside. "I don't think I'll get an argument from your ladies."

"You're getting one from me." She stood her ground. "You can't have all this installed on someone else's property. It's beyond pushy."

"I'll give you pushy, but I am having it installed. You, your grandmother, and your mother will have more peace of mind. And so will I." He waited a single beat. "You wouldn't take the dog."

"Oh, for God's sake!"

"What about when you're working nights and they're here alone?"

"That's not fair."

Those eyes, those tiger eyes, went jungle fierce. "I don't care about fair. I have no fucks to give about fair. I thought about what it would be like to lose someone I cared about, someone who mattered. I don't like it, so it's not happening. You matter."

"That's really not fair." She turned away, scrubbing her hands over her face.

"I agree there. I didn't want you to matter, but you do. So this is happening. It's pushy, it's not fair. Deal with it."

She'd never had anyone just order her around. The Colonel hadn't cared enough; her mother had cajoled.

Now she tried to figure out how to handle it.

"You could have suggested we do something like this. We'd have thought about it."

"While you're thinking about it, it's getting done. If your grandmother wants to have a conversation with me about it, I'll make myself available.

"I don't like these damn systems," he added. "I don't like the whole idea of them. But right here, right now, it's necessary."

"I don't like being rolled over this way."

"Don't blame you a bit. It sucks, and I'll apologize after that son of a bitch is in a cell. If it's any consolation, when he gets done here, he's putting one of these systems on my place. I don't like it any more than you, but you spend time there."

She turned back, dropped into a chair. "It makes me feel helpless."

"That's stupid, and you're not. You dented his shield, remember? Now you'll have one, and he won't dent yours."

He sat across from her.

"Part of you still feels coming here, living here makes you a failure, a weak one. That's bullshit. Coming here, starting over after what happened to you is what proves you're strong. Strong enough, Morgan, that when someone hands you a shield, you take it and you use it."

"It's really unfair when you're logical." She pressed her fingers to her eyes. "It's just been a day, and still has a ways to go." She dropped her hands back on the table. "I got an update from the FBI."

"Okay."

"I need to walk. Can we just walk around? I need a little Zen."

"Sure. Give me a second first."

When he took out his phone, she pressed her fingers to her eyes again. "You have to get back to work. We'll do all this later."

"Don't be ridiculous. Give me a second."

He rose, moved away. As he worked with his assistant on some rescheduling, he wondered why a sensible, grounded woman like Morgan found it so hard to accept help.

When he walked back, he held out a hand. "Let's walk."

"They don't have him. I should get that out of the way first."

"But?"

"He wasn't in the hotel room when the police went in, but a lot of his things were—clothes, IDs, electronics. And the car he'd gotten when he sold or traded his last victim's was in the hotel garage. They have the name he used to book the suite. He'd gone out shopping, had some lunch. They have credit card receipts."

She paused by the fountain, so they stood a moment. He waited while the water fountained and the sunlight struck the copper.

"From the time stamps, they posit he saw the police going into the hotel when he was walking back from his lunch—charged on the card under the new name. It was all about the timing."

Miles rounded it up. "So they have what he left in the hotel room, have the car."

"Yes, and more. He walked some distance, caught a bus. They had his new description from the hotel—from witness statements and the lobby cameras. He caught a bus—and they have him on that camera, too. And from where he got off and when, they believe he stole a car from a Walmart parking lot. They have the make and model of the car, the plates. He used the ID he had when I met him to buy gas. They found the car in long-term parking at the airport in Omaha, Nebraska. That's where they are now."

"He's running."

"That's what they said, yes. They're canvassing hotels, motels, car rentals, stolen car reports in Omaha. He didn't go into the airport. They seem sure of that. He may have stolen another car from that same lot. They're not sure yet."

She hadn't just dented Rozwell's shield, Miles thought. She'd obliterated it. And that worried him.

"He lost his tools, his equipment."

"He was carrying a laptop bag when he left the hotel," Morgan told him. "He has something, but since he used the Luke Hudson Visa card for gas, they think he doesn't have any ID on him that isn't compromised. For now."

"He'd need supplies to make more, and a place to hide while he does. He's in or around Omaha, Morgan, and you're not."

"I know. And I know they're frustrated. I could hear the frustration in Agent Beck's voice even though she's good at sounding very matter-of-fact. Frustration that they were so close, minutes really. And excitement that they were that close.

"So . . . that's where we are."

"He screwed up, and he has to know it."

He may have felt frustration, but all Morgan heard in his voice was satisfaction. "For someone who knows so much about tech, he didn't remember to disengage the tracking system. He used the blown ID for gas when he should've risked going in, paying cash for it. It would've taken them longer to track him that way."

She hadn't thought of that. Everything happened so fast. "Maybe."

"Pretty likely. Some little pump-and-go off the highway. Then the long-term parking—he's used that ploy before, hasn't he? Better if he'd changed the plates and driven the stolen car off the road somewhere."

"Yes. I . . . Yes." The sheer coolheaded logic of it calmed her nerves. "It wasn't smart. He wasn't smart."

"He's headed into sparsely populated areas, why not use that to his advantage? Instead, he goes to a population center. Or take the car in for a cheap paint job, get more miles out of it before ditching it. Check the ads, buy a junker direct from the owner for cash, and get more miles."

Frowning, she turned to him. "If I'm ever on the run from the law, I want you with me. What would you do next?"

He answered without hesitation. "Change my pattern. Cheap, off-brand motel where nobody gives a shit. Get the supplies I need to change my appearance again and generate a couple of fresh IDs. He has to have access to his money."

Thinking out loud and wanting to distract her, he walked with her around the yard. "Time for a population center where I'd open accounts in at least two different banks so I could have some funds wired in. Ditch the junker, buy a new car through my new bank accounts. Then I'd continue breaking pattern by finding a scenic and remote area, renting a house or cabin. I'd settle in so I could think about the multitude of ways I'd screwed up."

He glanced back, saw Clark installing the camera on the back door.

"After enough time had passed," Miles continued, "I'd book a private plane and fly to . . . maybe the Canary Islands, and settle in for a nice, long vacation."

"The Canary Islands?"

"For instance. A lot of miles between here and there. But he's not going to do all of that."

"No, he's not. But why do you say that?"

"The evidence is pretty clear he can't admit mistakes. If he realizes they tracked the car from South Carolina, it's not his fault. It'll be the guy who took the car in trade who's to blame. Whoever he stole the next car from—their fault it wasn't filled up with gas so he had to use the old ID."

"And my fault most of all because I'm alive."

"That's right." He took her by the shoulders, turned her so she could see the installation. "So this is happening. He's also not going to do all that because the pattern is who he is. He needs the pattern. He may change it briefly, but only because someone else is to blame. But he'll go back to it. He hasn't got the guts to uproot his life and plant it somewhere else, in some other way."

"What you're not saying is because of that, because of who he is, he'll have to come here."

"I don't have to say what you already know. But the odds have shot up, Morgan, way up, they'll find him first."

"Do you really believe that? I'd rather have hard truth than a gentle lie."

"I do. With everything you've just told me, I do believe that. He's running, he's panicked, and he's fucking up. You're not doing any of that. And he's alone." The hands on her shoulders ran down her arms, up again. "You're not alone."

"But I have to learn to live with having cameras on the doors."

"Millions do, apparently, and like it."

"They'll help keep my ladies safe when I'm not here at night." She looked up at him. "But it was pushy."

"Right. And your point?"

She only sighed, then tipped her head toward his shoulder. "I guess he'd better show me how it all works so I can show the ladies. But I'm not saying thank you, at least not yet."

"I don't care. Just like I don't care you're going to balk when I say you're going to start texting me when you get home after closing."

"Oh, for—"

"One quick text—'I'm home,' 'All clear,' 'Fuck off'—sent after you're inside and locked up."

"You do know what time I get home."

"I'm aware."

Because she couldn't help herself, she reached out to stroke his cheek. "I'm just going to wake you up."

"That would be my problem. I'm only asking you to text a couple words. Don't make me pull out my mother's rarely used but highly effective guilt power."

He knew he had her when he saw amusement rather than annoyance in her eyes. "What's the power?"

"You asked for it." He adopted a long-suffering tone twined with glittering affection. "I just can't understand why you'd want me to worry this way. It's not like you to be so selfish. It's such a little thing to ask, and would do so much to relieve my mind."

"Oh, that's . . . that's masterful."

"She doesn't use it often. Doesn't need to," he added with a hint of aggravation, "as the aftereffects can last for years. Possibly decades. Just a quick text, Morgan, after you're safe inside."

No, no one had ordered her around before. And no one but her family, her ladies, had ever worried about her like this.

"A remote version of you watching until I drive out of sight or go into the house. Okay, fine, but don't blame me for messing up your sleep cycle."

"Let's go get that tutorial. He claims there's nothing to it."

"I'm not going to thank you for the camera and doorbell thing, but." Taking his face in her hands, she kissed him. "I'm glad you came by so soon after I got the call about Rozwell. I'm grateful I had you to talk it through with, and appreciate you rearranged things at work so I could. So I'll say thanks for that."

"I told you, you matter. Now let's go find out how this damn thing works, since I'm getting stuck with one, too."

She took his hands again. "I like that part."

"Can't blame you."

When he left her, Miles called his office and rescheduled something else. He'd work late, make up the time. Unlike a psychopath, he could change patterns and habits when necessary.

So he drove back into town and to the police station.

He considered himself lucky to find Jake in his own office, coffee at his elbow as he scowled at his computer screen.

"Thank Christ! A distraction. Paperwork, the root of all evil. Close the door." He waved at it. "I'm taking five. Who let you out of the cage at this time of day?"

"My door's always open." Even knowing it would taste like overheated tar, Miles helped himself from Jake's coffeepot. "Have you heard from the feds today?"

Jake propped his feet, clad in his usual black Converse low-tops, on his desk. "Why would you ask?"

"Because I just got an update from Morgan."

"I haven't gotten any new information since Morrison let me know they missed him in Kansas City, but found a nice treasure trove in his hotel room. Fucker's luck's got to change, but from the look on your face, I'd say it hasn't changed enough for them to have bagged him."

"Not yet."

While Miles filled him in, Jake sat back, sipped his coffee. Someone who didn't know him well might've thought he was drifting off. Miles knew him and very well.

"He's not only running, he's leaving a trail. He's breaking down. He's not used to things going south on him, and in a lot of ways they've headed there since he missed Morgan."

Not just the same page, Miles thought, but the same paragraph. An advantage of knowing someone a lifetime.

"Do you think he'll keep running?"

"For a while. He needs to find a hole he can live in, and with, and replace some of what he lost. He needs all that not only to continue what he sees as his work, but to regain his confidence. How can you feel superior when you lost some of the tools that help you feel superior? He's got to be scared, and he's got to be pissed."

"And?"

"If you piss off a rabid dog, Miles, that dog's bound to go for your throat. Still, there's a human brain in this rabid dog, so he's going to do whatever he needs to do to protect himself before he goes for her throat."

Jake drank more coffee. "You don't have to ask. We'll keep patrolling by the house, and I'll add to that."

"I had Clark install one of those home surveillance systems—that you can check on your phone. He's putting one on my place now, since she stays there sometimes."

Jake let out a snort. "Miles Jameson's putting one of those smart and fancy security systems on the old homestead? Son, you've got it bad."

"I've got what I've got. Plus, it's temporary."

"Morgan or the system?"

Miles started to speak, then settled for a shrug.

"Well, I gotta say, I never figured you'd settle in on anyone like that high-end brunette. The blonde now, yeah, she's right up your alley."

"I don't have an alley."

"Pal, we've both got alleys. She's a looker, no doubt, but that runs second or third in your personal alley. She's fucking resilient, and that lives in your alley along with smart, responsible, and rooted."

And, Miles realized, the disadvantage of having someone know you for a lifetime.

"She hasn't had a chance to root."

"Wants to, though, doesn't she? That's easy enough to see. I like her, but even if I didn't, I'd make sure we do our best to keep her safe."

"I know it." Counted on it. "I've got to get to work."

"Me, too. But before that, I should tell you, since I live in the friendship lane of your alley."

"Alleys have lanes?"

"Ours do. So I'm telling you, I talked your sister into having dinner with me."

Miles had started to stand, and now sat back. "What?"

"It took some doing, but we had dinner last night, and having worked a chink in that wall, I convinced her to go kayaking next Sunday. None of that should be a big surprise to you, seeing as I told you when we were—what, ten, eleven?—how I was going to marry your sister."

"You also told me you were going to climb Mount Everest and pitch for the Red Sox."

"Well, some dreams fade with time, some don't. Or, in this case, some fade for a while, then come back in strong, bold colors."

"I don't want to think about this," Miles decided. "I don't want to think about Nell being right up your alley, or the two of you in strong, bold colors. It's . . . disturbing."

Jake only grinned. "I've been your best friend for twenty years or so. If you can't trust me with Nell, then who?"

"You don't have a sister."

"That's true."

"So I'm not going to think about it." Now he stood. "Except to say . . . she's got soft spots. They may not show, but they're there."

"Miles, I've known Nell for twenty years, too. I know who she is. I'm going to tell you, the unvarnished truth is she's a hell of a lot more likely to hurt me than I am her, as she's been my soft spot off and on since I was ten."

"Either way I end up pissed off at one of you." Shaking his head, Miles walked to the door, then stopped. "You and Nell haven't—"

When he broke off, Jake smiled again, lifted an eyebrow.

"No, no, forget I nearly asked. I don't want to know."

He drove back to the resort, intended to go straight to his office, then walked into Nell's.

"Miles, great. I was just finalizing some of the changes for next week's picnic, and—"

"Why didn't you tell me you and Jake were dating?"

Nell angled her head. She looped one of the trio of chains she wore around a finger, smiled at him. "Because that comes under the heading of—what is it now? Oh yeah. None of Your Damn Business."

"You're my sister, he's my oldest, closest friend. That sounds like it falls right into my damn business."

She picked up the bright blue resort water bottle from her desk. "Miles, you're not seriously going to attempt to dictate who I date?"

"No, but this is different."

"In what way?"

"Sister." He lifted one hand. "Best friend." Then the other. "And you know Jake's had half a thing for you for years."

"One he's contained admirably, or annoyingly, depending on the viewpoint. Either way, we had dinner and enjoyed ourselves. Alert the media."

"Knock it off. You're going kayaking on Sunday."

Eyes slitted, she slammed the water bottle down again. "Does he tell you everything?"

"No. And I don't want to know everything. But there's a goddamn code, Nell. A friend's dating your sister, he lets you know. It would've been nice if my sister let me know she was dating my friend."

"He's my friend, too, and it was *dinner*. Just dinner. If I decide it's going to be more, that's my choice and my business. So butt out."

Now he sat. "I had one date—one—with that . . . I can't remember her name. That girl who was part of your high school pack."

"Candy."

"Yeah, and the name should've put me off. But anyway, one date and you snarled at me for weeks."

"I've matured. How about you?"

"I love you."

"Back at you, moron."

"I love Jake."

"Jesus, Miles, I'm not going to drag him into bed, use him up, then toss him away. Or vice versa. You should know both of us better."

"Don't talk about bed."

Temper dissolved into amusement. "I'm going to sleep with him. There may or may not be a bed involved."

"Please shut up."

"If," she added, "we decide to have another date or two, and if we're both of that frame of mind. Meanwhile, I've gotten to be friends—outside of work—with Morgan. It's hard for me to find—or make—time to have friends outside of work and family. But we've had lunch, and we had drinks. You could almost say we're dating."

Now he just covered his face with his hands, scrubbed hard.

"You're sleeping with her. Should I be worried?"

"Nell—"

"Miles," she said in the same overly patient tone. "You and I don't take or make relationships lightly. And though it falls in that same category—None of Your Damn Business—I'll tell you I've had half a thing for Jake for a while."

"Well, hell. You never said."

"Remember the heading," she shot back. "I'm also going to say that seeing what Morgan's been through, how she's dealt with it, brought it home to me how quick life and plans can change. If Jake hadn't asked me out, I'd have asked him. I want to see where it goes. You'll just have to live with that."

"I'm going back to not thinking about it."

"That would be very wise."

"Morgan." He got up to grab a Coke out of her cooler. "I was just over there."

"Notice me not asking you what you were doing over there in the middle of a workday."

"I'm having one of those camera systems installed on the house."

"Ah." She considered, nodded. "That's a very good idea."

"She doesn't like it, but she'll deal with it. She'd just gotten an update on Rozwell right before I got there. I'm going to give you the highlights, then I have to get going. I'm way behind today. You could fill in the rest of the family."

"All right."

She took notes while he told her.

"I'm meeting with Mom in . . . shit, five minutes. I'll tell her. Look, let's grab dinner later, talk this through. You told Jake."

"Yeah, which is how . . . all the rest. I'm late."

"Me, too." They rose together.

"Hey." Anger forgotten, she crossed over to hug him. "Don't worry too much. The more I get to know her, the more I realize how self-reliant she is. Then add she has us, the FBI, and the local police on her side."

"A rabid dog with a human brain. That's what Jake called him."

"That sounds accurate."

And something, Miles thought, to worry about.

Chapter Twenty-three

Every time Morgan thought she'd found the sweet spot in her workout routine, Jen devised some new form of torture.

Today's pyramid of dead lifts, kickbacks, military presses, and biceps curls in the goddess position ranked as the worst yet.

She sweated her way to the top of the pyramid, indulged her inner camel in a thirty-second—all Jen allowed—water break, then did her best not to weep her way down again.

Getting strong, she lectured herself. Getting strong enough to punch Rozwell in the throat. And after the last vicious rep, she set down the weights.

But did it end there? No, it did not.

She suffered through twelve agonizing minutes of core with crunches, bicycles, the detested inchworm, and more until her abs burned along with the rest of her.

Breathless, limp, done, she lay on the mat, eyes closed. "When will I stop hating it?"

Helpfully, Jen tossed her a gym towel. "Why are you doing it?"

Behind her lids, Morgan's eyes rolled. "To get strong, be strong, stay strong."

"And it's working. You've doubled your weights and reps since you started. Packing some nice guns these days."

Morgan turned her head, opened one eye. With it she studied her arms. "Sort of."

"Very nice guns for your frame and body type. Now hydrate and stretch." Smiling, Jen held out a hand. "Body by Jen. I'm liking what I see here."

Morgan clasped hands, groaned her way to her feet. "This body by Jen feels like it's been pounded with a thousand tiny hammers."

"Hydrate and stretch," Jen repeated, "and it won't. You've come a long way. Keep it up. Hey, Nell."

"Jen. I've got a free hour."

"And the world shudders on its axis."

"I know, right?" In her black shorts and tank, Nell grabbed a pair of fifteen-pound weights. "I'm squeezing in some fun."

She took her stance, started with a swimmer's press, and sent Morgan a look. "You look like you've finished the fun."

"I'm done. Done in. She's a monster."

"I wear the badge with pride. Stretch," Jen said again, her beaded braids swaying as she walked away to find another victim.

Morgan started her stretches and scowled at Nell in the mirror wall. "Show-off."

"A badge *I* wear with pride. I was hoping to run into you before your shift. Mom just told me the Friedman event, that's Sunday, wants another bar."

"They already have two."

"And now they want three. One for mixed drinks, and instead of the second for wine, beer, and soft drinks, they want to split that. One soft bar, one wine and beer bar."

"I'll ask Bailey to take it."

Smoothly, Nell switched to Crazy Eights. "Is she ready?"

"More than for a wine and beer bar. It's a good way for her to solo at an event. I'll let you know. If she can't take it, I'll see if Nick wants it, or can switch shifts with me and I'll take it. Becs has her Friday night art class, and I wouldn't ask her to miss it unless we're stuck. Tricia's on vacation until Saturday."

"I'll leave it to you. How are you?"

With her hands clasped behind her back, Morgan drew them down and let out a sound that signaled relief. "I think my bones are burning."

"Keep stretching, and that's not what I meant."

"I haven't heard anything for a couple of days. The last I did, they found the car he stole when he dumped the first one at the airport in Omaha. He ditched that—he'd switched the plates—at a truck stop in South Dakota. They think he might've gotten a ride from there, heading west, as they had a possible sighting in Wyoming they were going to follow up on."

"So he's still running, and in the opposite direction from here. That's a good thing."

"I'm trying to think of it that way."

"I'd try that, too. I don't know if I'd succeed." Switching to twelve pounders, Nell started triceps extensions. "How's the new security system working out?"

"The ladies love it. Go figure." As she stretched her own triceps, Morgan had to admit—as usual—the burn had turned to warmth, and her fatigue to smugness. "They baked Miles a damn cherry pie."

"I love cherry pie. He did not share. It was intrusive of him, Morgan. Miles doesn't intrude unless his feelings outweigh his pretty rigid sense of stay-out-of-it."

"I get that. And along that line, how are you doing with your triangle?"

"I have a triangle?"

"You, Jake, Miles."

With a laugh, Nell set down the lighter weights. "I'm doing my best to enjoy one, ignore the other. *And* along that line, why don't we all go out to dinner, make it a foursome? Maybe next Sunday night when you're off."

"Oh." After rolling her shoulders, Morgan lowered into a runner's stretch. When Nell picked up the heavier weight again for another set of shoulder presses, Morgan wondered how Nell could lift steady without breaking a sweat. "Wouldn't that be a little awkward?"

"I don't think so. I think it would be good for Miles to see me and Jake as a couple."

"Are you?"

"I think we're cautiously approaching that destination. I can set it up, keep it casual."

"Have Miles grill," Morgan suggested. "He likes to, and it's not only casual, it fits the dynamics. Friends and family."

"That's brilliant. I should've thought of it."

"Maybe ask Liam to join with a date. That turns the triangle into a hexagon. I think."

"Really brilliant. I'll set it up."

"Let me know. Now I'm done with this hellhole for another day. Listen, when you have time, drop by Après. I have a couple of candidates for the fall specials to run by you."

"I'll do that. Keep the ideas coming, Morgan."

"I've got an endless supply."

She headed out, deeply considered the elevator rather than the steps. And weighing guilt against convenience, turned toward the steps.

Miles came down them.

"Is Nell in the fitness center?"

"Showing off with her fifteen-pound weights."

"Good. I need to go over something with her, and she'd have blown me off if I texted while she's lifting." He angled his head, studied her with those amber eyes. "You look good."

"Are you serious?"

"Almost always. You're kind of rosy and dewy."

"It's called sweat."

"It looks good on you."

To her complete surprise, he moved in, cupped her chin, and kissed her. A long and serious kiss.

"Really good. I need to catch Nell."

He strode off, leaving her standing at the base of the stairs, holding her gym bag. And within the eyeline of the spa check-in staff, who pretended not to notice.

Morgan spent most of Friday afternoon working in the garden with her ladies. A brief storm the night before had the weeds pulling up like butter—and reminded her how the blasts of thunder had waked her in Miles's bed.

And how the two of them had rolled together like that thunder even after the storm passed. She glanced over, watching her mother deadhead roses. How she hummed to herself as she worked, how content she seemed.

As if those years of uprooting, moving, searching had all come together here. This time, this place.

Swiping sweat from her forehead, Morgan sat back on her heels. "How does it feel to be Audrey Nash again?"

"Just right. I guess Albright never really fit me—or I didn't fit Albright. Who knew it could be so easy to take back what was mine all along?"

Now she glanced over. "You did. How does it feel to be Morgan Nash?"

"Like I've closed an old door and opened a new one. I didn't expect that, not really. Like I didn't expect to be happy here."

"Oh, Morgan."

"I came because I had to, and that first night, Mom, everything in me felt so dark and hopeless, sort of frozen in place, just like the winter. Now, moving toward the end of summer, it's the opposite. I'm heading toward thirty and living in my grandmother's house, but I feel light and hope and movement. These past months have shown me who you are, who Gram is, and who I am. I like who we are, we Nash women."

"So do I."

"Time for a break," Olivia called out as she carried a pitcher of sun tea to the patio table. "That sun's fierce, and no complaints, because winter's long and cold. But it's fierce. Time for a break."

"I hear that."

Morgan started over while Olivia set her hands on her hips. "I don't think this yard has ever looked better. The things you added, Morgan, brighten up the bright. I'm going to take time to sit and enjoy it while it lasts."

Audrey sat, pulled off her hat, and fanned herself with it. "No complaints, but whew! We're due for another storm tonight, and this one might cool things off a bit."

Morgan thought of storms, and Miles, and smiled as she poured tea.

"I like a good storm. I wouldn't mind it cooling off a little. Miles said to bring my hiking boots tonight."

"You haven't really taken the time to hike. You always liked going with Pa." Audrey took the glass of tea, rubbed its cold surface over her cheek before drinking. "I'm glad you're doing something fun, something that isn't work—even gardening's work."

"I have a suspicion Morgan and Miles find something to do that's not work. And," Olivia added, "I bet it's not a frisky game of gin rummy."

"Besides that," Audrey said with a laugh. "It's important to have shared interests when you're with someone. Besides that," she said again before Olivia could speak.

"I made a mistake there. You and Dad didn't. You shared so many things. The Colonel and I, well, we just didn't. Morgan and Miles share interests. Gardening, the resort, they both like dogs, and now hiking. And you're having your first dinner party as a couple on Sunday."

"I don't know if I'd call it a dinner party."

"It's dinner, and you'll have fun."

"I feel like I'm deserting both of you, spending so much of my weekends over at his house."

"Don't be silly." Olivia waved that away. "Your mother and I like knowing you're with a good man. And you need to spend time with people your own age. Make friends. Friends are part of the roots, too, baby, and keep what grows happy and healthy."

"Mom and I have our monthly book club, yoga classes, the shop, now the café. It's fun to grab lunch with a girlfriend. We both make time for that."

"And tomorrow afternoon we're heading over to Tom and Ida's potluck cookout. Where we'll eat too much and gossip the day away." Olivia sighed with pleasure. "We're not old fogies yet who need looking after."

"And we have the magic doorbell. I love that thing."

Shaking her head, Morgan glanced at the back door camera. "I know. I don't understand it, but I know you do."

Spreading her hands, Audrey smiled at Morgan. "I got an alert last week and watched FedEx deliver a package to the front door. It's like a secret window."

"The sun's fierce, the gardens are beautiful, that damn frog makes me smile every time I look at it, and we're all going to get our party on. That's a good deal, girls. Let's embrace it."

Morgan promised herself to do just that. Embrace it.

On a busy Friday night at Après, she enjoyed the work, the crowd, and looked forward to a Saturday hike, a Sunday gathering.

"We're going to switch, Bailey."

"Sorry, what?"

"I'll take the backbar."

"Oh, but—"

"I'm right here if you need help, but let's see how it goes for an hour."

"Are you sure?"

"I wouldn't say so if I weren't." Morgan nudged her forward, stepped back. "You've got the stick."

And she did fine, just fine, so Morgan let the hour run to ninety minutes.

"That's the way it's done."

"I forgot to be nervous."

"You've only got a few weeks left before you go back to school, so let's have you do two hours for your next shift with me. Now take a break. You earned it."

Satisfying, she thought as she filled orders. Satisfying to teach somebody how to do a job, and do it well. Not for a career, not in Bailey's case, but to earn a solid paycheck until she forged that career.

"You let her handle it." Opal stopped by the bar. "You got out of her way and let her handle it. When I'm wrong about somebody or something, I say so right out loud. I had you wrong."

"There might've been some of that on both sides."

"Yeah, might've been. Two summer specials, fizzy water on ice, double Bombay tonic."

"Coming right up."

"I've got a nephew just turned twenty-one. He's working in the Lodge kitchen the last six, seven months. Doesn't much like it, but he works. If he wanted to train at the bar, would you take him on?"

"If Nell approves the change, I'll take him on."

"Good."

She didn't expect to see Miles until she got to his house, but he walked in at closing.

"Worked late."

"I'll say."

"We'll get your bag out of your car. You can ride with me."

"Then my car's here where I'm not."

"We'll get it tomorrow. You've got your hiking boots?"

"As requested." She shut off the lights on what she considered an excellent shift. "I got a call from a friend today," she told him as they walked out.

"Oh."

"Sam. He and Nina . . . they'd gotten serious. He loved her, was on the brink of asking her to move in with him when it all happened."

She stopped at her car, took out her bag.

"You've kept in touch?"

"Yeah, and he has dinner with Nina's family at least once a month. He wanted me to know he's met someone."

In his car, he waited until she'd strapped in. "Is that a problem for you?"

"No. God, no. He's been seeing her for a couple of months now, and it's, well, gotten serious. So he wanted me to know. He's a really good guy, Miles. I'm happy for him. It's been nearly a year and a half—that hit me. It feels longer in some ways, then in others like yesterday. Her name's Henna. She's a paralegal. She has a cat named Suzie she spoils, likes old movies—like, really old black-and-white movies—and reading thrillers."

"A lot of information," Miles commented.

"Once he got my initial reaction he really went on and on about her. So I'm happy for him. Oh, she also skis, so he's going to bring her up here next winter, stay at the resort, introduce us. God, I hope I like her. I'll fake it if I don't, but I hope I do."

"You're predisposed to like her, so unless she's not anything like what he told you, you'll like her. Any problems tonight?"

"The opposite of problems." How she loved these late-night drives through the quiet dark while the world slept. The air blowing in the open windows, an owl calling somewhere deep in the trees.

"A busy summer Friday night," she continued. "I took the backbar with Bailey for about an hour and a half, and she handled it. Oh, and I had my first repeater—I mean for me. This couple who stayed at the resort last March, back for a week with their son, his wife, and their two grandkids."

"You remembered them?"

"Their faces. I blanked on the names, but I got the faces, so enough to say welcome back. And since they charged the drinks to the room, I could look up the names. James—Jim—and Tracey Lowe."

"They've been coming twice a year since their son—that's Manning—was in college. Manning met his wife, Gwen, at the resort on one of their summer trips. They got married here—sentimental. Their kids are Flynn—must be around six—and Haley, about four."

As he pulled into the drive, she shook her head. "And I think I bank data. I got some of that when they came in for their nightcap."

"The resort runs on loyalty and personalized service. The Lowes have been twice-a-year guests since I was in high school."

As they walked to the door, Howl let out a trio of barks followed by his signature howl.

"Better than an alarm system, cameras included."

"The offer to take him's still open."

When Miles opened the door, the dog stood, dancing in place, then rushed to Morgan.

"Did you miss me, did you? Yes, you did!" While she lavished Howl with love, Miles locked up for the night.

"Do you want anything?"

"Just this sweet dog." And, tilting her head, gave Miles a sidelong look. "Maybe you."

"The dog's got his own bed." So saying, he scooped her up, tossed her over his shoulder.

It made her laugh as Howl muttered and dashed for the steps in front of Miles. "Well, this is new."

322 ◆ NORA ROBERTS

"Just getting you off your feet after a long shift."

"Is that it? Most men would've gone for the romantic sweep instead of the over-the-shoulder."

"I'm not most."

"So I've noticed. You know, your house looks good even upside down."

He carted her to the bedroom, where the light came from cloud-misted stars and a three-quarter moon. And dumped her on the bed, covered her with his body.

"How do you like it now?"

"I've grown fond of this particular view."

As she studied him and he studied her, she ran her hands down his back, then up again.

"I like mine better." Eyes still on hers, he brushed her mouth with the lightest kiss. "You've got a face."

"I definitely have a face."

"It's a damn good face." Now his mouth brushed hers, lingered a little longer. "I thought so the first time I saw it."

"Behind the bar."

"No, the first time. At your grandfather's memorial."

"Oh. I don't think I saw you. Honestly, I'm not sure I saw anyone. It's one big blur."

"Everything showed on that face. The grief, the guilt, the wish you could go somewhere else, anywhere else, alone and deal with it. And I remember I wondered if I saw that because I felt exactly the same."

He kissed her again, just a little deeper, just a little longer.

"The next time I saw that face, and that was behind the bar, I saw something else. Something under the friendly, efficient bartender."

He switched to the pulse in her throat, pleased to feel it start to race. "I saw grit mixed with vulnerability. Just fascinating, that face. I like seeing it when I've got my hands on you."

"I want your hands on me."

He closed his over hers and used his mouth, just his mouth, to arouse.

"They'll get there."

He released one hand to flip open the buttons of her shirt, then slowly followed that gap down with his mouth, then roamed up again.

This time the kiss spun out and out and out until he felt her go lax.

He hadn't taken enough time with her, he thought, not with the late nights, early mornings. Now he would.

He flipped open the front hook on her bra, the deeply cut white lace he knew she wore for him. And trailed his fingers over her, light, light, light, while his tongue skimmed over hers, while her hum of pleasure spilled into him.

And he looked as he took that time with the crisp uniform, the black and the white in disarray. With her skin trembling under his mouth and hands, aroused.

As he eased her zipper down, his mouth took her breast, but gently, gently. No rush, no hurry as his fingers slid down to tease, only to tease even as she arched up against them, even as the hum in her throat became broken sighs.

As he traveled down her, sliding those trim pants over her hips, pressing his lips to her belly, he found it unspeakably erotic to be fully dressed while he peeled those layers away from a body that shuddered with need under him.

He took her up, watching her—that face—as he met those needs. She quaked under him, shuddering, just as the first flash of lightning turned the room white, and on one of her broken sighs came his name.

Thunder followed after.

He took her over; she let him. And with surrender she found power. She could take what he gave her until the pleasure of it shook through her like the sudden gusts of wind at the windows.

Her body felt as liquid as the rain, as if she could pour through his hands if he willed it. Under those hands she rose up where the world ran hot and the air thick, then floated down to the impossibly soft and warm.

When he levered up to drag off his shirt, she pressed her hands to the hard, strong wall of his chest. There, though he took his time, such exquisite time, his heart raced.

"That face," he murmured, and it moved her to hear his voice breathless. "I like how it looks when I'm inside you."

"I want you inside me."

Lightning flashed again, illuminating her as she reached for him.

He covered her, and he watched her as he slid, slowly, inside her. And held there as she flew up again, as she tightened around him.

"Miles."

"Easy." He murmured it as he took that exquisite time.

While the storm raged, he gave her that time, to build again, to break again.

Then he took her hands in his, took her mouth with his, so linked, joined, they broke together.

He lay over her, more content than he could remember being in the whole of his life. The storm, already passing, tossed the last drops of rain at the windows. Where lightning had flashed, moonlight returned.

From the library, the clock that had been his great-grandfather's struck three.

He lifted his head to look down at her, and yes, saw contentment there.

"That face," he said again, and watched her lips curve.

Chapter Twenty-four

She slept like a rock and woke to the scent of coffee.

"Time to get your ass up."

After blinking her eyes open, she stared at Miles. He stood beside the bed, fully dressed.

"What time is it?"

"Get-your-ass-up o'clock." Taking her hand, he pulled her up to sitting.

"Why do women do that?" he wondered, when she dragged the sheet up with her. "I've seen you naked. I've seen your breasts, which, I've observed, are very nicely proportioned to the rest of you."

"Because," she said, and left it at that. Then she saw the mug on the nightstand. "You brought me coffee!"

"I brought you something pretending to be coffee. Knock it back, get up. You've got thirty minutes."

"How long have you been up?"

"Long enough to grab a shower, drink actual coffee, get dressed, and make whatever it is you drink in the morning."

"Okay, I can do all that in thirty, no problem. And I appreciate you bringing me coffee even if you don't respect it. Where's Howl?"

"He's out on patrol. Thirty minutes," he said as he walked to the door. "I have to make a couple calls."

In thirty, because she considered it a challenge, she walked downstairs. She wore her hiking shorts and boots, a blue T-shirt, and a red ball cap. She'd hitched on a light backpack holding bug spray, a water bottle, a traveling first aid kit, a bag of trail mix, along with what she considered other essentials.

She found him in the kitchen, downing another cup of coffee.

"All set?"

He turned, looked at her. "What is it about women in boots and shorts? Sunscreen, bug juice?"

"Covered and coated—with more in my pack." She went into the mudroom for the leash. "We are taking Howl."

"Yeah, he's expecting it."

After Miles shrugged on his own pack, they went out the back. And when the dog spotted the leash, he sat where he was, looked deliberately away.

"He considers the leash insulting."

"Of course he does. As if you wouldn't be a good boy," she crooned as she went to him. "The very best boy. But we can't take you on the adventure without it."

He suffered the indignity.

"We'll take the car."

"Oh, I figured we'd hike the trail about a half mile from here."

Since she had the dog, Miles grabbed her free hand. "The Birch Trail's a good loop, and when we're done, we can pick up your car."

"Works for me. I'm bound to be rusty," she said as they piled into the car. "I haven't been on a serious hike in a couple years. Time to get back in gear there so I can hike in the fall when the leaves change— and that won't be long. I've never been here in the fall."

"Tourists jam the place."

"Which is good for the resort, and the town."

"Yeah, but the trails get crowded. We'll have some company today, summer brings them, too. But not like September and October."

"I'm looking forward to it. Not summer ending, but seeing the fall."

After he parked next to her car, she got out, shouldered her pack again before getting Howl out of the back.

"It's a five-mile loop," Miles told her, "but there's a cutoff to shorten it to three."

"I can handle five." Another challenge.

"We'll add to that walking down to the ropes course, zip line. The trailhead's right there."

"I rented a bike in the spring, a couple times, so I could tour the resort that way, get a better sense of the layout. I really thought about buying one, but it's just too far to bike to work, and too late to risk biking home."

"You don't have to get a bike just for transportation."

"No, guess not." But she couldn't justify just-because expenses. Not yet.

"Anyway, the way things are laid out? The walking trail around the lake, the hiking trails—at least the ones I've seen signposted. Then the zip lines, climbing wall, the cute little playground area. It all makes sense. I stopped in the Adventure Outlet, obviously, for the bike. Also smart to make it so easy to buy or rent gear, and right within sight of the ski lifts and runs. Then there's the lake."

She stopped to look out at the blue water dotted with kayaks and canoes. The mountains, green as their name, reflected on it. "I've never kayaked. I guess you have."

"Sure. We'll squeeze it in some weekend."

"It's something, to have all this at your fingertips really."

"My great-grandparents bought the land and built the first lodge, the first couple cabins, because of the lake and that view."

"You're lucky they had that foresight. And what your family's done with it. Building on it, yeah, but with respect. When I biked through, I'd spot a cabin, but it looked like it grew there."

Howl, forgetting the insult of the leash, strolled and sniffed his way along the walking trail.

"Word is you're going to transition to electric shuttles."

"Yeah, by the fall peak. We're putting in more charging stations."

"Also smart."

They came in sight of the ropes course, tucked in the trees. Morgan shook her head at the guests climbing, balancing, swinging high above her head.

"I can see doing that," she said as Miles steered her to the trailhead, "when the zombie apocalypse hits, or the inevitable invasion by aliens hell-bent on exterminating the human race. It might be necessary to build rope bridges and walls, learn to balance on swinging tires and wood planks. But until then?"

She shifted her pack. "I'll stick with hiking trails for my adventuring. And this is why," she added, as they started the climb through the birch trail that gave the trail its name.

"It's beautiful, already beautiful."

"It gets better. Let me know when you're tired of handling the leash."

"We're fine. I'm going to take a million pictures, so be prepared for it. Like now. Oh, I remember this. Wild lupine." When she crouched down to frame the spears of purple, Howl licked her cheek.

Miles waited, patient enough, each time she stopped to capture some spotted joe-pye weed, or whatever she found interesting in the bark on birches, old-growth maples.

They passed a group heading down, were passed by another couple heading up.

He liked her company, liked she didn't chatter endlessly, but could appreciate the quiet and the song of birds. He hadn't made enough time for this lately, he admitted, for just walking through the hills and forest he loved.

She stopped, held up a hand. "Wait, I hear . . . Is that a waterfall?"

"Around the next bend in the trail. It's small but scenic. Little White Falls. Resort property ends there, so we have the cutoff to loop back, or we can take the longer that runs through the national forest. It gets steeper."

"Definitely the longer, but I want to see the falls."

They tumbled down, dashing into the river below and foaming white against the weak-tea brown.

"It's beautiful. It's like music."

And it sparkled over the rock, beat water against water so the river showed its floor. Where the shade spread, moss-carpeted limbs turned the light soft. Yet the sun struck the tumbling water, bright as a laser.

The couple who'd passed them took a couple selfies, then turned to take the trail back down. A group of three rose from a low rock ledge, then continued on up the trail.

Miles took the leash so she could pull out her phone yet again. While she got her pictures, he pulled the collapsible cup out of his pack, poured water into it.

A grateful Howl lapped it up.

He glanced up in time to see her take their picture as he crouched down to offer the dog a second cup.

"Sorry, couldn't resist. I tossed an old plastic bowl in my pack. The cup's better."

She lifted her face to the sky. "This is the most perfect spot. I hate selfies," she said looking back at him.

"I'm with you on that."

"But it's a waterfall, and I'd like to make an exception to my no-selfie rule."

"Go ahead."

"It includes you. It's a waterfall, Miles, and the light's perfect. So please, just this once."

He should've known it would happen, just as he accepted refusing made him a jerk. He didn't mind being a jerk, but he'd mind more spoiling the moment.

He stepped over to her.

"Thank you." She held out the camera, turning it until she got the angle she wanted. "On three. Don't scowl."

"I'm not scowling."

To solve it, she turned her face just enough to press her lips to his cheek. When his lips curved, just a little, she took the picture.

"What happened to 'on three'?"

"That was better. Look." She brought the photo up. "We're adorable. And I'm going to do more of this." She pocketed the phone. "That's my solemn vow in front of the magic waterfall."

They continued up. It did get steeper, and Morgan supposed she had Jen's relentless workouts to thank for the fact she climbed without muscles twinging.

A group of teenage boys bounded by like antelopes, cackling like hyenas.

"It's all fun and games," Miles commented, "until somebody breaks an ankle."

"What were they, about sixteen? The age of indestructibility."

"Where were you at sixteen?"

"I honestly can't tell you. I used to keep a book to write down the place and the dates. After the divorce, we kept moving around so much, I kept writing it down. Then I tossed it—which was stupid—when I went to college.

"Done with that." She flicked her hand as if tossing something away. "But it was mostly a minor temper tantrum, and I regret it."

"Your mom probably knows if you ever want to put places and times together."

"Maybe, but . . ."

She went speechless when the world opened up. "Oh God! You didn't tell me."

"Makes a nice surprise. Not a half-bad view."

"It's *glorious*."

A world of mountains, valleys, hills, rivers spread out in vivid greens, tender blues, the sturdy gray of rock in jutted outcroppings. The soft peaks as they rolled on spoke of age and endurance.

I'm here, and have been long before, will be long after.

She could see the folds and cuts of land and water, the rise of trees, the climb of trails, all so clear under the wide bowl of sky. And like a gift, the white tumble of a distant waterfall.

A painting, she thought, unframed and open to anyone who stood at this spot.

She wondered how it looked when fog crept through and rose in mists to blur the hills. Or when the trees turned vivid in the fall, or the winter spread its bright, blanketing white.

Today it said summer, with life at its peak.

The silence was music.

"I have to do it again." She turned to him. "Sorry, but it's too perfect not to." She held up the camera. "It's your own fault. I don't even care if you scowl."

She slid an arm around his waist, angled the camera.

When she'd taken the shot, she pointed at Howl.

"Your turn. Sit down. Good dogs sit."

She crouched down to frame him in, with his eyes full of happy, head angled in anticipation.

That might've been the moment, Miles would think later, just the moment when he started to slip. Watching her convince the dog to pose—and damned if he didn't—with her absolute pleasure in the moment, in the place, in the quiet soaring like the hawks overhead.

The moment when she looked up at him, glowing, simply glowing while surrounded by the world that had always been his.

Then she stood, put her phone away, and took his hands. "Thanks. You couldn't have picked a better day, a better trail."

"That's a killer in the fall." He nodded toward the view.

"I bet, but right now, it's just so full of summer." Looking out again, she tipped her head to his shoulder. "Fall's bounty, winter's waiting, spring's beginning. But summer? It's fruition."

The silence broke as voices carried up the trail, so he moved on. Putting the moment aside, he walked with her and the dog.

"Now you've done it," she told him as the track wound downward. "I'm going to have to make a lot more time for this. Even an hour now and then on a day off. How do you feel about camping?"

"I feel humanity's progressed through work, innovation, necessity, and luck since they were cave dwellers or pioneers, and I respect their efforts, and value those efforts toward indoor plumbing, thermal windows, sturdy mattresses, and broadband. I don't see a reason to choose to ignore those innovations and sleep in a tent."

"That would be a no to camping. I'd say it's nice that I also have a healthy respect for progress and innovation. But I bet you know how, which would be handy in the event of that zombie apocalypse or alien invasion.

"And that's a bear," she said, stopping dead when one crossed the path about two yards down. "An actual bear."

"He's not interested in you." But Miles took the leash as Howl began to mutter and wag. "Brown bear, usually not aggressive. We're not taking another selfie with it."

"The thought never occurred. It's a bear. It's a really big bear."

But it lumbered its way into the trees.

"We'll give him a minute. You hiked with your grandfather a few times, right? You never crossed paths with a bear?"

"I did not. He told me what to do, what not to do if we did. I remember being disappointed we never saw one. Now I wonder why."

"We have some wander onto the resort now and then, especially around the cabins."

As they walked she looked toward the direction the bear had taken, but didn't see a sign of it.

"I'd probably be excited to see one—if I were sitting inside a cabin."

He shrugged. "They were here first."

It made her smile at him. "Dear Diary, today I saw a waterfall, stood and looked out over miles of mountains, and had a bear walk by."

"Do you do that? Keep a diary?"

"No. Who has time? But if I did, I'd add in the bear. I'm going to stop by the bakery after we pick up my car, get something for dessert for tomorrow."

"Nell's doing this cake thing she does."

"Nell bakes?"

"Sometimes. Plus, I'm grilling—you're doing the potato thing. She's not about to be outdone."

"I like that about her. The way she competes. It has to be challenging, being sandwiched between two brothers."

"Maybe it's challenging to be the oldest."

"Is it?"

"Not really. But it could be."

"It's not, because when it comes down to it, you're a team. There's one of your cabins. Look how it's all nestled in there, with rockers on the big front porch. I didn't realize we'd circled back so close to the resort."

"Nearly back where we started."

"I see that now."

They crossed the little bridge over the narrow stream, and the trail opened up to the ropes course.

She spotted Liam carting a couple of harnesses over to a bench.

"Good hike?" he called out as they crossed to him.

"It was wonderful. Waterfalls and vistas and bears. No takers this afternoon?" she asked as she scanned the empty course above.

"We're booked for a private run."

He held out a harness.

"What?" Nell clasped her hands behind her back. "No."

"Just the thing to cap off a hike."

"No, it's not. It's just the thing to make you squeal like a five-year-old or curl into a ball and whimper for your mommy."

"You're not afraid of heights." Miles picked up a harness, began to strap it on. "Not the way you stood up at the lookout."

"No, I'm not afraid of heights, but—"

"If you were, we'd skip this."

"I'm not afraid of heights, but I have a healthy respect for gravity."

"You won't fall. See this?" Liam held up the harness, showed her the carabiner on the belay system. "You clip this on, and it locks. It can't unlock until you physically unlock it. You'll always have at least one safety line attached at all times, even when you're standing on a platform."

"I question why I'd stand on a platform up there."

"It's fun!"

"If she's afraid . . ." Miles let than hang, started to remove his harness.

"'Afraid' is a strong word." And one she *knew* he'd used on purpose. "Wary. I prefer 'wary.'"

"What're you going to do when the zombies swarm?" Miles asked her.

"Die a horrible death, then spend the rest of my zombie existence eating brains. Damn it, this is an ambush." She grabbed the harness. "Show me how this thing works."

As he hooked it on her, Liam smiled into her eyes. "This'll hold easily three times your weight. We're both going to be up there with you, but first, I'm going to go over the basics right here on the ground."

"I like the ground."

Liam was thorough, and the basics didn't seem too complicated.

"What about Howl?"

Miles hooked his leash to the leg of the bench, set out water and a chew stick. "He's fine," he said, and handed her a safety helmet.

She wasn't that competitive, she thought, but found herself climbing to the first platform behind Liam with Miles behind her. On the platform, with Howl far below, Liam went over the belay and safety system again.

"The bridge will sway some as you step on those wood crosses, but you're hooked on."

"You go first."

"Sure. I'll wait on the next platform."

He might as well have walked across a solid stone bridge two feet above a lazy stream, Morgan thought as she watched him.

"You're fine," Miles said from behind her.

She spared him one dubious look, held her breath, stepped off the platform.

It swayed all right, but she kept her eyes on the second platform, even when Howl howled from below.

She didn't fall, and didn't end up dangling in humiliation.

"You did great! Want to go across first this time?"

"No, second's fine with me."

"Remember what to do?"

"Yeah, I've got the not-falling part down solid."

She watched Liam walk over vertical logs that seemed unnecessarily narrow and spaced unnecessarily wide, then glanced back to see Miles cross the bridge with the same ease as his brother.

Show-offs, she decided, and carefully unlocked her first carabiner, switched it to the next wire, gave it a nice testing tug before she did the second.

The logs swayed, too, but the idea of freezing halfway across kept her moving, kept her stretching a leg out to step from one to the next. The fact she swallowed a couple of squeals before they sounded boosted her confidence.

There were narrow wood swings that swayed, a rope net to traverse.

Liam let out a hoot of approval as she managed them. "You've got it! We could sign you up on crew!"

No, she thought as she made her careful way over a long vertical log, then what was, essentially, a tightrope. Definitely no to that.

She climbed a rope ladder, felt her abs sing as she swayed and balanced over the course of tires.

But the trapeze got her. She watched Liam grip it, swing like a circus act from perch to platform.

Her heart hammered; her muscles trembled. This was work! But she gripped the trapeze, sucked in her breath, and pushed off.

And it was like flying. For a second, maybe two, like flying with the air on her face, her body—as the song said—defying gravity.

When she landed on the last platform, her laugh rang out.

"That!" She threw her arms around Liam before she turned to where Miles waited on the trapeze perch behind. "Who knew?"

And that, he knew, was the moment. She stood, face flushed with the effort, with the sudden delight, her arms still around his brother.

Her smile could've lit the world.

He didn't slide out of affection into love, didn't slip from attraction into forever, but fell long and hard. No safety system could have stopped the fall.

It left him breathless, stunned, and a little bit pissed off.

So he'd think about it later, he told himself. Later, when he'd cleared his head and she wasn't right there distracting him.

When they'd started down, he swung over, then joined them on the ground.

"Fun, right?"

"More than I expected," she told Liam. "A lot more than."

"Wanna go again? There's time before the next group. I wasn't sure how long it would take you, but you're a natural."

"Once is enough. Absolutely."

"There's the zip line, the rock wall."

"Get out of here." Laughing, she gave him a shove. "Those are definite nos."

"Next time, zip line. It's such a rush and you can see for miles."

"You're a maniac. Your brother's a maniac," she said to Miles. "I'm going to free Howl."

"She's great," Liam began when she walked away, then shifted his feet. "Look, I wasn't hitting on her or anything."

"I know that. And let me add, as if she'd go for it."

"Well, you look a little pissed, so—"

"No, not that, and yeah, she did fine."

"I really like her. I mean, sure, in general, but for you. I like her for you."

"So do I." Miles unhooked his helmet while the dog greeted her as if she'd been to war. "And maybe that pisses me off a little."

Liam just slapped his shoulder. "You'll get over it. The pissed part, I mean."

"Maybe. Thanks for doing this. I figured she'd be more comfortable with you than one of the Adventure crew."

"It was fun." He took the harness from Miles. "She's gutsy. You gotta give her gutsy. Before we go over, any more on that asshole?"

"Nothing definite. They're still following leads out west. Maybe Oregon."

"Maybe he'll run out of room and take a dive into the Pacific."

"I could live with that, but it's better if they find the bastard. She's never going to be all the way steady until she knows he's locked up."

"He can't run forever, Miles. Nobody can."

No, Miles thought, but that was the problem. Sooner or later, Rozwell would stop running and try again.

At home, he lured her into the shower. Not just because he wanted her, and Christ knew he did. But with the hope the sex would clear his brain, return his balance.

It didn't.

When she went to work, he wandered around his house wondering how it was she filled so many spaces even when she wasn't there.

He went into his office, looked out of the turret view that had so captivated her. He sat, worked awhile. That filled spaces, too.

But he kept returning to those moments. The moment at the lookout when he'd felt that slip. Then the moment on the ropes, when he felt the fast fall.

And other moments, he admitted. The first time he'd seen her working behind the bar. That little click inside him he'd ignored. Watching her drive away in that rattletrap excuse for a car and wondering. Just wondering.

Seeing the way she worked out in the gym because she was determined to get strong enough to protect herself.

A lot of moments up to the one he'd stepped outside and seen her standing in his front yard with her tub of cookies.

"So what now?"

Beside his chair, Howl muttered his opinion.

"I don't need your advice. She's got you wrapped, or you've got her. Hell, I guess it's mutual."

He sat back, closed his eyes. "So that's just the way it is."

Absently, he laid a hand on Howl's head, and realized his little brother had it right. He'd pretty much gotten over the pissed part.

"She'll be home in a couple hours."

And that was the way it was, too, he realized. She'd be home, and he'd be waiting when she got there.

"You might as well do your last patrol."

They went down, and while Howl did his last patrol, Miles poured a glass of Cab. Thought of her.

Waited for her to come home.

Chapter Twenty-five

The bitch had ruined his life.

Gavin Rozwell stared at the never-ending rain outside the window of the crap motel stuck off the back roads in Oregon, and thought of sunny Mexican beaches. He thought of luxury hotel suites with down pillows and terrace views of sunsets over blue water.

Of champagne nestled in silver ice buckets.

He thought of how it felt to simply snap his fingers for service, and of strolling sun-washed streets knowing he could have anything he wanted.

Everything he was entitled to.

Morgan Albright—or Nash, as she called herself now—had taken that from him. Temporarily, oh yes, temporarily, but she'd taken from him.

He could feel the fucking federal agents breathing down the back of his neck. Literally feel their breath when he woke in some lumpy bed in some dingy room. Woke in a cold sweat in the dark, afraid and disoriented.

He'd taken to leaving a light on because the dark had too many moving shadows.

He couldn't shake them, couldn't quite shake them. No matter how often he told himself they'd never look for him, never find him in some dump of a room in the rain-soaked back of beyond, he felt them inching closer.

Twice he'd hacked into the state cops' system—once in Idaho, and again in Oregon—and found to his fury and his fear they'd updated his description.

The sketches didn't hit home, but hit close enough to force him to change his look, again.

He'd restyled his hair, added a beard, both shaggy and nondescript brown. He wore glasses with cheap black frames, and hated the face he saw in the mirror.

With the help of makeup, the lines around his eyes had deepened, and his skin carried the pallor of a shut-in. He'd already gained weight from all the fast food and lack of hotel fitness centers.

He changed locations and vehicles every other day. Rusty pickup trucks and rooms that smelled of must.

And the bitch lived her life on the other side of the country, laughing at him as she sat in that big-ass house.

He heard her laughing even when he left the light on at night.

He imagined killing her countless times, in countless ways. But those sweet, sweet dreams shattered to shards when he heard her laughing, when he felt the breath hot on the back of his neck.

It couldn't go on. It wouldn't go on.

He needed a place. Luxury might have to wait, but he needed a decent place where he could huddle in for a couple of weeks, maybe three. A month.

A place with a decent shower, where the rain didn't pound headaches into his skull. A place where he could think, plan, prepare.

He'd head south, south into Nevada. The desert heat would bake the mold out of his brain and warm his blood again.

He'd leave now, tonight, under the cover of dark and rain.

Excitement rose up as he thought of it. South, toward the sun, while they looked for him in the soggy Northwest. But west first, toward the coast. Dump the banger he'd stolen only the day before, get himself a truck. He could leave the fucking feds some bread crumbs so it looked like he headed north toward Washington State.

But he'd double back south. South toward the sun.

Where he could think, where he could plan.

Now he smiled out at the rain as he brought Morgan's face into his head.

Sitting in that big-ass house, thinking she'd beaten him. Thinking she'd won.

"Enjoy the rest of your summer, bitch, because I'm coming."

Now he was the one who laughed.

Miles reached for her when he woke Sunday morning. When he found the space beside him empty, he opened his eyes, studied what had become her side of the bed, at least on weekends.

And realized he didn't like that empty space. He'd gotten used to having her fill it, gotten used to the way she slept. On her left side, one hand under the pillow as if she held herself in place.

Annoyed, and more annoyed to find himself annoyed, he sat up and noted the dog had deserted him, too.

He got up, pulled on a pair of gym shorts with the vague idea of working out after coffee—better yet, after sex. Downstairs, as he walked toward the kitchen, he caught the mutter of the great room TV.

One of those home improvement shows, he identified. The woman loved HGTV.

And there she was, in baggy shorts, a baggier T-shirt, standing at the counter she'd littered with bottles, whole and juiced-out lemons and oranges. His grandmother's big cut glass pitcher glowed a deep, almost purple red with whatever she'd mixed in it.

Now, with one eye on a bunch of people ripping out ugly, shit-brown kitchen cabinets, she sliced an orange.

"What're you doing?"

Still slicing, she glanced over. "Morning. Why, I'm waxing my surfboard, of course."

"Ha."

He went straight to the coffee maker.

"I'm making sangria. The flavors need time to blend. I was going to make it when I got home last night, but you had other ideas, so I'm getting it together now so it'll have blending time."

He looked over his shoulder as he reached for a mug. "I had other ideas this morning."

That got a smile as she dumped the orange slices in the pitcher.

And picked up a lemon. "That'll have to wait. We have a dinner party to prep for."

Coffee. Coffee. Coffee, he thought as the scent of it brewing made him yearn. "It's not a dinner party."

She'd said the same, she remembered. But now she embraced her ladies' definition.

"We're having people over for dinner, that we're making. Hence, dinner party. And I know I'm more wound up about it than you are, but I don't get to do this kind of thing often. Mostly at all. The last time . . ."

She slid the lemon slices in, started on the lime. "The last time was when Nina and I made dinner for Sam and the man I thought was Luke Hudson. Today's going to wipe that one right off the books."

It mattered, he thought. What he considered just a casual summer evening with family mattered to her. For so many reasons.

He stepped away from coffee, stepped to her, wrapped his arms around her.

"Is that the biggest pitcher you could find?"

He felt her laugh, felt her relax.

"You're thinking that while Nell may have one glass out of solidarity, the guys are going to stick with beer, because your balls may shrivel up if you drink something you consider too fussy and girlie."

"That wasn't my exact thought."

"Sangria's neither fussy nor girlie, but a perfect summer adult beverage. And in a few hours, you'll learn my sangria's exceptional."

He stroked a hand along her spine before going back for coffee. "Not fussy says the woman who's decimated a decent-size orchard and has multiple bottles on the counter."

"One of the many secrets of my sangria is fresh juice."

When the doorbell rang, Morgan put down the knife.

"I'll get it," Miles told her.

"I'm fully dressed; you're fully not."

He held up a hand to stop her before picking up the remote and changing the channel to security.

"It's my mother. Why the hell is she knocking?"

He switched the channel back and started out of the kitchen as Morgan looked down at herself. And said, "Shit."

When he opened the door, Drea lifted her eyebrows. "Sleeping in?"

"Why didn't you just come in?"

"In case you were sleeping in or otherwise occupied." She handed him a basket of peaches. "The Millers are up from Georgia."

"How many bushels this time?"

"Two. So I'm divvying up. I know you're seeing Liam and Nell later. You can share."

"Maybe. Jesus, come in, come back. We're in the kitchen."

"I don't want to get in your way."

"In the kitchen," he repeated, and started back. "Morgan's making enough sangria for Barcelona. We have peaches," he said as he set the basket on the counter. "You can't possibly want to stuff them in there, too."

"I went red wine and citrus, but if I'd known." Morgan plucked one out, lifted it to her face, and drew in the scent. "They're gorgeous. Thanks, Drea."

"Thank the Millers. Second cousins on my side. They grow peaches in Georgia. And your sangria's what's gorgeous."

"I'd offer you some, but it hasn't had time to blend, and wouldn't be right. How about an iced cappuccino?"

"I—that sounds like a lot of trouble."

"It's really not."

While Morgan carried the pitcher to the refrigerator, Howl raced in from the mudroom, wagged his way to Drea for a greeting.

"There he is." Drea bent down to pet. If she wondered what it meant how easily Morgan worked in her son's kitchen while he stood in ratty gym shorts drinking coffee, she tucked it away.

"How was the hike?"

"It was great." Morgan brewed the espresso, got out a bowl. "I didn't realize how much I missed hiking until I did it again."

"And the ropes course?"

"You mean the ambush?" Tossing her hair back, she whisked half-and-half, sweetened condensed milk, and a little vanilla with the coffee. "More fun than I expected. Have you ever done it?"

"Family pride demands, and once was enough. Are those coffee ice cubes?"

Morgan shook the bag she'd pulled from the freezer. "Why dilute a good thing with water?"

"She says who adds a little coffee to her milk and sugar," Miles pointed out. "And maybe I want an iced cappuccino."

"I'm making enough."

She got out two tall glasses, added the ice cubes, poured the coffee mixture over.

Drea took one sip, then another. "Maybe you should come live with me."

"And I'm wondering why this is the first time I'm having this."

"You drink black coffee," Morgan reminded him. "Really hot black coffee. I figured I'd make these for tonight, post-dinner. We should probably do something with all these peaches, right? Like make something, for later."

Miles pointed at his mother. "She says we have to share."

"Well, that would be sharing, and there's a lot of them. I don't have a clue."

"Peach cobbler," Drea suggested.

"Even less of a clue."

"Cobblers are cobblers because you cobble them together. Quick and easy. Not a stretch for somebody who just made a couple of iced cappuccinos in under two minutes."

"Beverages, no problem. Food's trickier."

"I can show you."

"Really?"

"I've got time before I deliver peaches to my parents, then go home and make coffee ice cubes. And you're going to text me whatever you did in that bowl."

"Deal!"

"I'm going to go work out."

Miles deserted the kitchen. And he thought how she fit, just fit in his life as if the rest of his life waited for her to slide right in.

By the time he'd put in a solid ninety minutes in his home gym, showered off the sweat, dressed, he found his mother gone. Peaches filled a bright blue bowl on the counter in a seriously sparkling kitchen.

"I made a peach cobbler."

"Okay."

"No, this is big. I made it." She pointed to the baking dish cooling by the stove. "Your mom just said, now add this, do that. I made a dessert from scratch. We'll have to warm it up again before it's served, she said. Maybe with a scoop of vanilla ice cream."

"Okay. I'd've given you a hand with the kitchen."

"Your mom helped. She wouldn't take no. She said your dad's going to worship her when she offers him an iced cap after dinner tonight so we're even.

"I really like your family, Miles."

"So do I, more than most of the time."

"It shows. I poked around," she continued. "I hope you don't mind, but too late if you did, because I already poked. And I found these wonderful dishes. I forget what they're called—all different colors."

"Fiestaware."

"That's it. I thought we could use them tonight. They're fun and casual."

And what his grandmother always used for backyard parties, he thought.

"And you have perfect glasses for the sangria. Short, thick, colored stems and napkins in bright stripes I thought—"

She broke off when he pulled her in and kissed her.

"I take that as a yes."

"Use whatever you want."

"I think we'll skip the Waterford and fine china. I know I'm obsessing, at least a little."

"At least. Morgan." She smelled of peaches. "Let's sit down a minute."

"All right. Wait! It's nearly two. They're coming around six for cocktails."

"That's four hours."

"Yes, but I have things. A lot of things. I saw this summer table setting idea on HGTV I want to try."

"Of course you did."

"So flowers, vases, and candles and all of it. I'm in charge of the potatoes, then there's serving dishes. And I have to get myself together so I look good."

"You look good."

"Please. I'm still dealing with the shame of this outfit when your mother dropped by looking like the cover of a magazine with the caption 'Casual summer chic.'"

"Are you going to be like this anytime people come over here?"

"I hope not, but I think I have to get over this hump, success-fully. It's your house, your siblings, the chief of police. It's a big hump for me."

"Okay then. What's next?"

She let out a long sigh. "Thanks."

He shrugged it off as she went to get the napkins to practice some clever fold for the table look she wanted.

It could wait, he decided. What he wanted to say to her could wait. And he'd take more time to think.

It took damn near the four hours for her to satisfy herself with every detail. Flowers, candles, napkins. Her focus remained intense, though she chatted away while she prepped her potatoes, while he marinated chicken, the vegetables he'd roast, made the barbecue sauce.

And again, as they worked together, it struck how well she fit. How her anticipation of the evening had him looking forward to it all more than he'd expected.

She put on a dress—she sure had the legs for it. Just a breezy num-ber in pale, pale green that made him give thanks for summer.

At last, when she stood outside, giving her tablescape a last, critical look, she nodded.

"It looks good, right? It all looks good."

"It ought to. You know, you spent all that time fancy folding the napkins, tucking a nasturtium in each one—precisely—and people are just going to open them up."

"The nasturtiums are pretty, and edible—so there's that."

"There's that. I'm getting a beer."

"Or," she said as he started toward the copper tub where, at her insistence, he'd nestled beer and wine in ice, "you could sample the sangria."

"I thought it was still blending."

"It's had six hours, so that'll do. Just a sample," she said as she headed inside. "If you don't like, you don't like."

He looked down at the dog, who looked up at him. "I just want a damn beer. I folded frigging napkins. Dragged out the ironing board I barely remember I have so she could press the table runner that's going to end up with barbecue sauce on it. I deserve a beer."

Howl muttered back, and Miles heard sympathy. Maybe solidarity.

She carried the pitcher to the table with the copper tub, the glassware, cocktail napkins, flowers, more candles.

"I added some club soda just now for a little sparkle."

She poured two fingers in a glass, walked over, and offered.

"Just see what you think."

He took a sip, scowled.

"Not good?"

"No, I'm irritated because it is good, and I wanted a beer."

"You can always have a beer," she said, and kissed his cheek.

He heard Nell's voice from inside. "We're here! I'm putting dessert on the counter."

"Crap." Morgan actually slapped the heel of her hand on her forehead. "I made cobbler. I forgot she was making dessert. We'll leave the cobbler inside."

"Hell no, we'll have both. It's fine."

Nell stepped out with Jake. She, too, wore a summer dress, and Miles did his best not to imagine Jake had "thoughts" when he'd seen Nell in it.

She stopped, stared at the table.

"Well, wow. Just wow." She looked over at Morgan. "It all looks so happy! Oh, is that sangria? Let's have some. Jake, if Morgan made it, it's going to be great."

Miles thought he caught Jake's longing glance toward the beer, but he said, "I'm game."

By the time Liam arrived, they sat around a third table drinking sangria. He brought a sloe-eyed, raven-haired beauty named Dawn. It took Miles about ten minutes to judge she didn't fit. Nice enough, but not someone who'd slide in when Liam was ready. Or when he wasn't.

On the other hand, he couldn't say the same about Nell and Jake. He knew them both too well to ignore what he saw with his own eyes.

They worked.

Liam kept the ladies entertained while Miles started the grill. And Jake joined him.

"You'll hurt her," Miles said. "She'll hurt you. People do along the way, can't help it, because people. And that's between the two involved."

"That's life."

"Yeah, but if you *hurt* her, I'll have to kill you."

"What choice would you have?"

"Exactly."

"Right now, she's running the clock. That's fine. I've got plenty of time." Jake glanced back at the table. "And when her clock runs out, I'll be ready.

"So how much did you have to do with all this? Table looks like a magazine."

"I was slave labor."

"You've got it bad, son."

"I've got it. Can't say about her yet. Rozwell."

Once again, Jake glanced back, and kept his voice low. "They think he's heading to Washington State. The federal task force, the local LEOs, they're all over it."

"Doesn't matter. As long as he's loose it's hanging over her."

He heard her laugh, shook his head. "But not tonight."

When they sat at the happy table with its flowers and candles, its food and drink, he thought again: Not tonight.

Nothing hanging over her tonight, because she was in the moment, sliding over her particular hump.

Laughing with Liam, engaging Dawn in conversation about Impressionism—Dawn's particular interest. She talked baseball with Jake, about anything under the sun with Nell.

He knew some of it was an innate skill, a tool of her trade. But it sprang from simply enjoying people and listening to what they had to say.

"All right, Miles, you've definitely mastered the Jameson secret sauce." Nell nudged her plate away. "You're head chef next family meeting, if I recall correctly. And I do. I vote for pulled pork. You can handle it."

"I'll vote for that. And these potatoes," Liam added.

"Those are Morgan's specialty."

"One of two," she put in. "If my ladies have anything to do with it, I'll eventually add at least one more."

"Your ladies?" Dawn sent Morgan a quizzical smile.

"My mother and grandmother. We share a house."

"Oh." She took a delicate bite of chicken. "You live with your mother. I thought you worked at the resort."

"I do. It's been fascinating and enjoyable to live in a three-generation household."

Though she obviously tried, Dawn kept digging the hole. "I'm sure your grandmother must feel safer knowing you're in the house. Being elderly, I mean."

Miles caught Nell's eye-cast to the sky, but Morgan just laughed. "You'd better not let Gram hear you call her elderly. She and my mother go to yoga class every week, and the couple of times I joined them, I could barely keep up. They own and run Crafty Arts and Wine Café."

"Oh. I've been in there. It's wonderful. I think I've met your grandmother there. She's very sharp."

Morgan lifted her glass, but didn't hide the smile. "She's all of that."

No, Miles thought, the raven-haired beauty didn't come close to a fit.

The sun settled in the west before dessert time rolled around.

"Confession," Morgan began. "I forgot you were bringing dessert, Nell, then your mom came by with peaches."

"You made something?"

"She walked me through a peach cobbler."

"A dessert-off!" Liam declared, and Nell shot him a look.

"No. It's not a competition."

"Isn't everything?"

Morgan threw in with Nell. "No. We'll consider it your lucky night, and you get two desserts. Would anyone like cappuccino? Hot or iced."

"I've never had iced cappuccino."

"You won't regret adding it in," Miles told Jake.

"Do you have skim milk?"

To her credit, Morgan smiled at Dawn again. "Sorry, not on hand."

"Maybe just a half a cup—hot."

"You've got it."

"I'll give you a hand." As Nell rose, she patted Jake's shoulder as a signal for him to stay at the table.

"She's young," Nell said when she and Morgan were in the kitchen. "Just a tad younger than her age."

"She is, and didn't mean any offense. She comes from money, you can tell—and nothing wrong with that."

"Hope not, because me, too."

"She's had an excellent fine arts education, and is enjoying her last summer before she takes her first real job, at an art gallery, in Chicago—though she really wanted New York."

"You got more out of her than I did."

"She's an easy read, and she's a very nice girl—still a girl, but not a mean one. Neither she nor Liam will give each other a second thought when she moves to Chicago next month."

"No, they won't."

"You and Jake, on the other hand, give each other a lot of thoughts."

"More than I wanted to, until I did. For a cop, his edges are pretty damn smooth, and end up smoothing mine."

"Plus, if you'll excuse me for noticing, he's got a great ass."

"He does. It's hard not to notice. Okay," she said when Morgan pulled the cobbler out of the warming oven, "that looks great. Just like my mother's."

"She step-by-stepped me. Yours looks great. What is it?"

"Cherry Dump Cake—don't be put off by the name. You dump cake mix over cherries, add a little this and that. Bake it, and done."

"I could do that. I could actually do that."

"I'll text it to you. Are those . . . those are coffee ice cubes? That's brilliant. Give me one."

Morgan obliged her, and Nell sucked it like a popsicle. "God, I could mainline these. Why didn't I ever think of doing this? I'll get the desserts. You deal with the coffee."

Successful desserts led to lingering before the good-nights. Stars swept across the sky when Morgan sat out with Miles.

"How's that hump?" he asked her.

"Smooth and level, thanks. It was fun. Was it fun?"

"It was. Even the new and soon-to-be-forgotten girl had fun. You could have squashed that for her. You didn't."

"She didn't mean to be critical. She was surprised. It never occurred to her a grown woman—several years older than she is— would choose to live with her mother, much less her grandmother. Liam obviously didn't fill her in."

"It's your business, not hers, so no, he wouldn't."

"I appreciate that. And I appreciate you putting up with me today. I know I was a pain in the ass."

"Yeah, you were." He liked her quick, easy laugh. "You should make it up to me."

"I can try. What did you have in mind?"

"What I had in mind this morning when you were too busy being a pain in my ass."

"I see." She rose, then straddled him on the chair. "I guess it's the least I can do."

"It won't be the least when we're finished."

He rose with her so she linked her long legs around his waist. "We should call the dog in."

"He has to finish his last patrol. He knows how to get in when he's ready."

"Can we do this again sometime?"

"Absolutely not," he said as he carried her inside, "if I have to fold napkins."

"You can be excused from that duty."

"In that case, I'll give you a chance to persuade me."

"Miles." She nuzzled at the side of his neck, sparked little fires in his blood. "You're so good to me."

He intended to be.

Chapter Twenty-six

Ten days after Gavin Rozwell left a crappy motel room to drive into the rain-soaked dark, Beck and Morrison worked in a less crappy motel room while rain pounded the night.

They'd pinned maps on the walls, marked trails they'd followed, trails local PDs and staties had followed. They'd highlighted confirmed sightings in red, possibles in yellow.

Along with the maps, they had photos and descriptions of stolen vehicles they'd traced to Rozwell, separated them into recovered and not recovered.

They had photos of the last motel room in Oregon, statements from the not-very-interested desk clerk, statements from the goggling-with-interest waitress who'd served him the fried chicken special in the rinky-dink diner squatting beside the motel.

They had the statement of the clerk at the Quick Mart—who'd smelled of pot and despair—where Rozwell had bought a six-pack of Coke Zero, a family-size bag of salt-and-vinegar potato chips, and half a dozen Reese's Peanut Butter Cups.

They had the rattletrap Ford pickup, flat tire, no spare—with his prints all over it—abandoned on a back road outside of Fall City, Washington. And the description of a Dodge Ram reported stolen from a driveway less than half a mile from the Ford.

All leads pointed north.

"We tracked him back to the motel outside of Alpine in Oregon because of the mini-mart stop. Got him on camera there."

Beck paced back and forth in front of their makeshift evidence board while Morrison worked on their nightly report.

Beck wore a sleeveless tee and drawstring cotton pants that served her for these late-night sessions and for sleeping.

In the past three weeks they'd had a scant forty-eight hours back in Baltimore in their home office, including two nights in their own beds.

In lieu of a desk, Morrison used a side table about the size of a manhole cover where he tapped away on his laptop. His reading glasses—picked up at a Walmart after he sat on his last pair—kept sliding down his nose.

"Why'd he go into the mini-mart?"

Morrison looked up, over the half rims. "Because he wanted sugar and carbs for the road."

"It's under ten miles from the motel. The motel has vending machines. But he doesn't get his fix there, he goes into the mart, and he damn well knows they'll have the camera on checkout."

"Mostly luck we hit on that wit in the first place."

"Can't argue there, but it led us to the motel, and it gave us the truck he ditched in the parking lot in Molalla. Still Oregon but clearly heading north. Major airport in Salem, but he doesn't ditch it there, so we find it pretty damn easy."

Morrison rubbed his eyes, made the cheaters bounce. "Nothing about this is easy."

"But look. North." She began tapping the map. "Clear trail. Yeah, yeah, it winds a bit, but always north. Into Washington, and it sure as hell looks like he might be looking to slip over the border into Canada, or find a way to get to fricking Alaska."

Morrison took the cheaters off, tapped them on the knee of his faded dad jeans as he studied the map. "We're not digging up the bread crumbs. We're just picking them up along the way."

"That's right. Has he gotten that sloppy, Quentin? Do we think he's dropping clues like rose petals for us?"

"Could be. He's rattled. We know he's rattled. Staying in dumps, driving pieces of shit. Porking up, too, according to witness statements. He's rattled and running. But . . ."

Now Beck nodded. "But." She sat on the side of the bed, folding her legs under her. "I've had this feeling, and it's getting stronger, he's playing us. That truck we found yesterday? It's like a goddamn neon sign pointing north."

Morrison rose now, stretching his back till it cracked. Oh, how he missed his extra-firm mattress in Baltimore.

"After he missed with Morgan," Morrison began, "he went essentially a year without a kill."

"That we know of," Beck qualified.

"That we know of. Going by what we do know, he hasn't had a kill since Myrtle Beach. He'd picked up the pace there—Arizona, New Orleans, Myrtle Beach. Three kills inside six months."

"He had to make up that lost time, that lost year." She stepped to the big map, tapped Arizona. "He planned this one, took his time, getting back in the swing."

"But Dressler in New Orleans. That was of the moment, impulse, a loss of control. That was release, so sloppy."

"He had to follow up, get his rhythm back. He took some time, yes, with the victim in Myrtle Beach, bagged a solid payday. But still, Quentin, without his usual precision. Slipping up on the tracking in the Mercedes, back to sloppy. He lost that precision, what he thinks of as his elegance, with Nina Ramos."

"And now he's slowed down again. He lost most of his fancy tools, all the IDs he'd generated, and he's been on the run since Missouri. So he's rattled, out of his element, screwing up. But . . ."

Again, Beck nodded. "He's also pissed off. And who's to blame for all of it?"

"Morgan Albright—Nash," Morrison corrected. "And us."

"And us. He could get a little payback having us chase the wild goose."

"Do you think he's going after Nash?"

"No." She shook her head. "No, not when he knows we're on his trail. He has to feel us behind him. Do you?"

"No. He is rattled, Tee, so he needs time to settle down, to plan it out. Somewhere in that sick brain of his he knows he's made mistakes. She's the big one."

He picked up the bottle of ginger ale he'd set on the floor by the table, since he didn't have room on it with his laptop and paperwork. Sipped, winced a little, as it had gone warm.

He sat again, turning the chair to face her. Her room smelled of the travel candle she always burned. They habitually worked in her room, as she claimed his smelled like a gym locker.

She wasn't wrong.

So he sat, stretched out his legs, let the scent—peonies, he realized, like in his mother's garden in May back home—quiet his brain.

Because she knew how he worked, Beck sat quiet, said nothing.

"We should contact Chief Dooley and the resort security just so they sharpen their eye."

"Agreed."

"But he's not a subtle guy. It's black-and-white with him. If he's leading us north, and the more I think about it, the more I think you've got something—"

"He's going south," Beck finished.

"Yeah, hell. He'd planned on Mexico. We got that from his room in New Orleans. Maybe he's finessed a passport. But that's a long way to travel."

"You're thinking closer. So am I. Listen to that rain, Quentin. I swear I'd kill for some real sunshine, some heat. I'll bet your left eye he would, too."

"Left eye's my weak one. South then. We've got enough coverage up here to follow your nose south. First light?"

She looked toward the curtained window, listened to the rain. "If there is any."

"We'll find some."

"And we'll find him. He's not going to slip through, Quentin. And he's not going to get to Morgan. But I'm worried he'll get another before we get him."

She shook her head, her shoulders. "Fuck it. You know what I'm going to do once we have that bastard?"

"What's that?"

"After I kiss you on the mouth—deal with it—I'm going home to my long-suffering saint of a husband and making a baby."

"Is that right?"

"Bet your left eye. One thing this case has taught me? Life is for living. Let's catch this motherfucker and start living."

"I can get behind that." He closed his laptop, gathered his things. "I'll finish this in my room. Let's get some sleep."

Gavin Rozwell, now aka Leo Nesser, soaked up the desert sun. He felt renewed, refreshed, rejuvenated. Even the lousy motel room didn't harsh his buzz.

He'd trimmed his hair—still shaggy, but more careless than unkempt. He'd combed lightener through it, drawn it back in a stubby tail. He'd worked on the beard until it was mostly stubble with a little soul patch. A self-tanner had turned the pallor into a mild glow. He liked the look with green contacts and John Lennon glasses.

Sort of a vagabond artist type with the Birkenstock sandals and frayed jeans.

He'd gone up a full size in the jeans, but he'd soon take care of that.

His head told him a paunch—even a fake belly—would add to the disguise. But he wanted his body back.

He took long walks in the baking heat, carting a sketch pad and a camera.

Vegas called to him like a siren with its swank hotels and crazed nightlife. Even Reno whispered. But he stayed away, hiked sun-blazed canyons—he'd melt those pounds away—and amused himself picturing the feds slogging through the rain and gloom in the north.

He'd left a trail a blind man could follow before he'd pushed the stolen Fiat into a lake, watched it sink.

They'd find it eventually. But eventually would be too late.

At night, he researched. He needed a place, and the canyons and desert would provide.

Plenty of off-the-grids in this wide world, and plenty of asshole prepper types bullshitting online in chat groups. He only needed one.

He took his time. If he intended to spend a few weeks, maybe even months in some weirdo's cabin, he had to make sure he found the right one.

Someone without friends or relatives who might check on him. Someone who took prepping seriously enough to have a good supply of food, water laid in. A decent roof overhead.

He joined conversations under the handle "nowhereman," asked for advice, stayed out of arguments. Advice led him to other groups, and other groups to more local pickings.

He researched the pickings, took the hikes and drives to get closer looks when possible. He ate burritos, greasy fries and hacked. He ate chips—the road had given him a serious addiction to chips he couldn't shake—and drove to another flop motel.

He invested in a drone, flew it in the canyons, and got some decent aerial videos of a couple of the off-the-grids.

When he had it down to two most likely, he dug up the occupants' names and researched.

And decided no contest between the forty-seven-year-old retired marine gunny—who looked as if he could eat boulders for breakfast—and the fifty-three-year-old widow with ropey arms who went by the handle "Prep4Jesus."

Jane Boot and her husband James had settled in the nowhere between Gabbs and Two Springs, Nevada, twelve years before. Apparently, four years ago, he'd died of cancer they couldn't pray away. Jane lived on. She kept a goat for milk, some chickens, butchered her own pigs, and had a smokehouse for the meat.

She believed, fanatically, in the Rapture, in Commies who ran all branches of the government, and in inevitable war that humanity would wage against aliens—either terrestrial or extra.

She devoured posts on QAnon sites faster than he ate chips.

Jane, and the not-so-recently-departed James, stood as anti-vaxxers, anti-government, anti-gay, anti-everything that didn't include God and guns.

A certified nutcase in Rozwell's opinion, with no children, one sister who had long since disavowed her, and internet access.

She'd had a dog, but she'd buried him alongside her husband the year before.

Rozwell expected she'd be well armed and more than willing to shoot an intruder dead as Moses. But he'd figure it out.

He lost three pounds—fifteen more to go—and his confidence built as he hacked into her accounts as smooth as a knife through soft butter.

She had a truck, of course, and from the ledger she kept on her computer, took a bimonthly trip, either to Gabbs or Two Springs, to sell eggs and goat's milk and trinkets she made from cheap beads and tanned pigskin.

Gross.

She didn't use Amazon, UPS, or FedEx, and had an iron gate and lines of barbed wire with plenty of KEEP THE HELL OUT signage guarding her dirt road and five dusty acres.

But she had a cabin, a shed, a well and indoor plumbing, and solar for power—something her handy husband had seen to before he took his dirt nap. Otherwise, Rozwell would've risked the marine.

He flew his drone. He watched. He waited.

One day he watched her go to the shed, and this time she drove out in the truck.

At last!

He watched her, like a vulture overhead, haul jugs of milk, cartons of eggs out of the cabin and into the coolers in the bed of the truck. Then she hauled out a crate—probably the trinkets—and loaded that in.

She had a shotgun and what he thought was a rifle in the gun rack in the back, and a gun of some sort strapped to her side.

She shut the shed door, snapped it secure with a padlock before going back to the cabin, another padlock on that door.

In her dusty boots and jeans, she looked skinny as a snake, but he'd bet she had some strength in her.

With the drone, he followed her as she drove down the dirt road, spewing up more dust. But he called it back before she reached the gate.

Since her last ledger entry listed Gabbs, he guessed she'd head east to Two Springs. He got back in his truck and pulled out a map as if consulting it if she turned his way.

It took time for her to reach the gate, unlock it, open it, drive through. Then get out, shut it, lock it again.

Then she drove east, and Rozwell knew his luck had changed.

He waited ten long minutes before assuring himself she wouldn't double back. He couldn't just bolt cut the padlocks, or she'd know. But he'd spent some quality time in his motel with padlocks and lockpicks and wikiHow.

He didn't find it easy, and by the time he'd finessed the first one, the sweat rolled. It took him nearly a half hour to open all three, but he opened the gate. He went back for the truck, drove through, then locked up again behind him.

He'd thought this part through in the hours keeping watch or sitting in that motel room. He needed to get his truck well out of sight. He drove around the house, had to all but shimmy it through the side and the lean-to where the goat stood in the shade. It scraped the paint some, but what did he care?

He drove it back to where she'd strung several lines of barbed wire, to where sagebrush huddled.

He'd figured the angles from the drone. She wouldn't see it if she drove to the shed, not with the house and brush blocking it. If she crossed to the chickens, she would.

But he'd be on her if she did that.

She had a lean-to at the back of the house—over another pad-locked door—and the three-legged stool she used when she milked the goat.

Every damn window had shades pulled down tight so he couldn't get a peek inside.

He got one of his water bottles out of the truck, went to sit on the stool in the shade.

He'd hear her coming in that rattletrap truck. He might as well relax awhile.

He played with his phone, drank water. Wished for an air-conditioned suite at the Plaza. No, a water view. The cacti and sand, the sheer canyon walls made him yearn for the water.

The Casa Cipriani if he stuck with New York.

Or he could imagine the Pacific. Post Ranch Inn, Big Sur.

Or . . .

And here she came. Rattle, rattle, clunk, clunk.

About damn time.

He got up, used his ears first, since he couldn't risk his eyes.

He heard the truck stop, and yes, there it was, the creak of the shed.

Now he waited for the truck to shut off, the door to creak shut.

He had to take her from behind, planned on coming up on her after she unlocked the cabin door. She'd have her hands full. She always bought fresh fruit, some vegetables on these trips.

He heard the door shut and the snap of the padlock. Heard her bootsteps approach the house, so he slipped around the shed side of the house and pinned to the wall, sidestepped down.

Then her bootsteps stopped.

He risked a peek.

Her back was to him, her arms holding the crate with cloth bags in it. A carrot top poked out of one.

She looked down.

And he saw it, too. His tire tracks, his footprints.

She dropped the crate, reached for the gun at her side. And he was running.

She'd pulled the gun, started to spin toward him when he barreled into her. Like hitting a bag of bones, he thought as the gun flew.

They landed hard, hard enough he heard her head crack against the side of the narrow front porch. But it didn't slow her down as she jabbed an elbow into his gut.

He didn't see the knife until it sliced down his arm. But the pain, the smell of his own blood brought on the rage. He gripped her knife hand, twisted. He felt her wrist snap like a dry branch underfoot. And he rode her high-pitched scream as he pounded his fist into her face.

"You cut me!" His voice was like her scream as he pounded again, again. "You bitch! You whore!"

Her screams turned to gurgling moans as he beat her head against the edge of the porch.

She stopped gurgling. She went silent, went still. Now she only stared at him as he shoved up and clamped a hand over his arm.

Blood slid down, dripped off his fingers, stained the dirt, as hers did. She'd opened him up six inches between shoulder and elbow.

"I'm going to have a fucking scar, thanks to you!"

Furious at the thought, he kicked her, kicked her, then stomped her.

"See how you like it, you stupid old *cunt*!"

He knew she couldn't feel the pain he wanted to give her, knew she'd been dead since before the first kick, but he couldn't stop. Not until the effort and heat combined to make him dizzy.

He picked up the keys she'd dropped along with the crate, and left her there as he walked up and unlocked the door.

She'd have medical supplies—any prepper would.

He crossed the living area with its swaybacked sofa, single chair, and into the kitchen. Double the size of the living area, it had long counters—butcher block, probably the work of the handy husband. Open shelves ran along the walls, packed with canned goods, jarred goods, dry goods in glass jugs.

An old cabinet, maybe handmade, had a first aid kit, boxes of gauze, bottles of peroxide, antiseptics, alcohol, pain pills, bandages, the works.

He cleaned the gash in the kitchen sink. It stung like fire, bled in streams of red. Then, gritting his teeth, he dumped on peroxide, and that stung like the fires of hell.

Tears coursed down his cheeks, but he kept at it, used butterfly bandages to close the gash, slathered it with antiseptic, wrapped it in gauze.

He drank cold water straight from the faucet.

She had Excedrin Extra Strength, and he downed three.

Then he walked out and stared down at her. He'd be damned if he'd bury her, but he couldn't leave her there. She'd start to stink, plus he didn't want to look at her. Or risk somebody else with a drone taking a look.

He dragged her around the house. She left a wide smear of blood in the dirt, but he didn't give a damn.

When he got to the barbed wire, he went through her pockets.

Disgusting, but necessary. He found a small wad of bills, more keys, an old pocket watch, and a penknife.

He got the bolt cutters out of his truck, cut the wire, and dragged her farther away across the brush, into it.

Vultures and crows, he thought, they'd take care of the rest of her.

He drove his truck back, unloaded it onto the porch. He'd never leave anything behind in a room again, so he had all he needed. He carried the bolt cutters to the shed, dealt with the lock.

A little gold mine, he thought. More provisions neatly shelved, tools, animal feed. No room for the second truck, but no worries.

Carrying the bolt cutters, he walked back to the house, sneering at the blood path. He hauled up the crate to take the groceries in.

Waste not, want not.

A glance at his throbbing arm showed he'd bled through, so he changed the gauze before snapping the bolt on the door in the kitchen.

He expected some sort of laundry space, but stood surprised and smiling at the locked room.

She may have lived like a hermit in a cave, but she had a lot of tech. Solid tech, and he'd make good use of it. In addition to the electronics, she had a banquet of solar tools. Fire starters; flashlights; chargers; water purifiers; some sort of mini, foldable solar oven. A spare solar generator.

Invasions, Commies, civil war, or Rapture, he thought, Prep4Jesus had it all.

Including what he thought was an AR-15, or whatever the hell those whacked-out mass shooters loved, hanging on the wall next to a picture of Jesus.

He wandered like a boy in a toy store. And spotted the safe.

"Isn't that a nice surprise?"

He wanted a shower, wanted to change, unpack, settle in. But tossed all that aside and began to hunt for the combination.

He did find a laundry space—an ancient washer, no dryer. A bathroom that would have to do, the single bedroom.

More pictures of Jesus, a tattered DON'T TREAD ON ME flag pinned to the wall.

In the closet, in a metal box with yet another padlock, he found papers. Old letters, copies of birth certificates, marriage license, the deed to the land he stood on, and the combination for the safe.

He went back, and since they'd bolted the safe to the floor, sat on the rough wood, followed the combination.

Inside he found cash. Smiling to himself, he sat there on the floor and began to count.

"Thirty-six thousand, three hundred and sixty-two dollars."

He threw back his head and laughed. "Jane, you dead whore, thanks for the tip!"

He got his shower, then dealt with his wound again. Put on fresh clothes.

Her towels were sandpaper, and a glance at her sheets said the same.

He'd make a trip into Two Springs—it was closest and nearly twice as big as Gabbs—buy new, Egyptian cotton. Some decent soap. With her money.

He tossed her clothes into the crate, and damned if he didn't find more cash. Just a couple hundred hidden here and there, but cash was king.

Since all the work stirred his appetite, he got a nice, fat plum from her recent shopping spree.

The goat was bleating, the chickens cackling, the pair of pigs snorting. He'd enjoy the fresh eggs, but damn if he'd milk a goat even if he knew how. And he didn't know how the fuck to butcher a pig.

Still, if the stupid animals starved to death, he'd have to deal with it.

To ward that off, at least for now, he went back to the shed, dug up the feed for the goat. He even pumped out water for its pail.

"I'm a frigging ranch hand, so I guess I'd better rustle up some grub."

He found eggs, and plenty of them, and in a chest freezer pig meat, chickens that would no longer lay eggs. Rounds of bread marked with the dates.

Bitch made her own bread, for God's sake.

He didn't know how to cook any of the meat, but that's what Google was for. Right now, he'd settle for eggs.

A hunt through her supplies netted him plenty of canned goods, and a couple of bottles of good whiskey.

He scrambled up some eggs, a little singed, but they filled the hole, had them with what remained of his bag of chips and two fingers of good whiskey.

While he ate, he made a list on his phone of what he needed when he went to Two Springs. Sheets, towels, soap, some good wine, cheese, flatbread crackers, more chips. Maybe some dip to go with them.

After dinner, he sat on the porch and realized, despite the burning arm, he felt relaxed for the first time in weeks. Weeks and weeks.

Part of it came from the kill. He'd felt just a little of that tingle, even though he'd killed her too hard, too fast. Like the eggs, it filled the hole.

And the rest? Knowing he had a place, had the time. They'd never find him here. Why would they even look? He was sun; they were rain.

They'd still be chasing their tails when he was ready to finish with long-legged Morgan.

That time would come.

But now? He thought he'd pour another whiskey and play with the toys Dead Jane had left him.

After all, he was now home sweet home.

Chapter Twenty-seven

Since Miles had his family meeting/dinner on Sunday, Morgan slept in on Sunday morning, then spent some time in the garden with her grandmother.

It amused her when she realized they both wore floppy-brimmed straw hats, sunglasses, shorts with big pockets, and battered high-tops.

"We look like a couple of hippie farmers, Gram."

"I come by my look naturally. You're just a copycat."

Morgan tossed more deadheads in the bright purple tub. "Mom always looks like a model for something you'd call *Gardening in Style Magazine*. That skill missed me entirely. I didn't know she was working today."

"Darlie woke up with a stomach bug—which I figure is a euphemism for hangover. She's a good girl, a good summer hire, and deserves to party now and then."

"You and Mom are good bosses." She swiped at some of the August sweat as she looked around. "You know, I'm never going to be satisfied with a tiny yard now. I'm thoroughly spoiled between playing here and at Miles's house. Nina started it, and we really did make our little yard pretty. But now I'm going to want rock gardens and shade gardens and cutting gardens."

"And Zen frog fountains."

"Absolutely. Vermont winters are long, so I want every bloom and blossom I can squeeze in for spring and summer and right through the fall."

"You're staying."

Surprised, Morgan glanced back. "Where would I go?"

"Anywhere you want, my baby's baby. I can hope it's here, but that's for me and your mother. You didn't have much choice coming here, but you've made the best of it. Now you've had half a year or so to settle in and get a feel, so staying's a choice."

"It is." Hunkering down, Morgan tugged up a few stray weeds. "I didn't know what I was going to do when I got here. You made that room for me, you and Mom, and I didn't know what to do about that. Then I got the job at the resort. It's not what I planned, all these years. Not my own place, but it's my place."

She shrugged, looked up. "I've had all these moments, with you, with Mom, at work, alone in this wonderful house. I've seen how you and Mom live together, as friends as much as family. And realize I blocked myself off from that because I had something to prove."

"And did you? Prove it?"

"I did. What happened with Gavin Rozwell was all about him and really nothing about me. I worked hard, and I made a life because I wanted to, because I could. But I was missing this, Gram, this moment right now, because I was so determined to do it all myself, for myself. I was missing really knowing you, really knowing Mom, and that means missing really knowing me, doesn't it?"

Smiling, Olivia reached down, gripped Morgan's chin, gave it a gentle wiggle. "You get your good sense from me."

"Mom's soft, isn't she? Softer than you and me?"

"Always has been. The glass is half-full for Audrey, and more, waiting to be filled up the rest of the way. That doesn't mean she doesn't have spine."

"I never saw it in her until I came to stay here."

"She held me up when your grandfather died." Olivia looked over toward the woodshop because she could, and always would, picture him there.

"She was my rock when the world fell out from under me. Took over the shop for weeks. I was going to sell the business."

"I didn't know that."

"I couldn't see past the next minute, much less into tomorrow. The love of my life, gone in a minute, and how could that be? But she wouldn't let me give up, kept holding me up until I found my feet again. She let you go," Olivia said gently, "because you needed to go. And that took love and strength."

Then Olivia sighed. "He fucked her up. Let's just say it and move on. The Colonel fucked her up good and proper. But she found her feet again. So have you. We're Nash women, after all."

"We are, so I'm going to tell you, woman-to-woman, Nash-to-Nash, I've thought about leaving because of Rozwell. Because if they don't catch him and he comes after me again, he'll come here. You and Mom are here."

Before Olivia could speak, Morgan held up a hand. "And I know what you're going to say. The Nash women can handle it, and him."

"That's exactly right." A finger poke into Morgan's belly emphasized the point.

"And I believe that. I want to stay here, so many reasons why, but I couldn't if I didn't believe that."

"Good." Straightening, Olivia stretched her back. "Now I'm going to poke in and ask if one of those many reasons is Miles Jameson."

"He's definitely in there. It's one day, or mostly one weekend, at a time, but he's in there."

"Is that enough for you? The one weekend at a time?"

"I didn't expect to have that. That's on me, too," Morgan added as they moved around the garden. "I didn't really make time for dating, much less relationships. I was so focused on the goals."

"Not a thing wrong with focus or goals."

"No, but if you can't adjust? Being here's shown me I don't have to do it all myself, by myself. I can have a fulfilling career and a real life at the same time. I can work hard and still have time and room for family, and for being with someone who makes me happy."

"Found your feet. You don't have your mother's—or what was your mother's—fairy-tale view. You're not looking for someone to sweep you off those feet. But that doesn't mean you don't love, and love hard."

"I didn't plan to be in love with him." On a sigh of her own, Morgan pushed the brim of her hat back. "Like a lot, be attracted to, enjoy being with. I was with a guy in college."

"I should hope so!"

With a laugh, Morgan rolled her eyes. "Gram. I'm saying that's what it was, that list: like, attraction, enjoy. There were two others along the way who made that list. Then I stopped making time, making room. Then there was Miles."

"And this time it's different."

"Yes, for me. For me," she repeated. "The attraction? That was bang, right from the jump. I mean, look at this guy. The 'like' didn't take long. For someone who claims he doesn't much like people, he sure knows how to look out for them. The 'enjoy being with'? Just wow."

This time Olivia laughed.

"The love just snuck up on me, little moments by little moments."

"Best kind there is."

"Is it?"

"I was going to bang your grandfather like a hammer to a nail," she remembered. And laughed at Morgan's muffled snort. "But he snuck up on me. Love snuck up on me."

When she looked over at the woodshop, she could all but see him standing in the doorway, grinning at her.

"Then one day he said, 'Livvy Nash, nobody's ever going to love who you are like I do. Let's get married.' I'm all set to say, 'Are you crazy?' But 'Yeah, let's do that' came right out of my mouth. He had a plan, Steve did, and pulled me right along into it. And made me glad he did, every single day."

Wasn't it miraculous, Morgan thought, to have someone love who you are, and never stop?

"I like a plan. I must get that need for a plan from Pa. And this wasn't the plan. Plus, Miles and I had a sort of agreement before we got started. So I'm okay with the one weekend at a time. It's enough. He won't crush my heart. He's not cruel, he's not cold. Whatever happens, I'll handle it because I've had those moments. And this is home now, Après is my place."

"I'm going to tell you something, then we're going to go cut a couple armloads of those hydrangeas. After that, we're going to put them all over the house, then sit ourselves down with a tall glass of lemonade."

"Okay, tell me."

"When you love someone, and love him hard, and you're ready for him, you go after him. If he doesn't love you back, and love you hard, if he's not ready for you, that's his loss. Love's brave, Morgan. Love stands up."

"That sounds true."

"Because it is. It's solid truth."

"I'm just getting used to being in love with him, knowing I am. I guess I have to work on being ready."

"When you are, you'll know what to do. You're no coward. Let's go cut some flowers."

They arranged those magic blue hydrangeas all over the house. But instead of lemonade, Morgan got out ingredients and bar tools.

"I need some help."

"Mixing a drink? I'm not above a drink before three on a Sunday afternoon, but you're the expert in mixing."

"Not mixing, tasting, followed by judging, then choosing which of the three wins for our fall special. Just two sips, because I'll use different liquors in the choices. Mixing liquors is a fine way to get Darlie's stomach bug."

"Been there, done that."

"I thought I had it down to two, then I came up with another, so you'll judge three."

"Did you have Nell or Drea sample?"

"Too busy, all around. Plus, this way I can take Nell the one that wins."

Rubbing her hands together, Olivia sat at the counter. "Let's have it."

"Okay, first up starts with a nice, dry Riesling, then pear brandy—pear's the spa fall deal. The pear eau-de-vie—"

"Water of life? I've got that much French in me."

"It's pear brandy, and gives the Riesling a nice kick."

"Who doesn't like a nice kick?" Enjoying herself, Olivia rested her chin on her fist to watch. "It already looks pretty."

"It's going to look prettier. A little orange curaçao for zest, some honey syrup for sweet, and five—not four, not six—dashes of bitters for that touch of licorice."

"It sounds as pretty as it looks."

"If we go with this, I'll serve it in the classic Cary Grant champagne glass, with a thin slice of pear as garnish."

When she'd finished, Morgan held out the glass. "One sip. Consider, let it sit. Then one more to judge. Oh, hey, here's Mom. Perfect timing. Two judges."

"Didn't expect you until four," Olivia commented.

"Darlie recovered, with apologies. What are we drinking and why?"

"We're Morgan's official judges for the fall specialty drink." Olivia sipped, considered as ordered. "That is very, very tasty." She sipped again. "Excellent, and I'm not a big fan of the pear."

"I am, and I could use a drink. We were absolutely slammed this morning, Mom. A group of day-trippers—twenty-three of them."

"Two sips," Morgan told her mother. "Because there are two more to come."

"Oh, that's really good. Sweet, but zingy. Am I really only allowed two sips? It was a morning. We had two sisters from the group who got into an argument—the edge of a serious fight—over who would buy Lacy Cardini's *Secret Garden* for their mother's birthday."

"That Cardini painting's priced at eight seventy-five." Olivia pumped her fists in the air. "Woo!"

"I convinced them to split it, but it took work and every ounce of diplomacy I own."

"Once I make the other two, you sample and judge, I'll make your favorite."

"What are you making now? I'm going to sit down."

"This one has a vodka base. I'm muddling pear, simple syrup, and nutmeg. Martini glass for this one, chilled. Now the vodka, some Tuaca, and B&B—Bénédictine and brandy mix, well shaken—so you're going to taste vanilla, citrus, but herbal notes that say fall. Garnish," she said as she poured and did so, "with three thin crescents of pear, unpeeled."

Olivia sipped. "Our girl knows her stuff. I can see the leaves changing."

"Let me." Audrey snagged the glass. "Mmm. Time to start the fire. It's just lovely, Morgan. I don't know which I like best."

"Don't decide yet. We've got one more in the running.

"This time, I'm muddling pear—peeled—honey, and lime juice into a thick syrup."

"It already sounds good," Olivia said.

"Bourbon makes it better." She poured it into the shaker, added ice, capped it, shook.

"All of them seem like a lot of trouble."

Morgan smiled at her mother. "That's why they're special."

She poured the drink into a wide-mouthed lowball glass. "We top it off with some ginger ale for effervescence, garnish with a pear slice."

"You go first this time, Audrey."

"I don't usually drink bourbon, but I'll try it." One sip and she closed her eyes, said, "Mmm. I think I hear kids at the door, trick-or-treating."

"My turn." Olivia's comment was: "Well, well, well."

"Okay, consider all three, and if you need another sip, go ahead. I want you to hold your hand below the counter, then lift it up with your fingers signaling one, two, or three. There is no wrong answer. Obviously, one of them goes out of the running."

Amused, Morgan watched them take one more sip of each candidate.

"Hands down, fingers ready. And reveal! Number three, both of you? Really?"

"It was hard to choose," Audrey admitted. "But that last sip did it for me. They all say autumn, but I thought that one almost sang it."

"I leaned toward three myself, so it's unanimous. Well, that was easy."

"From this side of the counter anyway. And as the oldest in this panel, I'm taking the winner for myself."

"I'll make you one, Mom."

"No, no, both the others are terrific. I just have to decide which one to claim. I'll take the middle one. Middle ground, that's me. And I can't believe I'm sitting here drinking a cocktail at, what, two-forty-five-ish in the afternoon. I was going to make bread. And we still have to make dinner."

"Let's drink cocktails and order pizza instead."

Audrey laughed at Morgan. "That sounds . . . really wonderful. What do you say, Mom?"

"I say: cheers."

While the Nash women sat on the patio with cocktails, the Jamesons sat around the dining room table holding their family meeting.

Nell studied her tablet. "All right, last item on my agenda is Après's specialty cocktail, virgin option, and coffee for the fall, which we'll introduce right after Labor Day. Morgan hasn't decided on the cocktail, but assures me she'll have that for my approval early next week. For the coffee she's going to do what she calls Coffee Incom*pear*able— get it?"

"Har har," Liam said.

"It's a combination of coffee, poached pear, cinnamon, cloves, and so on. I said complicated, then she made me one. I'm sold. I thought we'd bold and italicize the pear in 'incompearable.' We can price it at four dollars."

"It's clever," Drea commented. "But she's a clever woman. We've got the Stevenson wedding in October, and the bride's using pears in her decor. I'm going to ask Morgan to come up with a signature pear cocktail, something other than whatever we use for Après, and nudge the bride toward it. Has she told you what she's going to offer, Miles?"

"No."

She hadn't told him about the coffee either, which didn't sound like something he'd say "sold" on. But he didn't doubt it would sell.

They did talk about work, some, he thought, while his mother gave her Events report. But when it came down to it, their time together was . . . compressed.

That's how they'd worked it. So far.

He pushed it off, tuned back in, reminded himself this was work, and not the time to think about Morgan.

But wasn't she right here, in the flowers she'd put on the table Saturday morning?

The table passed from his mother to Liam and fall activities. Nature hikes, photo groups, team building, kids' weekends, fall packages. And from there to fall landscaping, to fall maintenance, safety checks, seasonal inventory.

Once business concluded, food took center stage. He'd made the pulled pork as requested—a lot of damn trouble in his book, but it spared him from doing anything else for the family meal.

And Morgan was there, too, as she'd told him the Sunday forecast called for a perfect afternoon and evening. So he should use the colorful dishes again. And damned if she hadn't sat at the counter and fancy folded a pile of napkins, and made another big-ass pitcher of sangria.

"This looks so pretty." After one look at the table, his mother gave him the eye. "I sense a feminine touch."

"Apparently, Morgan has a thing about napkins. And sangria."

"I'm going to try it." His grandfather poured a glass. "One for you, Lydia?"

"All right. I don't think I've had any since we went to Spain. What's that, ten years ago?"

"Must be. Don't know what I think about poached pears in coffee, but this is damn good. Tastes like summer, and it won't be here much longer. Well, look at that. Rory's taught Howl to fetch."

Morgan had, Miles thought. And that damn dog still wouldn't go after a ball for the one who provided him with room and board.

She was here, in the damn dog, in the stupid napkins, in the flowers on the table. The woman was everywhere.

They ate pulled pork, his father's coleslaw, his grandmother's potato salad, corn on the cob his grandfather tossed on the grill.

After, since he'd made the main and that excused him from cleanup, he drew his grandmother aside.

"Got a minute?"

"I hope I have more than one. Let's take a walk. The grounds look especially nice this summer. You're the best gardener out of my grandchildren."

"I guess the landscape training stuck."

"Apparently." She put an arm through his as they walked. "I had lunch with Olivia Nash last week. She tells me Morgan's added to their grounds as well. A Zen frog fountain. You helped with that?"

"I was just the muscle. I love this place, Grand. I don't tell you that often enough."

"I see it, and that's plenty. You want the ring."

He stopped, stared down at her. "How did you know that?"

"My darling boy, I know you. We all know you." She leaned a little closer. "I promised you the ring when you found the one you wanted to wear it. She may want her own."

"No." He shook his head. "It'll matter to her, that it's from you, from family. It'll matter. But I don't want to take it unless you're sure."

Lydia looked down at the wedding set she'd worn more than fifty years. She slipped off the one with the square-cut diamond that topped the band. "What matters is you're sure, and I see you are. I'm wearing the pledge and the life that goes with it. I'm giving you the promise of that pledge. Do you want to tell the others?"

"I figure to wait until I know what she says."

"For a smart man you can be very thick. They already know. I can't tell you what she'll say, because I don't know her heart, not all of it. I can say she's a very lucky woman." Lydia put the ring in his hand, closed his hand around it.

"It may not be what she wants. Not the ring—the package."

"You'll have to find out, won't you? Life's a series of leaps. Now, let's go tell the rest of us what they already know."

He didn't have to say a thing, not when they walked in and he saw his mother's gaze go directly to his grandmother's left hand. Then watched her eyes fill.

"Oh, don't do that."

"I'm entitled. Oh, Rory, our baby's getting married."

"I don't know that. Wait."

"Good thing I didn't hit on her."

That changed quick panic to derision for his brother. "Yeah, that would've worked out for you."

"We'll never know now. Good job, man. She's a winner."

Mick took Lydia's left hand, brought it to his lips. "My own darling. Good job, us."

"Everybody, please back up. If she says no, nothing changes."

"Just shut up." Nell moved in to hug him. "First, she won't. Next, what are we going to do, fire her? She's not only the best bar manager we've had, but she's a friend of mine now."

Then his father wrapped around both of them, murmured in his ear, "Don't get down on one knee. Not her style."

"I wasn't planning on it. Listen, I mean it. Everyone back up. I have to ask her, and until I do, nobody says anything."

The ring of the doorbell saved him. "I'll get it."

He should've waited, he decided. Asked her first, then asked for the ring. Now he had his entire family champing at the bit.

Then he opened the door to Jake and everything else took a back seat.

"Sorry, I'm interrupting. Rang the bell because I know it's family meeting day."

"We're done." He knew. Of course he knew. "Rozwell. Somebody else is dead."

"Not that we know of. But I'm on my way to update Morgan—I asked the feds to let me do it. I wanted to give you a heads-up first."

"Might as well give it to everybody. Want a beer?"

"I'm going to consider myself on duty."

The buzz of conversation died away when Jake walked in with Miles.

"You have news," Nell said quickly.

"More of an update. I stopped by on my way to Morgan's."

"Let's all go sit down." Rory gestured to the dining room.

When they had, Jake set his hands on the table. "They've been following Rozwell's trail north, well into Washington State. It looked like he might plan to try to get into Canada. The thought process was he'd try going east once he'd gotten over the border, then cross south again, into Vermont."

"'Was,' you said?"

"Yes, Pop." Jake turned to Mick. "Beck and Morrison, the leads on the FBI's task force, the ones who I have to figure know him best, suspect he's been baiting them. Leaving a fairly easy trail so he can double back, head south. I've got to say, they convinced me.

"They've gone south. The rest of the task force is in the field, the local authorities are still looking north, and they're keeping a close eye on border crossings."

"Why south?" Miles demanded. "Sum it up."

"He's out of his element, using off-brand motels, shit-can vehicles, and he hasn't had a kill since South Carolina. I'm sorry," he said immediately. "That sounds callous."

"It sounds realistic," Lydia disagreed. "Morgan's part of the resort family. And more," she added with a glance toward Miles. "Mick and I have done some reading on him, and on his type. He needs the rush of the kill. He rarely, if ever, rapes. The kill is his release and his power."

"That's it, Grand, exactly. They figure he knows they're close, too close for him to risk that kill. Too close for him to risk what he really wants."

"Morgan," Drea murmured.

"Morgan. But if he can throw them off—and that's part of the rush for him, too—he can regroup. And south, the exact opposite, is how they see it. He likes the sun, and they've had a hell of a lot of rain along this trail. So they're going to look in Nevada, Arizona, California. They calculate he'll get cocky if he thinks he's put one over on them. More important to those of us sitting here, they don't believe he's headed this way. Yet."

"We'll put resort Security on alert."

"Yeah. And trust me, Miles, Westridge police already are."

"It's a lot of area to cover," Liam pointed out. "Nevada, Arizona, California. You could add New Mexico, Utah."

"It is, and I wish I could tell you something more definite. But if they're right, or even if they're wrong and he's trying for Canada, he's not here."

"He'll change his look again," Nell said.

"Likely already has. But he's put on weight. About twenty pounds, and they've got him on a mini-mart camera. They sent me the feed, and I can tell you, it's wearing on him. And that's one of the things, the mini-mart. He didn't have to go in, just bought some junk food, and they tracked him back to the motel he left. Vending machines right there. He'd know about the camera, went in anyway, didn't try to avoid it."

"He wanted them to see him," Miles concluded.

"That's how it reads to them, and it reads to me, too."

"We appreciate you coming to tell us, Jake. You're going to go talk to Morgan and her family now?"

"Yes, sir," he said to Mick.

"Go." Drea put a hand on Miles's arm. "Go. You should be there. We'll finish up here, feed Howl."

"I will. Thanks. I'll ride with you, Jake."

"Come by my place later, Jake?" Nell asked him.

"I'll do that."

Miles said nothing until they'd gotten in Jake's car. "Are you leaving anything out?"

"Nothing, except what I could read between the lines. They think he'll kill first chance he gets when he feels he's shaken them off. And he's got a head start."

When no one answered the door, Miles felt his nerves start to fray. Their cars, all three, sat in the drive, but no one answered the door.

"Let's walk around back," Jake suggested. "It's a nice evening. They could be sitting outside and didn't hear the bell."

"It would send an alert to their phones."

They'd barely gone halfway around when he heard the laughter. Giddy, female laughter. And the weight in his gut dropped away so fast he might've staggered.

And there they were, all three of them, with a pizza box on the table, cocktail glasses. If he wasn't mistaken, all three were just a little bit drunk.

"Ladies," Jake began.

Audrey let out a squeal that turned into more laughter. "Oh my God, you scared ten years off me."

"Rang the bell. I guess you didn't hear it. Or have your phones handy."

"No, we . . ." Her laughter died, and she closed a hand over Morgan's arm. "Baby."

"Say it fast," Morgan said. "Please."

"They don't have him yet, but he hasn't killed anyone else they know of. I do have an update."

"Okay. Okay." Morgan rubbed her hands over her face. "Sorry. I guess we all left our phones inside. We've been drinking. Fall specialty drinks. Quite a lot, really."

"Pull up some chairs," Olivia invited. "We can all handle our liquor when we have to. Information's power, Morgan. We have the power here."

They listened. Miles said nothing while Jake ran it through, just watched Morgan's face as she took it all in.

"Nevada, Arizona in August." She kept her hands folded on the table. "That's not just sun, that's brutal sun and heat, isn't it?"

"Never been, but yeah. The hope is he'll believe he's shaken loose, treat himself to a fancy hotel. He doesn't look good, Morgan. I can show you if you want. They gave me the go on that."

"I would, yes. I would like to see."

Jake pulled out his phone, brought up the feed, then handed her the phone.

"Oh. I wouldn't have recognized him, not right away. He looks older—not just the hair, the facial hair, he just looks older. And the weight. He looks puffy."

"He looks crazy," Audrey said as she looked over Morgan's shoulder.

"But it shows, and it didn't. It didn't."

"I'd like to see." Olivia held out a hand. "So there he is. He knows the camera's on him." She glanced up at Jake. "We have security cameras in the shop. I've seen some think about a little shoplifting, look at the cameras, pretend they aren't looking, aren't checking."

"I agree."

"He's lost a lot of the style, and again I don't just mean the hair, the weight. He had style, confidence, charm. And I know now he used those as weapons. But he doesn't seem to have them anymore."

"Beck and Morrison agree with that. And like any addict, he's jonesing for a fix. He's not coming after you when he's in this shape. That's their take, and one I agree with. But we're going to keep a close watch. That's a promise."

He rose. "If you have any questions. If you want to talk to me about anything, you call me. Any time of the day or night."

"Thanks." Morgan looked at Miles. "Are you staying or do you have to get back?"

"I'll stay awhile. Thanks for the lift, Jake."

"Anytime."

When Jake left, Audrey shifted to Miles. "We had a contest to pick the fall specialty drink." She kept her smile bright, her eyes direct. "Not an easy choice, and we've taken our task seriously. Morgan, why don't you go in and make Miles a glass of the winner. He has a vested interest, after all."

"I do." Understanding, he looked at Morgan. "That'd be great. I've heard about your planned desecration of coffee, so that's a pass for me. But I'll take the drink. And don't forget your phone."

"Sure. Just give me a couple minutes."

She looked off, he thought, between the alcohol and the update, just a little off. But she got up, went inside.

"What do you want to tell me?" Miles asked when Morgan was out of earshot.

"Not tell, ask. Take her home with you, Miles. She needs to get this out of her head. If she stays here, she'll end up in her room with this preying on her mind. Mom?"

"Take her for a walk with the dog, take her to bed. Distract her."

Though he hadn't planned to, Miles took the ring out of his pocket. "I have a distraction in mind."

As Audrey pressed a hand to her lips, Olivia's eyes narrowed on the ring. "That's Lydia's engagement ring."

"Good eye. It'll be Morgan's if she'll have it."

"Oh no, you don't." She pointed at Audrey. "Don't you start, and make me start. She'll see and misinterpret, and he's sure as hell not going to give her that here and now. Suck those tears up, Audrey Nash, and we'll have a good, happy weep when she leaves."

"Okay. Okay. I'm so happy. Miles, I couldn't be happier."

"We'll see what she has to say."

"Audrey, put those sunglasses back on. We had three contenders," Olivia began. "Here she comes now, so you can judge for yourself."

He took the glass Morgan offered, studied it. "It's got visual appeal. What's in it?"

She managed a smile. "Try it, then guess."

Because he thought she needed it, he played along. "Bourbon," he said after he sampled. "Bourbon, ginger, and the pear comes through. Honey?"

"Very good, and some lime. What do you think?"

"I didn't make the cut to judge the other two, but it's good. Says fall or winter. What are you calling it?"

"It's basically a Prickly Pear—not the fruit, in fact it doesn't use prickly pears. Some slight adjustments to that, and I'm thinking maybe Pear It Down."

"Should work. Nell will like it."

"That's the hope."

"She claimed to like your coffee sabotage. It's nice out here. That frog doesn't quit. Makes me wonder where I'd put something like that."

"I need to get up in your attic."

He sipped his drink, watched her. "Do you?"

"There's bound to be all sorts of things up there. You could use a mirror, some old piece with an interesting shape, behind the daylilies in the back."

Conversation equaled distraction. It wasn't his best thing, but he could manage. "Why would I put a mirror in the garden?"

"Light, reflection, interest. You've probably got more than one up there."

"Maybe. Let's go look."

"Now? I didn't mean now. I should—"

"Go," Audrey said. "Between the pizza and the cocktails, I feel an early night coming on. You and Miles run along."

"He hasn't finished his drink."

"Good thing." Setting it down, he rose. "Because you've finished more than one, so I'm driving, and you're not. I rode with Jake, so this solves how I get home."

Taking her hand, he tugged her to her feet.

"I don't have—"

"You've got stuff at my place. You got your phone now?"

"Yes, but—"

"Enjoy the rest of your evening."

"Oh, we will." Audrey shot out a brilliant smile. "We'll see you tomorrow, baby."

She held it, held it while Miles pulled Morgan away. Then let it go.

"Oh, Mom. My girl. Our girl."

Chapter Twenty-eight

"I didn't clean up the bar," Morgan complained. "I take cleanup duty."

"So you get a night off. How big a mirror?"

He took her keys, nudged her into the car.

"What? Oh, I don't know until I see. Jesus, we had a lot to drink."

"I noticed. It's the first time I've seen you drunk."

"Not drunk, but definitely not fit to drive. We weren't going any-where." She rested her head back. "They were having such a good time. We were. I swear, Gram could drink both of us under the table, then under the floorboards. And she was on her way to doing just that.

"She was a complete wild child," Morgan continued. "Did you know that? I had some sense before, but holy shit, no real idea. They just seemed like, you know, grandparents. She went to Woodstock. She dragged my grandfather to Woodstock. *The* Woodstock. She claims she smoked pot with Janis Joplin. Maybe she's making that up, but who knows? And now she lives in that big old beautiful house and runs two businesses and makes roast chicken and pound cake.

"You have to wonder."

"Wonder what?"

"What twists and turns take a woman like Gram from Woodstock and Janis Joplin to this." She gestured at the town as they drove through. "To Westridge, Vermont. To starting a business, going to yoga class and book club meetings. To being not just content but happy, satisfied.

"Anyway, we were having a really good time."

"I noticed." He'd give her grief about not having the phone with her later.

"You didn't have to come with Jake, but I'm glad you did. And I hope my ladies do have an early night, and don't worry about all this too much."

"You saw that video. And you had it right. He's lost his edge."

"My mother was right, too. He's crazy. You could see the crazy. He'd buried the crazy in Maryland, Miles. I never saw it. No one did. He played darts and trivia, and bought rounds, talked gaming with Sam. No one saw the crazy."

"Now he can't hide it anymore." After he pulled into his driveway, Miles turned to her. "That's going to make him easier to catch."

"I hope so. I'm buzzed enough to whine I want it over. I just want it over."

"I'm not buzzed, and I want it over. And that wasn't whining. I'll tell you when you're whining."

That made her smile. "You would."

He got out of the car, came around as she got out her side. And from in the house, Howl howled.

Inside, he greeted Miles with a mild stare, a quick wag. Then greeted Morgan with a rush of adoration.

"Maybe it's the way you smell," Miles considered. "It's pretty appealing."

"Well, thanks. Who's a good boy? Did you have fun today? I bet you did. Did your big brother give you some of that pulled pork?"

"I'm not his brother. I'm his landlord."

"Don't pay any attention to him. Let's go up to the attic. Won't that be fun?"

"Let's wait on that. I want to talk to you."

She straightened up and, he noted, made her face absolutely blank. "All right."

"We should sit down."

With the dog all but pasted to the side of her leg, she went with him, took a chair.

"I was going to do this a different way. I hadn't figured out the way yet, but different than this. But I figure you being slightly impaired gives me a distinct advantage. And why are you sitting there like you're waiting outside the principal's office?"

"I'm not. Just say it. I'll deal with it."

"Fine. I'm in love with you."

Her face stayed blank even when she blinked. "What? What?"

"You heard me, but I'll say it again for clarity. I'm in love with you."

"I have to sit down."

"You are sitting down."

"I have to stand up." She stood, then immediately sat again. "I'm dizzy. It's not the drinking. Miles—"

"Just be quiet." Impatience wrapped around the words. "You talked all the way over here, so be quiet. I'm not done."

Since she didn't know what to say to that, she said nothing.

"I didn't plan on it. And I didn't see it coming. Should have, but didn't. I can't claim it crept up on me, not when it kept hitting me in the face over so many things. The way your hands move when you're working. That's ridiculous, but there it is. How your brain works, how your heart works, how your body works. All of it."

Because he focused on her, he didn't notice when Howl walked over to him, leaned against his knee.

"But the knockout punch wound up at the waterfall, then started coming at the lookout. And it knocked me flat at the end of Liam's goddamn ropes course. So I'm in love with you, Morgan. It wasn't in the plan, and it wasn't part of the deal we made. But it wasn't a deal so much as guidelines. I'm moving outside the lines, so now deal with that."

"I—"

"I'm still not done." He took out the ring in his pocket. "We'll get married."

He said it matter-of-factly, the way he might've said *We'll watch a movie.*

She stared, and her mouth moved, but it took a minute for it to form actual words. "That's—that's your grandmother's ring."

"Does every woman recognize a diamond at six feet? Since I'm in love with you, and we're already outside the lines, we'll get married."

She stared, then dropped her head between her knees.

"Christ, do you really have to get sick now?"

"Not sick. Need to breathe. Stay over there and let me breathe." She waved a hand in the air as if to push him away, though he hadn't moved.

"If you want poetry, I can probably still recite most of 'The Raven.' And I've got some Yeats in me."

"Shut up. Did you get that ring from your grandmother because of Jake—what Jake told you before you came over?"

"I asked her for it before Jake got there. On their fiftieth wedding anniversary, she told me to ask for it when I'd found the one. When I was sure. When I was ready. You're the one. I'm sure. I'm ready. Get on board, Morgan."

"Before," she murmured, and lifted her head. "Not because of."

The fact he scowled at her leveled her heart rate.

"It's not a force field against psychos. It's a ring. It's a symbol. It's a damn question I wish you'd answer."

She swiped at her face. "You didn't ask a question. You made statements. Wait." She held up a hand before he could speak. "It's funny. Just this morning, Gram and I were working in the garden, and I ended up telling her I was in love with you. It did sneak up on me. I didn't expect it, didn't look for it. I've never felt it before, but I knew what it was. I thought you wanted to tell me you thought we should slow things down."

"That was stupid."

"Was it? Maybe. Blame the vodka—that was the second contender. I stuck with that. Never had a real taste for bourbon."

He kept watching her, and smiled.

"King of the jungle."

"What?"

"Your eyes. They might've been what started the whole thing for me—or your sparkling, people-pleaser personality. We'll go with the eyes," she decided when he laughed. "Tiger eyes, I thought. Lions are king of the jungle, but whatever. That ring. I can't begin to say . . . you'd offer me *that* ring because I understand the power and meaning of that symbol. That particular symbol."

"I've been advised not to get down on one knee."

"Please don't. You'd look ridiculous. And just stay over there for right now so I can try to be coherent. Marriage . . . Miles, I saw for myself how cold and wrong my mother's was. And one of the reasons was me. A child," she corrected before he could protest. "Any girl child anyway. So, it's important we know how—"

"I want kids—that's where you're going. And plural. I don't care what type. I want kids. I want family. With you. It's a big house. We could fill it."

Now tears swirled. "I want that, so much. With you."

"Let's get the rest off the table. If you want to open your own place, you'll leave a major hole in the resort. It's still your choice, and I'll stand by your choice. So will the family if you're worried about that. But you should understand, Après is yours anyway."

She'd planned, and planned for so long. Then everything had changed.

And now?

"Après is what I want."

"Okay, good. You'll have to start coming to family meetings."

"Really?"

"It's part of the package." He hesitated, so briefly, she might not have noticed. But she did. "It's a big package, Morgan."

"I like big packages. Your family must know because you have that ring."

"They know. So does yours."

"You told my ladies? Of course you did." Overwhelmed, she swiped at more tears. "Just—just sit there, okay, until I get this under control. I don't want to blubber when you put that ring on my finger. Not that ring."

"Then hurry up."

"Rozwell."

"No." His tone went sharp as a saber. "Don't bring him here. He's not in this. This is you and me."

"You're right. Did you really do this now because I'd been drinking?"

"Yes."

"God, I love that, so much. Even though you didn't actually ask, the answer would be yes, impaired or stone sober. You can get up now."

She rose when he did, and held out her left hand. When he slipped the ring on, he gave it a wiggle. "It's a little big for you. We'll get it sized."

"I could just do this." She closed her hand into a fist. "Forever."

"Yeah, that'll work. I'll go in late tomorrow. We'll hit the jeweler's when they open." He took her fist, kissed it. "It should fit, because you do."

He slid the ring off, then onto her index finger. "There, that does work. Wear it like that until tomorrow."

"Problem solver," she murmured, and pulled his face to hers.

The kiss warmed everything in her, lit up everything inside her. She had love, and the promise to make a life with love.

No, she wouldn't bring Rozwell into it, but she knew now, without a single doubt, she'd do anything and everything to defend the life they promised each other.

"You could tell me again."

"Tell you what?"

She cupped his face. "Miles."

"I'm in love with you. You might as well know I've never said that to another woman. You're the first."

"It's my job to make sure I'm the last. I love you, Miles. You're my first, too."

He rested his forehead on hers. "Then I've got my own job to do." Then he scooped her up. "I say we seal the deal."

"Yes, please."

"I think we should do that where we started."

She laughed as he carried her toward the sofa. "Another thing I love about you. So sentimental."

"Practical. Couch is close."

"Practically sentimental."

He tumbled with her to the couch. "Quiet now," he said as he tugged off her shirt. "I'm busy finalizing a deal."

* * *

In the morning, with the thrill still so strong, she waited while the jeweler measured her finger, measured the ring.

When Miles offered to buy her what he called a stopgap, she nearly teared up again.

"No, I can wait. It's worth waiting for."

"You might want to select your wedding bands." The saleswoman, all smiles, beamed at them. "We could have those sized for you as well."

"I hadn't thought of that. Should we do that? Are you going to want a ring?"

"I ought to get something out of it," Miles decided. "Keep it simple—keep mine simple. Plain band, no stones. Like that."

"We could both get ones like that."

"You could." The jeweler kept beaming. "But if I could suggest? With a gorgeous vintage engagement ring, an heirloom, you might consider a vintage band. We have a few in this case over here."

And with that, she lured Morgan to the locked display case.

"Oh, oh, they're just stunning."

But Miles had seen just where her gaze landed, and pointed. "That one."

"Miles—"

"An excellent choice." Wasting no time, the woman unlocked the case. "It's from the same era as the solitaire, platinum setting, a double eternity band, two carats total weight, so the solitaire won't outshine it. They'll complement each other."

"See how it looks."

"You should do the honors." No fool, the woman handed the ring to Miles. "Good practice. And it looks like a perfect fit. You have the hands for it. Those long slender fingers."

"Looks good on you."

"It would look good on anyone. But—"

"You don't like it?"

"It's gorgeous. Of course I like it, anyone would. But you don't have to—"

"We'll take it. And the other one—the men's one."

"Oh God." Fast, she thought giddily. Lightning fast, but so right. "I might have to sit down again."

"You can handle it. Now give it back. You don't get to have it until the deal's final."

"I'll box it for you—such an exquisite choice. And we'll see if we have your size in the men's band. You can have something engraved on the inside—no charge."

"No, we'll just—"

"Get his size, and he can buy the wedding band. Then you go away, Miles. Go to work," Morgan told him. "I buy your ring— that's how it works. And I get to decide if I have anything to say inside it."

"I'm the one who'll wear it."

"Yeah." She tugged him down, kissed him. "And you're going to be stuck."

And she knew just what she wanted engraved.

A Deal's a Deal.

From the jeweler's she went straight to Crafty Arts. She saw her mother first, chatting with a pair of customers. Then Audrey saw her. Stopped, and when she read her daughter's face, began to bounce on her toes before she dashed over to grab Morgan into a hug.

"It happened. It happened. Oh, let me see— Where's the ring?"

"It had to be sized, just a half size down. It'll take a few days or so. But I have a picture."

"She has a picture! Can I tell, can I say? I have to. You have to let me," she said as Morgan started laughing. "This is my baby girl, and she just got engaged."

Every woman in the shop applauded, and several walked over to look at the ring.

"I only have a picture. It's being sized." She held up her phone.

"What's all this ruckus?" Olivia demanded as she came down the stairs. She walked straight to Morgan, kissed both her cheeks. "He's a good man, and almost deserves you. Mimosas on the house, staff and customers. We're going to toast to a brave new start."

* * *

Rozwell hated fucking Nevada. He hated the goddamn desert, and he hated the filthy, ugly shack he was forced to live in.

He hated the puckered scabby scar on his arm.

Most of all, he hated the solitude, the isolation, the constant nothing.

He had eggs, Christ knew, and he was sick of them.

He had to cook for himself, and clean up after himself, and he was damn sick of that, too. He'd opened cans—lots of cans—and even tried frying up some chicken parts from the freezer.

It turned out scorched outside, too pink inside, and he hated that, too. He did better with rice, carefully following internet instructions.

He'd made a few burgers out of what he thought—hoped—was ground beef, but he didn't have any buns.

He'd gone through the fresh stuff his dead hostess had provided, lived on eggs, cans, and boxed food. And knew he'd have to make another trip to get some food he could just heat up. And some snacks.

So what if he hadn't taken off the rest of the weight? Maybe put some back on. So the fuck what? When he had his life back, he'd get back in shape.

He didn't have anything to *do* but eat, do his research, play with the tech toys, watch TV on his laptop, and eat some more.

He'd forgotten to water the goat, so he'd had to drag the dead, useless thing back with the woman. What was left of her, and what was left stank so much he'd nearly lost his breakfast.

He'd bought the sheets and towels, but without a dryer, the towels dried stiff. So he'd make a list, make a trip.

Food, numero uno. And he was running low on liquor. Maybe he could get a decent meal—one he didn't cook or wash up after—in Two Springs. Nobody looked for him in this godforsaken desert, but he'd be careful, keep to himself, though he yearned for voices, movement.

He missed having conversations, knowing most of what he said in them were well-crafted lies.

He caught himself talking to himself, tried to stop. But like the chips, he just couldn't.

Make the list, drive in, get a meal, buy supplies, drive out again.

He mumbled to himself as he paced around the house, one that had become a cage. Except for that side room. So he went into it, as it always settled him down.

He'd pulled down the Jesus pictures because he didn't like the way some guy who got himself nailed to a cross stared at him with what looked like pity.

He sat, a man carrying extra weight in his face and belly, one who smelled of sweat, dust, and clothes poorly washed. Roots showed in his dyed hair. His nails needed clipping.

"We'll just do a little check on our good friend Morgan. Let's see what that skinny bitch is up to."

He tracked her usual charges, payments. Groceries, insurance, gas, the monthly payment to her greedy grandmother. And frowned over a charge for seven hundred and change at a jeweler in Westridge.

"What's all this, Morgan? Getting extravagant? We can't have that, no, we can't have that. Not while I'm stuck in this hellhole. Time for a little reminder. Time to touch base."

He sat back, drumming his unkempt nails on the rough wood table. "Let's see, let's see."

Closing his eyes, he nearly nodded off in the chair before he shook himself awake, scratched his belly.

He used her account, ordered some slutty clothes—she was a whore, after all. Then went to another site, and another to order whatever caught his eye. Garbage bags, because she was garbage, room deodorizers because garbage stank, always keeping the purchase under five hundred.

He had so much fun he kept at it, hit an online florist for a funeral wreath, and filled out the card.

Morgan, always remember.

"That ought to do it. Yeah, that ought to do it just fine."

The fun worked up an appetite, so he went in, opened a can of chili. He didn't bother to heat it up, but ate straight out of the can.

"Another few weeks, that's all. Just to make sure, make damn sure.

Head east before much longer. Maybe catch some of that Vermont foliage. That's the ticket. Catch some of that color, right? Catch it, kill her dead. Kill her dead and close that deal, collect that debt."

He tossed the empty can toward the trash, licked the fork.

"Get what she owes me, and it's smooth sailing again. She's bad luck, that's what she is. Brought me bad luck."

With his belly full, he decided to take a nap. He'd make that list, go into town tomorrow. He didn't feel like cleaning himself up now. Tomorrow was good enough. Tomorrow meant one more day closer to taking care of business.

As he lay down on sheets he'd sweated through the night before, Beck and Morrison made a pass through Gabbs, then drove to Two Springs.

They'd checked both outlying motels, the single twelve-room hotel in town, shops, eateries. They sat down with the local cops.

It took most of the day and produced not a single hit.

At the end of it, they sat in a little restaurant where the air ran blissfully cold and ate surprisingly good enchiladas.

"We're not wrong, Quentin, I swear we're not wrong. There hasn't been a sign of him in Washington since we started south."

"Not seeing anything this way either."

"Not yet. But it still feels right."

"Maybe he's gone well and truly to ground. Taking a frigging sabbatical. Or we're not altogether wrong, but he headed east. Montana, Colorado. Arizona."

"Let's do this. We give this another day, get a couple of rooms, work the problem again, get some sleep. Start fresh tomorrow and go into the national forest, brief the park rangers. We get nothing, we take a break. I want to sleep in my own bed with my husband."

"Another day," he agreed. "We could use a break, clear the mind, maybe find a new angle. It's starting to feel like chasing our tails, Tee. I think we were right about him baiting us up north, I think we had that right. I just don't know if we've got this right. Not a damn sign of him."

"One more day, a break, then back at it. Since we're staying, let's have a beer."

"I can get behind that."

At the resort, well before her shift, Morgan knocked on Lydia's door. She knew the matriarch was in, just as she knew word had already spread. She'd wanted to wait until she had the ring on her finger again, but since word spread, she opted for now.

"Come!"

She opened the door. "Could I speak with you a minute? I have a meeting with Nell coming up, but I wanted to speak to you first if you have time."

"All right, come in, sit. It gives me a chance to tell you Mick and I are very pleased."

"Thank you, thank you for that. But more, I want to thank you . . . I had a very coherent and heartfelt speech. I practiced. But it's just gone. I can't tell you what it means to me that you'd trust me with the ring Mick gave you. The one you've worn all this time. I promise you I'll cherish it, and I'll do everything I can to be a good partner to Miles."

"He wouldn't have asked me for the ring if I couldn't trust you. I wouldn't have given it so willingly if I didn't know you'd cherish him."

"I will. I do. The ring's magic. That sounds silly, but—"

"It doesn't." Lydia's signature red lips curved in a warm, warm smile. "Not to me. And it makes me very happy knowing you'll wear it, since you feel that, too. The Nashes and the Jamesons. I find I'm not surprised. Your grandmother and I are going to have a great deal of fun harassing you and Miles over your wedding plans. I asked, and he told me you plan to stay, managing Après."

"Yes."

"Then you'll be expected at the September family meeting, with a report. Nell can help you with the basic procedure."

"I'll be there." She rose. "Thank you, for everything."

"Come see me once the ring's sized. I'd like to see it on you."

"I will."

"Oh, and Morgan, I liked that you brought out the Fiestaware, and the clever folds of the napkins. Little details make a home. You've already started."

Chapter Twenty-nine

When Morgan walked into Après, Nick greeted her with a bone-crushing hug.

"Congratulations, best wishes, whatever the hell it's supposed to be. I'm so happy for you!"

"Thanks. I'm so happy for me."

"Let's see it. Let's— Hey, where's the ring?" Those deep brown eyes reflected bafflement and insult. "WTAF! He didn't give you a ring?"

"It's being sized."

"Oh." His face ran the gamut from relief to approval to disappointment. "I guess I have to wait till it is to catch the sparkle."

"I have a picture on my phone."

"Show! Wait." He shot a mile-wide grin to a stool sitter who'd cleared his throat. "Sorry. What can I get you?"

"We'll try two of the special cocktails."

"Coming right up! My friend—she's my boss, too—just got engaged. We're pretty excited."

"So did we!" The woman on the next stool shot out her left hand and the ring on it. "He surprised me with this at dinner last night."

"Congratulations. It's gorgeous. Drinks on me, Nick," Morgan told him as he made them.

"That's really nice of you."

"Solidarity."

"Her ring's getting sized," Nick tossed out. "But she has a picture."

"Oh, we'd love to see. Wouldn't we, Trent?"

"Sure." He looked a lot more interested in the drink, but did his duty and looked at Morgan's phone. But his fiancée gasped.

"It's stunning! It looks like an heirloom."

"His grandmother's."

"Holy sh . . . sparkle." Nick set the drinks down. "We'll talk later. Nell reserved a table outside for your meeting."

"I'd better get to it. Congratulations again. Enjoy your drinks."

On her way outside, servers waylaid her with more congratulations, more hugs. It felt, Morgan thought, very much like family. She'd barely taken a seat when Nell rushed over.

"Late. I hate to be late, but it happens."

"It's, like, two minutes."

"Late is late. I need caffeine. Can Nick do an iced cappuccino as good as you?"

"Of course he can."

"Great. Hey, Barry, iced cappuccino. Two?" she asked Morgan.

"Why not?"

"And I missed lunch. How about we split a cheese plate? I need something, since I'm going to sample your potential fall specialty cocktail for approval."

"I like cheese."

"Great. Thanks, Barry. Now," she began immediately, "we'll get to the business portion, but first I want to hear everything."

"About what?"

Nell gave Morgan a long, hooded look. "Please. All I got from Miles was yeah, yeah, he gave you the ring, and it's getting sized. I want details. How did he ask you?"

"He didn't really. He more told me."

Nell sat back, face covered with the unsurprised disgust only a sibling can manage. "Of course he did, the romantic fool."

"But that was after he told me he loved me. He did that part really well."

"Okay." Willing to withhold judgment, Nell picked up the sparkling water Barry had already served. "Start at the beginning."

"Well, the beginning really began when my ladies and I tested out the three finalists for the fall cocktail. Enthusiastically."

"Oh boy, I'm going to enjoy this."

And she did, laughing her way through half an iced cappuccino and a portion of a cheese plate.

"All right, he gets some points. And you're happy. We're all happy. I hope you know that."

"I am, and I do."

"So when and where? Have you decided?"

"In broad terms. I asked for spring and he said fine, as long as I move in with him by the New Year. He wants to end and begin the year with me."

"Okay." Cracker in one hand, Nell held up the other. "Major points for that. On Miles's scale, that's virtually sloppy romance. Spring. The where?"

"I know we could get married here, and it would be wonderful, but—"

"It's not business, but it edges that way."

"A little, but more, I'd like to get married at his house."

"Your house," Nell reminded her. "It would be your house, too. And I think that's perfect, if my opinion counts. A spring garden wedding. What does Miles think?"

"He said, 'Whatever you want is fine.'"

"You don't actually believe that? Say you wanted him to wear a lilac morning coat to coordinate with the lilacs you carry."

"I'm writing that down just to see his face. He doesn't want to be poked by every detail. I'd say as long as I don't want that morning coat or horse-drawn carriages—and I don't—all good."

"It's good you know who you're marrying. You should also know Mom's going to want to get her hand in. So am I."

"I'd be crazy to toss away experts, especially when I know I'm going to want and need help."

"Say that again." Nell tapped her phone. "So I can record it for the future."

"I want and need help planning the wedding," Morgan obliged. "Signed, Morgan Nash."

"Okay, that's on the record."

"Knowing Miles, he'll want Jake and Liam to stand up with him.

In fact, that's the one clear answer on all this he gave me. Nell, would you stand up for me?"

Reaching out, Nell gripped Morgan's hand. "God, I was hoping you'd ask. I'd love to."

"I'm so glad. How do you feel about puce? Kidding," she said when Nell's mouth fell open. "I expect to see a replica of that expression if I test Miles with lilac morning coats. I know I have to pick colors, but I swear whatever they are, flattering is key. Do you think it's weird I'd like to ask Jen to be an attendant, to balance it out?"

"I think it's perfect. Delicate question while we're on it. Your father?"

"No." That came easy, and without regret. "So many reasons, no. I'll send him a note, but not an invitation."

"Do you want someone to walk you down the aisle?"

"Yes. My mother and my grandmother."

As her eyes filled, Nell held up a hand again. "Okay, I'm no soft touch, but that got me. More perfect, and so lovely, Morgan. Have you told them?"

"They cried. We all did. And it was perfect."

"We're going to have so much fun with this, and it will be perfect. Nothing's going to spoil it."

After nudging her cup aside, Nell took a breath. "We won't say his name, not here and now. But I'm going to assume Jake gave you the update."

"He did."

"Morgan, you became family to us when you took over Après. That's how the Jamesons work. You're only more so now. We've got your back, your front, your sides. Anything we can do, anything you want us to do, it's done."

"I didn't know just how much I wanted family until I let myself have family. I keep coming back to that. And in that spirit, of family, I'm going to ask . . . you and Jake. Any thoughts?"

"A lot of them, since you ask."

Nell looked around the tables, at people having a drink, a bite to eat, relaxing as the summer day turned to summer evening. "He waited, and that was really smart of him, to wait until I was ready. Or close to ready, whether I knew it or not. I'm not ready, quite, to take the leap you and Miles are. I want to give it a test run—that's me all over. Live together first.

"He's got a nice place, but I like mine better." She shrugged, picked up her water glass again. "Mine's closer to my work, his is closer to his. And the practical part of me knows that he's chief of police, and being closer to town's important."

"Find a house you like between those two points. Then it's not Jake's place or Nell's, it's Jake and Nell's."

"Buy a house together? That's . . . really smart. A compromise and commitment all at once. He'd like that. I'd like that. Maybe. Yeah, maybe. I'm going to like having a sister."

"So am I."

"Okay, Sister, go make me a drink, and we'll get down to business."

Across the continent, Rozwell drove into Two Springs early to avoid the heat of the day. A joke, he thought sourly. The heat never left. But he wanted to get this trip over with, get those new towels, some fucking food, some decent booze.

He wanted to hear voices, even if they came from stupid desert rats.

The town wasn't much—he'd call it a hovel—but it had stores, including a barely decent market, a few tired excuses for restaurants, two bars with a liquor store attached to one of them. The western rube version of a sheriff's department—that didn't worry him—and a huddle of houses on the outskirts someone with a sense of humor might call the 'burbs.

It lay a few miles from the western edge of Humboldt-Toiyabe National Forest, which held no interest for him—and sported views of the mountains.

Close enough for bored day-trippers or crazed hikers and campers to pay a call, so some of those shops ran to souvenirs, camping and hiking gear. And plenty of guns for sale.

He might not be a fan of the gun, but he'd caught sight of snakes more than once. He'd tried shooting the hell out of them with the handgun he'd taken off Dead Jane, tried her shotgun, and the rifle he'd found in the cabin.

And tested out the AR-15, which obliterated the snake and scared the crap out of him.

He put that one back on the wall, stuck with the handgun.

She'd had a shitload of ammo, but he'd wasted some of it on the damn snakes, then shooting the shit out of a cactus just to hear the noise.

He'd written down the kind of ammunition for the handgun.

Wouldn't hurt to pick some up.

Since he'd woken hungry, he'd eaten half a dozen eggs and the last of the bacon he'd found in the freezer. Jane had marked it— helpful—but he'd had to slice it himself, so the slices were mostly too thin, too thick.

He'd just buy some damn bacon. And sausage. And whatever else caught his eye and appetite.

He bought towels first. No Egyptian cotton in Two Stupid Springs, he'd discovered before. But he settled. He bought a new frying pan, since he'd burned the one at the cabin, then tossed it as far as he could toss.

He hit the liquor store. Beer, wine, whiskey, vodka, mixers, tonic, and, hell, why not tequila?

"Having a party?" the checkout clerk asked with a little ho-ho-ho like fricking Santa.

Rozwell stared at him, lip curled. "Yeah. I'm the life of the party."

"Bet." Avoiding those eyes now, the clerk bagged the booze, handed over the change.

After loading the supplies in the truck, he went for the ammo. He bought three boxes of hollow points for his inherited Colt 45.

And thought: Yeehaw, I'm a gunslinging son of a bitch.

From there, he hit the market.

Chips, cookies, candy, frozen fries—why hadn't he thought of that before? Bacon, sausage, frozen pizza. The pizza made him think of Morgan.

"Bitch'll get what's coming," he muttered, and the woman standing two feet away headed in the other direction.

Frozen dinners—heat and eat! Cheese! Milk! Cereal, bread, butter. Lemons—for a nice tequila shot. Bananas. Potatoes, because anyone could figure out how to bake a damn potato.

He filled two baskets before he was done.

At checkout, the clerk started ringing him up. She had a face as round as a pie with glasses that kept sliding down her nose.

It irritated him so much he imagined punching her right in those stupid glasses, just driving them into her eyes so they bled.

"Looks like stocking up," she said cheerfully.

He spread his lips in what he believed made a friendly smile. "That's right. Stocking up. Man's gotta eat, doesn't he?"

"Yes, sir." She kept her eyes trained on the items. "He sure does."

He carted the bags out, loading the frozen stuff in the cab where the AC, such as it was, could keep it from melting on the trip back.

He loaded the rest, found himself nearly out of breath with the effort, the heat. He unscrewed the cap on the bottle of Coke he'd bought in the mart, and brought it with him as he got behind the wheel.

Another good glug and he nearly choked on it as his breath caught.

As he started the engine, he glanced in the rearview mirror.

He lost his breath again, and in the heat still baking the cab, went ice-cold.

He saw them, just walking out of a diner-type place, the place where he'd have had breakfast if he hadn't been too hungry to wait.

But it couldn't be. A mirage, a trick of the light. He rubbed his eyes under his sunglasses, but they remained—and moving his way.

The fucking feds. Those assholes, Beck and Morrison. Right here, walking down the planked sidewalk.

Panic had his ears ringing, his eyes watering as he hit the gas.

He beat his hand on the wheel as he drove. How? How? How?

The truck rattled and shook as he pushed it as fast as it could go. Because they were right behind him. Right behind him.

He had to get back, fast, to Dead Jane's place. He'd broken his new rule and left clothes, equipment, cash—too much to lose again. He'd broken the rule because they shouldn't be here.

Why had they come here?

When he reached the gate, leaped out, his legs nearly gave way under him. Fear had him sweat-soaked, shaky so his fingers fumbled with the padlock keys.

But he got the gate open, drove through, and gathered himself to lock it behind him again. Just in case.

He tore down the drive, struggling to clear his mind enough to think, just think. He'd take the old woman's truck. A beater, but a better beater than this one. And maybe, somehow, they'd tracked what he'd been using.

He'd locked the cabin—safety first—so had to deal with those locks. Inside, he ripped through, shoving laundry he hadn't done with laundry he had. His own breath sounded like a windstorm as he gathered up his equipment, disconnected some of hers to take.

The money, the money, the money, the IDs he'd completed.

The guns, the ammo, the knives—including the one the dead bitch had stabbed him with.

Chickens clucked and clacked as he ran to the shed, dragged the door open. He tossed tools into the bed of the truck, the clanging echoing as he threw in his bolt cutters, a pickax, a hatchet, a hammer.

Dust flew as he drove to the shack, tossed bags, suitcases, briefcases into the bed. He forced himself to take more care with the equipment, stuck the handgun under the driver's seat. The rifle and shotgun went in the gun rack.

Let them come. He'd shoot them to pieces.

He needed water, food.

When he remembered all the food he'd bought, rage leaped into the fear.

He ripped open the door to the other truck, dragged out frozen dinners, frozen pizza, milk jugs, heaving them into the dirt. Time and money wasted, wasted.

As he raged, he screamed. As he screamed, something already cracked broke inside him.

He stood, looking around him at milk glugging onto the ground, at the dented boxes of potpies and fried chicken and gravy, the Dove Bars and extra-sharp cheddar.

And began to laugh, and laugh, and laugh so hard tears ran down his cheeks. He chuckled to himself as he transferred the other groceries, the liquor, the towels, from one truck to another.

Fuck it, fuck this shit, he was *done* with it. Time to close the books. Time for a reckoning. Time for a bitch to pay the goddamn piper.

"The time's come, the walrus said," he muttered as he bungeecorded one of Jane's tarps over the bed of the truck.

He started to get into the truck, then decided what the hell. Walking over, he ripped open the box of Dove Bars, yanked one out, tore off the wrapper.

He ate it while he drove to the gate. "Adios, Jane!" he called out while he filled his mouth with ice cream and chocolate. "Thanks for fucking nothing!"

He unlocked the gate, drove through. And tossing the padlock keys out the window, started the drive east.

As Beck and Morrison walked across the street to their car, the grocery store clerk stood outside the market smoking a Marlboro to settle her nerves.

"Hey! You're those feds, aren't you?"

"Ma'am." Morrison stopped at the passenger door, as he'd lost the toss to drive. "Special Agents Morrison and Beck."

"Deb said there were feds poking around yesterday about some crazy guy. My day off." She took a long drag. "Had my own crazy guy just a bit ago. Crazy eyes. Bought enough food for an army battalion. Gave me a look, a smile that turned my blood cold."

"Is that right?" Beck felt a little hum, walked over. "We left a sketch of the man we're looking for with the manager. Have you seen it?"

"Nah. I clock in, do my job, clock out. Mind my own business like everybody should."

"Would you mind taking a look now?" Beck opened her briefcase, took one of the sketches out of a file.

"Guess I could. I'm taking my break because Crazy Eyes shook me up some." She took the sketch, shoved at her sliding glasses. Shook her head. "Nope. This guy had shorter hair, sort of dirty blond— what I could see of it. And he . . ."

Pausing, she frowned. "Wait a minute. I guess maybe. It's the eyes, those crazy eyes. But this one didn't have a beard so much as a lot of scruff, and I think he had more weight in his face. But those eyes . . ."

"How about his height?" Morrison asked. "How tall would you say?"

"About six foot. Maybe just under."

"Did he say anything?"

"Yeah, he said how a man's gotta eat. I said, 'Stocking up,' because he had two full baskets of food, and he said how a man's gotta eat."

"Did he have an accent?"

"Didn't sound like he's from around here." She shrugged and smoked. "More like back east, I guess. It maybe could be him, I can't swear to it. But something wasn't right about that guy. That I can swear to."

"Did you see what he was driving?"

"No, sorry. Usually I'd've called for Tiny—he stocks shelves—to help him load up, but I didn't. Just wanted him gone. Never saw him around here before that I noticed. At least I never checked him out before. Mustn't live too far, I'd think, as he bought a shitload of frozens."

Though she was reluctant, they got her name and contact.

"What are the odds?" Morrison wondered.

"Good enough to do another quick check. If you're Rozwell, somehow got a place close enough to town to come in to buy food, what else do you stock up on?"

"If I'm holed up here, I'm going to buy a whole lot of alcohol."

"Yeah, you would. Let's follow the feeling, Quentin, show his picture one more time at the liquor store."

When they walked into the liquor store, the clerk looked up from a paperback novel. Not the clerk from yesterday, Beck thought. Younger brother maybe.

"Help you?"

"FBI. Special Agents Beck and Morrison." Beck held up her badge.

The clerk slid off his stool. "Oh, hey!"

"We're looking for someone."

"As long as it's not me."

Beck offered her best smile. "No, not you. This man."

The clerk took the sketch, shifted from foot to foot. "That's funny. Sort of."

"What is?"

"He kind of looks like this fella who was in here about an hour ago. Around the eyes, he does. And yeah, the mouth, I guess. I didn't like him."

"No?" Beck leaned in, just a little. "Why?"

"Okay, he bought enough stock I could've closed the door for the day, and my brother—he owns the place—wouldn't have known because the daily take would be more than it ever is. But he had mean all over him—the vibe, right? And he bought so much I just said how it looked like he was having a party. He gave me a look made me wish I'd kept my mouth shut. I think this is him, with shorter hair. What'd he do?"

"Did you see what he was driving?"

"I looked out, saw him loading the boxes of booze in a pickup. Old Chevy, rusted-out red.

"Hey, what did he do?"

But they were already out the door.

"It's him, Quentin. I swear I feel it in my guts."

"Let's bring the sheriff in on it. He's got a place. You don't buy all that food and booze for a damn road trip or when you're in a motel."

"He could have hostages—not his style—but there are homes and small ranches within a half hour's drive of Two Springs. Or maybe there's a place that's been abandoned. Frozen food means he has refrigeration and a stove or a microwave. Coming into town, making at least two stops means he feels safe."

As they moved, fast, to the sheriff's office, they scanned the streets.

"He could still be here," Morrison said. "But that's unlikely. Frozen food."

"Is going to melt pretty quick in this heat. He has to be close."

The sheriff's office had an outer room with a dispatch desk, and two more for the pair of deputies who both worked part-time. In the back, it held two cells, a unisex bathroom, and a makeshift counter for a hot plate and the coffeepot on it.

The AC whirled madly, and sent the smell of bad coffee everywhere.

Sheriff Neederman, a rawboned, sunbaked man of about forty-five, had his own office—with the door open.

"Well, FBI." He stood from his desk. "Didn't expect to see you again."

"Lucy Wigg from Two Springs Market and Kyle Givens from Givens Liquors and Beer just identified Gavin Rozwell from our sketch. He was in both places this morning."

"Well, hell. Are they sure of that?"

"Sure enough. He stocked up on food—including frozen products—and alcohol, which indicates he's found a hole close by. Close enough. We need to start a search."

"We'll sure help with that. I've got one deputy out on a call, and I'll bring the other one in. I'll notify state, have some head in here."

"He's driving a red Chevy pickup. Older model, from what we're told. You know the area, Sheriff. Let's have some best guesses."

"Let me make those calls and think on it."

When he had, he spread out a map. "These houses here, here? Few and far between maybe, but people'll notice a stranger. Different story when you move out here, or into the mountains. Hardscrabble ranches, hardscrabble people who live that life because they don't want people around. And you'll have your preppers, survivalists, anti-every-fucking-thing types. They wouldn't set out the welcome mat for him—or us, come to it."

"Leaning to that, who lives alone? No family—too much trouble," Beck said to her partner. "Easier to take down one person. He'd want privacy if he decided to dig a hole."

"There's Riley—former marine—piss and vinegar in one package." Neederman tapped on the map. "His place is a damn fortress. And there's Jane Boot—her husband passed awhile back, but she stuck. Comes in, sells eggs, goat's milk about once a month. Tough as nails, prepping for war or the Rapture, whichever comes first."

"The woman," Morrison said. "He'd go for the woman before he'd take on a marine."

"Let's go find out."

"I'll lead the way. She's got no phone—doesn't believe in them—and she's got her place gated and barbed wired off. I've got bolt cutters in the truck. If she's back there milking that damn goat, she is gonna be pissed."

Twenty minutes later, they pulled up at the open gate.

Neederman angled his truck across it to block any exit, then stepped out. He picked up a set of keys, shook his head when Beck opened her window.

"No way Jane would leave this gate open. Keys on the ground. Son of a bitch."

"Do you have body armor, Sheriff?"

He tipped back his hat. "Yeah, yeah. Son of a bitch," he said again. "She'd never leave the gate open."

"Let's suit up. Call for backup. My partner and I will take the lead from here. He's our quarry."

He aimed a hard look at Morrison. "If he hurt Jane, he's mine now, too."

After they'd put on vests, they drove through the gate.

"He's not here anymore, Tee. He got a whiff of us, that's what this means."

Face grim, she kept driving.

"There's the red truck, and groceries all over the ground. Front door open, that outbuilding door open."

"Somebody had a temper tantrum," Morrison muttered.

"Looks like it, but let's not get shot being wrong."

She drove between the outbuilding and the cabin, and using the car as a shield, they got out.

"Gavin Rozwell! This is the FBI. Come out with your hands up."

No sound but chickens clucking, pigs rooting.

She picked up a rock, tossed it to draw fire. And nothing stirred. She tossed another so it banged against the house.

"Okay, Quentin, let's clear it."

They came out of cover, stayed low as they ran to the door. He swept first, went in high as she swept and went low.

The place smelled of sweat and dust and looked like the scene of a bar fight.

They cleared it, and the shed.

"She has a Ford Ranger pickup, a . . . 2015 or '16, I think—and I'll confirm that," Neederman told them. "Blue, a medium blue, and I'll get the plates. Would he have taken her with him?"

"That's very doubtful."

He rubbed the back of his neck. "I'm going to look around for her," he told Beck. "And the goat."

"He had to see us, this morning. He had to see us, or why run like this after buying all the food?" Beck had to stop herself from kicking the melting packages. "He came out of the market and saw us. Or he'd loaded up already. Likely that. He got in the truck, drove here, did this, got what he wanted, and went."

"Running again, Tee." Because they both needed it, he put a hand on her shoulder. "He's running again, running scared and mad with it. Let's get the alerts out on her truck."

"She's back here!" Neederman called out. "And the goat. Jesus, what's left of them's back here. He just dumped her on the ground," he said when they joined him. "Just tossed her on the ground for the scavengers."

Chapter Thirty

Morgan opened the door for Jake on a sultry midmorning that begged for storms.

"Come in. Should I make coffee? Are we going to need it?"

He shut the door behind him. "Why don't we go for something cold. Your ladies around?"

"No, they're at work."

Whatever he'd come to tell her, it was bad. She felt the bad crawling under her skin.

"I don't think the sun tea's finished yet, but we've got Cokes."

"That'll be great. Morgan, are you okay hearing about Rozwell from me? You can contact the FBI if you want it straight from the source."

"I appreciate you taking the time to tell me yourself." Steady, she thought, look how steady her hands were as she filled glasses with ice. The panic days were over.

"He killed someone else, didn't he? I can just feel it knotted in my stomach."

"Yes. Why don't we sit down here and I'll tell you everything they gave me. I'll tell you what happened yesterday in Nevada."

"Nevada. So they were right about him going south. I like knowing they were right. It's something."

As he told her, Morgan sat back, stunned. "I can't see it, I honestly can't see him living in some prepper's cabin in the middle of nowhere. I can see him killing her, and I'm sorry for it, but the rest?"

"You broke him. That's my take on it. You broke his streak, and that broke him. I'll give credit to the FBI, and Beck's solid instincts, but she and her partner would be the first to admit hitting that town the same morning Rozwell came in for supplies was just blind luck."

"And they think he was there a couple of weeks?"

"Close to three. They've tracked his victim to her last trip into town. It's not unusual for no one to see her for a month, even more. They have her coming in to sell eggs, milk, some leather goods. She bought supplies, gassed up her truck nearly three weeks ago. And they've tracked Rozwell back to a motel about thirty miles away, up until the day she went into Two Springs."

"I see. I see."

"She was active in online groups—preppers, survivalists, religious fringes. As they see it, he kept that up off and on, but they tell me they can see subtle differences in her posts and responses starting nineteen days ago—the night after she went in for supplies."

Jake hesitated, then went on. "They'll do an autopsy of the body, and may be able to determine when she died. Morgan, every person they interviewed that had any contact with him yesterday stated they saw something wrong in him. He either couldn't hide it, or didn't bother. She had guns, Morgan. A shotgun, a rifle—they found spent shells scattered around. And she habitually carried a Colt on her hip."

"A lot of good that did her."

"The point is, he took them. He left an AR-15, so we can be grateful there, but he has the rest. And he bought ammo for the Colt when he went to town. He's never used guns before."

"He's not the same as he was before."

"The profilers agree with that. Everything they found at that cabin says he's lost control." Because he considered them friends, because she would become a kind of sister to him, Jake reached for her hand.

"Their thinking is he'll have no choice but to come here."

"Part of that's a relief because you're always waiting to hear the door creak open, to see the monster leap out. It's always there, Jake, no matter what I do. It's like some rodent tunneling holes under a garden. It looks settled and pretty, but it's all just waiting to collapse."

She looked down at her drink, then up into his eyes. "You're worried, since he took the guns, he'll just shoot me. When I'm going out to my car or running errands. He won't. He can't. It's too fast and final."

"He's not the same as he was," Jake repeated.

"No, but you can't change who you are at the base, in the core. He needs to hurt me, to see me afraid. He has to pay me back for everything that went wrong for him since . . . since Nina."

After giving herself a shake, she reached for her drink.

"I can't believe I only knew him for a couple of weeks, and I see him so clearly. The idea of him living the way you said for weeks . . . No, he has to pay me back for that. Killing me isn't enough unless I suffer first."

"I can agree with you and still worry I'm wrong."

"He took everything from me, Jake, everything but my life. And look." She spread her hands. "Not even two years later, I'm okay. More than okay. I have a home, family, a man who loves me. I have a good job, a good life. I have friends. He's the one who lost. He's the one who's running and desperate. Killing me quick won't make up for that. It's personal."

As the doorbell sounded, she automatically pulled out her phone to check. "It's . . . flower delivery. It's . . ."

She passed the phone to Jake.

His eyes went cool before he rose. "I'll deal with it."

It took her a moment to gather herself and follow him. She knew a funeral wreath when she saw one. At the door while Jake questioned the stunned delivery woman, Morgan studied the wreath and its message.

Morgan, always remember.

She would, she thought. She would always remember.

Because he knew changing the plates wouldn't be enough, Rozwell bought a paint sprayer, some pea-green paint, and on a stretch of desert road, coated the blue of Jane's truck.

It looked like shit, and he had to spend time wiping paint off the head- and taillights, but his ride no longer matched the description.

He figured it would hold for a while, especially given the yahoo cops in this part of the world.

He couldn't risk motels, no matter how crap worthy, so drove straight through, into Utah, drove from day into night, fueled by rage and fear, and caffeine and carbs.

Time to reestablish good habits, he decided, so drove to the airport in Salt Lake to take a much-needed nap in long-term parking.

He woke, hot and miserable, before dawn, but decided his luck was back in when he spotted a minivan, complete with a BABY ON BOARD sign, that must've parked while he'd taken his siesta.

Easily fifteen years old, he estimated, but whistle clean.

It took him more than a half hour, but he got in, disabled the alarm, got it started—hadn't lost his touch!—and transferred everything from the truck to the van.

It had two hundred thousand miles on it, but it would do the job, get him into Colorado, a halfway decent motel—not hotels yet, he warned himself.

A hot shower, time to groom, eat, sleep, and map out the best route to Morgan.

With Miles, Morgan closed the bar on Friday night.

"Beck called me a few hours ago."

He stopped what he was doing. "And you're just telling me?"

"We were busy; you were busy. And now's as good as then. A security guard spotted the truck he was driving in long-term parking, Salt Lake City airport. He'd tried spray-painting it, but the blue bled through. It took them some time to identify what he'd taken from there. A red minivan. A Kia, I think she said. He'd covered a lot of distance, but they tracked where he'd stayed at a Days Inn, in Colorado."

"Why don't we sit down?"

"No, I'm good. I'm good. He dumped the van in a Walmart parking lot in South Dakota. He carjacked an SUV, at gunpoint, tied the owner—a sixty-year-old woman—with bungee cords, gagged her, shoved her into the van. He knocked her unconscious, gave her a concussion, but he didn't kill her. That's something."

"They're following up what Agent Beck says is a very credible sighting in Minnesota, and she doesn't think he'll keep the SUV long, doesn't believe he'll risk trying for any of his contacts to trade it. They've got the airport in Minneapolis on alert."

"Is that it?"

"That's it for now."

"Morgan." He took her hand, the one that wore his ring. "This means something."

"It means everything."

"And busy doesn't," he added. "When they tell you anything about this son of a bitch, I know about it. Not after busy. I know about it. No wait time allowed. Just like you text me every night you're not with me when you get home. Like that, this isn't negotiable."

"You're right. I'm sorry."

"I don't care about sorry."

"No, you don't." Smiling, she laid a hand on his cheek. "But I'm sorry anyway."

"You could move in with me now."

"I wouldn't feel right or easy leaving the ladies alone, not when it really does look like he's coming."

"I can move in with you."

He would, she thought. He'd hate it, but he would.

"The house is as secure as it can get. And tomorrow I'm going to ask Jen to give me some self-defense refreshers. Listen to me, okay? Because I've thought a lot about this. Maybe he could have killed me before. I wasn't prepared—and still, maybe not. He killed Nina, but he took her by surprise, and she was sick, and she was tiny, Miles. But now I am prepared, and he won't surprise me. And I'm stronger than I was. More? I'm pissed."

"All of that's good, Morgan. And still."

"The police are patrolling the street. I've got a deputy following me home from work every night. I expect we'll have a cop or a fed camped in the living room if he gets as far as the Vermont border."

"If he gets that far, I'm camped there with them."

"Deal. And don't be mad, but I need him to come. I need this over and done. I want to look at wedding dresses and bouquets, decide on what song we want for our first dance, and pick just the right shade of lilac for your morning coat."

"You're going to do all of— What? No."

"I was saving the lilac to throw you off. This seemed like a good time. Now let's close Rozwell away, and go home."

"Fine. No lilac."

"Well, if I go with peonies with lilacs, maybe just a little one for a boutonniere. Then I start thinking about delphinium and sweet peas or tulips and spirea. Don't get me started."

"Of things I want to do, getting you started on bouquets comes close to dead last."

Outside, he took her hand again, and thought he could smell the first real hint of fall in the air. "How about 'Stand by Me'?"

"You want to watch a movie tonight?"

"Not the movie. The song. First dance. Because I will, and you damn well better do the same."

Her stress dropped to make way for the gooey she felt inside. "You have been thinking about wedding stuff."

"The stuff occasionally crosses my mind."

"I accept your song nomination—it's a really good one—if you'll accept the lilac sprig if I go there."

"Just a sprig?"

She held up her thumb and index finger to indicate small.

"I can sign on to that."

She turned into him, wrapped around him. "I love you, Miles."

"Another thing you damn well better."

Later, while they slept, Rozwell crossed into Wisconsin driving a Dodge pickup he'd bought for cash off a used car lot in St. Paul.

He'd made some plans.

Morgan dealt with the packages that came, the charges to her account, reported them. And kept her own log of them.

As September arrived, she sat down with her ladies.

"I know this worries you, but that's what he's trying to do. Worry us, get under my skin. But what all this says to me is he's desperate."

"Desperate's dangerous," Olivia pointed out.

"Yes, and I won't be reckless or careless. He's been driving for days, barely stopping. They know what he's in now because he bought a pickup for cash in St. Paul. The FBI's working with the credit card company. I'm not using the card, for anything. And they reported a new charge yesterday."

"For what?" Audrey demanded. "What now?"

"He must've heard about the wedding. He ordered two dozen black roses."

"With a card? Don't sugarcoat it, Morgan."

"I'm not, Gram. I'm not. It just said 'No Wedding, One Funeral.' It's not smart," she hurried on, because her mother went pale. "Just not smart. All these digs. Every one's a warning when he should be keeping it quiet.

"There's more."

"Let's have it. All at once," Olivia told her.

"They've got security feed of him on the car ferry crossing to Michigan. He must've had the truck professionally painted, changed the tags, but they caught him on it. He's blond again, no beard. Still carrying the weight."

"It's like he's leaving them a trail again," Audrey murmured. "Like he did before."

"It does, and they're considering that because they've tracked him heading south and into Indiana."

"Why do that?" Now Olivia rose, paced around the kitchen. "Why not cut over to Ohio, skirt the lakes, and keep going toward Vermont?"

"I don't know, Gram. I talked to Agent Beck for a long time. They have theories. He's trying to throw them off again. He's looking for a place where he could hide for a few days, catch up on sleep, wait them out. Wait me out. Clean himself up, because they say he looks rough. What they know is he drove at least two hundred miles out of his way—if he's coming here. And I know they're practically on top of him."

"Not good enough."

"They agree. I can hear Agent Beck's frustration. I didn't want to leave for work without telling you. Right now he's over a thousand miles away, and possibly taking another time-out. I have to ask you to shift gears because I have to leave for work in a couple minutes. I want to show you the dress I found."

She pulled up her phone, swiped for the site.

"Oh, Morgan, it's beautiful! Simple, sleek."

Morgan felt her muscles relax at her mother's approval. Audrey knew what worked.

"I wanted simple. Gorgeous but simple."

"And you found simply gorgeous. I love the lines with just the subtle flair of the skirt. But you're not buying a wedding dress online."

"But you said—"

"The style's very you, and very spring garden wedding, but you're not going online for your wedding dress. We'll make an appointment at the bridal shop in Westridge next week. It's a lovely place. You need to ask Miles's mother, grandmother, sister—and Jen."

"Oh, but—"

"A lot of people, a lot of opinions, yes." Audrey patted her hand. "But it's an important rite. And you need to touch the dress, try it on, be sure."

"I can always send it back if—"

"How about this?" When she wanted to steamroll, Audrey mowed them down. "If you can't find what you love, what you want, what makes you glow, you can order the one online without a peep from me. And I'm buying the dress."

"Mom."

"Please let me." Now her eyes filled. "I want to, so much. I want to give you that."

"Don't argue, Morgan. It's rude to refuse a gift that comes with love. This wedding is our gift, your mother's and mine. It's not who's paying, baby of my baby. It's about being part of the love. And I expect any argument to come from the groom's family. And we'll be prepared to compromise. That's part of the love."

"I already started a spreadsheet, and a budget."

"Of course you did. Oh, she's so like you, Mom. She sure didn't get that practical side from me. Now you can toss those out and think of the fun stuff. Your colors, the flowers, the music, the guest list. We'll try for next Monday for the bridal shop appointment. That way you won't have to worry about going to work, and we can all have fun."

"We'll talk, but now I do have to go to work. I need to tell Miles everything I just told you—before. We made a deal."

He led them south toward Indianapolis, where he'd rented a garage with a fresh new credit card. He tucked the truck inside, then took an Uber to the airport's private terminal.

He'd donned a dark wig fashioned into a man bun, had taken time and care with a very trim goatee. He carried his laptop, a carry-on, and had them board his single suitcase. He didn't worry about his identification passing—he'd taken time and care there as well.

He had a glass of wine on the flight to Middlebury, Vermont, and ate two bags of chips from the complimentary snack basket.

He just couldn't quit them.

Private meant no security checks of his luggage. The Colt snuggled safe in his suitcase, as did the knife.

By the time they tracked him from Indianapolis—if they ever did—he'd have finished what he started. His luck would come in again.

The next time he flew, he'd fly to some lovely tropical beach with a five-star hotel. And these past horrible months would fade away like a bad dream.

"Something's off."

Beck stood in yet another motel room, studying yet another map. "It's off, Quentin."

"He's playing us again."

"You feel it, too. There's no other purpose for him coming this far out of his way. He's steadying up. He's not steady, but he's getting there. He's got a plan now. That's what I'm feeling."

"We should head northeast. Leave this area with the agents in charge here, the locals, and take a direct route to Vermont."

"I'm feeling that. But more." She turned to him. "Let's go wheels up and get there. I want to see her, see Morgan. I want to see the setup in the house, the resort again, talk face-to-face with the chief of police. Go over resort security point by point. I'm getting this sick feeling again."

"We'll have to clear it."

"Let's do that. I want to be there."

"And we can backtrack from there. I think he ditched the truck, Tee. He bought it, then he ditched it."

"So do I. Let's just go there, spend some time assessing. If we're wrong, we take a hit."

"We weren't wrong before."

Rozwell landed in Middlebury after a smooth flight. The rental car he'd arranged waited. When he slid onto the leather seats of the Mercedes sedan, he felt an almost giddy wave of pleasure.

"I am back!" Giggling, he stroked his fingers over the wheel, grinned at the loaded dash. "Now we're talking, now we're talking, now we're fucking *talking*!"

He hummed a little tune as he plugged in Morgan's address on the GPS.

Thirty-two minutes sounded just fine.

When Miles walked into Après, Morgan had a cocktail shaker in each hand as she engaged two women at the bar in conversation. A little showmanship, he thought as she poured the drinks, added a skewer of three fat olives to each.

She had a knack for it. Both women toasted her after their first sip, and she took a bow.

"It's all in the wrist," she claimed, then caught sight of Miles.

He walked up to the bar, but spoke to Bailey.

"Last night with us."

"Yes. I'm going to miss everyone. Morgan helped me land an interview at a club just off campus."

"Let us know, and if you want work next summer, you've got a place here. I need Morgan for a couple minutes. Can you take over?"

"Sure. I had really good training."

Morgan kept the thoughts bubbling in her head as she walked outside with him.

"I thought you'd left for the day. Is it—"

"Nothing to worry about, and I'm on my way out. The feds are on their way—or will be shortly."

"Here. Why?"

He steered her toward the paths winding through the gardens. The nights had cooled, and the first touches of color tinted the hills.

"Apparently, they want to assess your security. Jake—they contacted him, he contacted me—thinks they want to get a gauge on you as much as that."

"Okay, that's good. That's actually good. I'd like to see them in person. I can get my own gauge."

"Jake wants them to assign an agent to Westridge, and I'll add my weight to that."

"Miles, he could decide to come here tomorrow. Or six months from now. How long am I going to be guarded and watched over?"

"As long as it takes. You live your life, Morgan. That's what you've done, what you're doing, and it doesn't change. He's not going to change that. But when and if he comes here, we're going to have every available resource. And I'm going to talk to your ladies tomorrow."

"About what?"

"About me staying a couple nights a week. You're with me three nights, I'm with you two or three nights. It's a nice balance. We can argue about it later—you're on the clock—but it's happening."

"This is the second time tonight somebody just rolled over me. I don't like it."

"Can't blame you, but it's still happening. You can see the first hints of color in the trees." He looked out and away to the rise of hills and peaks. "Time passes, seasons change. What doesn't change and won't? You belong to me now."

"Oh, wait just a—"

"We belong to each other. We're people who take care of what's ours, aren't we?"

"I don't see that as as smooth a save as you think it is."

"Maybe not, but . . . it's still truth. I have to go feed the dog. You'll text me when you get home."

"As soon as I wave goodbye to Deputy Howe and close the front door behind me."

"Lock it behind you."

"Yeah, yeah, yeah. The next thing you'll want a code or some sort of safe word."

"We'll talk about where my mind went on 'safe word,' but it's not a bad idea." Frowning now, he thought it through. "The opposite of a safe word's not a bad idea."

"Great. If I'm in a struggle with Rozwell, who'd have managed to get past Deputy Howe, through the alarm system, and into the house, I'll just say hold on while I text Miles our unsafe word. Pineapple."

"Pineapple's stupid." He gave her an absent kiss on the forehead as he considered it.

"Oh, *pineapple's* stupid?"

"In this context. Work Howl into the text."

"You're serious?"

"Every available resource. Or I can hang out until closing, take you home myself."

"Then look under the bed and in all the closets?"

Even as she said it, she understood. He worried. Of course he worried when he wasn't right there. Couldn't control the situation.

"We'll try the other way instead. Go home, sit in your turret, and answer all the texts and emails and whatever else you didn't manage to get to in a normal workday. And if I text something like 'Say good night to Howl,' come running."

"Count on it."

* * *

In the kitchen, Olivia and Audrey dealt with the last of the dinner dishes and talked about what remained in the top of their minds.

Wedding plans.

"We can look for our dresses at the bridal shop." Audrey hand-washed the wineglasses they'd used at dinner. "We have to look perfect when we walk Morgan down the aisle. Or whatever's going to stand for the aisle. I still get teary that she wants us to."

"No flounces, Audrey. The girl wants simple."

"Simple—flounce-free—but perfect."

Olivia picked up a cloth to dry the stemware. "They better pick a solid band because I want to dance my ass off. Who'd have thought, baby, that when she came here last winter, we'd be planning a wedding for next spring?"

"We'll not only know she's happy, Mom. We'll see it. We'll get to be a part of the life she's building. I'll never take that for granted. Never."

"You're going to get sloppy and sentimental on me again, which makes me sloppy and sentimental. So I say we knock it off and go watch a movie."

"I'd like a movie."

"I'll make the popcorn."

"I'll just take out this trash. And let's pick something happy," she added as she tied up the kitchen bag, then pulled out the recycle bin.

She carried both around the side of the house, dropped the tied bag in its can, dumped the trash for recycling in its.

She never heard him, not until his arm wrapped around her throat and the gun pressed against her temple.

"Make a sound, and I'll shoot you in the head. You must be Mom. Let's go in the house, Mom."

"Morgan's not here. She's not here."

"I *know* that." Rather than press the trigger, he turned the gun, gave her a good smack with the butt. "You think I'm stupid? Did she tell you I was stupid? Move!"

Her vision blurred—tears, pain, fear—as he dragged her to the kitchen door.

"Got it going," Olivia said. "Making two bowls since you're fussy about the salt." Then she turned, froze.

"And you must be Gram. Down on the floor, Grandma, face-fucking-down, or I blow Mom's head clean off."

His sneer widened into a grin. "Hey! Is that popcorn?"

Chapter Thirty-one

He thought about just killing them both. Not with the gun—too much noise. But he had Dead Jane's knife, and he had other ways.

Wouldn't it be fun to watch her face when she came home and saw their bloody bodies?

But that's what happened with—what was the little bitch's name? Who cares. It hadn't been enough, just not painful enough.

This time, he'd make her watch him kill them. That way when he killed her, she'd have those images in her head.

She'd suffer, and she needed to suffer. She'd pay, and she needed to pay.

He had an ugly scar on his arm—her fault. He'd gained weight— her fault. And just a few hours before, one of his back teeth had started aching. Her fault.

Every hour he'd spent in a musty motel room, every mile he'd driven in some piece-of-shit truck or van, her fault.

He deserved the best, had earned the best. And once he killed her, it would all come back. All his bad luck lived in her.

He'd had the bitches drag the nice, sturdy dining room chairs into the living room, then made the old one zip-tie the other one to a chair. He'd had to give her a couple of smacks, but he didn't mind that.

He'd zip-tied old Grandma himself, nice and tight, then used a roll of duct tape for good measure. They'd tried to talk with him, all quiet voices or tearful pleas, so he'd just slapped more duct tape over their mouths.

He paced awhile, scoping out the house, shoving popcorn in his mouth.

When he heard the chairs rattling, he went back in.

"Keep it up and we'll see how you like a bullet in the knee, or maybe the gut." He sat on the sofa facing them, the popcorn bowl in his lap. "When she comes in, she'll see you. That's phase one. She'll know it's her fault. It's all her fault. Do you have any idea what she cost me? What she took from me?"

As anger built up, the rage spewed out. "I've been living like some derelict, some *failure*, and she's living here? I bet she's got a big, soft bed upstairs—I'll take a look later. Big, old house—got some antiques, I see, some fricking heirlooms. How come she gets that when she ruined my life? I'm here to take it back, you get that? I'm taking it all back."

He reached for more popcorn, found the bowl empty, and threw it across the room. Glass shattered, flew.

In a flash, his face went from fury to calm and contemplative.

"Now I'm thirsty. Let's see what you've got, and if I hear a sound in here, Morgan'll find you both dead in a pool of blood."

When they heard him moving around in the kitchen, Olivia shifted again—quietly—so Audrey could try to maneuver her hand, her fingers, to pull the cell phone from her mother's pocket.

The hard plastic tie dug into her wrist, drew blood, but she kept trying, felt her heart pounding when her fingers brushed against the top edge.

Then they heard him coming back.

"You bitches are loaded." He took a long pull from a bottle of Coke. "Some nice wine in there, but I'll save that for after. I need a clear head to do my work. And speaking of loaded."

He strode over, ripped the tape from Olivia's mouth, beamed at the shock of pain that ran over her face. "This house is worth a bundle, and you've got a whole lot more tucked into brokerage accounts, business accounts. No reason in this world a woman like you should have all that. Money's a man's privilege, Granny."

"I'll sign it all over to you. You can walk away with every penny and disappear. Live the life you deserve."

"That's what they all say—if I give them the chance. I don't want you to *give* me a fucking thing. I take. Understand?"

He closed his hand over her throat. "Understand!"

When she nodded, he released the pressure. "I bet you've got a nice laptop. You're going to tell me where it is, tell me the password, or I'm going to get one of those plastic bags you've got in the kitchen, put it over this one's head. And you can watch me smother her to death."

She told him.

When he went to get it, Audrey tried for the phone again.

Bailey stayed to close the bar with Morgan.

"You keep in touch," Morgan told her. "I want to hear how school's going, the job's going—because you will get it—how everything's going."

"I will. Promise. I'm excited to go back, but I'm going to miss you, and everyone. Maybe you can save a slot for me at the bar over winter break."

"If you want it, you've got it."

Bailey took a last look around. "Summer's really over."

"She's got a little life in her yet, but yeah, you can feel her starting to bow out. It'll be my first autumn in Vermont."

"I didn't realize that."

"Army, school. So Christmas, some summer visits. I'm looking forward to it." And to all the autumns that came after. "Ready?"

"Yeah. Until winter break."

They walked out together. Morgan saw Deputy Howe leaning on his patrol car, talking with one of the night security team.

Routine now, she thought. Cops and guards, all routine.

Bailey turned, wrapped her in a hug. "Please stay safe."

"That's the plan. And you kick grad school's butt."

"Also the plan."

She walked to her car. "Jerry, Deputy."

"Night, Morgan. You drive safe now."

"Hard to do otherwise with a cop in my rearview."

As she drove, she let the work portion of the day slide away, let herself think about the next. Some laundry, a hair appointment where she intended to show the stylist the type of dress she had in mind so they could strategize wedding hair.

Nell had recommended a photographer—one her ladies agreed on as well. She needed to set up an appointment. She knew a lot of couples did engagement photos, but she didn't think she and Miles were that couple.

And she had the selfies from the hike.

The little spikes of annoyance she'd felt for him earlier had smoothed right over. He worried, she reminded herself, because he loved her. If she accepted love—and boy, did she—then she accepted what came with it.

Maybe she thought the *un*safe word silly, but it could be something they'd laugh about years from now. While Rozwell sat in a maximum security prison.

He waited up for her texts. He didn't say so, but he must, as he answered them within seconds. Just: *Get some sleep.* Or: *Talk tomorrow.* Never just: *Good night.*

But he waited every night they weren't together until he knew she'd gotten home safe. She should be grateful.

"I am grateful."

She pulled into her driveway, locked her car. Deputy Howe idled the patrol car at the foot of the drive while she walked to the door. When she unlocked it, opened it, she turned, waved. Shut the door behind her, reset the alarm.

She started to walk straight to the stairs and up, but a sound from the living room had her glancing over.

And everything inside her turned to ice.

She saw the bruises on her mother's face, on her grandmother's, the fear and grief in their eyes.

Laughing like a lunatic, Rozwell jumped up from his hiding place behind the sofa. "Surprise!" he shouted, waving a gun in one hand, a knife in the other. "Go ahead and scream, go on and make a move, and I slit their throats, shoot you, and I'm gone before you hit the floor."

Whatever it took, whatever it cost, he wouldn't hurt her ladies.

"I'm not going to scream, Gavin. What's the point in that? And you won't shoot me. It's not your style. It's lazy." She looked into his eyes. If she looked into her mother's, she'd fall apart. "You're not lazy, and you haven't come all this way to shoot me and be done with it."

"You think you're so smart."

"Smart enough, but you're the smart one. You know there's nothing I can do when you have my family. As long as they're alive, there's nothing I can do."

Alive, keep them alive. It was all she had.

"That's right, you bitch. You can't do anything. I'm in charge. I'm always in charge. Hey, did you like the flowers?"

"No."

He'd gone back to the blond hair, but it no longer shone, and the cut was uneven, choppy. She could see he'd put on makeup, and where he'd rubbed at it, the redness—too much desert sun—came through. He no longer looked fit and stylish, but doughy and rumpled.

He had an ugly scar on his arm, puckered and puffy.

She tried to remember everything Jen had taught her. She couldn't run. No one would hear her scream. She couldn't hide.

She promised herself she'd fight if she got the chance.

He'd played her once, she thought. She'd play him now.

"You wanted to scare me. You did. You want to scare me now. You are. I can't be worth the risk you're taking, Gavin. I'm nobody."

"You ruined my life."

"I didn't—"

She broke off when the phone in her pocket signaled a text. And the gun he held pointed—rock steady now—at her face.

Slowly, she lifted her hands. "It's my phone. In my pocket. I won't touch it."

"Who the hell's calling you? It's two in the morning."

"It's a text—that's a text. It's nothing. I won't touch it."

He took one step back, jammed the gun under her mother's chin. "Who'd text you at two in the morning? Fuck with me, I blow her head off."

"All right. Please. It's my fiancé. I text him when I get home, to let him know I'm home. Don't hurt her, Gavin. I'm telling you, if I don't text back I'm okay, he'll call the cops. You don't want that. I'll show you. Let me show you."

"Bring me the fucking phone."

"I'm reaching for it. I'm going to give it to you."

But his hands held the gun, the knife. She counted on it, so held out the screen so he could read the text from Miles.

Where the hell are you?

"Asshole. Answer. Stand right here where I can see what you say. Fuck around and find out, Morgan."

"I won't. She's my mother. I won't."

"Yeah? I killed my mother. Fuck around and you kill yours."

sorry. She kept the screen angled so he could see. closing took a little longer but im home now say good night to howl and get some sleep love you.

"Who the fuck is Howl?"

"It's his dog." Letting tears swirl, Morgan blurted it out when he jerked her mother's head back. "It's just his dog. It's just something we say. He'd wonder if I didn't. Please. I did what you told me to do."

The phone signaled again. Praying, her hand shaking now, Morgan held the screen for Rozwell to read.

I'll do that. Good night.

He heard me, she thought. He heard me.

"Drop the phone."

When she did, he stomped on it.

"Now unless you want my finger to twitch, step back."

Miles was out of his house and in his car within thirty seconds.

As Morgan sent the text, Beck and Morrison got off the plane in Middlebury.

The head of the ground crew greeted them. "FBI. Coming in late."

"Weather in Indianapolis, delayed takeoff."

"Yeah, we got word on that. They sent a car for you." He gestured, then handed them the key fob. "We'll get your bags loaded in for you."

"The resort's what, twenty, twenty-five minutes out, right?" Morrison asked.

"This time of night, twenty'll do it. Funny thing. You're the second private to come in from Indianapolis tonight. First one got out before the weather."

"Wait." Beck gripped his arm. "You had another private out of Indianapolis? How many passengers?"

"Just the one. Some dude. Rich dude. Had a Mercedes C-Class rental waiting. Hey! Your bags!" he shouted as they raced for the car.

"Call Chief Dooley." Beck jumped behind the wheel.

"I'm on it."

As he sped through town, Miles called Jake.

"He's got her."

"What? Nathan reported in. He watched her go in the house just minutes ago."

"He's got her. He's inside. Get there."

"Wait for me."

"No."

"Goddamn it." Jake dragged on clothes. And so did Nell.

"I'm going with you."

"No, you're not."

"I have my own car, so I ride with you or alone. But I'm going. This is family."

Morgan did step back, and kept her hands up in a gesture of submission. "I know you've been through a lot this last year. Year and a half."

"You don't know anything."

"I know you didn't want Nina. You wanted me."

"*That's* her name! Jesus, it was driving me crazy."

"I broke your streak, and you haven't been able to live your life the way you want to since."

"The way I deserve."

"Yes, there's that. And I've been living mine. It's really not fair. Sure, I lost my house, my savings, all of that, but here I am."

She spread her arms, stepped back again. Bring him to you, she thought. Away from them.

"Living that life in this beautiful house. I bought a new car. But you know that. You know everything about me. You know I've got a hot fiancé. A rich one."

"Diddling the boss, Morgan." His lip curled. "It's so tired."

"Not when it works." She lifted her shoulders, let them fall. "And he has this amazing house. I've got a thing for houses—you know that. And look at this."

She held up a hand, wiggled her fingers so the diamond glinted. "Honestly, Gavin, when it comes down to it, I owe you for all of it. There I was, slaving away at two jobs, pinching every penny, living in that little box. Then you came along."

She moved back another step.

"Then I broke your streak. Sent your luck right down the toilet. Had the feds sniffing at your heels. You left me messages with the locket, with the bracelet. Message received."

"They should've been you."

"But they weren't. You used your hands on them because that's what you need. Not a gun, not a knife. It doesn't work for you unless you use your hands. It has to be personal, especially with me. It has to be intimate. That gun's beneath you, and it won't give you what you need. We both know it."

"I don't need a fucking gun." He set it on the mantel behind him. "I don't need a fucking knife." And stuck it in the sheath on his belt.

"I know, Gavin. I've dreamed of your hands around my throat. I've dreamed of begging you to let me live this life I've started, one you gave me. But you never do."

Now he smiled, stepped slowly toward her.

"Beg me now. I want to hear you beg."

"Please don't hurt me. Take whatever you want, but please don't hurt me."

"I'm going to take what I want. Finally."

She sucked in air as if to scream when his hands closed around her throat.

Then she did exactly as she'd been taught.

She brought her knee up hard as she dug her thumbs into his eyes.

And he's the one who screamed.

When his grip loosened, just a little, she drove the heel of her hand to his nose, watched the blood spurt, felt it on her face.

Then she drew back with all she had, rammed her fist into his throat.

When he went down, she ran for the gun, but he grabbed her foot, sent her sprawling. Instinct as much as those lessons had her kicking back. They screamed together when her foot connected with his broken nose.

When the door crashed open, she thought it was him and scrambled up, grabbed the gun.

She'd never held one, never expected to, but whirled with it. Only to see Miles standing over Rozwell, fists clenched and ready.

"Miles. Miles, please take this. Please."

"Point it down, Morgan. You're okay. It's okay now."

The minute he had the gun, she dropped down to pull the tape off her mother's mouth. "I'm sorry, I'm sorry. It'll hurt."

She pulled it off, did the same with her grandmother's.

"I'm sorry, I'm sorry. I'm sorry."

"Stop that," Olivia ordered.

"You saved us. Baby, my baby. You saved us."

Seconds later, Jake came in, weapon drawn, then lowered it when he surveyed the scene. "Well, Christ on a crutch. Nell, call for an ambulance."

"He can wait," she said as she walked in behind Jake.

"Nell, for God's sake."

"Shut up, Miles. I'll get something to cut them loose. I'll find something."

"First drawer next to the kitchen door," Olivia said steadily, though her eyes filled with tears. "And we could use some water. Please."

"I'll get that. He's got a knife on his belt, Jake."

"Yeah, I see it. I'll get it. Feds are coming," he said as Miles handed the gun he held to Jake and went for the water. "They contacted me right after Miles did. Morgan, did you do all this?"

She looked down at Rozwell and nodded.

"Good job. Are you hurt?"

"No."

"Ladies, are you hurt?"

"He slapped us around some. He hurt Audrey more than me."

"Their wrists and ankles are raw, Jake." With the clippers, Nell crouched down to snip the ties.

"First aid kit." Closing her eyes in relief, Audrey wrapped her aching arms around her mother and her daughter. "Mudroom cabinet, over the dryer. We're okay. We're all okay."

Rozwell groaned when Jake cuffed him.

"He's not." Olivia's hand shook a little as she took the glass of water Miles offered. "He came up against a Nash woman. You had his number, Morgan. She had his number. Got him to put the gun down, the knife down. Smart, and brave, and strong," she managed, and finally began to weep.

Morgan looked up at Miles. "You heard me."

"I heard you."

"I heard you back. I knew you'd come." She pushed up to stand, swayed a little. "My legs are going."

"I've got you." He pulled her to him, held, pressed his face to her hair. "I've got you."

Beck and Morrison arrived before the ambulance, walked through the broken door.

Rozwell lay curled on the floor, eyes going black, nose swollen, blood dripping. Audrey and Olivia sat hip-to-hip on the sofa while Nell tended their wrists.

"Miles, we could use an ice bag or two."

"I'll get them. I know where they are."

When he heard her voice, Rozwell tried to focus on her. "I'll kill you."

"No." Miles moved into his sight line. "You won't. She beat you. You get to live with that. Morgan Nash beat you."

"Are you hurt?" Beck asked her.

"No. I'm all right," Morgan insisted. "We're all right," she told the agents. "I need to get the ice."

"So we see," Morrison said. "Good work, Chief."

"Not me. Morgan. She's got some blood on her, and it's all his. We've got an ambulance coming—and here it comes," he added as he heard the siren. "He needs medical attention. Busted nose for sure, his throat's bruised up, and his eyes bled some. Jaw might be busted."

"I'll go with him." Morrison nodded at Beck. "You got the scene?"

"I've got it. First, I'm going to apologize for being two steps behind."

"No." Morgan came back in. "That's just not true. You stuck with me all along. And if you hadn't, if you hadn't let me know so much, I wouldn't have been able to do this. To string him out. If you hadn't been behind him, kept him running, he would've come here long before this. Long before I was ready."

"I can wish we'd taken him before you had to be ready. It can wait until morning if you'd rather, but I need statements."

"Here, Mom." Morgan laid an ice bag gently against her mother's temple. "I don't know how he got in, but when I got home, just before two, he had them in those chairs. Zip ties and duct tape. Gram." She laid the second on Olivia's bruised cheek. "I'll make some tea."

"Screw tea. Get me a whiskey. A double." She gripped her daughter's hand. "Make that two."

At dawn, just as light sprinkled in the east, Morgan sat outside, drinking wine with Miles. Howl, fetched by Nell, lay sleeping under the table, one paw on her feet.

"They're finally sleeping. I wish they'd gone to the hospital."

"No way they'd leave you, or this house. And the EMTs cleared them both."

"I know. I know. I just . . ." She tried to shove it aside. "First time I've had wine at dawn," she said instead.

"Long night."

"That stupid unsafe word wasn't so stupid after all."

"I'd have known anyway. You didn't use any punctuation, no uppercase letters. That's not how you text."

"I wasn't sure you'd notice that. Glad you did. I knew you were coming when you said good night. You never text good night."

"It's not a real good one when you're somewhere else."

Reaching out, she gripped his hand, and her voice went thick. "That explains that."

"Try not to cry, okay? I'm worn pretty thin myself. I'm buying Jen the biggest arrangement of flowers ever known to man." He kissed the hand that gripped his. "You cleaned his clock, champ."

"I was so mad, Miles. Seeing them like that, helpless, bruised, bleeding. He wasn't going to do to them what he did to Nina. And I could see he was weak and jittery, and really angry. I just had to listen and talk and gauge. I just had to be a really good bartender." She lifted her wine, sipped. "Then do what Jen taught me and clean his clock."

"You beat me to it. That doesn't seem quite fair."

"You broke down the door."

"Yeah. I'll fix it. I thought I knew how much I loved you before I got that text. I didn't. My world just dropped away for a minute. Just went out from under me. Don't do that to me again."

"That's definitely not in the plans. He'll never get out. Later, I'm going to call Sam, tell him. He deserves to know. And Nina's family. Sam should go tell them in person. Then we don't have to think about him again."

"I'm taking the day off. You're taking the night off."

"I don't have anyone to cover the bar."

"Nell will find someone to cover. That's her job. Your job right now is to get some sleep, look after your ladies, let them look after you. Mine's to do all of that and fix that door."

She felt a little floaty, as if she stood just an inch outside herself.

"You're rolling over me again."

"Because you need it. You can roll over me when I need it."

"That sounds like a reasonable deal. But let's watch the day come before we go in. Let's just watch it come. It's the first day."

So they did.

Epilogue

Flowers bloomed as if they held as much joy as she did. In her life, Morgan never expected to feel as she felt now. Thrilled, calm, steady, giddy, and absolutely sure all at once.

Her mother did up the hidden zipper under the crystal buttons that stopped just above her waist. Her wedding dress, she thought as she watched both of them in the mirror in the room Drea had designated Bride's Area Only. Perfect, simply gorgeous with those long, clean lines she'd wanted, and bought—with full approval—at the local bridal shop.

Her mother had that one right on the nose.

With it she wore the teardrop diamond drops Miles had given her for Valentine's Day, and a single diamond bangle—for something borrowed—from Nell.

She felt beautiful, and realized that was another first in her life. Not pretty, not attractive, not good enough, but just beautiful.

She turned to look at Nell, who supervised everything in her pretty lilac dress with its crystal straps. Jen wore the palest of pink.

She closed her eyes a moment, thought of Nina, who would have loved every second of all of this. Nina's family sat now, she knew, in the garden in one of the rows of white-skirted chairs. And she'd be forever grateful they'd come, along with Sam and his fiancée.

A full circle, Nina. He's gone, out of our lives, locked away, and we've come full circle. I love you. I'll never forget you.

Drea rushed in, the mother of the groom lovely in pale plum.

"We're right on schedule. Olivia, I have to say again, the flowers are spectacular. How about some champagne, everyone? Some champagne and a good, deep breath all around. My boy's getting married, and my God, Morgan, you are an incredibly beautiful bride."

"Our kids, Drea." Audrey took her hands.

"Our kids. Nell, pour the champagne, and let's have a drink to our kids."

"One more thing first." Olivia lifted the crown of flowers, those pale pink peonies woven with lilacs, and set it on Morgan's head before kissing both her cheeks. "You're marrying a Jameson, and I couldn't be more pleased. But you'll always be a Nash woman."

"Aren't we the lucky ones?" Lydia laid a hand on Olivia's shoulder. "To be a part of another beginning. Drink up," she ordered. "Then, Drea, let's go down and let those handsome men escort us to our seats."

When they left, Morgan picked up her bouquet. Simple and sweet—those peonies and lilacs, some baby's breath, some trailing and airy greens.

She walked downstairs in the house that had become her home. Heard the music she'd chosen for just this moment.

Jen sent her a wink, then walked out the doors. Nell turned.

"You're about to knock Miles dead."

Then Morgan linked arms with her mother, with her grandmother. "Here we go."

They walked outside, where Howl sat like a good boy in his collar of flowers, down the aisle formed by the white-skirted seats to where Miles stood, a sprig of lilac in the buttonhole of his black suit.

Behind him, the fountain they'd made together—a frog, of course, standing in a yoga tree position—sent water sparkling in the air.

She saw Nina's family, Sam, Nick, the Greenwalds, Agents Beck and Morrison, so many people who'd touched her life and helped to form it.

Then she saw only Miles. And he looked at her as if she was everything.

When she reached him, she turned, kissed her grandmother, kissed her mother. "I love you both."

They stepped back, linked hands. She stepped forward, took Miles's. "I've been waiting for you," he told her.

"Wait's over. Let's get started."

Roots already planted, she thought as they turned to make promises to each other. And from this day forward, they'd tend them, and watch them grow.

NORA ROBERTS

(c) Bruce

For the latest news, exclusive extracts
and unmissable competitions, visit

/NoraRobertsJDRobb
www.fallintothestory.com